freshmen

OTHER TITLES
EDITED BY JESSE GRANT
AVAILABLE FROM ALYSON BOOKS

Friction, Volumes 2–7

The Best of Friction

Just the Sex

Men for All Seasons

Ultimate Gay Erotica, 2005

AND THE FORTHCOMING

Ultimate Gay Erotica, 2006

freshmen

the best erotic fiction

EDITED BY

JESSE GRANT

alyson books
los angeles

Celebrating Twenty-Five Years

For Fred Goss,
former *Freshmen* editor,
a wordsmith who took gay erotica to new heights

f f f

MANUFACTURED IN THE UNITED STATES OF AMERICA.

THIS TRADE PAPERBACK ORIGINAL IS PUBLISHED BY ALYSON BOOKS, P.O. BOX 4371, LOS ANGELES, CALIFORNIA 90078-4371. DISTRIBUTION IN THE UNITED KINGDOM BY TURNAROUND PUBLISHER SERVICES LTD., UNIT 3, OLYMPIA TRADING ESTATE, COBURG ROAD, WOOD GREEN, LONDON, N22 6TZ, ENGLAND.

FIRST EDITION: JULY 2005

05 06 07 08 09 a 10 9 8 7 6 5 4 3 2 1

ISBN 1-55583-905-3
ISBN-13 978-1-55583-905-5

LIBRARY OF CONGRESS CATALOGING-IN-PUBLICATION DATA
 FRESHMEN : THE BEST EROTIC FICTION / EDITED BY JESSE GRANT.
  ISBN 1-55583-905-3; ISBN-13 978-1-55583-905-5
   1. GAY MEN—FICTION. 2. EROTIC STORIES, AMERICAN. I. GRANT, JESSE.
 PS648.H57F74 2005
 813'.0108358'086642—DC22   2005043619

COVER PHOTOGRAPHY BY BODY IMAGE PRODUCTIONS.

Contents

∫ ƒ ♯

Boys Will Be Boys

A trip to the lake after graduation is full of lessons that never cropped up during high school. *HOT MOMENT TO WATCH FOR:* "He's drunk, I'm drunk, Arby's drunk. He stares at me like he loves me, his gaze somewhere around my mouth."

It's not every guy who gets lucky enough to have his straight best buddy drops his girl for you. *HOT MOMENT TO WATCH FOR:* "Don't you worry about how big your dick is? Straight guys worry about it, and we don't ever get near another guy's dick. But you gay guys can actually compare another guy's dick while it's, like, in action. What if you're not up to scratch?"

He's only popular on Saturday nights, when the chaste girlfriends send their dates home frustrated. *HOT HOT MOMENT TO WATCH FOR:* "When they finally shoot, they cry out 'Cindy Lou' or 'Peggy Beth' as their loads splatter against the back of my throat."

It just goes to show you: Never lose "touch" with your old high school buddies! *HOT MOMENT TO WATCH FOR:* "He said you'd blow me for 3 cents. That right, Kyle?"

Those Hallowed Halls

Two superhot yet straight college buddies realize they have some mutual admiration for each other. *HOT MOMENT TO WATCH FOR:* "Sleep would solve everything, Paul told himself. The big running back would wake up hungover and not remember what had almost happened."

Contents

Road Trips and Wild Rides

CONTENTS

CONTENTS

It Could Happen

Contents

A Fresh Face Is Born

f f f

When *Freshmen* magazine was born in 1980 it was conceived as a "one shot"—a magazine that would probably have only one issue ever printed. It was supposed to be merely a special supplement to its big brother, *Men,* the long-reigning gold standard in gay erotica.

As the old saying goes, though, the rest is history.

Freshmen was so wildly popular that in only a year's time it was further developed and launched as a new title that would stand on its own and grow more popular every year.

It's from the pages of *Freshmen* that some of the most titillating pieces of erotic writing have been selected for this book. Whether you are reawakening your closely held fond memories of these articles or are reading them for the first time, we hope you enjoy them—over and over again!

And be sure to explore more about *Freshmen* on its site on the Web at www.freshmen.com.

Boys Will Be Boys

ƒ ƒ ƒ

$f f f$

In Between

BY

R.J. MARCH

"Stop looking at me," he says, bunching up my shirt in his fist. We're in the field behind Wysockie's again, and our buddy Arby's somewhere in the woods that edge the fields, looking for his daddy's field knife, which he thinks he dropped there. We're all supposed to be looking, but Jason's got me by the shirt instead, flattering himself. He says he knows all about me, his face sneering, and I figure Arby's been talking, although that doesn't seem much like Arby. The way Jason's got me, I could easily break his wrist, but I let him think he's got the best of me.

Arby comes back, towheaded, hopping through the goldenrod. He's found the knife and waves it in the air. "He'd have killed me," he says, winded. Jason lets me go and stands glowering at the east, and Arby kicks my shoe. His zipper's open, but I don't say anything. Jason's dungarees are tucked into boots, and his head is covered with an old felt hat. His hand, fisted again, is on his hip. I can't help looking at him, only Arby doesn't like it. He kicks at my shoe and says, "It's time for lunch, ain't it?"

My shirt, half open, has lost a button. The sun is warm enough, allowing me to take the shirt off. I ignore my strange red nipples, pretending they don't exist. The others have seen them before, down at the lake. I wish they were more like Arby's, brown and small, little beady dots that roll under the tongue. Or like Jason's, nearly covered over by his chest hair. Mine are red and naked and pulled out, and I hate them, except when Arby's got his mouth on one of them and is pinching the other and I'm rubbing my prick against his bare belly.

"Let's go to the Hotel," Arby says.

ƒ ƒ ƒ

The Hotel isn't much of a hotel. It has rooms to let, attracting a few fishermen and hunters—there isn't much reason to come to Leesport but to kill something, including time. More than anything else, the Hotel is a tavern with an old witch in the back making sandwiches and frying up potatoes.

The bartender's name is Stoolie, and he lays down three cardboard coasters. We order three beers. Stoolie eyes up Arby, saying, "Don't tell me you're drinking age now, Arby Willis. I remember you losing your diapers in the lake and swimming bare-assed."

"Christ, Stoolie, that was a hundred years ago," Arby says, his mouth going down sideways. "Anyways, you served me last night."

"I was drunk last night, kiddo," Stoolie says, giving me a wink. "How's your mom?" he asks me, and I tell him fine. He eyes Jason and gives him a nod. Jason takes off his hat and wipes his forehead on his shirtsleeve, darkening the plaid. He puts his elbows on the bar and leans down to sip the head of his beer, hair falling off the top of his head where it was combed back. A few strands fall and veil his eyes, and Stoolie cuffs his head like we knew he would, and Jason looks up, hard-eyed, a curse on his lips, and Stoolie points to the sign up over the register: ELBOWS OFF THE BAR, PLEASE. It was Stoolie's rule and one we all obeyed—he'd toss you out otherwise. "It's manners," he says, explaining. Jason slowly, grudgingly obliges.

The beer's cold, and Stoolie's white hair reminds me of my grandmother. He hitches his sleeves and presses his hands on the bar. He's not a big man but looks like one. He waits for our orders—liverwurst and onions all around—and Arby leans over to see what's on the television. "You going fishing with us tomorrow?" he asks Jason.

"I suppose," he answers, looking around me.

Jason has dark hair and eyes and a beard shadow that won't ever be shaved away. He gets up, looking for the toilets. Arby tests the keenness of his father's knife on the hairs of his arm, causing Stoolie to give him a look. I hear the hinges of the john door whine and fight the urge to look at Jason coming out. He walks toward me, watching my eyes. His shoulders, broadened by the plaid, move counter to his hips. His hands curl up into easy fists. He wears a silver I.D. bracelet and a cheap watch. His belt buckle reflects a few rays of light. Stoolie brings out our sandwiches, then gets us more beer. Jason sits on his stool with his legs on either side of it, his shoe toes resting on the chrome rung. He catches himself with his elbows, lifting them quickly. "Manners," he says.

He's drunk, I'm drunk, Arby's drunk. "I don't know why I don't like you, just that I don't," Jason says to me. His eyelids are heavy, and he can't keep his hair from swinging down and covering them. He stares at me like he loves me, his gaze somewhere around my mouth.

"How can you say that, Jason?" Arby says sadly. "How can you say you don't like my Pete?"

f f f

We're in my mother's kitchen. She's upstairs asleep. Arby's close to being asleep himself. There are cards on the table, thrown hands, discards, the detritus of poker.

"I like you, Pete," Arby says, staring at his beer bottle. "I like you fine."

He lurches to his feet and walks away from us, looking for my bedroom. "I'm staying here tonight," he says haltingly.

Jason and I watch Arby stagger and sway, struggling out of his shirt. He calls to me, and Jason's mouth jerks to the right. "I'm going back," he says, meaning back to Arby's house up the street, where he's been staying. I tell him we'll be by at 6 to pick him up. "Seven," he says, standing.

"Seven," I say. He doesn't move. He looks down at me, his belt buckle glinting. He wants to say something—something mean, I'm guessing from the look in his eyes.

"See you in the morning," he says.

f f f

When he's gone I go to my room. I hear Arby snoring already, all sprawled across my bed, stripped to shorts I've seen often enough. I nudge him ungently, wanting him to move over and make room, wanting him to wake up. His eyes open, and he says he wants some, but I can see he's too drunk. He casts a wavering eye on the front of my shorts and takes a swipe at me that misses by a mile. He gets up on an elbow, shakily propped, and points at my crotch. I uncover my cock for him, shaking it out, unfurling its folds. It fattens, getting heavy and dropping south before pulsing upward, going rock-hard and panicky. I kneel on the mattress, sinking into its softness and bringing Arby rolling toward me, his mouth open, tongue resting on his fat lower lip. I get a shiver like I always do when he breathes on me, and I feel the slip his tongue makes over my pink helmet.

I need this, I'm thinking, going deep into him. We haven't had a chance since Jason came to stay with his mother, Arby's stepmother, who had married Arby's father years ago after Jason's father and Arby's mother died.

"What did you tell him?" I ask now, not wanting him to take his mouth off my prick to answer. "You didn't tell him about us, did you?" I hold the back of his neck to keep him put. Arby grunts and tries to shake his head, and I wonder what kind of cock Jason has—if it's as big as mine, bigger, cut or not, crooked, skinny. "What?" I ask Arby, "You ever seen him naked?" Arby stops sucking enough to look me in the eye and nod, and then his eyes roll and shut, and he's gone, passed out. His mouth goes slack, but his cock is as hard as mine, and it seems like a fair trade-off.

I go down on his slender tusk, my throat tightening around the knob. I push my nose into his blond curlies and fiddle with his nipples with one hand while I poke into his asshole with the other. "I could fuck you good, Arby," I say out loud, liking the idea of it. He's yet to let anything but my finger in him down there, although I've had plenty of opportunities like this— Arby crocked and out, legs spread, pointer pointing. I scrape the tender side of his stalk with my top teeth, and his dick twitches, and his little pucker grips my finger, pulling it in. I taste the first salty seep, and his balls tighten. He makes a small whimper, his hips roll, and his hole sucks my finger, and all the while, staring down his golden-haired legs, I watch as his back arches one way and then the other, and I shoot well over Arby's prone body onto the floor on the other side of the bed.

f f f

Jason's in the kitchen with my mother when I get up in the morning to pee. I smell coffee and hear my mother's voice telling stories about Arby and me, and I see Jason's eyes on me, sparkling a little with something I always take for meanness. I'm wearing yesterday's briefs, the front filled with a piss hard-on that catches Jason's notice for a second. I give him a half-nod, but I feel weird seeing him so early in the morning. It's like waking up from a dream and seeing the one you were dreaming about. I feel strange like that.

My mother says goodbye and that she'll see me Sunday. The rest I can't really make out above the rush of my piss streaming into the bowl, and then I hear Jason saying, "You said 7," his mouth close to the door, startling me so that I miss the toilet and wet the floor.

"What time is it?" I ask.

"Almost 10," he answers. The door opens. "Your mother said to give you this." He hands me a $20 bill.

"She's going to my gram's," I say. He's looking at my nipples.

"That's what she said," he says. He stands in the doorway, and over his shoulder I see Arby stepping out of my room. Wild-haired, he rubs his eyes.

"Jas," he says, making it sound like Chase, and it must only be odd for me, standing here, prick in hand, with two guys looking in. Odd but not bad.

"I was ready," Jason says, "but you two fucks..."

"Let me pee," Arby says, shoving past Jason and sidling up beside me with all the familiarity of a Siamese twin. I pinch out the last few drops and cover up while Arby aims, having to press down hard.

There's coffee left in the percolator. It's getting too late for fishing, the sun too high, burning off the mists that hang in the fields between the houses on the road off the lake. "But what else is there to do?" Arby says. He doesn't want to get dressed until he knows what we're doing. I've put on some jeans and sniff at the steam rising up from my cup. "We could go into Syracuse," he says.

"What for?" I say. "There's nothing there."

"It's kind of cold," Arby says.

"It'll warm up," Jason says. He stands near a window. He wears boots and heavy socks, fatigues cut off into shorts, and one of Arby's dad's sweatshirts. His hair is a line of fringe over his eyes.

"We could take the boat out anyway, I suppose," Arby suggests. He's eating cereal out of a bowl without milk. His chest is dotted twice with those little brown nipples that have shrunk up even smaller from the chill, a little line of hair in the middle, a continuation of the line that stems from his crotch.

"Might as well," I say, thinking we could get some beer and get fucked up. That's all I ever really think of these days. I like what it does to me and what it does to Arby, how we loosen up and nothing seems to matter much except that we get off. And I am hoping I might see Jason stripped down to his undershorts again, rising up out of the water one more time.

"Bring the radio," Arby says, getting up to retrieve his pants from my room.

$$f\,f\,f$$

In the lake's center we cut the boat's engine and put down an anchor. Arby scrambles up the ladder to the roof. He strips down to blue trunks that are tight and look like somebody's father's, and I want to take them off, hook my fingers into the front and pull on them, dragging them down his fleecy thighs.

Jason doesn't have trunks but doesn't mind going down to his boxers. He's the only man I know other than my grandpa who wears undershorts like those, so it seems like dress-up to me, and I watch him the way he says he doesn't like.

Arby spreads a blanket just big enough for the three of us. Jason stands up over his pile of shed clothes. His body is white but swirled over with hairs that all line up and seem to make a pattern over his skin. His boxers are white but patterned with little green fleurs-de-lis, new-looking, baggy. I see him looking at me, holding his hair out of his eyes. He dives over the side into the murky green lake. I lean out to watch him surface and remember last night when Arby broke off from sucking long enough to tell me he'd seen Jason naked. "Tell me about him," I say now, and Arby looks over his shoulder as though Jason might be back there, even though we hear him kicking and splashing and gasping below us. "Cold?" I call down to him, catching a glimpse of him and his seal-slicked hair.

"I used to watch him jerk off," Arby says, coming close and whispering. I watch his lips. "He'd have me sit on his bed with him, and he'd be naked, and I'd be all dressed, and I couldn't even touch myself, or else he'd stop the whole thing. He'd sit with his back against the headboard, legs spread, knees bent, heels touching, and I could see everything."

"Is he big?" I ask, and Arby nods.

There's a creep in my shorts, a stiffening that I don't like hiding from Arby. I call attention to it, spreading my own legs.

"Oh, don't mess with me now," Arby says in his indiscreet blue trunks.

$$f\ f\ f$$

In between them on the stinking blanket, nothing makes sense. When I dare to, I roll off my stomach onto my back, ignoring the hump of hardness that is plain to see in my shorts, and I pretend I'm interested in the swirl of clouds over us. The radio plays our favorite songs—"Born to Run" and "Brandy" and the one I secretly like by the Cornelius Brothers and Sister Rose. I turn and look at Jason with one eye: brown nipple, black tangle of hair just below the navel, pale thigh. *I know you, Jason Cortland,* I say to myself, wondering how attached he is these days to the boyish game he used to play with his stepbrother.

When my hair is sun-dried, I jump off the roof of the boat into the shock of cold water. I swim in the dark green of it, and it's like swimming in a beer bottle. I swim under the boat to its other side. I whistle when I surface, and Jason looks over the side, his face all shadowed, hair hanging all around it.

We dodge horseflies and drink icy beer. Jason's boxers cling
sheerly when they're wet. He plucks the front away from him
until he finds a towel to wrap around his waist. He jumps
instead of dives; otherwise, the water would peel off his shorts
and leave them floating in his wake. When he climbs up the
ladder, the water runs off him and he shines. He catches me
watching him, his shorts going opaque though still plastered
to his crotch, the outline of his dick like a fist against his cold-
tightened balls. "Quit it," he says softly.

I shrug. Arby's on the roof, asleep. Jason comes close to
where I'm sitting, shaded, going into the cooler for another
beer, no towel now. You can see the shore all around us; it's a
lake you can swim across if you're a good swimmer. I'm not,
but Arby is. Jason's shorts stick to him, hugging the curve of his
ass. He swigs his beer, straightening, and it's all right there for
me to see, hanging like ripe fruit, all heavy and wet. His hand
covers it, and I look up his long torso, past his bobbing Adam's
apple to his downcast eyes. The bottle leaves his mouth with a
soft smack. Look at what the cold water and slight breeze does
to his nipples, those chocolate kisses. His dick grows, tenting
the front of his boxers. He swats at the swelling, watching for
my reaction.

"Ain't it a monster?" he says proudly, appreciating his gift
from God. I've gone to stone myself, the blunt-ended shaft having snaked itself up and out, creeping toward my belly button.
He sees it too and ignores it.

"He's going to burn up there," he says, looking up toward
the roof.

$$f\,f\,f$$

I wanted him then. I wanted to pull off those flimsy soaked
shorts and get him into my mouth, to feel those tight balls
against my chin, his slick-skinned shaft sliding along my
tongue. I'm thinking this at the Hotel, my dick all hard because

I didn't wear underwear. I'm in the middle again, and every once in a while Arby's leg comes to rest against mine. The bar's empty save for us three, and Stoolie gave us money for the jukebox. Arby's talking about getting a job in Cicero. "I can work my way up to management in no time," he says.

"From stock boy to manager," Jason says, staring at bottles.

"It happens," Arby says. "Don't say it, Pete." He swats at me.

"I guess it's possible," I say, letting go of my glass.

"Anything's possible," Jason says, lifting his shoulders, his left leg touching my right. "I wasn't saying anything about it not being possible, I was just saying— "

"What?" Arby says, standing up and wedging himself between me and the bar, my leg fitting into his crotch and driving me crazy.

Jason's eyes take note of everything, and his leg moves away from mine. "Nothing," he says.

"Elbows," Stoolie says, and we take them off the bar.

$$f\,f\,f$$

I forgot my mother was gone for the weekend, but Jason remembered. The house is ours.

"I don't ever want to work," I hear myself saying. We're at the kitchen table again. Arby's not saying anything, but when Jason gets up to take a piss, he leans over the table and tells me how bad he's got it, this need to screw. I need it too, I tell him, nodding, thinking about Jason's thick roll.

"Let's go to bed," Arby hisses. The toilet flushes. I point my chin at the bathroom, meaning, *What about him?* Arby shrugs.

Jason comes back, zipping his fly. I can see the lay of his dick in his jeans, and he knows it. I recall how he grabbed my shirt the day before, bringing me close enough for a kiss.

"I'm going to go," he says.

"Sleep on the couch," I tell him, wanting him to remain.

"Whatever," he says.

In my room Arby strips, his skinny cock pointing at me. He grabs at my clothes. "Take them off," he pleads. His eyes are crazy, and I love his face. I'd almost kiss him. His hands pull at my belt; he pushes his face into my shirt-covered belly. When I'm naked he pulls me down on him, my dick going into the trough of his thighs. He fingers one of my nipples until it's hard and aching like my cock, and he breathes in my ear.

I hear the door open, that soft sound it makes, and the air changes in the room—I feel it on my skin and wonder if Arby notices. My ass tightens for him, flexes, and I push myself between Arby's thighs, enjoying the soft rasp of hairs there. Arby's hands wander over my back; he uses his quick-bitten nails like a girl. His legs open a little more, a small invite, and my cock slides into the sweaty crack, the damp under his balls, his little pink. His legs slide up my flanks, and his little ass gyrates—he wants it. I have to take a look at his face to see what's going on. I feel his cold heels on my ass.

He puts his lips on my chest, and his tongue slides to one of my red pokes. I tilt my hips, wanting badly to get inside him, to slip it in and start a good, hard fuck. I push and push and get nowhere; he's dry, and I'm stuck. Every move I make pulls on his face.

"Spit on it first," we hear, and Arby's eyes bulge. I see him look around me and then at me. I pull out of his butt's hard grip and drop a gob of spit down onto my rosy knob and work it all over my shaft. "His ass too," Jason says, showing me where with his finger. He's stripped down to sleeping clothes, a pair of his funny boxers, the front all spotted up from the leaking his cock has done.

"Now, go gentle," he says.

"Yeah," Arby says.

"I know," I say, feeling cranky all of a sudden. Arby's wet, little pink as kisses my spitty head.

"There you go," Arby says tightly as I slide in.

f f f

I bounce off the backs of Arby's thighs. He closes his eyes, and I weave my fingers through his stubby toes. Jason's shorts fall down, and he's working on his thick, long shaft. He lets go of it and swings it around like a snake, and I am compelled to fuck Arby harder.

The man beneath me pinches my tits, and Jason touches my ass cheek almost tenderly. He steps up behind me, and I feel it, what he wants to do to me. I shake my head.

"I can't let you ruin me with that thing," I say.

"Relax," he says. "I just want to slide it around on you."

I feel the heat of him rest against the split of my rump. He takes hold of my shoulders while Arby tries to get some revenge by twisting and pulling my nipples. The sensations double and become almost unbearable—the gritty suck of Arby's hole and the tugging he's doing on my pecs and the friction of Jason's pole and the frigging he's doing to my asshole—and then I can't feel anything but my own cock as it rams Arby's gash, and I squirt and squirt into the hot insides of my best friend.

"Not yet, not yet," Arby calls out, pumping his fist. I'm useless, though, unable to keep from sobbing anytime my prick moves. Jason pushes me into him, wanting to get the job done, singing, "Come on, baby, come on," and Arby, suddenly silent, holding his breath, sprays me with his come. It's thin and runs off me like sweat, and Arby begins to pant, his legs stiffening, his back arching, and then he chugs out a thick clot of goo that lands like pudding on his chest and belly.

"Oh, my," Jason says to the ceiling. He backs away and starts using both hands to pull off a shot that nearly blinds Arby. I lap it, viscous and going cold fast, off the end of Jason's prick while he shudders under my tongue. I lick it off Arby's face too, while Jason sniffs at his fingers.

14

In Between

fff

We're hungry enough to make ourselves breakfast at 3 in the morning. Bacon pops and sizzles, and Arby ruins our over-easy eggs. "We're having scrambled," Arby announces, stirring up the mess.

Jason leans back in his chair, his cock hanging out the leg of his boxers and resting on the seat, reminding me of a pet. I want nothing more than to put my knees on the cold linoleum and get him into my mouth.

He catches my look and almost grins. "Later," he says quietly, and Arby wants to know what we'll do tomorrow.

"It is tomorrow," I tell him.

f f f

Patience Is a Virtue

BY

KEVIN JOHNSON

I think it's a universal rule that every gay boy develops a crush on his best friend. It's certainly true of Carl and me. When Joanne introduced us, I was dumbstruck—he was fucking beautiful! Taller than me—not difficult, I'm only 5 foot 6—with blond hair, a square-jawed face, and a great body. I had no doubt he was straight because Joanne was the kind of girl who settled that question pretty quickly. Joanne, Carl, and I always hung out together, and Carl had no problem with my being gay. We'd go out on our own if Jo wasn't free. He'd even flirt with me a little bit, but I knew it didn't mean anything.

Gradually, I started to realize how much I really liked Carl. A dozen times I drifted away while looking at him: at the biceps that stretched his sleeves or the rounded butt cheeks that filled his jeans. I imagined him stripping, offering his body to me to do with whatever I wanted, letting me touch him and lick his dick until it was stiff and dribbling on my face...and then I'd realize we were in the middle of a conversation. I'd stutter and blush and try to hide the bulge in my pants.

He was perfectly comfortable around me. He didn't even mind sharing a bed if he stayed over. I never got any sleep on these occasions. My head was swimming with lust, and I had to fight every urge to grab my raging dick and beat it. He was due to stay over one time when my parents were away. Carl arranged to have a crate of beer, and about eight guys came over. Carl had invited four of his buddies, and I invited J.P., a guy I had played around with once, and Paul, a straight friend. We sat and drank and talked, the guys telling how far they had gotten with various girls. While I wasn't interested in the gory details about sex with females, the others seemed to be fascinated to meet a real-life homosexual and couldn't stop asking me questions.

"How much have you actually done, Kevin?" Carl's cute friend Jason asked me. "I mean with another guy."

"Actually, not that much. There was this one guy I met. We just had oral sex, and I enjoyed it."

"How about you, Carl? How far have you gotten with Jo?"

"I...I haven't done anything with Jo," Carl responded. "It just never felt like the right moment. I shouldn't tell you this...but I think I'm gonna dump her." Everyone was amazed. Jo was not the kind of girl who got dumped. "In fact," he continued, "I think I have feelings for someone else. Don't ask me who, 'cause I can't say anything yet. And don't any of you dare tell Jo before I do."

We promised not to say a word. The guys asked more questions—how I knew I was gay, how early I had realized it, and if I've never thought about girls at all—but there was one question I didn't expect.

"Don't you worry about how big your dick is?" Paul instantly went red in the face, embarrassed he'd brought up the subject. "Every guy looks at other guys' dicks...just to compare. In the showers or whatever." He looked around at us all. "Don't look at me like that, you guys. You know we all do it." Reluctantly, they all agreed. "Straight guys worry about it, and we don't ever get near another guy's dick. But you gay guys can actually compare another guy's dick while it's, like, in action. What if you're not up to scratch?"

"I think I'd be OK," I responded. "As long as the other guy's not too small, anyway. I guess I'll get used to other guys being smaller than me 'cause, I tell you, I got a pretty big dick."

Carl's friend Dan laughed. "How can you have a big dick, little guy? You're only three feet tall."

"I bet I got a bigger dick than you, fat boy," I taunted. "I bet you can't even see yours past your fat belly."

"Who says you got a bigger dick? How much you wanna bet?"

"I got a ruler over there on my desk, and I can prove my dick is bigger than yours."

"Well," Carl said, "I guess there's only one way to solve this. Kevin, go get your ruler. Let's see for real who's got the bigger dick."

I went and picked up my 12-inch plastic ruler. I was already throwing a bone just from all this talk of dicks. Carl took the ruler and held it out. "Come on, Dan, you first. It was your idea, after all."

"You can't be serious!" Dan stammered.

"You started it, so you can't back out now," Carl snorted.

"I'll only do it if the rest of you do it," he muttered. "I don't wanna be the only one standing here with my dick out."

"Come on, boys," Jason said. "Let's show Dan how it's done!" After a few glances around the circle, Dan's little noodle of a dick made its first appearance. I knew I had won my bet right there, but now that we were at this stage, I was going to make sure I enjoyed it.

Dan pulled at his little pud, trying to get some life into it. The rest of us had no problems. I had been hard long before. J.P. was staring at the other guys, but I only had eyes for Carl.

From the time his dick first flopped out, it took maybe three seconds until he was standing tall and proud. Dear God, it was beautiful. As it arced up over his muscular stomach, I realized it was even bigger than mine.

Since Dan still wasn't hard, Jason took the ruler first. "I got seven inches, boys," he announced before passing the ruler on to J.P., who eagerly took it and held it against his raging stiff dick.

"Six inches," he said in a panting whisper.

Paul measured in at just under seven inches.

It was my turn next, my chance to prove that a little guy could still carry a dick to be reckoned with. I held the ruler next to my stiff shaft. "Eight inches."

Carl flashed a big smile right at me. It almost made me shoot my load right there.

Dan had worked up as much of a hard-on as he was going to get, so he took the ruler and quickly held it to his cock. "Five inches," he muttered, stuffing his already softening dick back into his pants. The other two measured at seven inches and six inches, and then my ruler made its way to its final destination.

"Looks like I beat you, Kevin," he smiled, "although you put up some stiff competition." I didn't even notice my dick sticking out while I watched Carl. There was no doubt his dick was easily the biggest in the room, but he took a perverse pleasure out of making us wait, saying, "Patience is a virtue, boys." Carl counted. "Six, seven, eight...my God, nine..." Carl looked up and smiled slowly. "Nine and a half inches. You got a big dick, Kevin, but you get second place."

The excitement of seeing Carl's beautiful cock finally pushed me over the edge. I urgently fumbled with my painfully hard dick, only just managing to get it back into my shorts before it began pulsing and jerking as I shot off a massive load. I prayed that the other guys didn't notice. Carl glanced at me with a look that could only have meant he knew what was happening. It was a really intense look, as if to say, *I know, Kevin, I know. And thanks.*

I was horrified. I could never look Carl in the face again. I sat in shock, barely noticing when the guys drifted out, making their way home. I guess after everybody had shown their dicks, there was nowhere else for the party to go. They caught cabs or walked if they didn't live far. Eventually only Carl and I were left. I had never felt so uncomfortable in my life. Carl was on the couch with his legs spread, drinking a beer. He looked up at me and smiled.

"Finally," he breathed, "I have you all to myself."

"What's that supposed to mean?" I asked, completely confused.

"It means I'm glad the other guys left 'cause all that talk of sex and seeing your big hard cock at last made me so horny I just wanted to grab you and fuck you right here on the couch."

"But..." I could hardly speak.

"I'm gonna dump Jo. I was never into her. I have feelings for someone else. I told you that."

"Who?"

He got up from his seat and came over to me. With a gentleness that belied his power and strength, he touched my face. "You, silly."

He lifted me with his strong hands until our bodies were so close, I could feel the heat of his skin. He slowly brought his lips to mine. Just a touch at first, the kiss blossomed into a passionate battle. I lifted his shirt and felt the hot, firm flesh underneath. Carl did the same, his hands roaming over my naked chest, stroking the smooth skin.

"You're...so...beautiful," I panted.

"I think you're beautiful too, Kevin," he whispered. "I've been wanting to do this since the moment I met you."

Carl knelt down, chuckling as he felt the dampness in my pants. Undoing them, he stroked me through my sticky underwear, then stretched out his tongue, and an electric tingle shot through my body. He pulled down my shorts, and my stiff dick sprang out. He smiled, stretched his lips wide, and slipped them over the end. He didn't stop until the head of my dick slipped into the hot, wet tightness of his throat. My breath caught, my legs went weak, and I nearly fell over. I never imagined anything could feel so good. It wasn't long before I shot another load, and he swallowed every drop. My dick didn't go soft for a second.

He stood up and led me over to the couch, urgently wrestling his dick out into the warm air. I pounced on it, licking it from head to base, going absolutely crazy over every beautiful inch. Carl threw his head back with a hiss of pleasure. He shed his jeans and pulled a small foil packet out of his pocket. Giving my dick a few more affectionate licks, he slowly rolled the condom down over it. I never imagined Carl would willingly take another man's dick up his ass, but that's exactly what he was getting ready to do.

He stood over me on the couch and squatted down. I felt the tight ring of muscle easing itself onto my shaft, and Carl moaned. I asked if it was hurting him, and he shook his head and forced himself farther down. As he settled into position, I realized that I could still reach his huge erection with my mouth. Carl began to lift and lower himself on my shaft, sending more incredible sensations through my body, while I sucked greedily at his dick. Then he stopped, lifted off, and got down on all fours, looking at me with glazed eyes.

"Come on, Kevin," he pleaded. "Fuck me like you really mean it."

I got behind him, pointing my shaft down toward his glistening asshole, and gently slipped back inside. He urged me on, to go faster and harder, to really give it to him. I couldn't help but do as he said. I drove my dick into him with an energy I never knew I had.

"I'm gonna come again..." I gasped. The spasms shook my body, and my dick swelled up inside Carl's ass, blasting out shot after shot. I collapsed helplessly onto Carl's muscular back. I couldn't believe it—my dick was still hard after three of the strongest orgasms I had ever felt. I was so exhausted, there was no way I could do any more. But again Carl had other ideas.

He gently laid me down flat on the couch, then covered me with his own beautiful body, kissing me passionately. The feeling of his giant penis, aching for attention between us, started to bring me around again. He hitched my calves up in the air, and I felt cool breath against my asshole. When he flicked at it with his tongue, I almost cried with pleasure.

Carl stretched a condom over his incredible dick and covered it with lube. "Don't worry, baby," he said, "I won't hurt you. I'll take it slow. You'll love it, I promise." I believed him with all my heart because his tongue had relaxed me so much, but more than that, because Carl had called me his baby. I was hopelessly in love. He slowly teased my hole with the tip of his dick, nudging and pressing until I was practically begging him to put it in. I felt the thick head slip through the ring of muscle. My head fell back, my mind went blank, and my eyes glazed over with a fog of pleasure. He was right; I did love it. No pain as I had feared, only exquisite pleasure.

Carl gradually slipped one inch after another into my body, and I rose higher into heaven with each one. Finally, he started to pull himself back out, grazing past my prostate, sending waves of ecstasy through me. His pace grew faster and faster, until he was slamming his enormous dick into my virgin ass. Only a few minutes later, Carl let out a howl, and his entire body tensed up. The sight of all that muscle straining over my body made my own dick puff up, and I shot yet another huge wad of cream all over my chest without having even touched myself. I felt Carl's big dick spasming in my ass, and it seemed to go on forever. Minutes later Carl slowly dragged his massive shaft out of my ass. He fell on top of me with a big goofy grin, his sweaty chest slipping against my come-covered one. We both began to calm down, stealing quick kisses in between gasping breaths.

"How do you feel?" he asked me gently. "Did you like it?"

"Oh, man, it felt wonderful!" I told him. "It was the most amazing experience of my life." Then, before I could stop myself, I blurted out, "I love you!" Carl breathed a sigh of relief.

"Kevin, I love you too. I want to be with you forever." He kissed me again, fastening our lips and tongues together like Super Glue. I was so excited by everything, I came again as we lay together, the sperm spreading its warmth across our stomachs. "My God, boy, what the hell are you made of?" Carl exclaimed in amazement. "Do you realize you've come five times tonight?"

"It's just what you do to me. I can't help it. I've been patiently waiting for something like this for so long. Like you said, patience is a virtue."

"Well, everything comes to he who waits, baby. You don't have to be patient anymore."

f f f

School Queer

BY

BOB VICKERY

Saturday night is my night to shine. All the guys neck with their dates out at Bass Lake or the drive-in over on Route 27 or maybe at Jackson Lookout. But because the girls here are all "saving themselves," they tend to get the guys wound up so tight that the poor young studs could fuck a knotty pine by the time they finally take the little virgins home. So with blue balls aching, they head to the back of the Bass Lake boathouse, where they know they'll find me waiting. I suck the hard cocks of these Southern Baptist boys. I let them frantically fuck my face as they clamp their eyes shut and imagine it's not my mouth wrapped around their stiff, urgent dicks but pussy.

They groan and whimper while their full-to-bursting balls slap against my chin, and when they finally shoot, they cry out "Cindy Lou" or "Peggy Beth" as their loads splatter against the back of my throat. When they've finally got the relief they've needed all evening, the guys pull up their jeans and walk away, disappearing into the bushes without so much as a "thanks." But before I can get too resentful, the next shadowy figure rounds the corner of the boathouse, and the ritual starts up all over again. Sometimes there are actual lines. Other times the guys stand side by side, and I work my way down the row and tend to the stiff dicks throbbing in front of me. During the week I'm shunned by most of the other students at the small Baptist college I attend. But on Saturday night the boys can't get enough of me. It's a lonely life, being the school queer, but I serve a useful function, so I'm tolerated.

I don't suck every dick that comes my way. And among the men I deign to suck off, I do have my favorites. At the top of the list is Bill McPherson—what a sweet, hot guy. I can tell he was raised right: well-nourished, muscular body, straight teeth, clear complexion, glossy brown hair, steady blue eyes that meet your gaze with honest conviction—and so earnest! That's the charm of these Baptist boys. They're so damn wholesome, you just want to eat them up. Bill is well-liked on campus, an unexceptional student but still a big fish in this tiny pond: captain of the wrestling team and vice president of the Kappa Gamma Chi fraternity. He dates Becky Michaelson, this year's Azalea Princess in the school's homecoming parade. Lucky for me, she holds on to her cherry as if it were a piece of the One True Cross. More Saturdays than I can remember, Bill has come around behind the boathouse, frustrated, shy, embarrassed, dropped his pants, and offered his dick to me. And it's such a beautiful dick: thick, meaty, veined, pink, and swollen with a head that flares out like a fleshy red plum.

I love making love to Bill's dick. I suck it slowly, drag my tongue up the shaft, and finally turn my attention to the head. Then I probe into Bill's piss slit, work my lips back down the thick tube of flesh, and roll Bill's ball sac around in my mouth as I stroke him. His cock is familiar enough to me that I'm able

BOYS WILL BE BOYS

to draw him to the brink of shooting, back off, and draw him even closer.

Bill gasps and groans, his breathing gets heavy, his body trembles under my hands as I knead and pull on his muscled torso. When he finally shoots—every time he shoots—he cries out "Sweet Jesus in heaven!" like he's offering his orgasm to God. When I finally climb to my feet, wiping my mouth, damn if Bill doesn't look me in the eye, shake my hand, and thank me. It's a small thing, maybe, but he's the only one who acknowledges me, which gives me just one more reason to like him.

$$f\ f\ f$$

Except for his final thanks, Bill has never spoken to me during our cocksucking sessions. So it's something of a surprise when one late-spring night while I'm on my knees before him, he clears his throat and asks, "Do...do you ever do this to Nick Stavros?"

I take Bill's dick out of my mouth and look up at him, but his face is in shadow, and I can't read his expression. I know from seeing the two of them around campus together that Bill and Nick are good friends. "Yeah," I reply. "Nick comes around here from time to time—not nearly as much as you do."

Bill doesn't say anything, and I pick up where I left off. I twist my head as I slide my lips up Bill's cock shaft. I know he likes that. He starts to pump his hips and slide his dick in and out of my mouth.

After about a minute Bill clears his throat again. "What's Nick's dick like?" he asks. I look up at him again, and Bill, seeing the quizzical expression on my face, laughs nervously. "Nick's always kidding me about what a ladies' man he is," he says, "and so I was just curious about how he...well, measures up to me."

"You don't have anything to worry about," I say. "Your dick is awesome." I put it back in my mouth.

26

"Yeah, well, OK," Bill says, "but what's Nick's dick like?"

This is weird, I think. "You really want me to describe Nick's dick?"

"Yeah," Bill says. "Do you mind?" By his tone of voice I'm almost sure he's blushing.

"Unlike yours, it's uncut," I begin. "And a lot darker. It curves down, which makes it easier for me to suck. Though I sometimes wonder whether that makes it harder for him to actually fuck someone. It's a mouthful but not quite as long as yours, though maybe a little thicker. His piss slit is really pronounced."

Bill listens intently—as if there's going to be an after-lecture test on all of this. I half expect him to start taking notes. When he doesn't say anything else, I return to blowing him. After another minute he clears his throat again. "And his balls, what are they like?"

OK, I think. "He's got some low hangers," I say. "They're a couple of bull nuts. When he fucks my face, they slap against my chin. I love sucking on them, washing them with my tongue, though I can only do them one at a time. They're too big to fit in my mouth at the same time."

Bill says nothing else during the remainder of his blow job. As his dick gets harder, right before he shoots, he winds his fingers into my hair and gently tugs at it. "Sweet Jesus in heaven," he murmurs, as usual, just before his dick pulses and floods my mouth with his load.

On my knees before Bill, I hold the post for a long moment as his dick slowly softens in my mouth.

Finally, he let himself slip out of me and pulls his jeans up. As always, he shakes my hand and thanks me before disappearing into the night.

From that night on we settle into a new routine whenever I suck Bill off. Bill peppers me with questions, asking for more details about Nick's cock or his balls or his ass or how he acts when he shoots. I carefully answer every question, describing in detail just what it feels like to have Nick slide his dick in my mouth. Eventually, I tell him how Nick likes to push my face hard against his belly to make me choke on his dick and to see my nose buried in his dense thicket of black pubes. We establish that the odor of Nick's balls is like the sweaty, pungent scent of a male animal in rut. I recount the low grunts Nick makes as his load squirts down my throat and what that load tastes like (salty, with just a faint hint of garlic). I watch Bill's dick stiffen whenever I give him a report on my sessions with Nick, and I think how strange it is to know Bill's secret: He is queer for his best friend.

One day Bill catches up to me on the main quadrangle. I try to hide my surprise. Normally, nobody as high up on the campus pecking order as Bill would be caught dead talking in public to the school queer.

"Hey, Pete," he says. "How's it going?"

"I'm OK," I say cautiously. We walk along the brick path in silence. The people we pass stare at us with the same astonishment I feel.

"Look, Pete," Bill says, lowering his voice but keeping his eyes straight ahead. "Can you be at the boathouse tonight? Around 11?"

I let a couple of beats go by. "It's a weekday night, Bill. I have a chemistry test tomorrow that I have to study for."

Bill stops and looks at me, and I can see the desperation in his eyes. "I'm begging you, man," he says. *This is all very weird,* I again think.

"OK," I finally say. "If it's really that big a deal for you, I'll be there."

Bill looks relieved. "Thanks," he says. He turns on his heel and walks off.

$$f f f$$

The moon is nearly full tonight, and its light bounces off the lake and flickers against the boathouse walls. I sit on one of the overturned boats, smoke a cigarette, and wait. I glance at my watch: a little past 11. There's a rustle of bushes, and Bill steps out into the light.

"Hi, Bill," I say. But Bill looks behind him, not toward me. Again the bushes rustle, and suddenly Nick steps out and stands next to Bill. He glances at me, scowls, and looks away.

Bill takes a couple of steps closer. "Nick and I were double-dating tonight," he says, "But our girls just wouldn't put out." He gives a laugh that rings as false as a tin nickel. "And, boy, do we have a nut to bust! So we just swung by here tonight on the off chance that you'd be here to help us get a little relief."

I look at Nick, but he's still staring at the ground, refusing to meet my eyes. My gaze shifts back to Bill. "You guys are in luck," I say coolly. "I'm normally not here on a weekday night."

Neither Bill nor Nick says anything. After a couple of beats, I decide it's up to me to get this ball rolling. "Who wants to go first?" I ask.

"Why don't you go ahead, Nick?" Bill says, turning toward him. "I'll wait."

Nick shrugs, still taciturn. He has on a pair of cutoffs and a school T-shirt that tightly hugs his torso. Nick can be a surly bastard, and I like Bill way better, but there's no denying Nick's the more handsome of the two: intense dark eyes, an expressive mouth, powerful arms, a muscle-packed torso, and tight hips. As always, I feel my heart racing as he unbuckles his belt. I pull his cutoffs down past his thighs, and his fleshy, half-hard dick swings heavily from side to side.

"You take care of my buddy, Pete," Bill says. "Suck him real good!"

I glance at Bill. His lips are parted, and there's a manic gleam in his eyes. If he were any more excited, he'd have a stroke. Because I like Bill, I decide to give him the show he so obviously wants. I look up at Nick. "Why don't you take off all your clothes?" I say quietly. "It'll be more fun that way."

Nick glares down at me fiercely. After a brief pause he hooks his fingers under the edge of his T-shirt and pulls it over his head to reveal his muscular torso. He kicks off his shoes and steps out of his cutoffs. "OK?" he asks sarcastically.

I glance again at Bill. He marvels at Nick's naked body like a starving dog eyeing a T-bone steak.

"Yeah," I say. "That's just fine." I wrap my hand around Nick's dick and give it a squeeze. A clear drop of precome oozes out of his piss slit, and I lean forward and lap it up. I roll my tongue around his cock head and slide my lips down his shaft. I feel the thick tube of flesh harden to full stiffness in my mouth. I begin to bob my head and turn at an angle to give Bill a maximum view of the show. Nick responds by pressing his palms against both sides of my head and pumping his hips. Ever the aggressive mouth fucker, he slides his dick deep into my throat and pulls out again.

Bill moves toward us and stands next to Nick. He unzips his jeans, tugs them down, and his dick springs up, fully hard. "Now me," he says hoarsely. I look up into his face, but his eyes are trained on Nick's rigid, spit-slicked cock. Bill's the big man on campus, and I may be the queer boy with zero status, but tonight the tables are turned. It's clear that sweet Bill wants nothing more than to trade places with me—to get down on his knees and work Nick's dick like I'm doing. He wants Nick to plow his face. But it'll never happen. The closest he can let himself get to this fantasy is to have me suck his dick with the taste of Nick's dick still in my mouth. I actually pity the guy as I take his frustrated prong in my hand and slide my lips down the shaft.

While I work on Bill's dick, I reach over and start jacking off Nick, who pumps his hips, fucking my fist the same way he fucked my mouth a minute ago. One thrust catches him off-balance, and to steady himself he reaches out and lays his hand on Bill's shoulder. Bill reacts as if Nick's touch is a jolt of high-voltage current—his body jerks suddenly, and his muscles spasm.

This poor guy wants it so bad, I think. With my hand still around Nick's dick, I pull him closer to me until his dick is touching Bill's. I open my lips wider and take both their dicks in my mouth, feeling them rub and thrust against each other. Bill trembles at the sensation of Nick's dick against his, and Nick's breath comes out in short grunts.

I wrap my hands around their ball sacs and give them both a good tug. Bill groans, I feel his dick throb, and my mouth fills with his creamy load. "Sweet Jesus in heaven!" he gasps.

Nick thrusts hard into my throat. His breath comes faster now, and his legs begin to tremble. Suddenly, his body quivers, and his dick squirts jizz. I suck hard on the two dicks as they pulse in my mouth, their combined loads splattering against the back of my throat. I roll my tongue through the double dose in my mouth, savoring it like a gourmet.

Nick and Bill pull away. For a brief moment the three of us are frozen in our positions—me on my knees, come dribbling out of the corners of my mouth, Bill and Nick on each side of me, buck naked, their dicks half hard and sinking fast, their eyes not meeting each other.

Bill is the first to break the silence. "Damn," he says, his voice low. I look to meet his gaze, and the strangest thing happens. For an instant there's a spark, a little jolt of connection. For that brief flicker of time, I'm not the school faggot and he's not the big man on campus. We're buddies who've shared the pleasure of Nick's flesh.

Nick pulls up his pants and breaks the spell. He picks up his T-shirt and puts it on. "Let's go," he grunts to Bill. He walks back into the bushes and vanishes without looking back at either one of us. Bill gets dressed hurriedly and rushes after him. Before he disappears into the night, he turns, gives me one last look, and plunges into the bushes after Nick.

I get up and smooth my clothes, take a comb from my back pocket, and tidy my tousled hair. I walk in the opposite direction down to the patch of gravel where my car is parked. I'm sure I'll see Bill again this Saturday night, with or without Nick. If he's alone, we'll have something to talk about. Either way, it should be fun.

$f\,f\,f$

Three-Penny Dare

BY

R.J. MARCH

I'd given Travis three pennies because he'd asked for them, and I watched him put them down his pants. "Davis said you'd get them for me if I asked nice enough. He said you'd blow me for 3 cents. That right, Kyle?"

"Fuck yourself," I said, feeling a flash of hate for him. I found it hard to believe that Davis would say anything about what he and I did, putting himself in any position so open to ridicule. But then Davis was kind of stupid too, and maybe he thought Travis would think it was funny, and maybe he didn't bother to mention how he'd lie back, letting me crawl between his legs to lick his crotch and jerk him off.

"They're in my underpants, Kyle. One's, like, in my pubes, and the other two are under my balls. I can feel them. Why don't you dig them out for me, Kyle?" We were in his basement. There was a game on television—Penn State was kicking the shit out of Michigan. It was such a slaughter, we lost interest, sprawled on old sofas, one for each of us, drinking beer because his parents were out of town.

I could have left, but we'd just smoked a bowl, and I didn't feel as though I could actually move myself. I looked up at the dumb little windows near the ceiling that were set in little wells outside; you couldn't see anything unless you stood just under them, and then all you saw was the overhang of grass from above. I was thinking it was just like being buried and having a window in your coffin, only your coffin was huge and had big old lumpy sofas in it and a TV and your ex–best friend trying to get you to feel him up.

"You are so stoned," he said.

"Quit fucking with me," I told him. *What the fuck am I doing here?* I wondered.

"I got a pudgy just thinking about it," he said.

"You're such an incredible asshole, Travis, you know that?"

"This game sucks." He switched it off.

"No shit now, Kyle," he said, sitting up, making his face look very serious. "He told me you'd blow me for a nickel. Is that true?"

I shook my head.

"It's not?" he said, sounding incredulous, and I wondered just how much that dumbfuck had told him.

He shut up then and didn't say another word about Davis or me or the three pennies in his undershorts. He got up awkwardly—to take a leak, he announced quietly—and walked funny to the bathroom back by the laundry room. I listened to him, liking the sound. In the middle of the room I saw the copper shine of a penny, and I scrambled for it and picked it up, sniffing it before putting it in my pocket. Truth was, I'd have blown him for nothing.

f f f

"You need to learn to keep your fucking mouth shut." I was up in his face, smelling the Italian sub he'd had for lunch, my finger tapping on the small patch of soft black hair that had grown on his sternum.

"What the fuck's wrong with you?" Davis said, backing up. He was my height and age, 19, but 20 pounds lighter—not that that gave me any advantage over him. He was unscrupulous and meaner than I could ever hope to be. "And my mom's in the kitchen, so watch it, asshole."

"We need to get out of here then," I said carefully.

"Just settle down, Kyle," Davis said. He wiped his palms on his warm-up pants, looking around for something.

"Hurry the fuck up," I whispered hoarsely.

He gave me a cold look that made me bite the inside of my lip. "You better cool the fuck down, Kyle," he said, pointing his finger at me. He walked across the room and grabbed a gray sweatshirt off the back of a chair. "Come on," he said.

Outside, he walked to his car. "Mine," I said.

"Cool," he said. "I need gas anyway."

$$f\ f\ f$$

"And you're the one with the fucking secret," I said—whatever the hell that was supposed to mean. I'd taken us up to Bigger's Rock, a series of cliffs and clearings overlooking the Wallkill River. It was a party place for underage drinkers in the summer, but it was too cold to do anything now but look at the scenery. We called it Dyke's Peak because we saw Travis's sister kissing Amanda Betts there, slipping her hand up Amanda's Catholic-plaid skirt. I turned off the engine and sat looking out the window. I wasn't mad anymore, mostly because I'd noticed that Davis wasn't wearing socks. I took my hands off the steering wheel, turning toward him, and he got out of the car.

"I didn't say anything, Kyle, swear to God," he said over the roof of my Nova. "Why the fuck would I say anything? And to Travis, for chrissake? He's just dicking with you."

I'd already considered this—he really would have been cutting his own throat by saying anything to anyone. He stared at me, his hood up, eyes dark inside. He had thin lips that seemed always to be locked up in a smile, and his nose had a hard hook that kept him from being pretty but made him all the more beautiful. "Are we going up or what?" he asked.

$$f\,f\,f$$

"Maybe he wants some," Davis said. "He's just fishing. He's trying to get in your pants. You guys have been buds since, like, second grade or something, haven't you?"

I said, "Travis isn't like that."

Davis stopped on the trail, and I nearly ran into him. "I wasn't either—remember?"

I considered what he was trying to convince me of, but there was no way I was ever going to believe that Travis would do such a thing, not ever.

The sky was bright gray, and the hill across the river was dark. I was thinking that it would snow soon. Davis walked in front of me with his hands dug into the pouch of his sweatshirt, trying to stay out of the muddy ruts and keep his Pumas clean. I watched the way his butt flicked back and forth, how he walked on the balls of his feet, his hooded head bobbing.

There was a clean-edged cliff we liked. He was leading us there. "It's fucking cold," Davis said. The wind cut through my thin coat. He hopped around me, shouldering me, telling me how cold he was. "I'm cold too," I said.

"I wish we had a sleeping bag," he said. He pulled his hands out of his front pouch, and his sweatshirt lifted, showing the impress of his cock against the thin nylon of his warm-ups. He had a gigantic prick; I couldn't imagine doing much more with it than handling the thing, stroking it with both hands and kissing the fat bloom of its head, using the thick spit at the back of my throat for lube. He gave me a brown-eyed look, and I felt myself going all shy and buttery inside. He looked at me from the corners of his eyes, his head at a downward slant, his lips almost closed, breaths slipping out of him in small puffs. I glanced down and saw his hands fiddling inside his pants. I reached out, and he held open the waistband for me.

It was too late to do what I liked best, which was making him hard, feeling him go from a little spigot to a lead pipe. Now, there was something I could do with my mouth, until he'd grow and grow and my lips would stretch and stretch. Not that I wouldn't have stayed on him and done my best, but he was always reluctant to have me stay on him like that—afraid, I guess, that he'd lose it and come in my mouth or something, like that was a bad thing. "Just jerk it," he would say, hands on his hips, bouncing on the balls of his feet, the muscles along his thighs going taut. Sometimes he talked to me while I pulled on him. "That Wallace kid on the team, remember him? Did you think he was good-looking? How about Secor—now, that kid had a hot fucking body." He missed being in high school, missed soccer practice and the showers afterward—the wet, hairy huddle of guys who'd eye his plumbing furtively, enviously—the thickening rod, the great lathered balls. He'd linger as long as he could, until his dick threatened full erection. I wasn't the only one to notice but apparently the only one to let him know I'd noticed.

We stood face-to-face. I tucked his waistband underneath his balls and pulled on the hard shaft. It seeped and smeared my shirt cuff. I reached under his sweatshirt, where his skin was feverish. I found his nipple and toyed with it, rolling it between my fingers, something I think I liked more than he did. His nipples were pea-size and went hard quickly, and I loved getting one in my mouth to chew on gently. His stomach muscles fluttered under my fingertips, and I took his cock in both hands, a stranglehold that made the head bulge and go dark, and I bowed to put my mouth on it, wanting to lap up the big rolling drop of precome that had welled up in his deep piss slit. From there, I licked down his shaft to nuzzle his furry balls, the bag gone wrinkly from the cold. He liked the slide my fingers made over his dick head—I could tell by the way he leaked and from the roll of his hips. I looked up to find him watching me, his brown eyes tearing in the wind. He had something to say but wouldn't let it out. I covered his cock end with my mouth, tonguing into his hole, letting my lips go slack to slip down over his shaft.

"Stop," I heard him say, but I couldn't. I got as much of him into my mouth as I could, and he tried to break free from me, but I held him close and choked myself on him until I felt the hot blast of his come jettisoned down my throat. He pushed me off roughly then, shuddering. "Shit," he said. "Why the fuck did you do that?"

"Wanted to," I said, his residue dripping off my chin.

He wiped himself off on the inside of his sweatshirt, looking around us. I felt the cold, damp ground under me and the hot hardness I had in my jeans and wondered if he was ever going to take care of me.

"Get up," he said, his teeth coming together, the cold getting to him finally. "Let's go."

$$f\ f\ f$$

"I'm telling you, he wants it," Davis said. We were at the mall, standing in the store Travis worked in. We could see him standing by his register, picking at something on his knuckle, looking bored. "He wants you," Davis said as Travis looked across the store and spotted us. "Look at the way he smiles at you."

"Shut up," I said. He was walking over to us, swinging his arms wide.

"What's up, dudes?" he said, looking at Davis, then at me. To my amazement, there was nothing on his face, no trace of a smirk, not a reference to last week's three-penny dare. "I'm done at 5—what are you guys doing tonight?"

Davis looked at me, and I shrugged. "Why don't you come over to my place?" Travis pursued. "My dad went to Charlotte, and my mom's at my sister's."

"Sounds cool," Davis said.

"I just bought Redneck Ram-page—we can blow the fuck out of cows and shit," Travis said.

"Awesome," I said. Travis hitched up his shirtsleeve, baring his biceps. "Security just caught two guys in our shitter here fucking," he said, whispering.

"No way," Davis said.

"Absolutely going to town," Travis said, beaming. "They didn't even hear the guard, they were so into it."

"Fuck, man," Davis said, shaking his head.

"You got that right," Travis said, smirking.

In the car Davis said to me, "He's so fucking fixated, man, I'm telling you. He wants it, I know he does."

"Whatever," I said, putting the car in reverse.

$$f\ f\ f$$

I changed my mind like 10 times about going with Davis to Travis's house. But there was something about the idea of the three of us getting together that was like an itch in my brain I couldn't get to. Waiting for 9 o'clock, I sat up in my room, listening to my mom and dad bitching at each other about where they were going for their vacation—Maine or Hilton Head. I sat on my bed, looking through a month-old *Rolling Stone*, wanting to call Davis up and tell him I wasn't going to go, and then I was looking at this Tommy Hilfiger ad—three guys playing at the shore in wet boxers—and I felt myself getting a little pudgy. I dug into my jeans and got a handful, loving the way the front of my briefs felt, all full and warm. I slid out of my jeans and went to the mirror on the back of my door. I ran my hand over the filled-up pouch, my cock hugging the curve of my balls, the whole neat and pretty package.

"No, wait," I heard. "Let's ask Kyle."

"Jesus," I said, yelling to my parents through the door. "Just leave me out of it!"

My father came walking down the hall. I made a lunge for my jeans on the bed and was trying to step into them when he opened the door.

"What do you think, son?" he asked.

"I think I'm going to Travis's," I said.

I walked over to Aeropagetica Road. Davis's car was parked out front, and the porch light was on. I let myself in.

I could hear the music from downstairs and Travis laughing. I walked through the living room and kitchen. "It hurts like that," I heard Davis say. I stopped still, standing at the door at the top of the stairs. My heart started beating hard in my chest, and I felt really, really stupid all of a sudden. "That's better," Davis said.

"I told you," Travis said.

I had to see them, to catch them in their naked embrace, because not only was I insanely jealous, I was also poking out the front of my jeans again.

"Fuck, my head's gonna explode."

"Let me help."

I eased myself down the first step. Travis grunted. All I was thinking was, *You couldn't fucking wait for me?*

"Holy shit," Davis breathed.

I crouched down, trying to find them. The couches were empty. The guys were nowhere to be seen. I crept down two more treads and saw Travis's calves. He was clothed and standing, and Davis, I figured, was kneeling in front of him, which pissed me off even more, considering that he had never once made an offer to go down on me.

"I'm stuck," Davis said, and Travis moved, and I saw Davis hanging, his shirt covering his face, his torso bared, in some sort of hanging-boot contraption. "Get me the fuck down."

$f f f$

"They had one in *American Gigolo*," Travis said later. "Remember? Richard Gere?"

"You were, like, 1 year old when that came out," I said, holding the joint that Travis had handed me when I came in. "Who rolled this?" I tried to pass it to Davis, but he waved it on. I held it out for Travis, who said, "It's all yours, bud."

"I'm fucking zonked," Davis said, yawning.

"You want to try the boots?" Travis asked me.

I shook my head. "I'm afraid of heights," I said, cracking Davis up. He lay sprawled on the couch, and I leaned against it, sitting on the floor. Travis went over to the boots that were lying on the floor.

"They're fucking antiques, man," Davis said, his arm swinging off the couch and coming to rest on my shoulder.

I watched Travis put them on and reach for the bar overhead. His stomach was uncovered for a moment, and I saw the cuts of his abs. Where'd the baby fat go, I wondered, and how'd I miss it? He swung his legs up and got the boots hooked onto the bar. His shirt fell over his head, like Davis's had, and he tucked it into his shorts, but it kept pulling free, so he took it off. And then he started doing crunches.

"Fuck," I whispered. I was awestruck and staring—I couldn't help it. His body was beautiful, and I'd never noticed.

Davis snored behind me, missing the show. I watched as Travis's stomach divided itself into neat, symmetrical sections, little rectangles of muscle. "Sweet," I said quietly.

And then he was done, getting himself out of the boots, asking me if I wanted to try. He had a mouthful of white teeth his lips struggled to cover. His hair, cut short, was the color of pennies. He twisted his shirt like a wet washrag, making the muscles in his chest jump.

"Your buddy's out, man," he said, looking at Davis's arm slung over my shoulder. Then his brows sort of came together, and one corner of his mouth went up. "He's like your best friend now, huh?"

I shrugged, feeling guilty. I couldn't pinpoint when it happened, when Travis stepped back and Davis stepped up. Maybe when Travis started dating Shawna Baylich and I realized we weren't going to be two boys together forever. Maybe when Davis started getting boners in the showers, looking at me from the corners of his eyes, maybe that's when I had to decide which was more important to me—dick or friendship? Isn't that what Travis had done?

"I'm hungry," he said.

"Me too," I said, not thinking.

𝆑 𝆑 𝆑

We went upstairs, leaving Davis on the couch. Travis went to the refrigerator, and I hit the cupboards. "Dude," he said, all excited, and I turned and got a blast of whipped cream in the face.

"Fuck!" I shouted, and Travis laughed, pointed and laughed. He took a swipe at some off my chin and licked his finger, giggling convulsively. He came back for more, and I grabbed the can from him and squirted him from neck to navel. He stepped back and looked down at himself, and then he looked at me, cocking his head. "Oh, man," he said slowly. I put a dollop on each of his nipples.

"You really suck," he said, shaking his head.

"So you keep telling me," I said, impressing myself with the quick comeback.

"Can't blame me for trying, can you?"

The air went crackly—there was this static in my ears. I felt the whipped cream sliding down my cheek. He touched some again and licked his finger, and then he stepped close and put his face near mine, licking the line of my jaw.

I felt his tongue like a blow and stepped back, feeling pushed.

"I've been wanting to do that since, like seventh grade, I think," he said.

"Shut the fuck up," I said.

He hooked his finger into the waistband of my jeans and pulled me close. "Is this going to piss Davis off?" he asked.

I shook my head. "I'm in shock," I said.

"Do you need a blanket?"

"I'm having a heart attack, I think," I said, looking at his frothed tits.

"Have a taste," he said.

"Do I know you?" I asked him, looking into his eyes.

"Better than anyone," he said. "Least you used to."

I tongued away the whipped cream, feeling a little shameful, as if I were doing this to my brother. I licked his little brown nipple into hardness, and he held my head, telling me to bite a little. When I did, he moaned and pushed his hips forward, and I put my arm around him. He laughed, and I heard it in the cave of his chest. He pushed his shorts down, and his dick switchbladed up between us. I touched the cold, smooth skin of his ass. I licked down the whipped cream line to his belly button then nosed into his pubes, his dick pressing upward against my right cheek. I got the tip of it in my mouth. He had a nice pointed little dick head, shaped, I thought, like a Hershey's Kiss. It slipped easily into my mouth.

"Wait a minute," he said. "This is my fantasy."

He pushed me back against the kitchen table and started unbuttoning my jeans. He stripped me to my briefs, caressing the front as I had done earlier in the privacy of my room. He went to one knee, baring my prick. "You got bigger," he said.

"How would you know?"

"I was always watching, asshole," he said as he put his tongue on it.

I started thinking about the times we were naked together: the first time we got drunk, at Lisa Dinino's pool party, the two of us slipping off our shorts when everyone went in the house to watch Derek puke; at Disney World when our parents took a joint vacation and Travis and I had our own room; and now.

"Sit on the table," he said.

He spread my legs for me. My cock stood straight up, perpendicular to my body. He licked down the shaft, pushing his face into my bush, getting my balls in his mouth. He rolled them over his tongue, licking underneath them, his tongue long and serpentine and flicking at the hairs around my asshole. "Jeez," I said sharply.

His head bobbed up. "It hurts?" he asked, incredulous.

"No, it doesn't hurt," I said.

He pulled my shaft back, trying to get the head in his mouth. "That hurts," I told him.

"Sorry," he said.

He stood, rubbing my thighs with backward hands knuckling against the pale skin. His cock poked up between us. He looked at me, my cock and stuff, and then he looked at my face. His face was almost sad.

"What is that supposed to mean?" he asked me.

I looked up at the ceiling.

"I mean," he said, lifting one hand to touch his hair, "I don't want to think too much about this, not right now anyway, but—"

"But what?" I said.

He made a smile out of his lips, glancing toward the basement, then he cocked his head in that direction. "Him," he said simply.

I closed my eyes, trying not to laugh. "Forget about it," I said, leaning forward. Our faces got close, and there wasn't anything else to do but kiss. At first it was tentative and foreign—I hadn't kissed another guy before, and I don't think Travis had either. We acclimated quickly, though, and soon our tongues were wrestling, and his hands went around my back and dropped to my butt.

"Come on, " he said. "Let's go to my room."

ƒ ƒ ƒ

I hadn't been there in a long time, but it hadn't changed much. He still had his Flyers pennants up, and his poster of the Bay Twats, and a bunch of wall-mounted hubcaps we'd found together. The nostalgia I felt was spooky, like I was little again, or 15 at most. Travis pushed me onto his bed and lay on top of me. He said something that was muffled, his mouth against my throat. He pushed his hips against mine, and I got his shorts down to his thighs, and he was naked underneath.

"Can I?" he said, his mouth closer to my ear now.

"Can you what?"

"Can I fuck you?" he wanted to know.

I'd thought about it, of course, but I never imagined that it would really happen—not with Travis anyway. I must have blinked up at him about 20 times before I actually answered.

"I guess" is all I said.

He pushed his cock against me, saying my name. I loved it. I closed my eyes, letting my head fall back against the pillow that smelled like him. His cock slid over my balls, and he pressed his belly hard against my dick. His hairs there were short and prickly, just trimmed, I figured. He licked my shoulder, across my clavicle, the other shoulder, biting me. His dick slipped under my balls, poking against my hole. I spread my legs for him, getting them around him, my calves on his cold ass, ankles hooking, drawing him closer.

"Does he ever do this?" he asked me, his face in my neck.

I said no.

"What does he do?" he wanted to know.

"He stands," I told him. "He stands and comes."

He leaned back as far as my legs allowed him, and he spat on the end of his dick.

"This is going to hurt, isn't it?" I asked.

"I don't know," he said. "It's different for everyone." He licked his forefinger and wormed it into my ass.

"Does that hurt?"

I shook my head.

He pulled it out and brought his hand to his mouth, sucking on his thumb, and then he put that in me. I moaned, and he looked at me. I got my hand around my cock. Every move of his thumb made me shudder, made me arch my back and want more of him inside me.

He reached into his nightstand and pulled out a rubber and a bottle of lubricant. I watched him roll the rubber onto his pecker. "You sure about this?" he asked me.

I shrugged.

"We don't have to," he said.

"I know."

He jacked himself with a little lube.

"You've done this before?"

He nodded.

"Who with?" I wanted to know.

"You don't know him," he answered.

He held himself, pushing against the spot he'd worked into softness. The slippery head eased in, but his thickening shaft made me gasp, and he stopped, touching my face gently. I turned away, not wanting any kindness that moment. I wanted to be fucked, and I told him so.

He pulled me to him, filling me with his cock, until he was in all the way and I was seeing stars. But there really were stars, these glow-in-the-dark stickers we'd put up on his ceiling years ago.

"Dude," he said. He put a thumb on my left nipple, rolling the little knob around. He shouldered my feet and managed to get more into me. I felt his balls bouncing against my tailbone, his pubes rasping my stretched-out ass lips, his breath blowing down on me, hot and sweet. He grabbed my cock and spat on it, drawing his palm up over the head. I touched his hand, shaking my head. "I'll blow," I said, and he smiled.

He fucked me slowly, bringing his cock head all the way out and pushing it back in. He leaned back to watch his own progress and the way my ass pulled when he tried to leave it. He gripped my ankles and lifted my bottom, slamming into me, making me grunt.

"Fucking beautiful," he said, turning us over on our sides and lying behind me. He held my hip and ground his dick up into me, rolling us over again so that I was on my stomach, my face in his pillow, and he was pounding me, licking my back, pounding and pounding my ass, his thighs between mine, spreading mine, coming up inside me.

"Oh, man," he said, pulling out, pulling off the rubber to show me. The end of it was filled.

He lay on his back and said, "Hop on." His cock was still hard, sticking straight up. He licked his palm and juiced up his stick for me, and I squatted on him, feeling a little self-conscious. He stabbed up into me, and I got my dick in my hand, jacking hard and fast and bobbing on his prong, keeping my eyes closed, not wanting to see him looking at me.

"Fuck," I said, and I started shooting. When I opened my eyes, his face was streaked, and he was laughing.

We took a shower together, washing each other's body. "I like this," he said.

Downstairs in the basement, we woke up Davis.

"We're hungry, are you?" I asked.

He nodded sleepily. "What time is it?" he asked.

Travis told him.

Davis sat up, rubbing his face, his cheek bearing the imprint of the Herculon weave of the sofa.

ƒ ƒ ƒ

We walked out to the car. "I forgot my wallet," Travis said. Davis leaned over the backseat, his arm against my shoulder.

"I'm kind of horny," he said.

"You are?"

He nodded, grinning just a little. I reached over the seat and touched his crotch, finding him hard.

"Later," I said as Travis got into the car with us.

"Let's go, man, I'm fucking starved," I said, and we were off.

Those Hallowed Halls

f f f

f f f

The All-nighter

BY

T. HITMAN

R-*i-i-ing!* Paul's eyes shot open. At first he thought it was the alarm clock that shattered the forbidden dream. His right hand still gripped his cock, which was half-hard, just a few strokes shy of getting him off into the sheets that had felt, in his dream, like the warm folds of a familiar mouth.

R-i-i-ing!

Paul's left hand reached for the snooze button. But when the ringing continued, his right-handed choke on his cock relaxed, dropping the moist, precome-soaked sock of foreskin from finishing off the unconscious jack job he'd been giving himself as he reached, now conscious, for the phone.

"Hello," he growled, his deep voice cracked and sleepy.

A young man's gruff baritone answered, "Pablo!" Paul knew right away who it belonged to. "It's me, dude. I'm at the police station. I need your help!" It was Buster, and he sounded like he was verging on panic. "I need you to bail me out! If my dad finds out, he'll tan my ass." Buster's voice rose even faster and higher, causing the ache in Paul's dick to pound.

"I'm fucked if you don't come help me out, dude!"

"Slow down, bro," Paul said. He pinched the tired corners of his eyes before looking at the clock. It read a quarter to 3, and one quick glance out the dorm window at the early-morning darkness confirmed it. "Did you say you're at the police station?"

"The campus cops busted me. I wasn't doing nothin'!"

Paul knew better. He knew Buster better. Stretching out on his back, Paul reached down and teased the slick, itchy flesh of his cock, causing the moist pink head to push its way out of his darker-colored foreskin. "So big man on campus got cuffed. Buster's been busted!"

"This ain't funny, Pablo," Buster huffed into the phone. "I'm in big-time trouble, dude!"

Paul sighed and let go of his recently awakened dick. He gave his balls an absent scratch and said, "What can I do, buddy?"

Fifteen minutes later, Paul Aguillara stood outside the bulletproof glass of the teller's window at the campus police station, checkbook in hand, $200 poorer, with two exams staring him in the face on Monday morning. He looked at his reflection in the glass. Usually, he was neatly kept, but tonight he appeared to have been hit by a freight train—or rather 200 pounds of full-steam running back that was Buster Varitek.

"He'll be out in a minute," the woman behind the glass informed him. Paul hesitated a second longer, staring again at his tired brown eyes, the day-old stubble on his square-jawed face, his jet-black hair, usually so perfect and gelled, now barely combed. Even his clothes—a T-shirt under his old leather jacket, his seersucker shorts—everything looked wrinkled. At least his black sandals, pulled on in haste, showed off his legs, so solidly athletic with their sheen of black hair, and his perfect size 11 feet.

Soon the electronically sealed door buzzed open and Buster was led out into the reception area in front of the uniformed storm trooper who had arrested him. A wounded scowl covered the big guy's handsome face. At that moment Paul had a rush of anxiety at the sight of his best buddy—Buster with the buzz-cut hair and baseball cap turned backward. Big muscle dude Buster, the pussy magnet, who sometimes drank too much and puffed his chest too much and who was always getting into trouble when he didn't score—on the field or off. Paul felt anxiety, because at that moment he remembered his dream.

"I'm releasing him to you," the officer growled. Paul only half heard the statement. "You can pick up your car Monday morning. You're gonna have to pay to store it Sunday. That's 40 more bucks each day it stays here."

"Yeah, whatever," Buster said, clutching his yellow copies of the arrest papers that matched the color of Paul's bond receipt. He didn't say much more until they reached Paul's Jeep and the doors were shut, the ignition started. As Paul drove back toward the dorm, he could smell the stale stink of beer on Buster. The punch Buster had taken to the side of his face was easier to glean in the warm glow of streetlights than it had been beneath the cold white fluorescents in the police station.

"So you were fighting again," Paul said. He was still pissed off. With everything on his plate, the last thing he needed was this. But he was also shocked by how much relief he had felt at seeing Buster safe, at helping him out—something fatherly, protective, maybe more. Dare he even think it?

"It wasn't like that," Buster said, folding the papers and raising his ass high enough off the seat to tuck them into the back pocket of his shorts. It took him several tries to finally accomplish the task, during which Paul's gaze couldn't help but be drawn to the fullness tenting the front of Buster's shorts, his crotch now thrust up, the outlines of his manhood, pure iron that hadn't accomplished its goal to hunt and conquer, to plug the choicest pussy at some pub in the campus town. Even before Buster settled his ass back down on the passenger seat, Paul had to look quickly back to the road. With a rising sense of embarrassment, he felt his cock begin to stir, constricted by the boxer briefs under his shorts. He had gotten half-hard before he could stop himself, the pressure working down to his balls, making it feel like someone was giving them a painful twist while alternately jerking the foreskin over his cock.

"So was she sweet?" he asked, hoping to divert his thoughts away from what it was that kept teasing his memory, that fucking dream, and what he had felt when he first caught sight of Buster at the police station.

"Real fuckin' hot, dude. Nice set of cans. Real small ass in a miniskirt so tiny, I swear you could see her fuckin' pussy lips crack a smile," Buster answered. "Only problem was that when I offered to buy her a drink, her townie boyfriend got a little offended."

"Did you think he wouldn't?" Paul asked, eyeing Buster.

"Not at me, dude," the big guy said. "He took it out on her! Pulled her off the barstool and dragged her to the door, calling her all sorts of names you and me only say to each other after we've fucked some hot piece of tail—and not to their faces. It ain't gentlemanly." Buster cracked a sexy smile that showed off his perfect white teeth. "See, like I told you, it's not how you think it was."

"You went to jail because some other dude was rude to a woman? Took a punch?"

"Yeah," Buster shrugged. "But you should see how many he took."

$$f\ f\ f$$

"You can sleep it off here tonight," Paul said, peeling off his jacket, then his shirt, tossing them onto the desk chair after closing the door behind Buster. "But, man, I've gotta study when I get up. You're out on your ass before breakfast."

Buster answered with a deep, sour burp. Over the next few minutes Paul watched Buster fumble as he tried to take off his shorts, his beat-up old sneakers, and finally his socks. Then, with Buster dressed in just a well-packed pair of white briefs, any trace of exhaustion vanished. The temperature inside the small dorm room seemed to double as Paul tried not to stare at Buster's hairy chest and solid athlete's physique. Paul kicked off his sandals and tucked both thumbs into the top of his shorts, ready to shuck them like the rest of his clothes. But when he realized that he'd thrown wood again in his boxer briefs, he left them on, sure he would push them down once the lights were out and the weird thoughts he kept trying to blame on lack of sleep could be forgotten.

Paul grabbed the folded-up quilt at the foot of the bed and one of his pillows and then tossed them onto the floor.

"Your bed," he yawned.

"Fuck that," Buster chuckled. "I'm the guest. You get the floor."

"No fuckin' way," Paul said.

"Wrestle you for the bunk," Buster said. Before Paul could argue, the big football player had him flat on his back on the bed. Pinned by the hair-covered tree trunks of Buster's solid legs, Paul watched in horror—momentarily paralyzed—as the big guy clamped down on his hands and ground his almost-naked body, putting them face-to-face, cock-to-cock, on the dormitory bed. Buster leaned down and grinned. At such close range, Paul couldn't deny it, couldn't say his tough-assed buddy wasn't the most beautiful fucker he'd ever laid eyes on.

"Get the fuck off me!" he half-laughed, pushing back against the pressure. For the moment, Buster's hands—and cock—had him pinned, and the longer Paul struggled, the harder Buster seemed to get. Soon the decent lump in Buster's briefs had tented obviously, its crown straining to the point that Paul noticed a tiny circle of wetness form on the crisp white cotton. Buster too appeared to sense something more than the usual routine had taken place, and at one point he looked down at himself. This was Paul's opportunity. He pushed up, and in a flash flipped the football player onto his back. The scratch of their bare legs, bare chests, near-bare cocks rubbing together filled Paul's eyes for a blinding moment with a shock of white light. Once the stars had cleared, there was Buster, looking just as dazed, twice as incredible and handsome.

"So you gonna share your bed?" the big guy asked with a sheepish grin on his face.

Paul drew in a deep breath. The air smelled strangely electric, of male sweat, beer breath, and the unrivaled jock scent of Buster's skin.

"It's almost 4 in the morning, fucker," Paul said, shaking his head and taking a deep breath.

"I know." The shit-eating grin on Buster's face flattened, becoming serious. "I really wanted to get some pussy tonight, Pablo," Buster sighed. Paul felt him push upward, just as he ground down. The action mashed both their dicks together, and even through his shorts Paul felt the warmth and wetness of Buster's excitement. Paul's dark-brown eyes fell into the big guy's baby blues. The room became silent, deathly so.

With his chest and dick pushing into Buster's, Paul grew aware of his racing heart and the way it was beating faster, faster. The moment could have erupted into something more. But just when it appeared it would, when Buster opened his mouth, ready to say something, Paul rolled off. The change in pressure on his dick was like a sucker punch.

"You get the floor," he said, now avoiding Buster's eyes. Standing, he flipped off the light, bathing the room in total darkness except for the poor glow of the alarm clock, the fucking alarm clock that kept telling him how fast the minutes were speeding by at some points, dragging slowly at others.

Saying nothing, Buster slumped to the floor on his back. Paul heard the big guy groan as he assumed the position, long legs stretching out on the floor. In the dark, however, he knew he couldn't conceal the truth that their wrestling match had caused him to get hard too. Paul dropped his shorts, even his boxer briefs, at long last freeing his uncut six-incher and the meaty sac of low-hanging balls that a minute earlier had been pressed into his best buddy's. He tried not to think about Buster and the fact he'd felt his cock, as hard as his own, pushing into his own, staining it with precome, inviting him to make a move.

Sleep would solve everything, Paul told himself. The big running back would wake up hungover and not remember what had almost happened. Paul would be too busy cramming for his tests to think about the incident. *Yes,* he thought, *sleep will solve everything.*

But it didn't.

$$f\ f\ f$$

Paul was half out of it when he heard the steady whap-whapping from the side of his bed. The longer he thought about it, the louder, wetter the sound grew, and the further he was pulled from sleep.

"Fuckin' wanted some pussy," a deep, whispered voice growled. This was accompanied by the sound growing louder.

Paul had nearly fallen asleep on his back, one hand at the side of the bed, the other draped over his forehead. He slowly lowered his hand, tipped his head to the left. There in the wan red glow of light from the alarm clock's digital numbers an image took form. Buster also lay on his back, but he'd arched one of his big, strong legs up and had pulled his underwear to one side. Poking up, above the egg-shaped balls that were hanging to one side, was the running back's stone-stiff cock. Each upward stroke by Buster's hand intensified the wet sound, and the rounded head glistened visibly in the red light. The big guy was getting himself off, right there at the side of the bed, within hand's reach.

Between his own spread legs, Paul felt his cock rising up at the sight of Buster's display. He took a heavy swallow, only to find that his mouth had gone completely dry. Part of him wanted to join Buster; the other was paralyzed by what such an action would mean. But the heavy swallow and the curious shift of Paul's weight on the bed again gave Buster the upper hand. The big guy tipped his head toward the bed and continued to jack his dick. Paul thought about closing his eyes, pretending to be asleep, but he didn't. He watched for a few more seconds, seconds that felt more like hours, until Buster aimed his dick toward the side of the dorm room bed—and Paul's open hand.

The warm, spongy skin brushed his fingers. Paul flexed his thumb, running it along the sensitive underside of Buster's cock head.

"That's it, Pablo," the big guy growled. It was all the urging Paul needed. Wrapping his fingers around Buster's shaft, he began to jerk the eight-inch cock the same way he'd done it to himself, teasing the knob with the skin of its shaft. Buster's cut cock reacted by releasing a trickle of fresh precome into Paul's palm. Before he could stop himself, Paul pulled back and licked the salty-sweet nut juice off his hand before taking hold of Buster's cock again. The big guy lurched up with each stroke, moaning deeply, but saying little else than "F-u-u-uck!"

The more Paul jacked on Buster's cock, the clearer it became to him that what he really wanted, needed was a better taste of his best pal's boner.

Paul slid off the bed. Buster must have known what was to happen. He maneuvered Paul's 180-pound mass of solid muscles into position, spinning him around into a reverse sixty-nine on top of him. This time Paul did not question it or worry about the outcome. He didn't care about the exams or losing a whole night's sleep or being awakened by a call from the police station. There was only Buster, Buster's cock, and the feel of it as he took it into his mouth, sucking the running back closer to getting off. The taste was salty and comforting, something that Paul had only imagined in his dreams before this night.

At one point Paul felt the rough fumbling of a hand down his bare ass, from his crack to his hole, from his hole to the sensitive skin between his can and his ball sac. Buster reached lower, freed Paul's uncut six-incher from where it was trapped between his own stomach and the big guy's pecs. Buster didn't say anything as he explored the moist folds of foreskin, then their hard center, gently stroking it, even once extending his tongue for a lick of it. This excited Paul almost as much as having Buster's cock in his mouth: the fact that the horniest and most handsome dude on campus wanted him so badly, he'd taken Paul's dick between his lips. Still, nothing got to Paul more than what came next.

Through the low moans and staggered deep breaths, Paul heard Buster grunt, "Fuck, Pablo, I really want to tea-bag some pussy."

The strong hands holding on to his sides pulled Paul back, forcing his ass flush against Buster's face. Something warm and wet inched its way between Paul's cheeks. Buster moaned again, as did Paul, but this time it got muffled up inside Paul's asshole. The big running back started to eat him out, tonguing him the same way Paul knew he licked pussy.

Paul thought about protesting; sucking cock was one thing, but getting his ass worked over was another. The incredible feel of Buster's mouth on his hole silenced any arguments. Paul resumed sucking harder and faster as the licks across his asshole went deeper, hungrier. With his mouth clamped on to Buster's dick, a hand teasing his foreskin, and the big guy's face shoved halfway up his crack, Paul knew it wouldn't be long for either of them. Buster confirmed it when he grunted an impassioned "Pablo!" up into Paul's butt. Right then Paul pulled back, catching the first squirt out of the big guy's cock between his lips. On the next blast Paul's body tensed, and the hand teasing his foreskin pushed him over the edge. He was still gulping Buster's powerful-tasting load when he blasted five scalding volleys of his own jizz across the running back's hairy chest.

f f f

"Here you go," Paul said. He put the Jeep in park and clapped the knee of his best buddy. Both of them seemed tense from the contact.

Buster forced a weak smile. "Thanks for everything, Pablo. I'll pay you back." That was all that Buster said as he reached for the door handle.

Most of the morning had gone the same way—few words, none about what had happened the night before in Paul's dorm. Still, when Buster closed the door behind him and leaned in, with his shiner, day-old stubble, and nervous, caged expression, his was—Paul conceded—the most handsome face he'd ever seen. "It's OK," he said, smiling back.

Buster lingered at the open window. "So, dude, you got anything lined up for the weekend?"

"A date, I think," Paul answered. "Nothing major."

"Why don't we go out together?" the big guy asked.

A sudden rush of warmth lit Paul's insides. He felt his cock begin to stir in his shorts.

"I mean," Buster continued, his smile widening, "I need you there to keep me out of trouble."

Paul chuckled and sighed.

"That all I'm good for?" he asked. "Saving your ass each time you get into some shit you don't want the old man to find out about?"

Buster shook his head.

"No, dude. You're a really great friend, and you're good for a hell of a lot more."

f f f

Boystown

BY

R.J. MARCH

Maybe we weren't getting a lot of studying done. Maybe we were always this close to academic probation. "But maybe ass really is more important than the social structure of England in the 16th century," McFeeley said in all earnestness, burning his fingers on what was left of a big fat joint.

McFeeley and I got together at orientation. We were standing in line to register for freshman comp. He stood behind me. I'd seen him all weekend—he looked like a man to me and not at all like some prefrosh 18-year-old. He'd worn the same clothes all weekend: a scruffy yellow Polo button-down oxford-cloth shirt and a pair of chinos with a tear in the ass that hung open like a toothless grin, exposing a variety of boxers throughout the three days. On this particular day I noticed tattersall, which tugged at me somewhere inside, becoming meaningful for no apparent reason. I had, I guessed, a tattersall fetish.

I straightened my shoulders and pushed out my chest when he came up behind me. I glanced back casually—you know, checking out the lines and shit, and mumbled a "How ya doin'?" He smiled, his green eyes on me, and nodded. He chewed gum, his dimples working in his cheeks.

It was a slow-moving line, inching up a little at a time. McFeeley was moving a little faster, though, and I felt the wind of his spearminty breath against the top of my head. I was afraid to move—I didn't want to turn and bump into him, and I didn't want to get any closer to the girl in front of me, and I didn't want to stop feeling the heat his body generated radiating toward me.

I got up to the table to register, my hands shaking, my cock just about hard. After a few moments of floundering, I found a class that sort of fit my schedule. I put the pencil down and turned, McFeeley having pressed up against me the whole time I was bent over the table.

"Wait for me," he said uncoyly. I nodded, a sudden slave to his whim and my boner.

I went with him to his room. His roommate for the weekend, an Asian he called Duck Soup, was at the getting-to-know-you party in the quad. McFeeley unbuttoned his shirt, his chest thick with hair and muscle.

"You gonna wrestle?" he asked, stretching out on the bed, his chino pants going taut over his crotch and accentuating the McFeeley log.

"Now?" I asked. "Oh, for school." I shrugged, feeling more than stupid. "Thinking of it, I guess."

"Me too," he said, his hand going behind the curtain of his shirt.

$$f\,f\,f$$

I still don't remember exactly how he got me on his lap. I recall his scratching an itch on his back and then having taken off his shirt. "Is this a fleabite?" he asked me, wanting me to come closer so I could inspect the thing. The next thing I knew, his big black-haired chest was tickling my ear, and his hand rumbled over my hard-on.

"You suck dick?" he asked. "You've got pretty lips. Pretty eyes too. Don't look like a cocksucker—that's why I didn't bust a move the first night at that asshole dance." We'd pissed together at the dance, wordlessly, shyly. I didn't look at him or anything. *A feat in itself,* I thought at the time.

His voice lulled me but not my cock. He played with it to distraction.

He had me stand for him, undoing my pants. My dick poked up stiffly in my briefs. He slid them down. My pointer vibrated as he regarded the pouting snout of my foreskin. "Cool," he said, leaning forward and taking the frilly end into his mouth, teething on it, pulling it, tonguing into the turtle-neck of it. His hands circled my waist, fingers resting in the crack of my behind. He pressed his cheek against my prong, inviting me to hump his face, and I did for a while, but I had to pull back.

"I'll shoot," I said, and he looked up at me, his face all serious.

"Oh, no," he said. "Don't do that yet."

He had me sit down to watch him strip off his pants. He was solid, already a man, and I felt so fucking pubescent looking up at him, with my boner all sticky between my thighs. He stood before me in his tattersall boxers, the front dotted with leakage. He was prickly with hair, his legs carved columns, slightly bowed. His toes lay on the linoleum like fingers, his feet wide and white.

He stepped up to me, pushing me backward, crawling over me, straddling my middle. He bent over and pushed his mouth against mine, the stubble of his face burning mine. He licked around my lips and into each nostril and then across my eyelids. I could feel the big press of him against my chest, still wrapped in tattersall. I wanted to haul it out and feel its hot skin and slimy leak; I wanted to taste it.

"Never sucked dick?" He pulled my arms up over my head, tipping his hips forward, butting the soft underside of my chin with his cock. I shook my head slowly to feel the head of it down there.

"You picked a roommate yet?" I had: Kevin Stein, bright and innocuous and unattractive—but only because he asked me.

"You wanna room with me?"

I nodded slowly, his huge dick restricting the full movement of my head. "OK," I said quietly, my spit thick and making it hard to speak. I wanted him fiercely, pointedly. All the things I'd ever wanted to do rushed through my head like a porn flick on fast-forward as his cock rested against my throat.

He rolled off and lay beside me.

"Go to it," he said.

$$f\ f\ f$$

McFeeley's log was thick and long and straight. It did not taper to a point like mine; instead, it stayed the same circumference from base to head, a frigging telephone pole of a dick. I held it in my fist, impressed with its being there. I'd always wanted to suck dick, forever and ever—I just hadn't had the opportunity. There had been a couple of close calls, I guess—jacking off with a buddy, trying to pretend it was a matter of course, meaningless. Cases like that, you just jack, come, and act like nothing ever happened.

But this time there was no pretending, no need to pretend. It pulsed in my hand, wanting my mouth. I pressed my lips against its flat red-rimmed head. I took it into my mouth and tried to swirl my tongue around it. His fingers played over my shoulders, and I laid a hand on his thigh, stroking the fur on it. His nuts, two racquetballs in a bushy bag, bobbed as I ran my bottom teeth along the tender front of his cock. There was no way I could take half of it in my mouth, but I was satisfied, and I think he was too. I used my hand to take care of the rest, a firm sliding grip that banged against his pubes.

"Oh, my God," McFeeley said, an arm slung over his face. "That's a sweet fucking mouth."

He rolled me over, his dick planted in my mouth, and began to fuck me that way. He screwed my face gently, taking care not to choke me. I gripped his fleecy ass, fingering into his crack, loving the feel of him in my hands. His bunghole pushed out like lips waiting to be kissed. I poked around it, the hairs there coarse, thick. "Touch it," I heard him say, and I fingered the plushness, the wrinkled, winking gash turning hard and tight. I pushed in and found him wet as a whore. He fed me a little more dick. He throbbed on my flattened, useless tongue; he throbbed into the aching cave of my throat. He stopped breathing, and his whole body tightened. He brought his fanny down hard on my finger.

"Oh, fuck," he whispered as his cock chugged in and out of my mouth, its split opening and hosing my tonsils with the warm pudding from his balls. His thighs tensed against my cheeks, and he pulled out to finish the job by hand, gushing sweetly over my lips and chin.

He turned around and grabbed my pecker. "Never played with one like this before," he said, fisting it, exposing the head. I shot up into the air between us, splashing us both.

"Jesus," McFeeley said, wiping his eyes. "You could have warned me."

fff

McFeeley liked games. His favorite was I'll Get Him First. I guess he made it up. I mean, it doesn't exactly sound like the kind of game you'd play in the backseat of the family car while your parents up front are trying to get to Disney World.

When we moved off campus from the room we shared in Boynton Hall—Boystown Hall, we used to call it—we realized the freedoms we just didn't have on campus. McFeeley liked loud sex, a lot of loud sex—something that living in the dorms didn't foster. And I liked screwing the swim team, but discretion made up a small part of their valor, and smuggling the breast-stroker Dickerson into my twin bed (with McFeeley feigning some pretty awesome snoring and drunken mumblings, all the while jacking off and watching us have at it) was no small feat. "No more mower sheds for us!" we rejoiced, toasting ourselves with shots of beer our first night, trying to get a quick buzz before Dickerson came by to our private housewarming party.

f f f

There was this new guy—Val Palmer was his name—a transfer from the Midwest. Mack and I spotted him at the student union. "Mine," I said, as though calling him first would give me dibs on this blondie with the falling-down socks and big switching ass, his homemade tank top riding his little pink nipples into some kind of hardness.

"To the victor go the spoils," McFeeley said with some smugness, and a week later I came home from biology and walked in on the two of them, McFeeley naked on his knees, his big dick disappearing into the fat-lipped mouth of Mr. Palmer, who lay spread-legged on the floor, his little flopper hanging out of his undone jeans.

I stayed where I was. Mack liked an audience anyway, although he didn't see me at first. He was too busy staring lovingly at Palmer's widened mouth. Val hummed and kissed the red end of McFeeley's joint and licked the thick shaft and slack-skinned balls that swung mid thigh. He took them into his mouth, and McFeeley lowered himself onto Val's face. He unbuttoned the boy's shirt, uncovering those now-famous—with me, at least—nipples, firmly puckered, like his lips.

Val's chest was free of hair except for a pretty feathering of the stuff narrowing up from the big blond bush that surrounded his impossibly white, nicely thick, and strangely soft cock. He moaned under the touch of Mack's fingers.

Mack was a big-ass monster. His beefed-up arms were leg-like in their girth, and he was more interested in the gym than the gridiron for a couple of fairly obvious reasons I don't feel it necessary to go into. But he didn't mind making the occasional tackle, throwing himself headlong at one of those big, sweating guards from Penn State.

Unlike Palmer, McFeeley was all haired-up with black curlies, but under it all his skin was as white as a salt lick. He was as pretty as a picture—to me, at least—his face nicely sculpted, his cheek and chin always carrying a shadow of beard no matter when or how often he'd shave, his mouth full and always smiling, reminding me of kissing. His green eyes were closed as he squatted himself on Val's face.

The boy under him squirmed and scrambled, his hands impotent weapons against McFeeley's sequoia thighs and boulder-like glutes. I noticed Val's prick twitching to life.

It was then that I also noticed that I'd been noticed, McFeeley blinking up at me with a shit-eating grin. He reached down and swung Palmer's little bat at me. "You snooze, you lose," he said.

"Hmm?" Val mumbled with a mouthful.

I gave Mack the finger.

"Feels awesome, baby," he said, his voice dripping with sex. "C'mon, buddy, clean me up."

I left them alone, myself in some sore need of attention. I drove fast to the bookstore on Route 222, where'd I'd stop every now and then after class. I walked sheepishly past the attendant, trying to look like I wasn't here for a blow job. My dick felt as obvious as a shoe in my pants, though. I got some quarters and roamed the place—it was a big room lined with stalls that had photo stills from the featured videos posted outside each stall's door. My peers today were familiar faces: two old men sucking Luckys and giving me the glad eye. "Cold enough for you?" they both asked as I walked past.

Out of a booth fell a thin boy wearing sad bicycle pants, wiping his lips with the edge of his T-shirt. He looked up at me like I was his next meal. From the same booth exited Monty Viceroy, patting the wet spots on his crotch and checking his zipper, his car keys already in hand. He saw me and glanced away quickly, but he knew he was busted, so he gave me a little nod. I'd seen him here before and in the library john at school, so I was not surprised to see the president of the student council looking so postcoital. He ducked his red head and did some fancy stepping around his trick and the two smoking fogies.

Present company did not present any likely or likable suck candidates save for Viceroy, him only for the sheer pleasure of doing someone in politics. I viewed some video sex and yanked on my pud. *McFeeley and Val are probably covered with goo and in each other's arms right now,* I was thinking. McFeeley had probably already turned on *Mighty Morphin' Power Rangers,* which he never missed, his dick soft and heavy and sticky and reeking of Palmer's ass.

I sighed, feeling lonely. I heard someone getting change and checked my watch. The screen went blank. My Sambas smacked on the sticky floor, sounding as though I'd walked in wet paint. I wondered why there weren't any good fuck films about hockey players. I tucked my rock away, the stubby, flat-ended thing with its frill of skin. I sniffed my fingers.

Standing to the left of my door, wearing a tank top and warm-ups and startling me when I emerged, was someone who looked vaguely familiar. I was pretty sure I hadn't boothed it with him before, though. His hair was cut in a flattop, and he had the long, stretched-out muscles of a basketball player. He looked at me, then away, his hands restless in his pockets— I could hear them rustling in the nylon. What I could see of his chest was free of hair; there was a russet peek of titty when he worked his shoulders into a purposeless shrug.

I left him standing there. As eager as I was to see him with his filmy pants about his ankles, he didn't seem the type to suck or be sucked. There were a lot of players who just liked to garner some attention, showing off their tent poles before secreting themselves and their cocks away in a video closet and adding to the sticky mess on the floor, going home chaste to the wife or girlfriend. I walked away from this one, trusting my judgment.

Sometimes I'm wrong, though, and so when this one turned and followed me, staying a few doors behind me, I figured I was going to have to reconsider my initial impression.

He mumbled a greeting. I said, "Hey," and he leaned toward me and said he felt the same way here that he'd felt in church when he was a boy. "You know—a lot of whispering and thinking bad thoughts when you're supposed to be praying," he said, his voice barely above a whisper. He had long white teeth and was clean-shaven. He looked to be about 30.

"You go to Kutztown," he said, and I looked at him a little more closely, wondering if I should know him. Had we already boothed it?

"I was coaching tennis there," he said. "Name's Nicholson. I remember seeing you around. You're what's-his-name's roommate."

And Nicholson was the one "what's-his-name" had told me about: the coach who had been let go when rumors of sexual impropriety had started circulating. "He was probably screwing Velakos," McFeeley speculated. "But fucking Velakos is fucking with fate, man, 'cause the fucker's nuts. Probably went to the dean with a butt full of the coach's come." McFeeley had a good eye for such things—Palmer, for instance, who was probably walking back to his dormitory room with a butt full of McFeeley's man juice. Good fucking eye, Mack.

I didn't feel right about this one, though, not trusting my own eye. He was nice to look at—very nice—with his short brown hair and his heavy brow and his pants rustling like a flag in the wind. I caught sight then of someone familiar, a black man whose dick never seemed fully engaged, who took a long time to come. We nodded—it was nice to be remembered. The huge vegetable-like curve of his dick was apparent through his zebra-stripe workout pants. I looked over at Nicholson. He scratched his bared tit.

The two old guys shuffled off, giving us whippersnappers dirty looks, and Bicycle Shorts left, miffed at being so completely ignored. It was just the three of us then, circling the outer walls, every now and then popping individually into a booth to refreshen our tumescences.

There was an alcove out of sight of the security cameras, which hovered and flashed little red lights over our heads. It was a favorite resting area for me when I felt like loitering outside a booth, and it was also a handy place to gather a small group of daring pud-pullers. I'd seen as many as seven guys in the tight little space doing all sorts of shit. I stood and waited. It was a proving ground—I figured if Coach came around and stopped too, it was a done deal.

He came around, parking himself in a doorway, gripping the front of his pants. He stepped into the booth and looked at me, but I stayed where I was. I fingered the outline of my dick, making it hard. He kneaded himself through the blue nylon, producing a sizable erection. He pulled it out and shook it at me, the second time I'd been wagged at like that today. *Second time's the charm*, I told myself and undid my jeans. My cock hit the air running, thrusting up with a snap. I did not have the coach's length or girth, but I made up for it with a wealth of foreskin. I could see his lips wet with drool, and I figured I knew what his favorite food was.

I pinched the end of my pecker and twirled it around for him like a bag of Shake 'n Bake. I skinned the head back and fingered the hard bluish head. I pushed my jeans down my hard-muscled quads and lifted my shirt. My chest and stomach were covered with a fine stubble of see-through hairs. I pinched my right tit and rolled it under my thumb, circling it, feeling the rasp of mowed-down hairs all around it.

Nicholson's prick was monolithic. His grip failed to cover half of it, and his fingers could not close around it. It was by far the longest johnson I'd ever seen. He worked it in his fist and squeezed out a ladle's worth of juice, leaking as much as I ejaculate. He wiped his sticky hand on his stomach as though the stuff were offensive, while I was thirsty for some of that.

There was the sound of someone getting change, $5 in quarters falling and reminding me of Atlantic City. Nicholson's cock was gone in a flash. I peered around the corner. Another old shuffler, probably a retired trucker, got himself into a booth and stayed there.

I gave Coach the all-clear. I still had mine out; it was buzzing in my hand. I watched the slow unveiling of Nicholson's member and decided then and there to bend at the waist and have a taste. I was not normally inclined to the act, though certainly no stranger to it. The fat gusher appealed to me—its fat knob, the trim and taut shaft that looked suntanned, a brown ring running around the middle of it, marking the beginning of the deep end.

"We could watch a movie," he said.

"I'm claustrophobic," I told him. "It's all right here; nobody can see." I liked it outside the narrow, coffin-like cubbies. I liked the chance of an audience, the dangerous thrill of being caught by the club-armed attendant.

The black guy pulled up like a shadow, soundlessly. Nicholson quickly turned shy, but I kept playing with mine. The man stepped into the alcove with us, between Coach and me, his back against the wall, and let out his hose. It was similar to Nicholson's in size and shape, and it was the color, almost, of an eggplant. He kept his eyes on my prong, which seemed hardy and useful and insistently hard. His head was shaved, and he wore a Tommy Hilfiger T-shirt through which he rubbed his rubbery tits. Coach eyed us both, shrugging his shoulders and dropping his pants, and we were all unimpeded. I reached out and plucked at one of Coach's rusty nipples—it shrank up and pointed at me. I twisted until I heard him sigh.

I wanted them side by side, their similar, contrasting bangers swinging toward my mouth. Tommy's curved downward as though tugged by gravity and its heavy purple knob. He smacked it against his thigh until it left wet marks. Coach's cock was bone-hard and ruler-straight. I decided then and there to blow them both. I wasn't much of a cocksucker—not much!—but when would this ebony-and-ivory opportunity present itself again? I went to my knees in the alcove between them, and they both stepped up.

I licked Tommy's salty tip and held on to Coach's staff, jacking the rocky thing as I nosed under the plummy hang of Tommy's balls. I looked up to see the two of them fiddling with one another's pecs, their hands pawing, their faces coming closer and closer. I switched to the concrete head of Nicholson's dick, forcing it to the back of my throat. I heard his sigh and the smack of lips, and I squinted up to see Tommy's snaking tongue bathing the stubble of Nicholson's chin. I felt my own leaky piece twitch. Tommy thrust his dick in my face, and someone's fingers tangled in my hair.

I sucked one and then the other, switching back and forth. I was pretty pleased with my performance, and my cock was feeling as though the head would come off in a gooey blast. I pulled on it until I felt my nuts suck up into my insides, and my pecker vibrated over and over again.

Coach was close too, I could tell, but there was no telling when Tommy would get off. I decided to concentrate on Nicholson's sticky knob, using my hand to get to where my mouth couldn't. His hands cradled my head, holding it still, and he fucked into me, and I swallowed an amazing amount of dick. He made a noise, something between a moan and a growl, and he pulled out, swearing and panting, looking down at his pipe. He aimed for my mouth, his own gaping, and shot five or six blasts into me, thick and stringy.

Tommy grunted with approval and lust and turned my head with a finger and added his own deposit of come, adding to my already sizable postnasal drip.

"Ah, shit," I said, feeling like a cat stretching in the sun. I tossed a big load onto the gray linoleum, getting a little on Tommy's Filas.

$$ f\,f\,f $$

I got home after dark, and McFeeley was on the couch watching *The Ren & Stimpy Show.* He was wearing a pair of boxers and some dark-heeled socks. He lifted his hand in greeting.

His boxers were the tattersall ones, my favorites, and I found myself wishing I hadn't just wasted my time and come at the 222 Adulte Shoppe. I could see the warm, soft, fuzzy sac that leaked out of the leg of Mack's shorts. I felt a little wistful.

I went into the bathroom, ready for a shower. Mack followed me. I turned on the water and started undressing. Mack sat on the lidded toilet watching me. "What?" I said, getting down to my shorts and finding my dick glued to the inside of my briefs. I gave a little yank and felt as though I had ripped off a chunk of skin. I checked for bleeding. McFeeley snorted.

"Where were you?" he asked, smirking. "Who was sucking your dick?"

"Sex, sex, sex, McFeeley—is that all you think of?" I said, my cock pulsing upward.

ƒ ƒ ƒ

Down the Hall

BY

PIERCE LLOYD

$\mathbf{B}$eing the only out student in a men's dormitory at a midsize private school isn't always easy. Being gay and attending a fairly conservative institution isn't always easy either.

When I began my senior year, I had been out to most of my friends for three years and to my family for two years. I had worked for the university every year since I began school but quit my job senior year to focus on my studies. I kept living in the dorms because it was significantly less expensive than renting an apartment.

I lived on the top floor of an all-male dorm. This became an asset to me because part of the research my professor and I were working on involved studying groups that share living spaces. We had received a sizable grant, and while Dr. Lawson had decided to conduct research in a nursing home, he asked me if I would help him to research a college dormitory. In addition to observing the students' socialization, my duties included checking on several students' well-being. As part of the study, twice a week I was required to go into each dorm room and ask all the students on my floor how their schoolwork was going, whether they were having any problems, etc. Then I had to fill out reports.

Unfortunately, as with most studies, there was a dilemma. I couldn't question any individuals without their permission, and few guys on the floor had any inclination to participate. It didn't help that, being older, quieter, and gay, I wasn't the most popular resident.

Then, after one unfortunate weekend of wild partying all over the building, circumstances worked out in my favor. A number of guys on the floor were written up for disciplinary measures—after being observed running through the building drunk and screaming. They were notified that they were in danger of being put on probation or even expelled from the dorm. The resident adviser offered them the chance to do community service to offset one of their disciplinary reports, and they all jumped at the opportunity.

He presented them with several options, including my project, and everyone chose to participate in the study. I guess answering questions twice a week beats picking up trash on fraternity row.

The first week went off without a hitch. I knocked on each door, reintroduced myself to the guys I had only met in passing, and filled out my reports. Most of the guys on the floor were on athletic scholarships. There were basketball players and tennis players and one or two hockey players. The rest were all thinking about pledging fraternities.

Then at about week 2, I noticed that something was up. Rumors began buzzing about my sexuality. Now, let me be upfront about this: I'm not a very political person. I come out to those I want to come out to. I don't worry about the rest. If someone asks me honestly, I'll be happy to tell him. But I don't make any big announcements. It's easier that way.

Anyway, I began noticing that the guys were watching me more closely. Maybe I'd left an issue of a national gay newspaper lying around when my door was open, but I'm sure I've been careful about where I keep the latest *Freshmen*. Maybe one of them had class with someone who knew me. Maybe they'd heard me through the walls the night I picked up a muscular stud at the gym.

None of my neighbors approached me specifically, but these guys weren't particularly mature. Most of them were just 18, and they'd brought with them the usual stereotypes and misconceptions that their high school buddies had instilled in them. Eventually, the university experience would open most of their minds. It just takes a while.

Every group of guys has a ringleader, and on our floor it was Gavin. He was a tennis player, tall and lean with dark hair, intense brown eyes, and a pathologically mischievous personality. Some of the guys hung on his every word, and the rest seemed to at least respect him. I soon got the impression that he'd never met a gay man and found the prospect not threatening but somehow hysterically funny. With Gavin in charge of the social climate of the floor, things began to take a turn for the bizarre.

It started one evening as I was doing my reports. As I approached the room that Gavin shared with his roommate, a shy blond swimmer named Patrick, I heard a voice say "He's coming!" and then the sound of giggling. I knocked at the door, which was slightly open, and heard a melodious voice say "Come in!"

The first thing I saw when I opened the door was Gavin, a big smile on his face, wearing only a pair of boxers—around his knees. His soft dick was big and circumcised.

"Hey, Steve. What's up?" he said. I glanced around the room and saw there were four other guys present, all standing around facing me, all with their underwear at half-mast.

Gavin was the best-hung. Patrick had real blond pubic hair, and he was blushing bright-red. He looked pretty uncomfortable, but he was exposing himself just the same. All of the guys were pretty well-built, particularly Joey, who stood only about 5 foot 6 but had massive pecs and arms. He also had a pretty big ball sac, I noticed.

"Having some trouble getting dressed?" I asked.

"Gosh, it's just been a long day. I like to get back to my room and let it hang free," Gavin swung his big cock around.

I knew they were taunting me, but I was determined not to let it faze me. I wanted to prove that I was above this childishness, that it didn't bother me.

"Whatever makes you comfortable," I said. "It's your room." I forced myself to look at his eyes and nowhere else as I asked my list of questions. I moved on to the next boy, and the next. When I got to Patrick I heard Gavin say loudly, "Oops. I think I dropped your pencil. Better pick it up." I turned just in time to see Joey bending over, pointing his well-formed ass in my direction.

If I had been at all in doubt before, by now it was quite obvious that they were trying to get my goat. I quickly looked away and pointedly said, "You guys have a good night— whatever it is you do in here." When I shut the door behind me, I heard Joey and Gavin collapsing with laughter.

Soon the joke spread to the entire floor, and within two days the guys were naked nearly all of the time. They even walked down the hall naked, their tight bodies presumably meant to tease me and get some kind of a reaction. The resident adviser soon put a stop to the hallway nudity, since the hall was a public place. But all the guys started answering their doors in various states of undress—the shy ones stripping to their underwear and the bolder ones, like Gavin and his crowd, going buck naked. Soon most of the guys abandoned the use of shower curtains in the bathrooms, preferring to soap up their muscular frames in full view of the entire room.

Technically, it was sexual harassment. These young men were using their bodies to try to get a rise out of me. If I were a female, it would have been a clear-cut case. But I wasn't a female, and I guess that's what kept me from taking any kind of action against the guys. I may be gay, but I'm just as much man as anyone else, and I was determined to take it like a man.

Besides, although I hate to admit it, it's not often I get treated to such a smorgasbord of young male flesh. Practically every day I was confronted with beautiful bodies daring me to look at them.

I also began to suspect that the constant nudity was increasing the camaraderie on the floor 10-fold. Most first semesters were tense times, and it seemed like these young men were bonding in a way unlike any other dorm floor I'd seen. One day, I observed the only uncut guy on the floor, horse-hung Sven, giving a demonstration of his foreskin to four fascinated onlookers. He showed them how it retracted, and many of them were surprised to learn that his dick head was moist, not dry like theirs. In a way, the atmosphere was even educational. But the sexual tension for me was fierce and continued to be stepped up.

f f f

I knocked, as usual, on Gavin and Patrick's door. When I came in they were all completely nude, as was their custom now. I was asking Gavin about his week, looking directly at his eyes (my custom) when I realized he had taken his cock in his hand and was stroking it. I tried not to look, but out of the corner of my eye I saw that it was growing under his touch. Joey, who could never control his laughter, began giggling, and when Gavin's attention was on Joey, I stole a glance at his prick.

Completely erect now, Gavin sported about eight inches of prime cock. I looked up to find Gavin meeting my gaze.

"Problems, Gavin?" I said drily, trying to project the image that I was simply bemused by his efforts.

"I don't know what it is," he began. "I just have this...itch." He began stroking his dick faster, really jerking off now.

"Well, that's too bad," I said, moving to the next guy in the room. I tried to ignore the sounds of Gavin masturbating. The other boys smirked and pretended nothing was happening. When I finished talking to Patrick (who looked as shy as usual, although I allowed myself to notice that he had the most amazing abs I'd ever seen), I heard Gavin moaning.

"U-u-ungh...I think I'm gonna shoot a load!"

I looked over to see that Gavin's lying on his bed, spread-eagle, furiously spanking his cock.

"Anyone...here...want...to watch...me...come?" he grunted. In fact, we were all watching as he arched his back and shot spurt after spurt of creamy white semen onto his chest.

He sighed. "I feel much better now." Joey was laughing so hard he fell to the floor and kicked into the air, his nuts jiggling in my direction as he did so.

I excused myself and went to my room. Once there I pulled out my cock, which had been hard but hidden by my briefs during the whole encounter. I jerked off, the image of Gavin's orgasm burned into my brain.

Late that night there was a knock at the door. I threw on some shorts and answered it. There stood Patrick, clad only in a pair of boxers.

"Can I come in?" he asked. "I want to talk to you about something."

"Sure, come on in," I said, ushering him in. Fearing this could be another game, I left the door open.

"Can we please shut the door?" he asked. "I really want to talk to you in private." I let him shut the door.

"What's up?" I asked brightly.

"There are two things I wanted to tell you," Patrick said. "First is that I'm...I'm really sorry about what the guys are doing to you. I think it's stupid and mean, and I wish I had the guts to stand up to them and say something about it. But I don't know many people here, and I don't want to be the odd man out."

"Oh, it's no big deal. They'll get bored with it in time."

"No, it is to me. It feels wrong, and I'm sorry I've been a part of it."

"Well," I said, "I appreciate that, and I accept your apology. And the next time you greet me at the door with your cock hanging out, I'll try not to stare too hard."

He laughed at that. "So," I said, "what's the second thing?"

"The second thing I want to tell you..." His voice trailed off. He swallowed. "I want you. I've wanted you since I met you. I've never told anybody this, but I think I'm gay."

He was trembling. I reached out to put a hand on his shoulder reassuringly, but he threw his arms around me and embraced me.

My mind raced. On the one hand, he was attractive and I wanted very much to kiss him. On the other hand, it could still be part of an elaborate joke. On the one hand, I was four years older than he was. On the other hand, he was an adult with a mind of his own. On the one hand, his hand was rubbing my back as he buried his head in my chest. On the other hand...

Well, his other hand was working its way down into my boxers.

I gasped when he grabbed my cock with his right hand and began fondling it with a feather touch.

"I want you so much..." he said. I answered his unspoken question by kissing him deeply.

I came up for air and joked, "Now, this isn't just another game, is it?" In response Patrick knelt on the floor and started kissing and licking my cock head.

I liked this game.

"I guess not," I said as I sat down on my bed. Patrick pulled off my shorts and continued giving my crotch a tongue bath.

I allowed him to do this for a while while I remained passive, then I stood him up and stripped off his boxers. His naked body was a sight I'd seen several times before, but the seven-inch erection he was sporting was a new touch. We lay on my bed in a sixty-nine position, and I slurped greedily at his hard-on.

I pried apart his ass cheeks and located his tight hole with my fingers. I massaged and stroked it until it relaxed a little. I wet a finger with saliva and poked it inside, just up to the first knuckle. Patrick gasped at the sensation.

"Do you want me to stop?" I asked.

"No," he said, "Don't even think about stopping."

More confident now, I slipped more of my finger into his virgin butt. When the whole finger was in, I inserted another one and probed around inside his ass. I kept sucking his cock. He paused in his oral ministrations to moan.

"I'm gonna come," he said. No sooner were the words out of his mouth than he was shooting a hot load of semen at the back of my throat.

I was more aroused than I had ever been. I was thinking of things I wanted to do with Patrick that I would never before have allowed myself to think.

He lay motionless on the bed as I fished a tube of my favorite lubricant out of the nightstand. I squirted some into his butt and he giggled.

"That feels funny," he said.

"I'll make it feel all right," I said. "Roll over."

Obediently, he rolled over onto his stomach. I put a pillow under his crotch so that his ass was sticking up in the air. With two fingers I eased his hole open again and spread the lube around inside him.

When he was good and greasy I straddled his butt. "I've never done this before," he said. "Be gentle."

I was surprised at the ease with which his hole opened up for me as I slid my cock head into him. Then, just as I slipped the first inch and a half of my erection past it, his ass ring clamped shut around my manhood. Slowly, I massaged it into relaxation and eased the rest of myself into him.

His virgin ass took all of me in and then gripped my dick like a vise as I pumped rhythmically into him.

I took a long look at Patrick, his tight little body strewn out on the bed for my pleasure, his back arched and his ass raised to greet me as he moaned into my pillow. I turned around to see his toes curling up from the sensations I was drilling into him.

I leaned forward as I fucked him faster. I breathed in the sweat and shampoo smell of his hair as I shot my load deep into him.

I withdrew and collapsed next to him on the bed. He put his arms around me and pulled me in tight.

Later that night he sneaked off to his own room. We were fuck buddies for the rest of the year.

The sexually charged, naked atmosphere on the floor never did completely go away. The guys just got so used to it, they kept it up. And more than a few of them caught on to the fact that they weren't just teasing me but also each other. If you were to walk through the hall late at night, at many doors you would hear beds creaking, a youthful voice moaning in pleasure or the distinctive sound of balls slapping against an ass.

And my door was no different.

♩♩♩

Spice Up Your Life

BY

NICK MONTGOMERY

"Now, young man," the doctor said. "Tell me what is bothering you."

He was a kindly looking Asian man, no more than five feet tall with patches of gray at his temples. He looked to me to be in his mid 60s, although he seemed unusually spry and alert for someone that age.

"I don't know what's bothering me," I answered, glancing nervously around his office. The room was a dark, cluttered enclave, with weird posters on the wall depicting human anatomy and charts of plants and herbs. There was no examining table, only two mahogany chairs with red silk cushions. Instead of being the usual glare of sterile white, his walls and ceiling were a heavy, dusty brown. Exotic music trickled faintly from a small adjoining room in the corner. *God only knows what's in there*, I thought.

"Then why did you come here?" the doctor asked. Noticing

my nervousness, he smiled gently to reassure me.

But the smile didn't help much. I was already beginning to think it wasn't the best idea, coming to him for help. I had been under the weather for weeks. Not sick, mind you, just slow and sluggish and tired. Everything seemed to be blurry around the edges, as if I were observing life from under water.

"A friend recommended you," I replied. "She said you were an herb specialist, or something like that."

The doctor nodded. "I specialize in a number of things." He smiled again, then asked, "What are your symptoms?"

"I just feet bored and tired and sluggish sometimes," I said.

"Lonely?"

I had to think about that one. I had a fair number of friends and acquaintances, any one of which I'd go out for a drink with on a Friday night. But when it came down to basics, that's really all they were—minor friends and acquaintances. I guess my only real friend was my roommate, Eric. Only I wasn't quite sure what it was I felt for Eric.

"I guess I'm lonely," I said.

"Horny?"

I laughed out loud at that one. I couldn't help myself. What kind of doctor was this guy?

"Um," I managed to sputter, still giggling, "I don't know...."

"Do you masturbate?"

"Yeah," I said.

"How often?"

I stopped laughing. I didn't know what to tell, him. The truth was, I masturbated more than the average 21-year-old should, especially one in college, where sex was practically considered a major. Believe me, I'd had many opportunities, with both men and women. But I didn't feel like engaging in a few random nights of cheap sex with strangers. It was unhealthy, for one thing, but it also wasn't what I was looking for. So I usually ended up settling for my right hand and a bottle of lotion.

"How often?" the doctor asked again, his gentle smile never wavering.

"Very often," I quickly answered.

"What do you think about when you do it?"

"I'd rather not answer that," I said quietly. "If that's OK."

I felt bad, hiding things from the guy. But I didn't feel like revealing everything. I already assumed he knew I was gay. He seemed pretty astute. And I really didn't want to tell him that I usually thought of my roommate—and the time I caught him jerking off in his bedroom.

I had come home from class early, thinking the place was empty. I took off my shoes and padded down the hallway past Eric's door, which was slightly ajar. Apparently, Eric thought the place was empty, too, because as I swept past his room, I heard a slight moan. I stopped. There was another moan. And another.

I turned. Carefully, quietly, I peered through the crack in the door.

Eric was naked, standing in front of a full-length mirror. His back was facing me and I had a prime view of his incredible ass, clenched and thrusting slightly. I also had the advantage of being able to see his reflection in the mirror. While I had admired Eric's body from afar many times, I had never seen him naked before. What I saw amazed me.

He was obviously a guy who had seen plenty of time both in a gym and on the playing field. I knew he had been an athlete in high school, and it still showed. His chest was hard and well-defined, with rock-solid pecs punctuated by dark, dime-sized nipples. His stomach was a rippling wave of muscles, a tight washboard beneath his skin. His legs were hairless tan columns, the muscles flexing slightly as he thrust himself in and out of his hand.

The biggest surprise, though, was Eric's cock. It was a good eight inches, and he could barely get his fist around it. Its shaft curved seductively upward, the tip swollen and succulent.

At first, I was afraid Eric might notice me and suddenly stop, embarrassed. Or even worse, he would see me and grill me about why I was watching him. I was about to leave when I noticed that his eyes were closed and his head was tilted back. I decided to chance it and moved in closer to get a better view.

Eric moaned again. He ran a large hand across his massive chest, fingers fumbling with his nipples. His other hand was equally as busy, a clenched fist working his cock.

By this time my own cock was hard in my khakis, pushing against the fabric, threatening to break free. Keeping my eyes glued to Eric's body, I lifted my shirt, cautiously unzipped my pants, and pulled out my hard-on. Eric aside, I was no slouch in the cock department, packing eight solid inches and an ability to stay hard for hours. I lightly palmed the head, feeling a dab of precome stick to my hand. Then I started stroking, slowly at first but gaining speed and force the more I watched Eric.

He was close to coming, I could tell. His face was flushed and a thin sheen of sweat covered his body. Also, his cock was pointing skyward, the head turning a light shade of purple.

I jerked myself harder, thrusting my cock in and out of my closed fist. I could feel a heat building in my scrotum, that pleasurable feeling that only meant more pleasure was on its way. The sensation moved through my balls and up my shaft, and before I knew it, my hand was dripping with nine full spurts of jizz.

I heard Eric grunt and looked up to see him douse the mirror with his own supply of come. Spurt after spurt hit the glass and splattered back onto his legs. He grunted and bucked until every last drop had been forced from his cock.

And then he looked up.

To this day, I don't know if he saw me or not. I thought I had been quick about it. I jumped from the door and shuffled into the bathroom, closing the door as hastily and quietly as I could. I stayed in there a good 10 minutes, washing all traces of come from my hands. When I emerged, Eric was gone. But it fueled my fantasies to think of that day—not only of what I saw but what fun it might have been if Eric had seen me and wanted to experiment more.

"It's all right if you don't want to tell me, young man," the doctor said.

"Thanks," I said, slightly embarrassed. Just thinking about that afternoon had given me a raging hard-on, one that I attempted to hide by crossing my legs.

"Besides," the doctor said, getting to his feet, "I know just what you need," he said. He shuffled off into the small adjoining room and returned a moment later with a small pouch tied shut with a blue ribbon. He plopped the pouch into my hand and smiled.

"This should do the trick," he said.

"What is it?"

"It will make you more attractive to people," he applied.

I was confused. I had no problem with my self-image. In fact, I thought of myself as a good-looking guy—sexy, even. I liked my tousled brown hair and blue eyes. I liked the way my summer tan never seemed to fade. And I particularly liked what a year of going to the gym every day had produced: a solid body that could honestly be described as "ripped."

"I don't understand," I said.

"It's an aphrodisiac."

"Oh," I said, still confused, if not a bit startled. "Like Spanish fly?"

"It's similar, yes." The doctor flashed me a mischievous grin. "Only more potent."

I studied the small pouch in my hand, kneading it with my fingers. It made a slightly crunchy sound as I felt the herbs being jostled around inside. Would this really do the trick? I doubted it, but I thanked the doctor and asked him how much it cost.

"No charge," he said, that ingratiating smile of his now at

full beam. "I never charge for the first time. Try it and tell me if you enjoy it."

"Thank you very much," I said.

"You're welcome." The doctor shuffled into the little adjoining room and closed the door. I turned and headed out the front door into the street and toward my apartment.

At home, I plopped onto the couch and examined the pouch in my hand. I sniffed it. It smelled pungent, spicy, exotic. I began to feel a little light-headed and warm. What was this stuff made of? The doctor was right; it was definitely potent.

I thought about having a tiny bit and treating myself to an uncontrollable jerk-off session, but remembered my 4 o'clock history class. I had missed it too many times to skip it that afternoon so, reluctantly, I closed the pouch and left for class.

When I came home an hour later, I saw that Eric had invited three of his friends over. Austin, Pete, and Steve were your typical fraternity jocks—backward baseball caps, wardrobes from Abercrombie & Fitch, and bodies you couldn't help drooling over. Austin had jet-black hair and eyes to match. He always had a growth of stubble—which went well with his dark Italian features. Steve was a redhead with a freckled face and farm boy physique. And Pete was a brown-haired, green-eyed party boy. The most well-built member of the bunch, he had a habit of lifting up his shirt unconsciously and showing off his washboard abs. It looked like they all had just sat down to dinner.

"Hey," Eric said. "I just made some spaghetti. Want some?"

"No, thanks," I said, making my way into the kitchen. I was about to get something to drink from the fridge when I noticed the pouch sitting on the counter. It had been opened, the blue ribbon curled next to it. I picked up the pouch. It was empty.

I practically sprinted back to the dining room. "Um, Eric," I said. "What did you do with the stuff in that pouch on the kitchen counter?"

"The oregano? I put it in the sauce. I hope you don't mind."

Before I could protest, I saw Austin shovel a forkful of pasta into his mouth. Then Steve did the same. Pete was chewing, a good third of his plate already empty.

"I don't mind," I said, wondering what the hell I should do next. "It just wasn't oregano."

"Whatever it is, it's damn good," Pete said. His face had reddened and I noticed beads of sweat forming on his forehead. "Is it hot in here?" he asked.

"I think so," Austin said. "Don't you have air-conditioning in this place?"

"It's fucking unbearable," Steve added. He stood up and pulled off his T-shirt, revealing a freckle-specked chest taut with muscle. He ran a hand over his chest and down his stomach. "That's better," he said, before sitting back down at the table.

Austin and Pete stood up and did the same. Austin's chest was solid and dark, a thick mat of hair tapering down his stomach. Pete's was hairless and pale, with rosy-pink nipples that pointed straight ahead. Like Steve, their pecs and stomachs were nothing but muscle.

I stood speechless and motionless. Three incredible-looking guys were sitting shirtless at my dining room table, all under the influence of a mightily potent aphrodisiac. I could tell by their body language that something was going to give—and soon. I didn't know whether to run or fetch my video camera.

It turned out I didn't have time to do either. Pete and Austin began to eye each other, wicked grins forming on both their faces. Austin smoothed a hand through his chest hair then dipped it into the waist of his jeans. Pete pinched his nipples slightly, never taking his eyes off Austin's roaming hand.

"Shit, I'm horny," Austin said, his hand moving furiously inside his jeans. "I could sure do with a blow job right now."

"Me too," Pete said, standing up. "I'm *real* fucking horny."

He slid off his pants and boxer shorts and stepped out of them. He had a great-looking cock, long and narrow, that stood straight out from his body. In no time, Austin was on his knees, twirling his tongue around the tip of Pete's dick. Pete tilted his head back and gave a long, guttural moan.

"What the fuck are you doing?" Steve asked, springing from his chair. But, instead of trying to break them up, he stood next to Pete and whipped out his dick. His was shorter than Pete's but thicker and more veined.

Without missing a beat, Austin moved from Pete's cock to Steve's. He alternated between the two, wrapping his luscious lips around one then the other. Steve put an arm around Pete's back and moved in close. The two began to kiss passionately, their tongues snaking in and out of each other's mouth. Low, animal-like grunts escaped their locked lips.

I started to speak but, due mostly to pure shock, couldn't produce any words. Obviously, it was an incredible sight, watching these three studs go at it. I didn't know whether to break them up or join in. So I decided to watch a little more and see what happened.

Pete, meanwhile, moved behind Austin and slid him out of his jeans. Austin's cock outdid both of theirs in length and girth. It pointed skyward, rising out of a thick bush of pubic hair. Austin continued to deep-throat Steve as Pete huddled behind him and began to tongue his ass. Soon, Pete had Austin's ass cheeks open wide and was plunging his tongue in and out of Austin's hairy hole.

"Yeah," Austin moaned before cramming his throat with Steve's mighty cock again.

I looked to see what Eric's reaction to all this was. He didn't say a word, only stared wide-eyed. It wasn't until I saw him pull out his own monster dick that I realized he was staring more out of pleasure than shock.

"Hey, Austin," he said sharply, cock in hand. "Suck this."

Austin crawled over to where Eric was sitting and immediately took all of his shaft down his throat. Eric tore off his T-shirt and grabbed Austin's head, guiding him up and down his saliva-slicked dick.

I glanced over at Pete and Steve, who were contentedly engaged in a frantic sixty-nine, each of them trying to take as much of the other into their mouths as possible.

"Take off your clothes," Eric told me. "Let me see your cock."

"I don't like this, Eric," I said, although my raging hard-on inside my pants was obvious to anyone with two eyes. "Make them stop."

Eric smiled at me and pushed Austin away. Then he stood up, cock still hanging out of his jeans, and came over to me. He grabbed my belt buckle and pried it open. Then he undid my jeans and yanked out my erection, bending down and running his tongue up and down the shaft.

"Stop," I muttered weakly. "We shouldn't...be...doing this."

I closed my eyes. Eric opened wide and I could feel my cock slide deep into his mouth. His tongue rolled around my head, my shaft, my balls. It was obvious he had done this before.

"Don't stop," I heard myself saying. "Don't fucking stop."

Eric didn't. He continued to gorge himself on my hard-on, seeming to take it in deeper and deeper every time. His tongue moved constantly, exploring every inch of my shaft. He cupped my balls in one hand, the other resting on my lower back, pushing me closer to him. All the while his masterful tongue didn't stop.

I suddenly felt my cock slide out of his mouth and slap against my stomach. I opened my eyes.

Pete was on his hands and knees, Steve standing in front of him, fucking his face. Austin had gotten a condom from somewhere and was behind Pete, stuffing his huge dick into Pete's tight hole. Pete grimaced and cried out at the initial penetration. Then he smiled and eased back onto Austin's cock.

"Yeah," Steve said. "Fuck him. Fuck his tight ass."

Austin, hands on either side of Pete's waist, began to plunge his thick rod into Pete's hungry hole. Pete, enjoying it now, once again went down on Steve.

Eric stepped in front of me. He was completely naked now,

his body just as solid and beautiful as I had remembered it to be. He grabbed my head and pushed me toward his hard-on. His cock was so huge, I could barely fit it into my mouth. But I soon managed, sliding my lips down it inch by inch until my face was pressed into his patch of pubic hair.

Eric moaned and moved his fingers through my hair. He bucked his hips, ramming his cock deeper down my throat. He tasted good—a mixture of salt, sweat and precome. I wrapped my tongue around the head, dipping into his piss slit. I worked his balls with my hand, kneading one, then the other. His thrusts grew more forceful. He had a grip on my hair now and was pushing me down, impaling me on his cock. I had to hold my breath, but I didn't want to stop, didn't want to do anything but feel his meat sliding in and out of my mouth.

And then, he came. He body began to shake and he shouted in ecstasy, the come shooting out of his cock and down my throat. I kept my lips tight around his shaft, making sure none of it got away from me, all the while swallowing, swallowing as spurt after spurt hit the roof of my mouth. When he was finished, I licked his cock clean.

Eric went to the table and shoved the plates to one side. He bent over, his ripe ass tilted upward. "Fuck me," he said.

"Eric, I don't think you want me to."

"I need it," he said. "I need it."

He reached a hand behind him and inserted his index finger into his tight hole. I glanced over at Steve, Pete, and Austin.

Pete was still on all fours and Steve had just deposited a load of come onto his face. Pete licked at it hungrily. Austin, also still on his knees, pulled out of Pete, ripped off the condom and sprayed Pete's back with a massive amount of semen.

Eric, meanwhile, wasn't watching any of it. Instead, he was thrusting his hips back and forth, his finger going deeper and deeper inside him. "I have to have it," he moaned.

I grabbed his arm. "Come on," I said.

Quickly we made our way into Eric's bedroom. He closed

the door and immediately grabbed me, his mouth pressing down on mine. His tongue parted my lips and slid into my mouth. His hands roamed freely across my body, pinching my nipples, cupping my balls.

My mind was reeling with pleasure when he produced a condom from his bedside table and slid it onto my hard, hungry shaft. He made a quick flip onto his back and before I knew it, I was fully inside him. We moved slowly at first, Eric savoring the way my cock slid in and out of him. Then we began to move quickly, frantically. With his legs flung over my shoulders, I gripped his thighs and rammed my meat into him again and again. Eric made a series of guttural moans, meeting each of my thrusts with one of his own.

And then, in a flurry of sweat and groans and tongue-filled kisses, Eric came again, sending a geyser of come onto my chest, neck, and face. Tasting his sweet jizz on my lips, I felt the rumble of an orgasm deep inside me and filled the condom with an eruption of my own come. I landed on top of Eric, my cock still inside him. We exchanged one sweet, sensual kiss before drifting off to sleep.

Eric was still asleep when I awoke. I studied his handsome angel-face and began to dread what would happen when he woke up. I had quite a bit of explaining to do and wasn't looking forward to any of it.

I slipped on a pair of Eric's boxers and padded into the living room. It was dark outside. The clock on top of the TV said it was almost 9 o'clock.

Steve, Austin, and Pete had left. I glanced over to the dining room table. It was still cluttered with half-full glasses and plates of spaghetti. There was also a note:

> Eric,
> Thanks for dinner. We have to do it again.
> The Guys

"Are they gone?"

It was Eric. He stood silhouetted in the bright hallway. He had a towel wrapped around his waist.

"Yeah," I said.

An awkward moment passed between us.

"I'm sorry, Nick," he said. "I don't know what got into me."

I sighed heavily. "I have to be honest with you. It was the spaghetti sauce."

"What about it?"

"That pouch I had sitting on the counter—it wasn't oregano, like you thought."

Eric had a concerned look on his face now. It was beautiful, the way he squinted his eyes in confusion, the way his lips parted slightly. "What was it?"

"An aphrodisiac," I said. "An herb doctor gave it to me."

Eric laughed. "You mean, I put Spanish fly in the pasta sauce?"

"Yeah. Only the doctor told me it was more potent."

"Jeez," Eric said. "No wonder the guys were fucking their brains out. I've never seen them that horny."

He paused, and that gorgeous, concerned look filled his face again. Then he said, "But you didn't have any sauce."

I looked into his eyes; I knew what he was getting at. I had been caught red-handed. My secret was out. Eric knew.

"No," I said. "I didn't."

Eric began to walk toward me, slowly and with purpose. He smiled, then dropped his towel.

"Good," he said. He put his arms around me and pulled me to him. He was erect, and I felt his steel-hard cock press against my stiffening one. "Because I didn't either."

Road Trips
and Wild Rides

f f f

f f f

Ready

BY

R.J. MARCH

By the time Kevin and Billy
reached Cape Cod, they had broken up. They hadn't really
known each other long, and neither was particularly impressed
by the strange twist this vacation had taken.

"I think it's a good idea," Kevin said. He'd been skeptical
all along—it hadn't seemed the best idea, the two of them as
a couple, from the start. (They'd seemed rather mismatched,
in his opinion, but the sex was fucking awesome.) And so the
breakup seemed justifiable until he started calculating the
cost of it, what with the vacation and all: a house for the
week, rental car, souvenirs—he'd gotten off cheaper in the
past. "So we're going to go through with this?" he asked, just
to be sure.

"The trip or the divorce?" Billy asked facetiously.

Kevin laughed. "Both," he said.

Billy looked at him for a moment—looked into him, it felt

like—before answering. Kevin had to force himself to keep an eye on the road.

"We're amiable, aren't we?" Billy asked. "I mean, it's not like we hate each other, right?"

Kevin shook his head.

"We just want different things," Billy continued. "I think we can still have fun. What do you think?"

Kevin turned his head and nodded. *I hope so,* he thought to himself, wanting to smile.

$$ f\ f\ f $$

They rode in silence for a while, Kevin driving and then playing with the radio, searching for a good song, as Billy looked out his window at a landscape that was becoming less and less dense. The thing Kevin hated about road trips—or maybe this was actually one of those love-hate relationships, like the one he'd just ended—was the boners he'd get. What was it about being in a car that made him want to play with himself? He glanced over at Billy's legs, the hem of his silky basketball shorts raised high, sunlit, and he felt a moment of remorse—*Was that why I loved him,* he asked himself, *his thighs?* It hadn't been love, though, not in the real sense of the word. It wasn't consuming or anything like that. He knew consuming—he'd been there. He put his hand out the window and let the rush of air drag it back. He opened his hand and felt as though he were holding something wild and light. But still he had the hard-on of a lifetime, sticking up like a telephone pole planted firmly in the crotch of his pants.

He looked over at Billy again, this time to see if he'd noticed his sudden burden. Of course, he hadn't. He was too busy looking out the window, cruising every man they happened to pass. *It would have been nice to have rented a convertible,* he was thinking, but he probably would have gotten a terrible burn, anticipating what fate had in store for him in the week to come.

He looked at himself in the rearview mirror, furtively, not wanting to be caught by Billy, whom he'd always considered a bit vain. Of course, the boy had every right to adore himself. Physically, he was well put together, lanky, casually muscled. But his eyes—that was what had drawn Kevin to him from the start—those green eyes and their crowd of black lashes, his sensually shaped brows, all seen in a nanosecond, Kevin running the last of a five-mile race and Billy handing out cups of water, standing in the sun like some sort of...angel. He regretted the word, but there was none better to fit how he looked at that moment, holding out the plastic cup, wearing baggy basketball shorts and a red-trimmed V-neck T-shirt (like he was wearing now—turned out it was something of a uniform for the boy). Everything stilled, and Kevin ran in slow motion toward the dark-haired youth, who held out the cup to him like wine, like elixir, and he took it from him, and their hands met roughly, and the boy said to him in a voice like a man's, "Way to go."

What he saw, getting back to his own reflection, was the gray in his hair, a multitude of gray that seemed untimely, unkind, and unnecessary at this point in his life. He wasn't yet 35, so what was the point? he wondered. He didn't feel mature enough to warrant anything that marked maturity so pointedly. He realized that sort of thing was relative—he had an aunt who went silver-haired in high school; that was the story, anyway—and besides, it didn't really mean anything.

But it caused him to look sideways at Billy, whose hair was coal-black, like glistening tar, when he overdid the gel. He loved—the word nearly made him wince; not anymore did he *love*—the way Billy's scalp shone so whitely through the black bristles of his hair when it was cut like it was now, close to the sides and back of his head. It was longer now than it had been on that day in July when Kevin had run through the crowded streets of Brewerton, begrudgingly admiring the hilly terrain he'd failed to notice when he'd driven the course the week before. He sought the boy out afterward, panting, the muscles in his legs already starting to stiffen. He searched the crowd until he'd found him. He was eating a hot dog. He got himself a cold drink, lingering, following the boy, who, on closer inspection, was more into his 20s, Kevin decided, than he'd originally figured. He got himself close enough and finally into the boy's field of vision, close enough to be noticed, close enough for the boy to say, "Hey, it's you! How'd you do?"

"Just over 30," he answered, walking up to the boy with his hands on his hips, pleased with himself for the first time that day—both for his time and for the fact that Billy had remembered him. The boy—maybe he should say *man* or *guy*, but *boy* just fit—was wearing a name tag: WILLIAM, VOLUNTEER. "Is William your first name or your last?"

The boy blinked.

"Huh?"

"Nothing," Kevin said, the dumb joke aborted.

$$ f \, f \, f $$

They'd fallen into Billy's unmade bed quickly—too quickly, Kevin thought now and at the time too, tasting the beer on Billy's mouth and saying to himself, *This is a bit early*—but Billy's motto that week was "Carpe diem" or "Carpe whatever tickles your fancy," and Billy was feeling rather ticklish that day, which was why he brought Kevin to the houseboat where he lived during the summer, docked at his uncle's marina. He'd tossed him onto the tousled sheets and drawn the blinds, pulling off Kevin's running shorts, fumbling with the laces of his shoes until he was frustrated by the intricate knot Kevin had tied earlier that day. "Your feet," he said, almost breathlessly. "I want to see your feet."

"They're ugly," Kevin said, grimacing. "They're callused, ugly feet."

Billy pulled off his own T-shirt, revealing a nearly smooth torso. His nipples were small but defiant the way they jutted out, with a fringe of hair, and a dark line rose up out of his shorts and into the dimple of his navel. Kevin struggled to shake off the shackle of his ankle-bound shorts, and Billy knelt on the bed.

"I like your place," Kevin said. "I could use a shower, though—I stink."

Billy put his nose close to Kevin's chest. "You smell fine," he said, drawing his tongue up against the fine spread of hair that grew across his pecs. "You taste fine too."

"But still—" Kevin said, squirming.

"We could swim," Billy offered.

"We could," Kevin said.

"Now?" Billy asked, looking down at the moist package of Kevin's groin, his underwear a sodden mixture of sweat and precome.

"Why not?" Kevin replied.

$$f\ f\ f$$

They walked down to the fuel pumps. The sun was just setting, and the effects of the beers they'd had at the Oyster Shuck—"A typo?" Kevin asked. "No," Billy answered, "a tool"— were on the wane as well, but Billy had yet to lose the boner he'd sprouted at the sight of Kevin's bared feet: bony, well-used toes, long and articulate, with trimmed nails and hardened tips. He possessed high arches, a network of blue snaking veins and a dusting of hair across the tops. The feet, Billy theorized, were the windows to the prick. He walked ahead, keeping an eye out for his uncle, who could at any moment pop out of nowhere and commandeer Billy and his new friend into the bacon-smelling front room of his house by the lake, regaling them with interminable stories about the Second World War and how he'd accidentally slept through Pearl Harbor.

He wouldn't have minded a can of Old Milwaukee, though.

The pumps were the best place to swim because the water was deep, the channel cleared for some of the bigger boats that sailed Oneida Lake and berthed at Dickson's Happy Harbor, which sounded to Kevin like some sort of funny campground rather than a marina. It turned out that the place was home for more than Billy; Kevin met Billy's neighbors the next morning, stepping out onto the back deck (they'd had occasion to "meet" Kevin the night before, Kevin a self-avowed "noisy fuck" who didn't realize how easily voices carried across the water) to admire the sunrise. "Morning," they said narrowly, an elderly man and woman, minding their fishing poles and cups of coffee.

They jumped into the dark lake like boys, with flailing arms and running feet. They splashed each other and flirted underwater, and Billy put his foot between Kevin's legs. They hid against the pilings and kissed, Billy looking up, waiting for the sudden appearance of his uncle.

"What's that?" Kevin asked, pointing to a zigzag on the water's surface.

Billy looked. "It's probably just a snake," he said.

Kevin swam to the ladder.

"They're really more afraid of you," Billy said.

"I don't think so," Kevin replied, scrambling up onto the dock.

$f\ f\ f$

In the houseboat Billy had Kevin lie on his back on the bed. He knelt at Kevin's feet, placing them on either thigh, and he massaged Kevin's legs, his fingers kneading the long muscles of thighs, inching closer to the hairy, inert sac that lay between them. Although his balls rested heavy, his dick was anything but motionless. It hopped across his belly like a teased dog on a leash, leaving a sticky trail of drool everywhere it went. Kevin grabbed the rammy thing in his fist, holding it like a stick, and brought Billy's mouth to the head. "Nice," he breathed, as Billy took it all into his mouth with one swallow, his throat constricting around the glans. He jimmied his hands under Kevin's buttocks and squeezed them until Kevin gasped.

Kevin held on to Billy's head and fucked his mouth, and—rolling him over, never leaving the hot orifice—he did push-ups into it. Billy was incapable of choking—born without a gag reflex, he explained the next morning—and could have deep-throated Kevin all night long, if that's what Kevin had wanted, but Kevin had other things in mind. He pulled himself out of Billy with an audible pop and went to work on Billy's own tool of trade. It was a formidable handful, squat and blunt like a school yard bully, and it tested the elasticity limits of Kevin's lips. *Imagine getting plugged by that,* Kevin thought, not that he would ever, unable even to imagine it, because he was born, he would later explain, with a very strong fuck reflex—"I can barely tolerate a finger," he told Billy down the road, a confession that would play a part in the relationship's unfortunate and untimely demise, as Billy was as avid a top as he was a bottom.

On this night, however, Billy was content to be porked—more than content. He was determined to enjoy the night on his back, feet planted on the low-hanging ceiling of the bunk, Kevin well-placed between his thighs, filling up Billy's hungry asshole with his hard dick. Billy spread his legs wide, inviting Kevin softly to go hard at it, encouraging him with savage tit play. He cupped Kevin's pumping ass and played in the culvert between his muscled cheeks, just touching the tightened bud of Kevin's hole, sending him into a fury of fucking. Kevin lifted himself up on his toes and plowed into Billy, making the boy grimace, his mouth frozen in a silent wail. He wanted to stop, to draw it out, prolong what was turning into a beautiful fuck, but he was locked into it now, thrusting toward the end, his skin sticking to Billy's skin, his cock sucking out Billy's insides, withdrawing to make the hole puff air, only to slam back in and make Billy grunt.

"Fuck," Billy said quietly. He sent a flying stream of come between them.

Kevin gripped Billy's ankles and strove into the soft heat, pressure building behind his balls, which had tightened and taken on the appearance of a brain, thanks to the shave he'd done that morning. He opened his mouth to express delight, and Billy bolted up and shoved a thick tongue into it, and Kevin mewed, capped off like that, his cock leaving the buttery hole and unloading a wild spray of semen.

f f f

The drive now taking its toll, they stopped at a restaurant and ate a quiet meal. It was almost 5 o'clock, and they were nearly there, almost in Hyannis, where they'd rented a house for the week. The real estate agent had said it was a cottage, and it had definitely looked cottage-like in the fax they'd received, but in all actuality it had the appearance of an overgrown tool shed in somebody's grandmother's backyard, according to Billy, who would have preferred the amenities of a hotel with a balcony and a swimming pool and a bar downstairs. Still, it was nice inside, however small, and suited Kevin and did not disgust Billy, who surveyed the cottage with a buyer's eye. "It's cute," he said. "It's Martha Stewart-y. I like it. Let's make some pot-au-feu."

They unpacked. The bedroom was small, most of the space taken up by the iron bed. Billy sat on the double mattress, testing its give, and sank deeply. "We'll be hunchbacks by the end of the week," he said.

Kevin liked the matelassé spread and the celadon-colored sheets and the way the curtains were pulled back from the windows and draped over simple hooks. He sat down on the bed and leaned into Billy's back, forgetting for a moment that they were no longer intimate. He inched away from the stiffness that had crept into Billy's body and closed his eyes, thinking that it was going to be a long week and not that easy to ignore the siren's song that Billy's body unwittingly emitted. Kevin covered his eyes with his forearm, tired from the drive, and fell fast asleep.

He awoke from a dream that seemed to be continuing into his waking state—Billy on his knees between Kevin's legs, his mouth covering the whole of Kevin's engorged prick. Billy pushed his lips into the feathery brush of Kevin's pubes, his hands roaming the contours of his chest, fingering his nubby nipples. Whatever their status, the one thing Billy couldn't resist was a sleeping Kevin. He'd deftly undressed his ex and coaxed him into a state of arousal in a matter of two seconds. *He was like a sexual pickpocket,* Kevin was thinking, still feigning sleep, going so far as to fake a little snore, watching through half-closed eyes the bob of Billy's head. *Amazing,* he thought, feeling a bubble of orgasm rise up from his testicles and spread across his stomach. It smacked him between the eyes, and he stretched his legs out, making the muscles of his thighs taut, and Billy chugged down a swallow or two of Kevin's baby juice.

"I wish you wouldn't call it that," Billy said later on.

"Why?" Kevin asked, smiling. He'd had one more beer than usual and was feeling tart, if not exactly bitter. He was upset, in his state of slight inebriation, to be bereft of the finest man in town. "In this town, anyway," he'd said—there was that tartness—and then he brought up Billy's "chugging the baby-juice cocktail."

"Is that really necessary?" Billy said, glancing up and down the bar.

Kevin smiled. "That's the vehicle, though, the medium," he said, "the stuff babies come from."

"You always do that," Billy said, pushing his drink away from him. "You're always trying to teach me something I already know. You think you're fucking Jean Brodie."

"Fucking her? I don't even know her," Kevin said into his beer.

"You are an asshole," Billy said, getting up.

f f f

Back at the cottage, which Kevin could think of only in quotes now, there was a little sitting room that barely contained a weak-looking wicker settee. Billy grabbed an extra blanket and the pillow from his side of the bed and tried to make a bunk for himself on the settee. Kevin watched him carefully arrange himself on the cramped cushion.

"You don't have to do this," he said quietly. The light from the bedroom shone on Billy's face, which he'd shut down for the night. His lashes, dense and black, rested on his cheeks and turned Kevin to mush. He went over to the rickety wicker sofa and squatted beside Billy, putting his hand on the man's shoulder. "Come to bed," he whispered. He uncovered Billy then, and the boy opened his eyes.

"You're not going to pick me up, are you?" he asked.

"Well, I was thinking about it," Kevin answered.

"Don't you have a hernia or something like that?"

"You think I'm old," Kevin said, leaning back on his haunches.

"Well, you think I'm immature," Billy replied.

"You hate me."

"I hate wicker," Billy said. Then he smiled broadly. "We're in love again," he said sweetly.

f f f

He let himself be picked up and later said that it was the sexiest thing anyone had ever done to him. "If I'd known that, I would have done it a long time ago," Kevin said.

In bed their bodies met in the center of the rutted mattress. Billy ducked his head under the covers and put his mouth on Kevin's chest, lapping around and around the left nipple, bringing the little thing up hard. He licked down Kevin's hair trail to the bush that lay at the base of his cock, also up and hard, and worked his tongue into it. He moved himself, snaking down under the sheet that covered them, and got himself turned around, his head burrowing into Kevin's crotch. Kevin twisted, arching his back, and offered his rear end to Billy, who obviously had not gotten enough to eat at dinner.

"What's with you and this sudden turn of events?" he heard the covered boy say.

"I'm not sure," Kevin said. "I won't be sure until it happens."

"Happens? Do you mean as in 'going to happen'?"

"I think so," Kevin said.

"Wow," Billy said, sitting up, ghost-like.

$$f\ f\ f$$

Billy offered some advice and did his best to make Kevin's transition from unfuckable to easy lay as easy as possible.

"Relax," he intoned, pressing his smallest finger into the well-lubricated pucker of Kevin's anus. He stroked the small of Kevin's back.

"Easy, easy-easy-easy," Kevin panted, nearly hyperventilating.

"I think we have issues here that go beyond my capabilities," Billy said. "I think you need ass therapy."

"I'm doing fine. I'm doing fine," Kevin breathed. "Just go on to the next finger and keep quiet."

"I'm trying to keep your mind off your troubles," Billy said, slowly withdrawing his pinkie and replacing it with his middle finger out of spite.

"Christ almighty," Kevin said, and his ass cheeks clenched with a ferocity that cracked Billy's knuckle.

"Take it easy," Billy snapped.

"You do the same," Kevin snapped back, "and I know that's not your ring finger either."

It might have taken an hour, maybe a little more, but at I A.M. Kevin announced his readiness. "I really think I'm going to like this," he said, grinning, straddling Billy, who did his best to disguise a yawn as an expression of excitation. After getting Kevin to explore himself with his own finger, to feel for and find "that little ball" that becomes stimulated—"It'll harden right before you come," Billy explained; "I know that much," Kevin griped, his left arm underneath him—he advised that Kevin opt for the man-on-top position. "You get to control the whole thing," he said brightly.

At the first touch of Billy's thick-headed prick, Kevin balked. "I'm really not ready, not ready, definitely not ready."

"Oh, shut up and take it like a man," Billy bitched.

"It's like a fucking can or something," Kevin said. "You can't take a can like a man. Can't you do something to make the end pointier?"

"Are you fucking serious?"

"It hurts. Take it out."

"It's not in," Billy said, his voice taking on an edge.

"Maybe this isn't such a good idea after all," Kevin said, trying not to let himself rest on Billy's hips.

"Yeah," Billy said, wiggling his body out from under Kevin, who stayed squatting precariously on the edge of the mattress.

"Just where do you think you're going?" Kevin asked.

"Back to bed," Billy replied from the sitting room, trying to make himself comfortable on the settee again.

f f f

Kevin nudged Billy awake. "I'm really ready this time," he said. Billy opened one eye. "I am not," he said simply.

Kevin grabbed the boy's arm. "Please," he said. "You've got to now. I really am ready." He put his hand under the blanket, finding Billy's now-soft but greased-up cock. He tugged a few times and put his mouth on Billy's, his lips sticky with sleep. Billy put his arms around him, opening his mouth, accepting Kevin's probing tongue. His cock responded as well, growing in Kevin's grip, thickening enough to make Kevin swallow hard, becoming limb-like.

Kevin took a deep breath and some of Billy's as well and got himself on top of him. He took hold of the bully between Billy's legs and gripped it firmly, positioning his fanny so that the head touched the pinched opening. He let his hips drop and felt the first inch enter him. And then he felt the hole blossom, opening like the aperture of a camera, as fast as that, and the head slipped in. He didn't say what he wanted to say, which was "Oh." It hurt some, but not nearly as much as he'd expected it to. He felt the slow slide of Billy's exceptionally fat shaft, his ass lips rasping, and he pinched on his own nipples, turning them sharply, the equivalent of bullet-biting, he guessed. When he'd taken the whole thing, the whole big fat goddamn motherfucking thing, he took a deep breath. "See," he said, "I told you I could do it."

Billy put his hands on Kevin's hips. "Ride me," he said.

"Ride you," Kevin said, biting the inside of his lips. He twisted his tits one last time and lifted his ass, and Billy's cock swizzled his insides. "It's...excellent," he said through clenched teeth.

And then, all of a sudden, it was excellent—well, maybe not all of a sudden. It took quite a few squats for Kevin to get used to Billy's circumference, but after that Kevin was jockeying Billy's beer can, bopping on it like a bronco buster, hooting and hollering and giving Billy cause to blush even—the things he said, begging for it loudly, proudly, wanting more, more, more!

"The neighbors," Billy reminded him quietly.

"Fuck them," Kevin answered. "We're on vacation."

And so it happened that Kevin and Billy enjoyed their trip to Hyannis, known forever thereafter to Kevin as "Hi, anus."

f f f

Riding the Train

BY

DALE CHASE

I saw him through the window: He was running toward the train as the doors began to close. It was a desperate sprint. But I saw exuberance in it too. I guessed he enjoyed cutting things close.

He leaped into the car just as the doors shut, and he stood grinning for a moment, obviously pleased with himself. I wondered what had delayed him and how far he'd run.

It was near midnight, so the car wasn't crowded. I was headed back across San Francisco Bay to Berkeley after an evening in the city. I was all alone and very horny.

He glanced up and down the car with an expectant look on his face, as if he expected applause. When none came his gaze caught mine, and he lingered on me for a moment. Then he took a seat at the other end of the car.

I let the sparks from our brief connection course through me as he settled in. He faced me, riding backward and looking out the window, even though we were still underground. Our moment had electrified me, and I relished its lingering charge.

He had fair skin but dark, curly hair—a mop of it—and boyish features. He looked a year or so younger than I was—around 20, maybe. He had clothed his slim physique in a yellow windbreaker and a pair of jeans. He seemed very at ease with himself. I watched him lounge in his seat as if he was in front of a television. I pictured us watching TV together.

I dreaded each stop the train made, growing increasingly anxious that his would be the next one. We passed through the remaining stops in San Francisco, then into the tube under the bay, then up above ground in West Oakland. I kept him in my sight the whole time.

How many times did I look at him directly? Enough to let him know? Had I piqued his curiosity? Was he indifferent to my attention? He fidgeted in his seat, propped an elbow against the window for a while, and finally settled down again. Three more stops and I would have to leave him. Or maybe I wouldn't. Maybe he'd get off with me. Maybe he was a student. Maybe he was on his way to his dorm.

He rose suddenly, moved toward the door, and plopped down into the seat across from mine. He grinned at me, and I smiled. He chuckled as if he did this all the time. For a second I hated that possibility, but he stood as the conductor announced my stop: Rockridge. I found myself standing beside him, though I couldn't remember leaving my seat. An erection crowded my jeans.

The cool air on the outdoor platform refreshed me. Only then did I realize how hot I was. The guy ambled along, and I fell in beside him, matching his stride. He said nothing. I couldn't say anything. I wasn't deft at casual pickups. My attractions never felt casual, and I invariably clammed up just when I most wanted to be open.

We shared a step on the escalator, descending to the plaza and always bustling College Avenue. I liked coming back to the cozy neighborhood and often lingered amid the crowds, caught up in the sights, smells, and comforting din of the lively community. Now, however, I found the hubbub intrusive. I wanted quiet; I wanted to be in my own little world and to take this guy with me.

I was pretty sure he sensed my desire for him as we walked along; he didn't alter his pace or turn his gaze to any of the many distractions that might have caught his eye. He looked straight ahead, and I spent a few blissful blocks believing he was following me home—until I began to wonder whether he wanted me to follow *him* home. How could I ask for clarification without betraying myself as a complete dolt?

As if on cue, he asked, "So where do you live?"

"Next block," I told him. When he just nodded, I added, "Want to come up for coffee?"

"Yeah, sure."

That was it. He asked nothing more and, as much as I wanted to begin a conversation, I kept quiet. When we reached my apartment I couldn't even get my key into the lock. The physics of the maneuver was just too much to handle.

"Take it easy," he said, and I laughed and turned the key. *Easy?* I thought. This kind of thing was never easy for me.

Once we were inside I discovered he was way ahead of me; I need not have worried whether we were both feeling the same thing. He tossed his jacket aside, undid his jeans, and pushed them to his knees. His cock was short, thick, and already wet. He reached down to his balls and played with them while his cock bobbed up and down, beckoning me. I stared at him so long he laughed.

"So?" he asked, and I almost apologized for my mental fugue.

Instead of heeding my impulse to fall to my knees and suck him madly, I moved slowly. Fully dressed, I pressed myself against him and trapped his cock between us while I kneaded his butt cheeks. I looked into his eyes and thought to kiss him but hesitated. He grinned, then opened his mouth in invitation. As I went in—tongue first—he began to undo my pants. As our kissing heated up, he wedged a hand into my jeans and onto my prick. He began to pull. We went at it like that for several minutes before he pulled back and asked, "You got a bed?"

His question made me feel clumsy and inexperienced. He was leading me along when I wanted to be the one with the moves. I let those useless thoughts scatter as I took him to the bedroom, where he stripped. After watching him, I did the same.

He rolled onto the bed with such nonchalance, I knew he'd done this hundreds of times. He was experienced and proud of it. He lay on his back and raised his knees. His dark hole winked at me.

"Well, c'mon," he urged gently as I stood there, naked and transfixed by the sight of his ass. "It's all yours."

I fetched a condom and some lube from my night table and suited up. Then I crawled onto the bed and got down between his legs. I pushed a gob of lube into him with a finger. He squirmed and said, "Gimme two." I added a second finger and more lube and began to work him a bit as he stroked his stiffening dick. After a minute or two he said, "For chrissake, fuck me, will you, dude?"

I slathered my swollen prong, guided it to his hole, and pushed in.

"Yeah," he moaned as his sphincter muscle clamped on to me. When I settled into an easy stroke, he asked for more. "C'mon, give it to me. Ride my ass."

As turned on as I was, something held me back. Maybe it was the swiftness of it all. I wanted to come in the worst way, but more than that, I wanted to connect a bit — even though I knew this was pretty much a fuck-and-run scenario.

"C'mon," he pleaded again, pushing against me until he got me where he wanted: pounding him steadily and forcefully. "That's it," he coached. "Ream my ass good."

At that point I let myself go and forgot about any connection other than my dick screwing his butt. I pulled out and let my wet cock slide up between us, then speared him again. He let out a cry, and I saw how gone he was—totally into getting done.

I grabbed his feet and pushed them up toward his ears to angle for maximum torque as I gave him his fuck. As my load started rising, I slammed into him, growling with each massive thrust. He began to pull his dick frantically. Seconds before I let go, he shot an impressive wad onto his stomach. He kept pumping himself as I unleashed my own torrent deep inside him.

Exhausted by the fuck, I slumped forward onto him, then slid out. He wrapped his arms around me—loosely, as if the embrace were a token gesture.

"Some fuck," he said as he worked his way out from under me.

I didn't get up. I watched him dress and fought the urge to ask him to stay; I knew that wasn't his thing. I could feel it. He was headed elsewhere—either back onto the train or to a club or to the baths. Wherever there was fresh cock.

"See you around," he said from the foot of the bed.

"Yeah, sure," I replied, and he was gone. I rolled over and reminded myself he'd been just what I needed. Soon I was fast asleep.

ƒ ƒ ƒ

About a week later I found myself on a late-night train again. I'd met friends in San Francisco for a show, and I'd just managed to catch the last train home. It was sparsely peopled, and the end car I entered was empty—or so I thought. We were in the Transbay Tube before I realized there was another guy onboard.

Amid the low railroad rumble, I heard the unmistakable

sound of a hand working on a cock. Knowing that lowlifes occasionally frequented the cars, I hesitated. But when my dick began to get hard, I decided to take a chance and look.

He was sprawled in an area where two seats faced each other, with his feet up on the seat opposite him. His coat was open, his jeans were undone, and his sizable cock was wet with spit and precome. His eyes were closed, and he seemed perfectly content to work over his meat in this very public place. As I appraised him, I guessed he was about 19. He had long dark lashes, olive skin, short medium-brown hair, and an uncut cock that looked intensely inviting. I slipped in beside his feet.

He sensed my presence and opened his eyes. He boldly met my stare. "You're not taking me off this train till I'm done," he said.

"I'm not a cop," I assured him, "just an interested bystander." He took a long look at me and apparently liked what he saw.

"Want a taste?" he asked.

I got up and leaned toward his crotch, and he let go of himself.

"Suck my dick," he murmured as I hovered over him. I reached down to his dark bush and grasped the base of his shaft, then closed my mouth over him. "Oh, yeah," he moaned, pushing up at me.

The train made a stop at West Oakland. Fortunately, nobody got on. The doors closed, and we started moving. I kept him in my mouth the whole time, playing with his delicious foreskin, tonguing his piss slit, caressing his sweet, sensitive underside. Then I sucked him into my throat.

The train arrived at the 12th Street station in Oakland. Again, no one entered the car. It was a good thing because he was getting vocal. He told me what he was going to give me— and that he was going to give it to me more than once.

I sucked him dry, then sat back with my hand still on his cock.

"Now me," I said as I pulled open my khakis. He got down between my legs and fished out my swollen, throbbing prick.

When the car was back above ground, I glanced out the window as bits of Oakland flashed by. I relished the sensation of a good blow job. The experience was even more titillating for the public venue—never mind that nobody was actually there to see us. The doors opened and closed with each stop, but I made no move to cover myself; this guy was good, and I was about to let go. I told him when I was about to unload, but he held on. When my jizz started to erupt, he kept gobbling. Even when I was done he still sucked.

We were through the Berkeley Hills Tunnel when we sat back and really looked at each other.

"Where you headed?" he asked me.

"Actually, we passed my stop. How about you?"

"Concord. I was at this party in the Mission, but it was a bust. There was one really hot guy and a bunch of losers, and the hottie took off with someone else. I got so turned on thinking about him that I couldn't wait till I got home."

"I'm glad you couldn't. You know, I ride the train all the time, but I've never done anything like this."

He stroked his cock, and I watched it start to fill again. "How about we do a little more?" he asked. When he handed me a condom I understood what he had in mind. I rolled it over his rigid prick, and he said, "Climb on."

He lubed himself with spit while I pushed my pants down. He spread his legs and eased me onto his dick. As it inched into my rectum, I looked out the window. For a while we rode along quietly anchored as I sucked him with my muscle and he gave me just the slightest thrust. Silence filled the car. When he started to ram his cock up into me, everything else disappeared.

He dug his fingers into my hips and held me while he thrust his big dick up my chute. The familiar, squishy sound of a skin-on-skin fuck slap filled the car. I jerked my cock furiously, knowing he was about to drive the come out of me.

When we reached Walnut Creek, he relented. I settled down onto him as doors opened and closed. Again, nobody entered the car. It was unlikely we'd have company now; we were deep into suburbia. Here, everyone was already securely tucked in for the night.

When the train resumed its pace, so did we. As we sped toward the stop before Concord, he reached a frantic pace, obviously ready to blow.

"Oh, man," he said with a grunt. I knew he was shooting cream inside of me, and that knowledge took me over the edge as well. I pumped myself and watched my juice shoot onto the seat beside him.

It was a long climax, considering what we'd already done. When I finally dismounted and slumped into the opposite seat, my ass tingling and my pants at my ankles, I saw he was still hard. He pulled off the rubber, tossed it under the seat, and fingered the residue of spunk on his cock head.

"Why don't you come with me?" he asked. I didn't respond immediately; I just sat there looking at him and that dick. "I've got a whole lot more," he added, "and you look like you could handle it."

The conductor called the Concord station. I watched him stuff his erection into his pants. After only a moment's hesitation, I quickly dressed and followed him out. In the parking lot he unlocked the doors to a late-model sedan and climbed into the backseat.

"Here?" I asked.

"Yeah, I can't take you home. I'm still crashing with my parents." He was already out of his pants. I knew I could get what I needed; here in the emptiness of the deserted lot, I could really let go. I unzipped and climbed in.

"You've got one sweet ass," he said as he ran a finger up my crack. He got my pants off and positioned me on my knees, facing out the back window. He moved behind me and worked two fingers into my hole. He prodded until I began to beg for it, then he suited up and shoved his cock into me again.

As he began to thrust in earnest, I heard a train pull into the station. In a dim corner of my mind I recalled that the suburban trains stopped running at midnight. I banished the thought; at that point, nothing else mattered. All I wanted was a good fuck. I squeezed my sphincter muscle and heard an appreciative moan behind me, then the sound of the departing train. I hoped I'd missed the last one.

fff

Scottie

BY

R.J. MARCH

We decided to put Darren on top because he didn't mind sleeping so close to the ceiling. I wouldn't have been able to close my eyes, and rolling over would have been a problem because of the cast. I was knocking it into everything—furniture, doorjambs, people.

The table folded down and became a bed; covered with its cushions, it slept two. That's where Paulie and I were sleeping. Paulie found some blankets in a cupboard and put them down. I stepped out of the little camper, clipping my elbow on the way out. Darren was poking at the fire with a stick, listening to the radio. He looked at me, his face lit by the flames, framed darkly by his shoulder-length hair. His shirt was unbuttoned, and I could see the shadow between his pecs, the patch of hair that grew there, narrowing as it went down, making a thin brown line that rolled over the muscles of his stomach before making a sharp drop into his jeans, which were big and hung low, showing his hip bones and the dark fringe of his pubes. He'd been looking at me lately and not saying anything, as though he knew something about me, and I wondered what it was he thought he knew. Maybe he'd seen me go into the bathroom at the mall and not leave for an hour. Or maybe Joe Panotti had let something slip about me—he didn't care anymore what people thought now that he lived in New York City and was practically married to a guy. I think he loved the looks he got from his old high school buds who'd named him "Pussy King." Everyone but me.

I wasn't gay like Joe. No, I was going to settle down and get married eventually. I thought my taste for dick would pass when I met the right girl. As far as I was concerned, I was still young enough for it to be a phase.

The way Darren looked at me got me all undone in a second, though, and I was going to say something—I just didn't know what—but then Paulie stepped out of the camper. Paulie was like my little brother; he was most definitely my best friend. He walked across the sand to where Darren and I silently faced off, the fire going between us. I could hear the waves—we hadn't seen the lake yet, having come in so late. Darren had gotten us lost outside Watertown, and then we were heading south again and passing signs that said Syracuse was 50-some miles ahead. That's when things had got a little tense, and Darren and I had exchanged some shit, and Paulie, sitting between us in the little pickup cab, had told us to cool it.

Darren stopped then, skidding into the gravel on the side of the road. The little Scotsman camper we were towing—Scottie, as we called it—nearly came up alongside us. "If you know the way, then you drive," he'd said to me. He got out and stood in the headlights, pulling out his dick to take a leak; I watched the arc glistening in the halogen spot. Paulie had stayed where he'd gotten thrown—right up against me. He was always doing stuff like that—putting his arm around me, playing with my hair, leaning into me when we walked together. I guess some guys would have taken it to mean something, but coming from Paulie, it was like coming from your cousin or your brother or something like that.

I think, though, that his ease with me like that had something to do with the frustration I felt around other guys. I wanted to touch them the way Paulie touched me—casually, intimately—and that just didn't happen. It tied me in fucking knots sometimes, and I'd have to take a trip to the mall, sitting in a stall to sort things out, waiting until someone would try the door and find it unlocked and not mind that it was occupied. That's when the touching became easy, my hands doing their own thing, and I could relax for a while, my pants undone, my dick getting worked over, and I'd touch whoever's head, finger his hair the way Paulie sometimes touched mine. Those weren't the highest moments of my life, but the times I felt some sort of release—and I don't mean the obvious one—I would feel free for a while. But it was a short-lived feeling, and then I usually felt like shit, swearing that was the last time, I was going to shape up and act like a man, and I'd call whatever girl I was seeing—because I was always seeing some girl—and ball her brains out. But the things I would think about while I was fucking had nothing to do with the woman underneath me. It was a phase, just a phase.

Paulie said we ought to check out the lake. Darren didn't move from the low folding chair where was sitting in front of the campfire. I picked at the frayed edge of my cast.

"Who's coming?" Paulie asked. He looked at me. I nodded. "Darren?"

Darren shook his head.

Paulie shrugged, but I was thinking, *What a fucking baby.* We were going to get punished because he fucked up and got us lost—he would be angry all week. I shook my head, tired of the asshole. It was going to be a long week.

SCOTTIE

f f f

We passed the dying fires of campers gone to bed. There was a moon in the sky, just a bit of it shining through some gliding clouds, and Paulie said something about it being late. We passed a trailer that was lit up, a couple inside playing cards, and I wondered if Paulie was still seeing that girl from Marcellus, the one with the braces and the mosquito-bite tits.

Paulie had been here before, so he knew the way. But the road was rocky and rutted, and the moon slid behind a heavy bank of clouds. Paulie led the way, and he kept swinging his hand back and hitting mine, screwing around or just making sure I was keeping up. I stubbed my toes a couple of times and cursed the fucking sandals I was wearing, and then the road went soft and sandy, and the waves sounded as though they would take us away. I saw the lake then, Lake Ontario, and it was black, and the breakers seemed almost to shimmer when the moon reappeared. Paulie's hand swung back and caught me hard in the nuts.

"Christ," I gasped.

"What'd I do?" he asked.

I fought the urge to crumble to my knees but went down anyway. Paulie's hands went to my shoulders. "Are you all right, Chris?" he asked. I nodded, wondering how this simple movement could add to the most incredible pain I'd ever experienced. It seemed for a couple of minutes that the only way to be rid of the agony would be to have my balls removed. Then they dislodged from wherever they had gone, and some of the pain subsided, but I felt like a castrate anyway.

I stayed on my knees a while longer, and Paulie delivered a litany of remorse, but I could almost straighten up and walk again. "No big deal," I said, trying not to squeak. "I never liked kids enough to have any of my own anyway."

We walked over the sand, which still held the heat of the day's sun. The water was warm too, washing up over my feet.

My groin ached dully, and I wondered if you could actually bruise your balls. Paulie put his hand on my shoulder.

"I'll tell you," he said as he leaned closer, "if Darren is going to be an asshole all week, he can leave now."

I agreed but kept my mouth shut. Besides, Paulie's lips moving so close to my ear caused my dick to flutter. I was wearing shorts that were thin and baggy, and the wind went up my legs, blowing around my crotch like a horny old man. I went bony then, my dick twitching up and doing a little dance. I was glad for the dark and hoped my hard-on would go away before we got back to the campfire and Darren's moody eyes.

"Where's the toilet around here?" I asked. Suddenly, I felt I needed a little time to myself.

"We'll walk back that way," Paulie said, facing the water.

"The waves are really a lot bigger than I expected," I said.

"How are your nuts?" he asked.

A tongue bath wouldn't hurt, I thought right away, giving myself reason for a stupid grin. "They're OK," I told him.

"We're going to have a great time," he said. He pinched the long muscle at the top of my shoulder in a sort of Spock grip, and I pulled away.

$$f \, f \, f$$

I saw the lights of the bathroom up ahead on the left. "There you go," Paulie said, but he followed me in anyway.

The place stunk and buzzed with mosquitoes, reminding me again of Paulie's girlfriend. There were showers at one end. Paulie stepped up to a long trough that passed as a urinal, and I got myself into a stall. I took the one by the wall; the one in the middle was occupied. I looked down—force of habit— listening to the steady stream of Paulie's piss ringing. I could see my neighbor's foot, bare and tanned, toes lifted off the concrete, the tendons along the top in sharp relief. The foot tapped soundlessly, making me wonder. In a mall the foot wouldn't be bare—I'd be looking down at a loafer or a Nike—but the tapping was usually some sort of sexual Morse code. Or not. I'd been wrong before.

"I'll meet you outside," I heard Paulie call out. I thought about Paulie getting undressed in that little trailer and sliding under the blankets with me, and I got a fatty all over again. The foot tapped some more, toes pulled up, tanned and sandy, a young foot. I moved mine, pivoting on the heel, bringing the toe of my sandal closer to the invisible line on the floor that separated our stalls. My cock was too hard to ignore. I started dry-jacking, listening to the papery noise of skin on skin, imagining what the man beside me looked like and if he could hear me. I wanted him to be young, my age, and I wanted him to have a chest covered with short dark hairs, and I wanted him to stick his fat cock down my throat.

I listened for bathroom noises from my neighbor—grunting or the use of toilet paper or even a trickle of piss—but there was nothing, although I did hear him sigh. And then I heard the sound that spit makes when it's used to jerk off.

There were no holes to peer through, no way to judge what this person looked like except for his foot, which I deemed beautiful. The toes were long, and there were sprigs of hair on each. I'd never thought much about feet, but seeing this one made me want to have it in my mouth, toes curling on my tongue.

His foot moved closer to that boundary. I squeezed my prick, and juice leaked out. I cleared my throat. I watched his toes flex and heard them crack. He sighed again, deeply, and my knees began to shake. I heard Paulie whistling outside—I was taking too long; he'd get suspicious. I moved my foot closer to his, wiggling my toes. And then he put his foot on mine.

I started dribbling, unable to control myself. Come bubbled up and out of my prick, running down my hand, falling on the toilet seat. I shuddered, holding my breath, trying to clean up with toilet paper, his foot still resting on mine. I felt the first drops before realizing he had come across our feet.

I practically ran out of there, barely able to compose myself. My cock tented the front of my shorts, and I was thinking there was no way Paulie wouldn't notice the big wet spot. My cock felt gigantic, the way it bobbed and swayed in my loose shorts, and I tried to push it down, but it wasn't going anywhere yet.

"Jeez, Chris," Paulie said, laughing.

I said, "What?" trying to sound innocent. Paulie laughed again. My wrist started aching the way it had been doing lately as we walked back to camp.

I dreamed about that toilet that night—that I went there to piss when everyone was asleep and all the lights were off. I felt around for a light switch and touched something that felt like a hard cock. *Well, it couldn't be anything else,* I thought, touching it carefully, fingering the loose sac of nuts that dangled beneath the firm rod. It was as hard as wood, jutting out at an angle from the wall, hanging like a trophy. *Not real,* I thought, although it certainly felt lifelike, and I decided, since I was alone, that it would be all right to suck the thing a little. *Need one of these at home,* I was thinking, touching my lips to the fat helmet. It was sticky with juices, and its end felt like the real thing, a cushion that gave way to a hard bluntness. I got it into my mouth—it felt bona fide to me, the real thing, thick and quivering with a life of its own—and started sucking it, getting my lips all the way down the base. I took hold of the balls and held them gently, letting them roll on my palm. With my other hand I gripped the shaft and must have tugged too hard because there was a sudden flood of light. I blinked in the white glare, making out an audience of guys— some I recognized and some I didn't—all of them laughing. And there was Darren in the back of the room, a huge grin on his lips.

"See what I mean?" he said, laughing. "I told you he was a cocksucker."

$$f\ f\ f$$

I awoke, and it was dawn. Paulie snored softly beside me, hugging the wall, keeping to his side of the bed. I listened for Darren in the back, pressed up against the ceiling. My wrist itched, and my balls still ached from Paulie's accidental blow the night before, and of course, my cock was bone-hard again. Paulie said something, a mumbled nothing, caught in some dream. I put my cast-encased wrist between my legs, giving myself something hard to hump against. It hurt less that way, and I held my breath. I closed my eyes and pictured someone—that hot Orioles baseball player—and rubbed my dick against my cast.

Darren moaned, and I stopped dead still. There was a thud. "Shit," he said, looking around the corner, rubbing his head. "Fucking bed," he said. "Paulie's sleeping here tonight."

He threw his legs over the side of the bunk, letting them dangle. They were long and covered with hair. He threw back the covers, and I saw the hard poke of his cock sticking up out of his boxers. It was tall and leaned to the left, its head shaped a little like the end of a baseball bat, blunt and flanged.

"Where's the toilet?" he asked.

"Up the road," I said. "Not far."

"What time is it?" Paulie said, rolling over, not opening his eyes. Darren looked at his watch but didn't say anything. He noticed his bared dick and gave me a look as though it was somehow my doing. He eased himself down to the floor, covered himself up, and walked to the door. He stood there, not a foot away from me. His back was wide and brown, and he had dark hairs growing in a spade at the small of his back. Paulie pulled on the blankets. Darren held his hair back, twisting it into a ponytail. I always thought he'd look cool with a brush cut like Paulie's and mine.

"Where is it?" he asked me.

"The toilet?" I said. "It's, uh...Paulie, where's the toilet?"

"Might as well be in a fucking tent," Darren said.

Paulie lifted his head. "It's just up the road, asshole. There are signs all over the place. Even you should be able to make it there."

Darren smirked, looking down at us.

"You two look cute together. Ever think about coming out? Moving to Hawaii? Getting hitched?"

"He's an asshole," Paulie said to me when Darren was gone. I sat up, looking for my shorts, feeling the need for some cover. Paulie stretched across the mattress, stealing the extra room I'd given up. His arm lay across my pillow, tanned and copper-haired.

"He's got issues," I said, looking at his arm, wanting to put a finger on it where I could see a vein pulsing.

"You sound like that Danny guy," Paulie said.

Danny was someone I worked with, a really cool gay guy. He had said that about Darren the first time he met him—that he's got issues.

"What the fuck does that mean?" Paulie asked. "That's bull- shit anyway. Darren fucks more chicks than the both of us."

Just like Joe Panotti, I thought. Fucking Joey and his sweet little prick—there was no end to that guy's libido that summer after we graduated, right before Joe went to college in New York. I remembered almost each time we dicked around because it was nearly every day: Joe dropping his pants in the car for a quick knob job during my "smoke" break at the restau- rant; the times he took me to the mall and pimped me out in the men's room, joining in when he found someone he liked; the night he almost fucked me.

"Whatever," I said to Paulie, trying to shake the horny walk down memory lane I was taking.

"Danny would say that too," Paulie said. "You're hanging

out with him too much. He's rubbing off."

"I work with him, for chrissake," I said. Danny was the gayest gay guy I knew. What I liked about him was that he didn't have the faintest idea of what I was all about. He'd flirt like crazy with me, then throw his hands up and shake his head. "I'm wasting my time with you, Chris, just wasting my time." He was always telling me all guys were bi, they just didn't know it. "Ask Freud, honey—he knew the score. Probably got his salad tossed all the time."

On the beach that day, I looked for my toilet buddy, and I thought I'd found him about 20 times. Every time I thought I'd nailed him, some other guy with hot-looking feet, long and hairy-knuckled toes, came walking by. I stayed on my stomach most of the time. "Your back's getting burned," Paulie said. "I know," I said, staying put.

"I'm hungry," Darren said, glowering, like it was our fault. I looked at his feet. His toes were stubbed, blunt-ended things. They didn't seem to have anything to do with the rest of him. They dug into the sand like pale and fat slugs.

There was a concession stand at the other end of the beach, close to the toilets, which were set back from the water. It was funny to see where everything was in the light of day, how close things were when they had seemed so far apart the night before. I wasn't moving from my blanket at that point, so I threw my wallet at Darren and told him I wanted a couple of hot dogs and something to drink.

"I'll go with you," Paulie said.

I closed my eyes, the sun crisping my back. I could hear the waves and the music that Paulie brought along and could feel myself being pulled out and away. Paulie put his foot on my stomach. The wind blew across my shoulders. Darren whispered in Paulie's ear; I could see the white flash of his teeth. He asked if Paulie would shave his head. "It's lemonade," I heard someone say. I opened my eyes.

"Dinnertime, Sleeping Beauty," Darren said to me.

f f f

I went back to the toilet that night, hoping to relive the experience of the night before, but the place was empty. I sat in the stall for nearly an hour, waiting, getting hard, going soft, waiting. Someone came in and took a quick shit. I could see by his yellowed toenails that he was not the one from last night. And someone came in to brush his teeth. I squashed a mosquito that landed on my thigh and waited until I was too bored to wait any longer. I got up, flushed the unused toilet, and went to wash my hands—force of habit. I looked into the mirror, wondering when I would shave again, when this guy came walking in wearing soccer shorts and Adidas sandals, a towel over his shoulder. He nodded, glancing down at my feet, I thought, and I looked at his. My heart started pounding. It was him—I was sure of it. He walked over to the showers, throwing his towel over a bench. He slipped off his sandals and pushed himself out of his shorts. I stood at the sink, staring, hands drip-drying. He stretched his arms up over his head— his rib cage hollowed. He scratched the top of his head. He was ignoring me, acting as though he was by himself. He stepped behind the partition that provided some privacy, and I heard the water being turned on, the splash of it on the concrete floor.

I'm not sure exactly what I was thinking or if there was in fact any thought process at all. I went over to the bench and started undressing, standing in front of him, watching him, his wet skin, the water that ran over him, off him. I had no towel, no showering accoutrements. I turned on the shower directly across from him and stepped under the shock of cold water that took my breath away. I quickly stepped back.

"It takes a while for the water to warm up," the man said.

"Christ," I said, hugging myself. I stuck my foot into the falling ice-cold water. "How long is a while?"

"This one's hot," he said, his back to me. His ass was high and tight-looking, his crack a thin line. He reached back and soaped himself up. "I'm almost finished," he added.

"It's getting warmer," I said, going under the spray. I had to turn away from him because my cock was hoisting itself up, pulsing with blood.

"Pressure's good, at least," I heard him say, and I looked at him over my shoulder, ready to agree. His dick was lathered. He was facing me. He handled himself casually, sliding the tube of his palm up and down his shaft. He looked at me with green eyes, brown shoulders, his flat stomach feathered with dark hair. Soapsuds gathered in his pubes, dripped from his balls, ran down his long thighs. He leaned back in the water. I liked the way his toes curled against the concrete.

The door pushed open, and we both about-faced, a poor attempt to hide what was dangerously apparent. I listened to whoever taking a piss, and my cock deflated, and I was able to turn and look over at my shower partner. His ass cheeks shined. He looked over his shoulder at me, winking. It was a little too public for me, though, and I gathered my stuff together and wiped as much water off me as I could and left.

f f f

I went back to the little camper in an agitated state. My dick flopped around in my shorts like a salmon in spring. The guys were playing cards and passing a bottle of Jack Daniel's when they weren't chugging back beers.

"You're going to have to catch up," Darren said, shirtless, handing me the bottle.

"Did you swim?" Paulie asked.

"Yeah," I said. I took a swig and put the bottle on the table, looking at Paulie's hand. I got a bottle of beer from the cooler and took it outside. I needed fresh air and something to look at besides Darren's bare torso.

It wasn't long before I was joined by him anyway. "Help me put Paulie up in the bunk," he said.

I looked up at him. "Are you sure that's a good idea?"

"I'm not sleeping up there again," he said, "and you sure as hell can't."

I looked back at the fire. "He'll be all right," Darren said. "Come on. Just help me get him up."

Paulie wasn't all that drunk. He probably could have gotten himself up there by himself. He acted helpless, though, and stupid, and let Darren and me push and pull him out of his clothes. Stripped to his briefs, he was smooth, compactly muscled, a little wrestler. I spied his soft prick, the way it lay cradled in his underwear.

"Get up there," Darren said.

"I'm trying," Paulie whined. Darren put his hand on the white cotton of Paulie's ass, pushing him upward. Paulie tumbled into the bunk, one of his arms and one leg hanging over the edge.

I went to where Darren and I were going to sleep and started clearing the table. Darren stood behind me, taking off his shorts. He was naked underneath. I saw the bright white strip of untanned skin, the dark brown beard that surrounded his long prick. "You sleeping like that?" I asked.

"I never wear anything," he said.

Did last night, I thought but let it go. The thought of climbing into bed with him bare-assed like that wasn't exactly going to bother me much, or else it would bother me too much. I stripped down to the ratty old boxers I had on and got under the covers, hugging the wall.

"Fucking Paulie," Darren said, turning off the light. Paulie sucked up a snore and started coughing, mumbling something about an airplane, and Darren slid into the makeshift bed with me, his feet brushing against my legs electrically. He settled himself, nowhere near me, and I listened to his breathing. It stayed shallow and nasal, and I wondered what he was thinking. And then he spoke:

"You ever hear from Joe Panotti?"

I swallowed hard.

He accepted my silence. I thought I could hear him smiling, lying there beside me, flat on his back, his long legs bent at the knee to fit the short bed.

"He was a horny motherfucker," Darren went on. "I remember when we went up to Cross Lake for Senior Weekend, and he and I shared a tent. Fucker was all over me as soon as he thought I was asleep. His hand crawled into my boxers like a fucking spider. He started jerking me off once he got me hard. It was fucking insane. I mean, there we were with half the fucking ball team, and some of them were still up, drinking around the fire, you know? And besides, everyone fucking knew that Panotti had just gotten his dick sucked by Titties Janson."

I lay there in disbelief, my eyes crossing in the dark, my dick throbbing, trapped between my thighs. I didn't dare move, not wanting to betray myself or to give him any reason to quit his narrative. He shifted, bringing his arms up over his head. "And then he put his head under my sleeping bag and started blowing me." He kind of giggled. "It was my first one, man, I am not ashamed to admit it. I've had a few since—chicks only—but not like that one. Joey could suck the dimples off a golf ball, man."

Tell me about it, I was thinking, remembering a couple of blow jobs when he seemed intent on taking my dick off.

The next thing I knew, Darren rolled over me like a wave, and I felt his skin all over me, hot, a little sweaty. His mouth found mine surprised, and I tasted his tongue for the first time, never having imagined his flavor. He pumped his hips, digging his hard-on into my boxers. His hands found mine and held them to the foam rubber mattress.

"He told me all about you," Darren whispered.

"Yeah, me too," Paulie said, slipping under the covers, sliding up next to us.

"This is a hallucination," I said.

"Not exactly," Darren said.

"Move over," Paulie said, pushing Darren off me and coming closer himself so that I had them on either side of me. I tried to move myself to give them more room. "Ow," Darren said when I hit him on the head with my cast. Paulie's hand slipped into my shorts—at least I think it was Paulie's hand—and Darren kissed me some more until he leaned back and said, "OK, who's going to suck who?"

"It's *whom*, I think," Paulie said.

"I think he's right," I added. Paulie cupped my balls, his fingers edging the furry surroundings of my butthole.

"Everybody could do everybody," Paulie said.

"I'm up for that," Darren said.

"How come you never let me suck your dick?" Paulie asked him.

"Wait a minute," I said, trying to sit up and shake this image out of my head. There was no way this was really happening—I was having some intensely realistic dream, I was sure, and then Paulie stood up, hitting his head on the cupboards overhead—"Fuck!"—and tried to stick his dick in my mouth.

"Open up," he said.

"I want to turn on the light," I heard Darren say, feeling him reach for it. The pointed tip of Paulie's cock brushed the stubble over my lips, and he complained. I put out my tongue to taste him, the moistened slit of him. He could have used a shower, but the smell of him was almost like perfume, and I opened my mouth wide just as Darren ducked under the covers and nosed around the opening of my boxer shorts. He pushed them down my thighs and licked my sudden boner, humping my calf with his sticky prick. Paulie's cock hit the back of my throat, nearly choking me, as Darren took me down to the pubes with all the ease of a sword swallower, and I made a noise that was supposed to sound appreciative.

"Did that hurt?" he asked.

I uncorked my mouth long enough to say "Unh-uh."

Paulie started pumping himself into me, trying sex talk.

"C'mon, baby," he whispered, "take it all. That's a good boy; suck my big dick. Suck that dick, baby. Oh, fuck, yeah. Fuck— that's awesome. Fuck!"

"Paulie," Darren said, "just shut the fuck up."

"Sorry," Paulie muttered, and then he began to moan and groan.

"Paulie!" Darren barked. "Get down here." And Paulie dropped to his knees to chow down on the bone Darren offered. I watched Darren's lips come off my dick, a string of drool connecting us. He gripped my shaft in his fist tightly. "I want to see you sit on this," he said to Paulie. Paulie looked up from his suck, looking at the fat head of my prick and the five or so inches that stuck up out of Darren's fist, then he looked at Darren. Then he looked at me. I don't know why, but I winked at him. He looked cute down there with his mouth all full. And then he nodded, winking back.

The sight of his ass coming down on my pole was almost enough to make me lose it. He squatted over me and lowered himself slowly, and I saw his asshole glistening from the gob Darren had spat there, my head touching the wrinkled puss. He slid on like a tight glove, and I heard Darren whistle. He licked his palm and started jacking, watching the two of us for a while, and then he got himself behind Paulie and lowered his ass until it was right in front of my face. I tongued his tiny hole and fingered it too, and it was tighter than anything I'd ever touched. He gripped the tip of my finger and wouldn't allow any further access.

Paulie rode me, and I pulled Darren's thick pecker back through his legs and sucked on it, alternating between that and his little rosebud pinch. Paulie's ass lips made my hips buck, and I fucked into him, tonguing up Darren's hole, making him grab my head and jam my face into his ass crack. "Fuck," he breathed, and I felt him shudder as he unloaded across Paulie's back.

My nuts tightened, and my knob caressed a tender button

inside Paulie's cunt, and I let him pull the come out of me with his sliding ass lips. He stood up quickly, his hole gaping and dripping with gobs of semen. "Ouch," he said, bumping his head again, and he jacked off over Darren and me, hosing us down with his hot spray of jizz.

"Hey," Paulie said, his shoulders heaving. "We need a shower now!"

f f f

We walked to the showers together in clothes we threw on. I think I was wearing something of Paulie's and of Darren's. There was much hooting and towel-snapping and soap-dropping. I was still convinced that I was in some walking dream state, that this would all make for a nice morning erection. I was ready to open my eyes for real and see the sun pouring in through the camper's funky crank windows—*What is it that they're called, jalousie? Jealousy?* It didn't matter to me what the windows were called or how this dream was going to end up. I looked at Paulie as he stood under his showerhead and Darren standing under his and got hard all over again, and Darren said, "Looks like we've got a long night ahead of us, Paulie."

"Next time, you're getting fucked," Paulie said.

"What the fuck ever," Darren said.

"Christ," Paulie asked, "can't Darren get fucked next time?"

"Forget about it," Darren said, turning his back.

"Whose dream is this, anyway?" I said, and Paulie laughed.

f f f

I woke up the next day to the snuggle of Darren's back. He wriggled his behind. I turned, looking for Paulie, and found him up in the bunk, his foot hanging out of the covers. I was thinking, *Dream or real? Dream or real? Dream or real?*

SCOTTIE

And then Darren rolled over and said, "Would you do me the kindest of favors and get your dick the fuck away from the general vicinity of my ass?"

"Sure," I said.

"I told you no last night, man—you ain't gettin' in," he said, sort of smiling.

"What?"

"You heard me," he said.

And then we heard a bump, then, "Shit!"

"Hey, guys," Paulie said, rubbing his head.

fff

Street Smarts

BY

PIERCE LLOYD

I found myself driving through an unfamiliar neighborhood as rain spattered my windshield. I had just finished an evening seminar titled "The Sky's the Limit: Changing Your Career Path, Changing Your Destiny." I do corporate training seminars, teaching middle-aged men how to get ahead in business. It's a good gig to have at 26, and I was lucky to have found a lucrative niche in the corporate world.

Driving back from the seminar in the growing darkness, I feared I would get lost, which was ironic because I had once lived just a few miles from where I now was. We moved a lot when I was growing up, and I spent the eighth through 11th grades at a school on the other side of town. Unfortunately, my bad sense of direction, coupled with the fact that I had never owned a car in high school, now left me wandering in an unsavory neighborhood. So I pulled over to get my bearings and realized I was already lost.

I decided to continue along my current route, figuring I would only get more confused if I turned down a side street. After a while I spotted a bookstore that was still open. *Better ask directions,* I thought. *Only straight men are afraid to ask directions.*

It was a porn shop, of course. No other kind of bookstore would be open in this neighborhood this late at night. As I parked, a couple of street youths—hustlers—whistled at me from the other side of the parking lot.

"Wanna play?" one of them called out.

Ignoring them, I entered the store, which had an extensive gay section. The hefty and friendly overnight clerk gave me detailed directions back to my hotel. I wrote them down, not quite understanding, and thanked him.

After a few minor purchases, I was on my way back to the car. The hustlers looked bored, and I wondered how much business they got on a night like this. I scanned them, feeling a little guilty, until I saw a guy I found attractive. He had a small goatee and looked young. He had a narrow waist and defined biceps. He wore wide-leg jeans and a baseball cap.

He noticed me checking him out and called out to me, "Like what you see?" He raised an eyebrow, and I couldn't help but feel sorry for him. I mean, I thought my job was tough.

"You know your way around this area?" I said.

"Well enough."

"I just need help getting back to my hotel. I can't find my way back."

"I can show you," he said. "I can show you around. I can show you a good time. I can show you whatever you want for a hundred bucks."

"A hundred bucks is a little steep for me," I said, "especially since I just need a tour guide. Tell you what: I'll give you $50, and I'll buy you dinner. And don't tell me that's not the best you're gonna do tonight."

He grunted. "Sit-down dinner?"

"Sure, sit-down dinner."

"Fine," he said, ambling up to my car.

"Whoa," I said. "Before you get in my car, I need to know that you're safe. Open up that backpack."

He grumbled but complied. Inside his backpack he had an extra pair of clothes, some condoms, lube, and a worn copy of *Catcher in the Rye*.

"Satisfied?" he said.

"Sure. Good book?" I asked.

"Got it from a trick," he said. "S'OK so far."

We got into the car.

"Got a name?" I asked my new guide.

"Chas," he said, enunciating the *ch* sound so it wouldn't sound like jazz.

"Short for Charles?"

"Yeah, but I don't like Charles, and I don't like Charlie. So it's Chas."

"It has a nice ring to it."

Chas gave me directions, and we drove in silence for a while until he spoke again.

"You know, you look kinda familiar. Have I been with you before?"

I assured him that he hadn't.

"Oh. Maybe I'm wrong."

Another bout of silence, then: "How about a hand job?"

"Do you want to give or receive?" I queried him, mostly jokingly. Mostly because I have to admit that sex had crossed my mind. I'm not a saint. I had no explicit intention of getting into his pants when I asked him to get into my car, but at the same time I had picked him because he was cute.

"I don't know. Either," he said. I guess it was a question he didn't get very often.

"No thanks. I'm fine for now."

"Whatever. You sure I don't know you?"

I looked at him. No recollection. Then I looked more closely and realized that he was familiar to me. His face, his sneer...I'd seen him before.

And then I remembered him. I had gone to high school with him. It was a big school, and we hadn't really known each other. He was Charlie then, a jock without a personality.

"I think we went to high school together. Charlie?"

"It's Chas now. Where did you go to school? What's your name?"

I told him.

"Yeah, maybe...did I used to make fun of you?"

When Chas was still Charlie, his locker had been across the hall from mine. He was two years younger than me, but it didn't matter; he was still higher on the social pecking order. As I recalled, he and his friends had made fun of me once or twice.

"You used to call me a fag," I told him.

"I think you're right. I'm sorry if I did. I didn't mean anything by it."

"I know you didn't." I understood. When we're adolescents, we all do things that don't make sense, that we feel we have to do. I'm sure I had whole months in high school that I wasn't proud of.

We drove for a while. I got bored.

"Take off your pants," I told him. He looked at me warily.

"Look, you offered. And I'll pay you...and still buy you dinner."

"Yeah, yeah, OK," Chas said, sliding his jeans down quickly. His T-shirt was long enough to cover his genitals. His legs were pale and thin, but his thighs and calves had the tautness of a guy who spends a lot of time on his feet.

I reached over and lifted his shirt. His penis was flaccid, just a few inches long in this state. It was topped by a smattering of neatly trimmed brown pubic hair.

I rested a finger on his shaft, gently, and caressed him. He began to stir, slightly at first, then more and more as I teasingly kept touching him.

Driving became difficult as I rubbed Chas's cock more vigorously. Neither of us said a word, but soon he was sporting a raging erection. As his penis throbbed, I inched my fingers down to his ass, where I found the tender lips of his hole. I pushed one finger inside curiously, and Chas slid his hips forward to accommodate me. Soon I had plunged my index finger deep inside him, and he grunted at the sensation. I inserted another finger. His breathing grew heavier as my hand dry-fucked his warm hole.

As we neared the hotel, I stopped and put both hands on the steering wheel.

"Who's the fag now?" I asked. It came out a little nastier than I had intended.

Chas snorted and said, "Shut up." Sensing that I was done with my game, he pulled his pants back up, although his hard-on was still pretty evident through his jeans.

Dinner at the hotel restaurant started with the two of us silent. As Chas ate, however, he became talkative, and I soon learned more about him. He had gotten into drugs in high school and avoided college. After a while his parents ordered him to leave their house, which he did. He started turning tricks shortly thereafter.

Now, he claimed, he had been sober for two months. He lived in an apartment with four other guys.

"It's kinda crowded, so we sleep in shifts," he said. It's all right for me, I guess, 'cause I work nights,.

When dinner was over, we both looked around kind of hesitantly.

"Hey, bud, I owe you some money," I said. "Let's not settle our debts here. Why don't you come on up? You can freshen up, maybe use the shower if you want."

Chas and I retired to my room, where he accepted my offer of a hot shower. When he came out wrapped in a hotel towel and looking just a bit more appealing now that he was freshly scrubbed, I handed him a $50 bill.

"Here ya go," I said.

"Thanks." He put the money in his shoe.

"Listen..." I began, "you can crash here if you want to. I mean, it's a terrible night out. You might as well get some sleep."

"Serious?"

"Sure." I added, "Watch some cable if you want. I'm going to take a shower."

I half-expected him to have run out with my luggage by the time I finished showering. He hadn't, though. Instead, he was curled up under the covers, asleep.

I put on a pair of boxers and slipped into bed. Chas awoke and whirled around. I saw that he was sleeping in the nude.

"A little edgy?" I smiled.

"A little."

Once I was settled in, he sidled up next to me and put an arm around me.

"Hey, it's OK," I said. "We don't have to—"

He shushed me. "Will you hold me? It's been a long time since I've fallen asleep with somebody holding me."

So we spooned, his back to my chest, and in that position we drifted off to sleep.

I woke a few hours later, my arm slightly numb and my cock stiff from a piss hard-on. I gently extracted myself from the bed and crept to the bathroom. When I returned, still half-hard, I tried to approximate the position I had been in before.

Chas stirred. "You have a hard-on?" he asked, sliding his hand up my leg to my penis, which responded by becoming fully erect again. He spun around in bed, and I felt his erection rub my own. "Me too." He smiled.

I smiled too, saying nothing, and felt my boxers sliding down my legs. Chas disappeared beneath the covers, and I felt his lips embrace my cock.

Nothing had ever felt like this before. I vacillated between moaning and making mental notes on how to improve my cocksucking skills. Suddenly, Chas stopped sucking me; moments later, his lips were on my ass.

I had never been rimmed before and didn't know that it could feel like this. I bit into the blanket in front of me as Chas's lips formed a seal around my asshole and his tongue worked its way up into my crevice.

What am I doing? The thought entered my head and was then quickly forgotten. Chas emerged from under the blankets and kissed me, giggling, as I realized he was letting me taste my ass on his lips. I could feel his cock, hard and urgent against my abdomen. I put my arms around him and pulled him to me.

Soon I eased a curious finger down his back and into his fuzzy butt crack, where I began to play with his asshole. I pressed and found his ass once again yielding.

"Aw, yeah, that's it..." Chas said in a throaty voice.

"You don't have to talk dirty for me, Chas," I said. He smiled.

"So noted. Aah...yeah..." he moaned as I continued finger-ing his ass.

After a few minutes of hot and heavy making out and finger-fucking, Chas spun his ass around toward me. He didn't have to tell me what to do next.

"You want it in you, don't you?" I asked. As a response, he slid his crack up and down against my cock. Reaching into his bag, which was on the floor next to the bed, Chas retrieved a condom and some lube and handed them back to me.

I'm not terribly well-hung, but the head of my cock is fair-ly thick. I eased it into his opening, and then tried to nudge it carefully past his limber sphincter. He still let out a gasp, but was soon welcoming my whole shaft into his butt.

"Yeah, that's it," he sighed.

A minute later I was fucking him. It took me a moment to get in stride as I contemplated for a second the absurdity of the situation. Here I was with a former classmate turned prostitute, and I was having the time of my life. It was unquestionably the most erotic sex I had ever had, partly because I could now clearly remember lusting after Chas when I had known him as Charlie.

To hell with memories. Living in the moment was just as much fun, and the way Chas's ass gripped my cock was definitely better than any memory. I plunged in as deep as I could, over and over. I reached around his tight abs and grasped his hard cock, stroking it with my clenched fist.

"Oh, babe, I'm too sensitive," he gasped. "Gotta slow down."

I tried, honestly I did, to temper the pace with which I manhandled his meat. But his engorged prick must have been pretty damn near close to exploding already because within seconds he was spasming in my hand.

"U-u-ungh..." he moaned as I felt spurt after spurt of semen flood past my fingertips. Within seconds, the sheet beneath us was covered with a warm, milky puddle.

Chas seemed exhausted for half a second, then devoted all of his energies to making me come. He arched his back and tightened his butt's hold on my cock as I tried to pound into him as forcefully as I could. I wanted to hold out, but I was no match for his increased friction, and I soon blew my load within him.

We collapsed, spent, and kissed briefly before drifting off to sleep.

When I awoke, groggy, Chas was not in bed next to me. I worried that perhaps he had gotten up and slipped off with my wallet and watch...but then he emerged from the bathroom, freshly showered again.

He looked sheepish.

"Good morning," he said.

"Morning," I replied.

He sat on the bed and dressed, then stood up.

"I want to give you this," he said, handing me the money I

had given him the previous night. "I...it's stupid, but I make it a rule not to take money from friends."

I looked at him. "You're right," I said after a moment. "We are friends."

He smiled about to say something.

"However," I said, pressing the money back into his palm, "this is cash I agreed to pay you to help me with directions. Whatever happened after that, well, if you don't want to charge me...that's your loss." I winked.

He blushed. "Thanks, I guess." He continued, "I gotta head out...I'm supposed to meet a friend."

I nodded. "Is this the part where I ask you if this is really what you want to do with your life?"

"I think this is that part, yeah," he said with a smirk. "And the answer is no. But right now I gotta do what it takes to survive."

I nodded again. "I want you to contact me," I said as I gave him my card, "for more than one reason. Of course, I'd like to see you again. But more importantly, I'm an expert at helping people find better jobs. That's what I do for a living."

"Really?" he asked. "No kidding?"

"Funny how things work out, isn't it?" I said.

"Yeah," he said, still smirking. "Funny."

f f f

The Whole Truth and Nothing But

BY

DEREK ADAMS

"Turn off that fuckin' music
before I twist your fuckin' head off and cram it up your fuckin'
ass. Fuckin' fruit." I spun the volume dial to the left, reducing
the sound to a whisper—I sensed that a person who doesn't
appreciate Barry Manilow isn't a person who'd listen to reason.
I heard two or three other muttered grunts of approval from the
other cells, then an explosive fart.

Before I try to tell you what really happened that fateful
night, let me introduce myself. My mama taught me to always
say "please" and "thank you" and to introduce myself to
strangers. "The Hutters've never had anything to be ashamed
of, Jimmie Jack," she'd tell me, "except maybe for your Aunt
Verleen—and that wasn't really her fault. She never would've
become a nympho if it hadn't been for the Bulldogs winning

147

the homecoming game that year. Nobody expected that." So now you know. I'm Jimmie Jack Hutter, and my being here at the state honor farm is just a great big horrible, ugly mistake.

Well, unless you've been out of the county for the past two months, you already know I was in that car out in front of the Big Pit barbecue restaurant and convenience store. I never disputed that, not for a minute. I was in the car, and I was driving, but I didn't know a thing about the plan that Lyle and Bobbie had cooked up to rob the place. And I sure as hell wouldn't have forced Lula Rose Hicks to strip naked and get into that meat locker. I mean, Lula Rose and I went to school together up until she dropped out her freshman year when she had to get married. If Nona Dinks hadn't gone in to get that shoulder roast out of the self-storage, poor Lula would still be in there. No telling what might've happened. Sorry, Lula Rose.

When Lyle Driscoll pulled in to the station for a lube job that afternoon and told me he was a Hollywood agent, I believed him. I mean, I'm just not a suspicious person. Hell, he was driving an imported car and was wearing this big diamond ring and some clothes like the ones in that catalog I keep under the mattress. Well, when he told me he was looking for a guy to star in this new picture he was working on and mentioned that I was perfect for the part, it sounded legit to me. After all, I've been working out real hard for years—and I had been voted runner-up for Best-Looking Guy my senior year. Anyhow, when he gave me his business card and told me he'd be by that evening at 8 o'clock to take me out to meet the film's backers, I just knew he was for real.

Well, Lyle was there in front of my place that evening, honking the horn, right on time. I strode across the yard to his car, aware that he was watching me intently. I was wearing a real tight pair of shorts, white socks, my good tennis shoes, and a baseball cap, turned around backward. It was just exactly what Lyle had told me to wear. Since it was sort of like an audition, I walked up to the car real slow. When I was about three feet away, he rolled down his window, tossed out his cigarette butt, and flashed me a big sincere smile. He had real nice teeth.

"Goddamn, Jimmie Jack. You look hot enough to melt paint. Fuckin' shit."

"Thanks, Lyle," I replied modestly. "You're looking mighty good yourself." He was too. He had changed out of his good clothes and was wearing a sleeveless T-shirt that showed off his arms real nice. He had big biceps and dark hair on his shoulders. It looked real hot. I peeked in the car and saw that the fly of his faded jeans was unbuttoned and something that resembled a flesh-colored hose was draped over the seat between his legs. My heart skipped a beat.

"Get on in the car," Lyle said, jerking his head in the general direction of the passenger seat. I walked around, opened the door, and climbed in. Lyle hit the gas and sprayed a rooster tail of gravel about 10 feet in the air. I'd have to remember to rake the yard before I mowed on Saturday or risk busting out every window in the damned house.

I forgot all about windows when Lyle reached over and put his hand on my neck. "You suck cock?" he asked as we drove past the Tastee-Freeze out near the end of Main Street. I was waving at Carl and Cal Macks, hoping they'd see me in the big car, but they were too dumb to look up. Well, when I realized what Lyle was asking, I snapped my head around and stared, my mouth gaping. "I'm gonna assume that means yes," he said, tightening his grip and pulling my head down into his lap so hard, I damn near chipped a tooth on his zipper.

Well, I should've grabbed his balls and punched them up his ass, but I didn't. I'm not a violent guy, and his balls were so big and furry and heavy in my hand that I just sort of wanted to fondle them instead. While I was doing that, his dick started stirring, so I settled down to investigate. I started back at his bush and began working my way out to the end. It was a long enough trip to warrant packing a lunch, I'll tell you. I've seen a few dicks in my day but never anything to hold a candle to

Lyle's man handle. It was as thick as my wrist and had veins twining around it like vines around a tree trunk.

"Get on that damned pole, Jimmie Jack. Show me what you're made of." I opened wide and got on. "Shit, yeah. Feels fuckin' hot, man. Suck that big dick. Lick it. Fuck!"

Lyle bucked his hips and grabbed at the back of my head, ramming his prick so far down my throat, I could feel the fist-size head pulsing in my belly. I grunted and groaned and struggled a little, but then Lyle smacked my ass real hard and jammed a finger right up my hole, which calmed me down considerably. I wondered for a second just how the hell Lyle was managing to drive that big car with both hands busy, but he started knuckling my prostate, and I forgot all about it.

I have to admit, I've always prided myself on my cock sucking, so I set out to give Lyle the blow job of his life. I just got him to let go of my head so I could maneuver around some, and then I got right down to it. I locked my lips tight around the shaft and came up off of him nice and slow. By the time I got out to where I could knob him, Lyle was so far away, I could barely see him. Hell, if I'd thought about sucking him before we'd started, I don't think I'd have been able to manage it.

I was managing now, though. I ran my tongue around the bulging dome of his cock head, swabbed his piss hole, rasped away at the bundle of nerves tucked right below it, then started down on him again. I rode it slow, letting his immense girth stretch my throat muscles to the max. By the time I was rooting in his pubes, I was beginning to see stars—and judging by the sounds he was making, so was Lyle.

I kept on after him, hard and fast. I'd ride the rail from end to end a few times, then grab his cock with both hands and jack it while I licked all around the end and tried to catch my breath. After about 10 minutes, Lyle's nuts were trying to climb up on top of his hard-on, and judging by the sounds of the engine, I figured we were going about a hundred miles an hour.

"Unh! Fuck! Jesus!" Lyle let fly with a mighty load. His cock slipped out of my grip and flexed, pointing straight up. A huge gush of white cream pumped out of him, hitting the roof of the car. It splattered against the gray fabric and hung there like a stalactite. "Christ!" Lyle let loose with another one. This time his splooge blasted the windshield, right in his line of vision. He leaned forward to wipe the glass, and his big come cannon pointed right at me as Lyle squirted out a third shot. It hit me on the neck and sprayed the side of my face. It was hot and thick and smelled like a man's sweaty balls. I grabbed for my crotch, ready to work myself over, but Lyle grabbed my wrist.

"Save it, pal."

"But I'm horny," I protested. Hell, I was too. I'd just sucked a cock that was damn near as tall as I was, and I wanted some relief.

"Shit!" Lyle slammed on his brakes, and I flew off the seat, getting wedged under the dash. The floor wasn't any too clean either, and a whole bunch of dirt and twigs got stuck in the gummy mess that smeared across my neck and shoulder. "We're here," Lyle said. "Get out." Lyle opened the driver's door and took his own advice.

"Lyle," I spluttered, crawling out on all fours onto the sharp gravel of the driveway, "I gotta get cleaned up before I meet these—" I looked up and saw a semicircle of guys, all staring down at me. I scrambled to my feet and crammed my hat back onto my head. My hair was a mess. This screen test sure wasn't getting off to a great start.

"Hi, guys," I said sheepishly.

"Christ," somebody muttered.

"This is it?" A guy who looked like Lyle, only with bigger muscles, walked around me, staring hard. I felt like some live-stock exhibit at the county fair. "Can he fuck?"

"I've been fingering him on the drive out," Lyle replied, clearing his throat and hawking a wad of spit. "You could park a tour bus up his hole."

"Pardon me?" I couldn't believe my ears. If I'm anything, I'm tight. Just ask any of the guys down at the truck stop at Four Corners.

"Shut up and get inside," Lyle grunted. Somehow all his manners had gone south on him. I was revising my opinion of him by the minute. I would've given him a piece of my mind, but I didn't want to act ugly in front of important strangers. I just gave him a look and followed him inside.

I'd been expecting an office. What I saw was a big old warehouse with some lights set up around a platform draped in black plastic sheeting. One of the guys had a video camera with him, and another guy walked over and started turning on the lights. Several of the others started taking off their clothes. I had no idea what they were going to do, but I had to wash my face.

When I got back—after using a toilet that hadn't been cleaned since maybe World War II—there were four guys, all naked, all hard, up on the platform. There was a redhead with great pecs and a scarlet pecker; a blond with enough muscles to start his own gym; a black dude with skin the color of coffee with a lot of milk in it and intense gray eyes; and a big guy without a hair on him, head to toe, and a cock that put Lyle's prong in the shade. It was bigger than anything I'd ever seen growing between a man's legs—and that includes that truck-driving redhead from Kansas City I met last month—and it was hard as a rock. It was a wonder the poor guy didn't just up and pass out.

"Onstage, buddy," the man with the camera snapped. "Hurry it up."

"Hey, guys," I said, stepping up onto the platform, hand outstretched. "I'm Jimmie Jack Hutter. I—" My introductions got cut short when the tall black man gripped my wrist and pulled me up against his hard body.

"Suck me," he growled, his voice deep and sexy. He pushed me to my knees and began smacking my face with his meat. After the first few smacks it was starting to hurt, so I opened wide, and he slid in deep, bouncing his balls off my chin.

While I was starting to suck, somebody grabbed my shorts. I reached back, but by then my shorts had been torn off, so I ended up grabbing my own bare butt. I wasn't the only one with that in mind, as it turned out—within five seconds the blond and the redhead had followed suit, and I had enough hands on my ass to play piano duets. Those hands all had fingers, and most of them ended up in my crack, pulling my cheeks apart, spreading my ass lips wide.

"Move the camera in closer, Jack. Get that butt in focus."

"Guys, I—" The black man's prick popped out of my mouth, only to be replaced by the bald man's huge schlong. The black man began prodding at my ear with his spit-slicked hard-on. I was so busy trying not to choke on all that cock while keeping my ass ring clenched tight that I completely forgot the audition piece I'd been practicing. I was planning to knock 'em dead with this scene from *Little House on the Prairie*, but I had a feeling they weren't interested.

"Got those fingers up in him?"

"Yeah."

"Pick him up." Before I could dislodge the huge horn crammed down my throat, the two guys behind me lifted, suspending me above the platform. I managed to get my feet on the floor and would've stood up and given them a piece of my mind, but the shaved guy had a grip on my ears that was constricting my movements. As it was, I snorted and wiggled my butt angrily.

"OK, men, loosen him up for Harry." I felt something pressing against my hole; then my ass pipe was full of cold, slippery lube. I wiggled around, but it didn't seem to slow anybody down. The nozzle disappeared; then I felt furry thighs against the backs of my legs. A second later I had a cock up my ass, and I was getting fucked.

"Got a good angle," the cameraman grunted, slithering beneath me on his back, his camera pointing up toward my crotch. "Little tomcat has a nice dick. Photographs nice. Balls pulled up tight enough so they don't interfere with the penetration shots. Change partners, guys." Dick number one popped out of my ass, its place quickly taken by dick number 2.

The three of them fucked me to within about an inch of having me shoot my wad all over that camera guy. Hell, I was leaking lube, my nipples were swollen up in thick points, and my hole was grabbing frantically at whatever prick was poked up inside it at any given moment.

"Go for the final scene, men. Do it!" All of a sudden I was empty, fore and aft. I stood up and looked around dazedly. Harry, the bald muscle god, had lain down on the floor and had his fist clenched around the base of his pecker. It glistened with my spit and Harry's own dick lube, rising up to the level of my kneecaps. The other guys grabbed me by the arms and walked me over to Harry. When I was straddling his hips, they started to push me down.

"I don't think—" My speech was cut short by the addition of two big hard pricks to my mouth, both ripe with my own funky ass juices. I sucked them noisily as the third guy brought my asshole into contact with Harry's big knob.

Believe me, nobody was more shocked than I was when his belly smacked against my ass. Man, I felt like I had two spines all of a sudden. It was beyond intense. I had a feeling that the pricks going down my throat might just meet up with the one coming up my asshole. There was a whole lot of bucking and pumping and groaning going on for the next few minutes. The guy who'd sat me down on Harry was now up front, taking turns with the others fucking my face. I was twitching and slobbering, personally taking care of five cocks, counting my own hard-on. I felt a little like a trained seal I'd once seen playing these horns at the circus—only the seal hadn't been taking it up the ass.

"Come shot!" the director yelled. Suddenly, I was flat on my back, asshole snapping at the air, staring up at the camera and four bulging stiffers. The redhead erupted first, his load splashing down on my chest and neck like molten lava. He was still spitting when the black man blasted off, creaming all over my face. The blond got my left leg and my arm, shooting hot ribbons with the force of a garden hose. Finally, Harry got off, aiming his load at my cock and balls. One touch of that hot, manly load of his, and I blew my own cork, laying a line from my Adam's apple to my belly button.

"Cut!" The guys surrounding me all stopped flogging their hogs and walked away, leaving me lying in the middle of a lake of jizz, totally dazed. I looked up and saw the cameraman counting money into Lyle's hand. Lyle stuffed it into his pocket, and the man left.

"You know how to drive?" Lyle was standing over me, hands on his hips. He wasn't talking near as nice as he had before the audition. I nodded. "Get a move on. We've got things to do."

I got out to the car and found Lyle in the backseat with this guy he called Bobbie. I thought he'd been the one working the lights, but I wasn't sure. He had lots of blond hair and sort of a dumb expression on his face. I didn't think he was handsome at all. Lyle directed me to the Big Pit and told me to wait. If he'd told me what he was up to, I could've warned him that Deputy Stallings came in for coffee and doughnuts every night at midnight, regular as clockwork. That was strictly his fault.

The rest is all there in the court documents. I don't know how Lyle's lawyer talked that jury into believing that I had been the brains behind the whole thing, but he did. And to think I went to high school with those people. They should have known better.

"Hey, Vergil!" That was Pete, the dude in the cell to my right. He and Vergil—the guy to my left—talked across me all the time. I might just as well have been a big old hole in the atmosphere for all the attention they paid to me. "My pals Lyle and Bobbie sneaked me in a new video this afternoon. You gotta see it, man. It's wild!"

"What's it called, Pete?"

"Hell, I don't know. Wait." There was rustling in Pete's cell. "Get this, Verg—*Jimmie Jack Hutter Takes It All.*"

"That's a dumb title."

"Wait'll you see it. I'll stick it in the machine in the lounge tomorrow night. That'll get the guys stirred up—seeing some hot little sleazeball get his butt poked. Shit, they'll be trying to screw the sofa cushions."

Vergil laughed and said something back, but I didn't pay any attention. I was all of a sudden starting to feel a little dizzy.

Working Stiffs

f f f

ƒ ƒ ƒ

The Ice Cream Man Cometh

BY

T. HITMAN

On hot summer Saturdays, I sometimes drive into downtown Boston, park my car, and head over to the Charles River Esplanade. I like to sit under a tree on the bank of the river—more often than not dressed casually in a T-shirt, shorts, and slides (no underwear)—and do some work at my leisure while watching the boats and the world drift by. I usually get a lot of writing done, and the guys blading, rowing, jogging, or just walking past makes for much better scenery than I could enjoy sitting at home.

ƒ ƒ ƒ

I met Freddie on one such Saturday afternoon late last summer. I didn't know his name was Freddie when I drove past his battered old ice cream truck on my way into the city or that he'd end up playing such a significant part in my life. All I was aware of at the time was that he was undeniably one of the most handsome guys I'd ever seen.

Because the truck had no driver's side door, his whole body was visible as he sat behind the wheel. But I had to lean over to get a look at his face. "Whoa!" I gasped when his astonishing visage came into view. This ice cream man was a young stallion. He looked like he was a couple of years younger than I— 20 or 21 but no older. His black hair was short and neat, and there was a trace of a scruffy goatee on his chin. Tan cargo pants, white socks and sneakers, and a white T-shirt covered his trim, perfect body. The pits of his shirt were slightly damp, and I could see the fullness of a nicely packed crotch at the center of his pants. His most dazzling feature was the infectious smile he flashed when he noticed me noticing him. It took my breath away.

I gave him a flirtatious grin and fanned myself. He replied with a thumbs-up, then turned on his truck's calliope music. We gestured back and forth a few times—a wink from him, a blown kiss from me—before we reached the exit for the waterfront. As I turned off, I waved goodbye to him, seemingly for the last time. Still dazed by the encounter, I parked my car, slung my backpack over my shoulder, and set off for a day of peace and quiet work under a maple tree in a remote corner of the Esplanade.

A few hours later I was out of mineral water and had edited a good 20 pages of work. When the sound of an ice cream truck reached my ears, I figured it was time for a break. I packed up my stuff, dusted off my butt, and trudged to a bend in the road where a handful of adults and their kids flocked to buy something cold. I didn't recall my morning encounter until I saw that the truck had no driver's side door. Then I realized that the same handsome young man I'd flirted with on the highway was doling out cold drinks and ice cream to the crowd. Up close, he was even more handsome.

As the crowd thinned, the ice cream man looked around and recognized me.

"Amigo!" he exclaimed playfully as he flashed that beautiful smile.

"You talking to me?" I countered.

"If that was you riding my tail out there on the highway, then yeah. Come here," he said, waving me over. "I got something special for you."

I strutted over, folding my arms. "What could you possibly have in there for me?"

"Something cold," he said, handing me a frozen Rocket Pop. "On me."

"If it was on you, it would be melting," I said with a chuckle. Then, grinning as widely as he was, I accepted his gift.

The ice cream man ignored my comment. "It's just a little thank you."

I licked the tip of the Rocket Pop seductively. "You're thanking me? For what?"

"For making me feel like a macho hombre." He pumped his arms, and his smooth, tanned biceps bulged out of his damp T-shirt. I licked my ice cream faster and marveled as a single drop of sweat trickled down his forehead onto his nose, then from his nose to the counter.

"Damn, dude," I sighed.

The ice cream man relaxed and leaned down to face me, locking his eyes on mine. "Do you usually come on to strangers like this?"

"Only if they're really cute," I answered simply. "And you, amigo, are the cutest."

The ice cream man glanced around to make sure we were still alone and then declared, "I'm not gay."

The impact of that statement was as painful as the ice cream headache that set in after I accidentally swallowed a mouthful of cold slush.

"What are you?" I managed to ask after I recovered from the temporary trauma.

"Curious, I guess," he said, extending a hand. "My name's Federico, but my friends call me Freddie. You?"

"Jake," I replied, studying his long, strong fingers for a moment before taking his hand in mine. His grip was warm and firm.

"So, Jake," Freddie sighed in a lower voice, "you ever do it in an ice cream truck?"

I was so surprised by the question that I lost my grip and dropped the last of the melting Rocket Pop on the pavement.

"I thought you weren't gay?"

"I said I was curious," Freddie growled under his breath. His expression suddenly seemed very serious. "And you're really cute."

A wave of embarrassment rushed through me, heating me up and driving out the last of the iciness inside me. "Now I need to do something to thank you."

"Yup," Freddie replied, his infectious grin returning. "So why don't you come on up here in the truck?"

I started to argue about not being such an easy catch, to tell him that I truly, honestly was looking for something a little deeper than a onetime fuck with a curious straight dude—even though I'd been so flirtatious with him out on the highway. But before I could utter a single word, Freddie tipped his head toward the missing front door.

"Don't worry," he said. "The back closes up. We'll be alone in here, just you and me."

It hit me that he was serious. I looked around, shocked. As remote as our shady spot on the Esplanade was, it was still broad daylight in the heart of a busy city.

"Are you nuts?"

Freddie reached down and grabbed the full, obvious bulge in his cargo pants. "Maybe a little," he laughed. "Aren't you up for a little adventurous sexperimentation?"

I hesitated a moment longer, then tossed my backpack through the open window. "Maybe," I said, my insides twisting into knots in anticipation of having sex with such a gorgeous guy. "Yeah, just maybe."

I stepped through the driver's side door and, from there, into the refrigerated rear of the truck, where Freddie waited. It was a tight fit, but the air—a mix of cold from the freezers and warmth from Freddie's body—proved to be intoxicating. Freddie quickly closed the vendor's window and pulled a curtain across the rear of the truck, effectively cutting us off from the eyes of the outside world.

"So now what?" he asked. "I'm new at this, remember?"

"How about we start with the basics?" I said playfully.

"Like kissing?" he asked with a slightly nervous quiver in his voice.

I took one of his hands in mine. He squeezed it before bringing it to his lips. "Yeah," I said, reaching for his shoulders and pulling him closer to me, "kissing."

Freddie wrapped his arms around me and backed me against the nearest freezer, roughly crushing his lips against mine. His movements were frantic and awkward at first, but the longer we kissed, the softer and gentler he became.

"That's it, Freddie," I sighed between kisses, running my hand through his hair. His arms, at first clasped around me in a death grip, slowly relaxed. He slid one hand under my shirt to explore my chest. The other slipped down the back of my shorts to squeeze my hard runner's butt.

I opened my lips wider to accept Freddie's tongue into my mouth. We pressed our bodies together, and I realized we were both rock-hard. As the handsome boy ground his cock against mine, I swept my hand across his chest and the taunt expanse of his six-pack abs. Freddie yanked off his T-shirt, and his warm, sweet scent filled my nostrils.

Taking my hand in his, Freddie guided it down the front of his cargo pants into the tangle of crisp, black curls beneath the waistband—and then to the prize just a little farther.

"Yes-s-s," he huffed. His Adam's apple slid up and down in his throat as he swallowed. I cupped the straining bulge in his pants and gave his goods a firm squeeze. Looking down, I saw a small circle of precome spreading across the tent between Freddie's legs. "Do it, amigo," he begged in a deep, breathless growl. "Go down on my *verga!*"

I sank to my knees as I unzipped Freddie's pants. Like me, he was free-balling, since it was a hot summer day. I had an unobstructed view of his manhood.

"Fuck," I sighed.

As I'd expected, Freddie's respectable tool was uncut, capped by a crimped hood of foreskin. Two meaty nuts dangled below it in a loose sac covered with curly black hair. I gripped Freddie's cock and pushed back its hood, forcing the moist pink head from the folds of musky skin. Leaning in, I took a tentative lick. A bittersweet taste tingled on my tongue.

"Yeah," Freddie groaned. "Suck it!"

I glanced up at his face—he looked almost deliriously happy. Reaching around, I gripped one of his hard butt cheeks in each hand, then pulled him forward and drew his cock between my lips. The salty tang of his foreskin and precome exploded in my mouth. I swallowed him until my nose was buried deep in his pubic patch and his low-hanging nuts were bouncing against my chin.

As I knelt at Freddie's feet, slurping his uncut prong, I worked my shorts partway down my thighs and began grinding my boner against his leg. After a while he pulled his tool out of my mouth and replaced it with his balls.

"Lick my nuts, amigo," he commanded.

I lapped at his sweaty bag while he rubbed his drooling cock against my cheek. As I got ready to gobble his rod some more, Freddie reached a hand between my legs and pulled me up to my feet by my dick.

I wasn't sure whether he planned to suck on my pole or just

jack me off. He yanked down my shorts and stood there in front of me, admiring what he saw: another man's cock and nuts. Giving in to his curiosity, Freddie toyed with my bag and rubbed our cocks together, teasing both our knobs with his spit-soaked foreskin. Instead of taking me in his mouth, he made it clear that he had something completely different in mind.

"Turn around and bend over," he growled. "I want to fuck that hole!"

I was more than willing to give up my ass, but only if we played safely. I pulled a condom out of my backpack and rolled it over Freddie's cock. I applied a bit of lube from a small tube I had with me, then turned around to await his assault on my ass. To my surprise, he lowered his head and stuck his tongue in my crack to get a taste of my funk. Bent over the ice cream freezer, I ground myself against his face. The tickle of his goatee on my most sensitive flesh drove me right to the edge of shooting my load.

"Fuck," I heard him say as he exhaled. His warm breath teased my pucker.

I reached around and stroked his sweaty mop of hair. "What is it, man?"

"I never thought a guy's ass would taste so sweet," he groaned. He plunged his face back into my crack and tunneled his tongue deep into my hole one more time. Then he stood up and prepared to mount me. Breathing heavily, Freddie lined up his sheathed cock with my freshly tongued hole. A swell of anticipation rushed through me when I felt the tip of his dick poking at the outer ring of my pucker.

"Yeah," I moaned.

Freddie leaned forward as he pushed into me, pressing me down on the freezer until he was flush on top of me and his mouth was right at my ear. The pressure of his firm, strong body against mine, the smell of his breath, and the sensation of the cool metal of the freezer beneath me made every square inch of my flesh tingle. In my excitement I flexed my sphincter around the cock nudging its way into me. Freddie inhaled sharply and pushed in farther. When he was all the way in, his nut sac banged against mine.

"Oh, man," I sighed. "Do it, Freddie. Fuck me!"

Freddie shuddered and eased out of me just enough to tease my prostate with the head of his cock before shoving it all the way in again.

"I can't believe how fuckin' tight you are," he huffed between gasps. "Your stuff is way tighter than any chick's!"

Freddie fucked me with passionate abandon. Locked together with my chest pressed against the cold metal and his hot body grinding against me, we grunted and sweated until the action sent us both over the edge.

Freddie shot into the rubber up my ass, and I blew one of the biggest wads of my life right there on the floor. He was still stiff inside me when the sound of a fist banging against the outside of the ice cream truck brought us out of our reverie.

As Freddie pulled himself together and went to take care of his customer, I quietly savored what we'd just shared. I knew it was a one-in-a-million chance, but I was hoping we'd made more than just a physical connection. As it turned out, we had.

$$f\ f\ f$$

Almost a year has passed since Freddie and I met. He is no longer just curious. In fact, he's become something of an expert when it comes to making love to another man. On Saturdays in the summertime I still head down to the Esplanade to write. But now I usually ride shotgun in the ice cream truck, right next to the greatest guy alive, my Freddie.

♪ ♪ ♪

On the Run

BY

DALE CHASE

Eric always cooked. I never thought much about it until he left and I started losing weight. I'd wander into the kitchen, stomach growling, and open and close cupboards and stare at the fridge. All I could see was Eric in those white cutoffs. All I could think of was pulling them down and taking him right there, with pasta boiling and lettuce and tomato on the cutting board.

Food was important to Eric, and during our four years together he tried to impart his enthusiasm to me but never quite succeeded. I ate what he prepared, praised his efforts, and followed the healthy regimen he suggested, but I didn't do it because I loved food. I did it because I loved Eric. He was everything I wanted, and right up until he told me there was someone else he was my life.

In the month since he'd gone, I'd thrown myself into working, exercising at the gym, and riding my motorcycle.

Eating was something I wanted no part of, and only when my stomach got vocal did I give in. I also considered moving back to San Francisco but as yet couldn't make myself leave the suburban retreat we'd shared. Tucked high into the eastern side of the Berkeley hills, it offered a woodsy privacy and held enough traces of Eric to make departure seem like abandonment. And at night I'd hear raccoons foraging among trash cans and deer coming down to nibble the roses—everyone eating. Sometimes I'd lie awake and try to figure out where I was going. Dawn would arrive without answers.

And then one Monday night I skipped the gym and ordered a pizza because there was a flier in with the mail, and the picture was so realistic, the cheese looked like it was about to run off the page. I phoned in for a large with everything; the guy on the phone said 45 minutes.

Eric hadn't liked pizza, and as I waited for mine I realized I hadn't eaten any in four years, and for the first time since he'd been gone it occurred to me that the relationship might have been just a bit confining. I had to laugh. A pizza, of all things, had pried open my eyes.

The house was small, on stilts, and fronted by a long balcony, and as it was a warm night I sat outside awaiting my dinner, anticipating a meal for what seemed like the first time. No more than 30 minutes had passed when a little green Geo Metro pulled into the driveway below. It had a red and white banner on its antenna, and the deliveryman who stepped out wore a white painter's cap with the same logo.

I watched him stretch as if he'd been in the car for hours, then reach back inside to pull a single box from a large vinyl warming envelope on the seat. While I'd already noted his trim build and tan, it was this rear view that got me, and I experienced that same catch in my chest, that same rise I'd gotten so often with Eric. And then I absolutely knew this boy was mine.

He couldn't have been more than 20 and wasn't especially tall, maybe 5 foot 8, but he was put together, clad in a white

T-shirt and khaki shorts. His feet were bare. "Up here," I called, standing, and he gave me a smile and started up the stairs.

"It's $18.90," he said when he reached me. He seemed shy about the price, glancing down at the receipt.

"Money's inside," I said. "C'mon." I slipped through the open door without a backward glance, aiming for discretion while my body accelerated to readiness like a missile primed for blastoff. Money in hand, I hesitated. I could feel him behind me, teasing me with his proximity, and I feigned a search for cash as my cock prodded below. "Just a second," I said finally, now rock-hard. I wanted some measure of control when I faced him.

When I turned I did so with $25 in hand but made no move toward him. He gave me that smile again, boyish and brilliant, put the pizza on the table, and pulled out change. "Keep it," I said, and he took my money, hesitating just long enough to let me know what I wanted to know—a split-second confirmation that set my blood racing. It had happened once before, on a beach with Eric, and an hour later I'd had his dick in my mouth. Flushed with anticipation I managed only a question: "Been doing this long?"

"Couple of years."

"What's your name?"

"Rob."

"I'm Greg."

"Nice to meet you, Greg, but I've got to get going. The pizzas are getting cold."

He was out the door before I could say anything more, and I stood paralyzed for a moment, caught in the aftermath of a collision that hadn't happened. Had I misread him? Had my wires frayed during my time with Eric? I ran to the balcony and watched the Metro back down the driveway and stop, my breath stopping as well until a passing car swept aside any notion of Rob changing his mind. Seconds later he was gone.

I lasted about a minute before going after him, enduring in

those agonizing seconds nearly the same sense of loss I'd felt when Eric told me it was over. "No way," I said aloud as I scrambled back into the house, grabbed my keys, and slammed the door. I was on the Kawasaki in seconds, tearing after a boy I scarcely knew as dusk began to fade.

Roads are narrow up here, snaking through tight curves among pines and oaks, and where I usually enjoyed the lean and sway and sailed along easily, I now crossed the center line over and over, straightening curves and closing fast. I stayed a good distance behind yet kept the little green car in sight and saw it pull up a long circular drive and park in front of an aging ranch house set in a glade of trees. I parked on the street and watched Rob take two pizzas to the door. When he went inside I climbed off the bike and crept into the little forest, fully aware of how predatory my actions were. I felt like some nocturnal animal come out to feed and found it a comfortable role. Excitement was building even though I had no clear idea how I'd approach my prey when it reappeared.

The erection that had diminished on the ride renewed itself, and when Rob emerged from the house and stood on the porch, taking a long look across the grounds, I realized he knew he'd been followed. And more, that he approved. I stepped into view just as the porch light went off, and we were left in half-moon shadows that offered enough illumination to find each other, enough darkness for concealment.

When he came toward me, his walk was sure and confident, and by the time he reached me, he had his fly open. "Here?" I asked, and he nodded. "I like it on the run," he said, and he dropped his khakis. The cock that sprang up at me was slim but substantial, and I sank to my knees and began to feed, oblivious to the fact that the owners of the ground where I knelt were eating pizza not 50 yards from where I took my nourishment.

Rob was oozing readiness, but I took my time, sucking first his knob, tickling the slit, then sliding down the shaft to taste the whole of him. As I pulled at this delicious dripping meat, his hands plowed my hair, and he began a slow thrust that was so exquisite I wanted to scream, but, hey, my mouth was full! I sucked and licked until he began to groan, and when he shot his salty load down my throat he let out a cry I was certain would bring the porch light back on, but all was quiet as I savored what he'd given me. Afterward he stood in the half light, prong slowly descending, and when I rose to embrace him, he put his mouth over mine and bore his tongue deep, lapping his own come.

I couldn't believe we were doing this in somebody's front yard, and yet I dropped my cutoffs and pulled him to me, squeezing his butt cheeks, because there was no stopping now. I had to have him, and he knew it and turned to present himself.

I wet my fingers and lubed him thoroughly, then went in, driving up his alley with such force, his legs nearly buckled. Recovering, he bent forward and thrust his ass back and let me ride him standing, receiving my pole with an expert rear thrust that pushed me toward eruption all too soon. As I held him at the waist and thrust, I enjoyed my first real fuck in a month, easing the pace to postpone the inevitable explosion. He murmured as I slid almost completely out, diddling him with my crown, then pushed back up his rectum and stopped completely. He responded by contracting his sphincter, which nearly did me in, and I ached with urgency until there was finally no choice. My sauce was rising, and I began to work him in earnest, slamming my dick in and out until I squirted what seemed like a gallon of cream. And even then, after I'd emptied myself, I didn't want to stop, and I stayed inside him until I went soft, kissing his shoulders and neck, caressing his long sweet cock. "Come home with me," I said, and he leaned back against me and said no. "Pizzas." He pulled away slowly, put on the khakis, and grinned.

"When, then?" I asked. "Let me have your number."

"Let me have yours. I'll give you a call."

"When?"

"Tomorrow night. You can meet me."

"Where?"

"I won't know till then. Depends on the order."

"You mean like this? On a pizza delivery?"

"I told you, I like it on the run."

I gave him my number because there seemed to be nothing else to do, and as I watched the little green car drive away, I replayed the whole crazy scenario. I rode home slowly, having no idea what I'd started—or, really, with whom. He was simply Rob, the pizza man, and for now that had to be enough.

f f f

By the time the call came the following night, I was a wreck. I'd been distracted all day at work, asking people over and over what they'd just said, and I'd skipped the gym because I didn't want any flesh around me that wasn't Rob's and also because I didn't want him to get my answering machine, where I knew he wouldn't leave a number. I still had the pizza but hadn't eaten any, couldn't eat any. So I sat until after 10, fidgeting, running the remote, and pacing the balcony, scaring off raccoons. Every time I thought of Rob, my dick stirred, and when the phone rang I almost went off as well.

"Bear Valley Road," he said without a hello. "Do you know it?"

"Sure."

"Vista Drive, about three miles up, 112, last house on the right. It's got one of those old-fashioned lantern lights on a pole at the road."

"And where will you be?"

"Delivering a pizza," he said and hung up.

I stared at the phone, surprised at the extent of his game, then headed for the motorcycle. In minutes I was on Bear

Valley Road, which wasn't in a valley but ran along a ridge. Small dark streets dropped away down either side, most of them populated by older houses on large lots. There were no streetlights. I had no trouble locating Vista Drive and the lantern light. Beyond it I could make out a cabin-like structure set at the end of a flagstone path. The little green Metro was nowhere in sight.

I parked to one side, near a rampant jasmine that had overtaken a small fence. I'd been there no more than five minutes when I saw the Metro speed up the driveway and heard its horn sound. A porch light came on, and an elderly woman stepped out. I watched closely, as she seemed to know Rob; a comfortable banter accompanied the pizza transaction. He patted the woman's arm before she went back inside, and then he was alone, caught in the light she'd failed to extinguish.

He knew I was watching. I wondered for a second if the old woman was too, wondered also if Rob liked it that way. He lingered beside a cane rocker, fingering its back, and then he took off his painter's hat and ran a hand through his sandy hair, burnished gold in the light. I started toward him, knowing it was his show, that whatever we were to do had already been carefully choreographed. When he saw me he unbuttoned his Dockers and slid a hand down inside and kept it there.

"Fuck me," he mouthed. I nodded and mouthed back, "Where?" He indicated the porch, and I shook my head and mouthed a "No way." He grinned and shrugged, came down the steps, and led me to the side of the house where an old chaise sat. In the thin glow of the porch light, I could make out a faded green-and-yellow pad. "OK?" he mouthed. I nodded.

We pulled away each other's pants and trapped our rigid cocks between us as we embraced, him biting my neck, me clutching his ass. As much as I loved his hard prong against mine, I wanted to be inside him, rammed to the hilt, and I turned him around, pushed him onto the chaise, and spread him, his dark bullet hole beckoning. I licked a finger and shoved it in, and he groaned, and I licked some more and lubed and probed until I had him ready, then climbed on, pulled him up to a good angle, and plowed in. He pushed back against me as if to get me in even farther. I savored his channel until urgency stirred, come boiling inside my balls. I picked up speed.

As I rode him I felt him reach for his dick and work himself, and the chaise squeaked as we pounded out a fuck, neither of us concerned whether the old lady might hear us. As I deposited my juice up Rob's sweet rectum, I felt a recoil run through him like that of a handgun, my cock surging in response even though quite empty. As we quieted I licked his neck. "Rocket man," I said, "you are truly something."

When I slipped from him and he got up, I saw a thick puddle he'd left on the chaise, and it made me want to fuck him all over again. "Come home with me," I begged, envisioning a repeat in my bed and more the next morning. He shook his head and pulled on his Dockers.

"So this is how it's going to be?" I asked. "I don't understand. I mean, we've got something here."

He looked past me, like an animal caught in a hunter's sight, and I knew I was losing. "Why the running?" I pleaded, but it was too much or too little, because he bolted past, headed toward the car. I knew not to follow. I watched the Metro drive away.

I threw away the stale pizza when I got home. I tore it to pieces and shoved it into the trash. But that didn't help, and my hard-on the next morning brought an ache of uncertainty as much as longing. I worked it slowly, almost absently, and thought of Rob doing it for me; I shut my eyes and saw his beautiful cock and felt hunger as never before. I had to have him, had to keep having him. I didn't go to work that day, knowing I'd be useless. When night fell I waited by the phone.

"610 Rohner Drive," he said. "At Camino Diablo." He didn't ask if I knew it or give me time to question; he just hung up. In seconds I was on the bike, headed south. Rohner Drive was at the other end of the hills, in a relatively low-rent area, but in these hills low-rent was still pretty high. When I found 610, however, that was all I found—a number painted on the curb. The lot was vacant, a tangle of weeds and untended shrubs. An old oak listed to one side, draping branches nearly to the ground. I could hear some small night creature scurrying in the dark. I pulled deep into the lot, parked, and sat on the bike, wondering at this new turn the game had taken.

I heard the Metro before I saw it, screeching around a turn, then flying past. Brakes squealed as it stopped down the street, and in a few minutes it reappeared, turned up the drive, and aimed its headlights at me. After a minute Rob shut off the lights, killed the engine, and stepped out of the car. There wasn't much moonlight—just enough for me to see he'd shed his clothes entirely. What walked toward me was a beautifully furred animal looking to rut. I was overcome by this overt need, so base that it hung in the air like a hot musky scent.

As he came to me, I dropped to my knees and drew his wet cock into my mouth. I devoured the proffered bone as my hand kneaded his balls, and when I looked up at him, my mouth full of his dick, he smiled and came, squirting a long delicious stream deep into my throat. I sucked at him until I had every drop, gorging myself, wanting still more.

When he withdrew he pulled me up to him, my rigid cock jabbing his leg. He reached down and wrapped a hand around it, then lowered himself and took it into his mouth, where his tongue began to work me as mine had him, and I began a thrust I couldn't control, fucking his mouth instead of his ass, his sweet and juicy mouth that swallowed my pulsing cock. I gripped the sides of his head and felt his jaw working me, and I looked up and nearly howled as I filled him with a load that felt like it weighed a pound. When I was empty I kept fucking him because he kept sucking me, his tongue working even when I went soft. When he released me I sank to my knees and tried not to say what I felt. I fought back the words as I looked into his eyes, looked at the mouth where I'd just been. When I started to speak, he pushed his lips to mine, and I knew he meant me to lick my own come as he had, and I knew then this was what we would always be, animals in the night. Rob's mouth pulsed against mine as he urged me on.

When he pulled back I reacted from instinct, trapping the animal before it escaped. I grabbed his upper arms and held on as he tried to break free. "Don't leave," I pleaded as we began to struggle, then toppled over. He thrashed beneath me, but I was bigger and heavier, and I held on, fueled now by desperation, unable to face abandonment. His struggle was fierce, but I fought him to submission, and it was only when I had him pinned that I realized it was I who had lost. When you defeat a wild creature, you steal its power, the very thing you are trying to possess. I rolled off him. "I'm sorry," I said as he jumped up. Sweaty and dirt-smeared, he stood above me, cock dangling. I reached up to claim what I wanted, but when I met neither resistance nor erection, I knew it could never be my way. I wanted to suck the life out of him but didn't. I retreated, as did he.

He walked to the car, turned on the headlights, and caught me in the glare, my own nakedness as dirty and bare as that of any creature prowling the night. I stood for him, displaying myself, and thought maybe this was where we belonged after all, maybe this was how it should be, and maybe it wasn't such a bad thing. When Rob drove away I stood listening to the night. Something shrieked, far away. A kill? Penetration? One something mounting another something, driven by sheer instinct?

†††

Stripped of Inhibitions

BY

PIERCE LLOYD

I lived with Tim for a semester. It was an incredibly difficult semester. Not because of school; I was breezing through my classes. No, the difficulty lay in sharing a room with a god-like hunk and trying to keep my hands off my swollen dick. And it was none too easy keeping my hands off of his dick, either.

Many nights he'd go to sleep early, sprawled on top of his covers, clad only in tight white briefs. I would stay up late to do homework or surf the Internet, and my eyes would inevitably sneak over to his chiseled form. He had a baby face, which made his enormous chest seem even more out of place. He had rock-hard abs and a narrow waist, and his obliques—his "Apollo's Belt" in classical terms—etched deep lines that led beneath his clean white cotton sheath. On more than one occasion, I gazed lustfully on his sleeping form and wanted nothing more than to rip off his underwear and slurp greedily on his balls and cock.

His modesty was frustrating. It was as though Tim was teasing me with his amazing body but was too shy to reveal himself all the way. So I fantasized about his cock, which he always kept hidden, even changing his underwear in the shower stall instead of in our room. Sometimes I envisioned his erect cock as big and menacing; sometimes I pictured it as small and cute. But I never got a chance to see it.

As it was, we were pretty good friends. Tim was a fun guy who enjoyed his beer, but never seemed to gain an ounce. Since we were close and I had few friends, I sometimes felt an urge to tell him how I felt about him—or at least that I was gay. But he was always talking about women, and I never could figure out quite how he'd react. I was only a sophomore in college, and I wasn't yet ready to come out to everyone in my life.

At the end of the first semester that year, Tim moved out to live off-campus with a friend. I ended up having the whole dorm room to myself. That was nice, but I missed Tim.

A few weeks into the spring semester, I bumped into Tim at the library.

"Dude!" he yelled, grabbing my hand. A nearby student, studying, shushed him. "How're things?" he went on, more quietly.

"Things are good," I said, noticing that he held my hand an extra instant before letting go. *Why do I notice these meaningless things?* I wondered. *Why torture myself?*

"What have you been doing with yourself?" I asked nonchalantly. "I haven't seen you around much."

"I got this new job," he whispered, "making, like, so much money."

"Really? Where do you work?"

"I'm a male stripper now."

I was taken aback. "Really?" I managed to say.

"Yeah. Dude, we've got so much to catch up on. You free later?"

"Sure," I said, not caring if I had plans or not.

f f f

"So your new job..." I said as we munched on pizza.

"It's the easiest money I've ever made. All I do is, I go on a Friday night or a Saturday night, I dance around a little, take off my clothes, and I get at least 100 bucks."

"All your clothes?" I asked, truly fascinated.

He smiled mischievously. "Sometimes, if the mood is right."

I wanted to ask, "So when can I see you perform?" I settled on, "So how did you land this job?"

"It was just dumb luck, I guess. This exotic-dance service in town used to just provide female strippers for parties, but they were always getting requests for men. So they hired a few. There are three of us now, and we can barely keep up. I found out from Tina, this girl who sits in front of me in chemistry. She's a dancer too, and she told me I had a good body and should apply."

"Wow. I never knew that was a business."

"Yeah. It's great. I make at least $100 for the dance, and then I usually make anywhere from $20 to $200 in tips. Sometimes I do two dances a night."

Suddenly, his face lit up. "Dude! You'd be perfect. You're just the type they're looking for."

"What? Me?"

"Yeah. You've got a good body. You haven't gone downhill since last semester, have you?"

I bristled. "Of course not."

"Then you should apply. It'd be great. We could do big parties together, get felt up by tons of hot chicks...."

It didn't really sound like my cup of tea.

Tim stood up and pulled me to my feet. "Come here." He led me to the bathroom, then locked the door with the two of us inside.

What's he doing? I wondered.

"Take off your shirt," he ordered. Confused, I did as I was told.

"Perfect. See? You've got great pecs. Women love pecs."

I looked down at my chest. While the work I'd been doing at the gym had begun to show, I wasn't really at Tim's level yet. Still, I had to admit I looked pretty good.

"I don't know if I'm comfortable with the whole thing."

"Aw, dude," he whined, sounding like the sitcom best friend trying to talk his chum into some crazy shenanigan. "Tracy says a lot of guys worry that their dick is too small, but most guys are just fine. They aren't expecting porn stars." He reached for my pants.

"What the hell are you doing?" I said as I mentally willed him to go further. He unbuttoned my fly.

"I'm checking you out. I'll bet your dick is bigger than mine," he said. He yanked my underwear to my knees, and I stood before him in all my glory. He checked me out for maybe two seconds.

"See?" he said. "You're plenty big. I'll give them your number, OK?"

"Uh, OK," I said, pulling up my pants. "But you've got to help me with the tricks of the trade."

"Absolutely, buddy. Rule number one, trim your bush."

We both laughed hysterically at that one.

ƒ ƒ ƒ

My interview wasn't nearly as seedy as I'd expected— or hoped. I was asked a few questions, looked up and down, and hired.

My first job wasn't nearly as seedy as I expected, either. It was some woman's 40th birthday, and her friends were determined to embarrass her. I stripped from jeans and a dress shirt down to my briefs, then did a teasing dance as I stripped to my G-string. The birthday girl turned bright red, and when my 20 minutes were up, I left—no nudity, but a $100 fee and $30 in tips just for shaking my butt. All in all, I guess it was a pretty good job.

I was at the agency picking up my check with Tim when the secretary got a call. She said "Uh-huh, uh-huh" a few times and then put the caller on hold.

"I got a party on the 25th," she said, chewing her gum. "They want two guys."

"We'll take it!" Tim chimed.

"It's an all-male party," she said.

Tim shrugged. "I got no problem with that." He looked at me.

"Fine," I said, secretly wondering, *What if I see somebody I know?*

I needn't have worried. The party was on the outskirts of town and consisted of 15 older men, all slightly bearish. I had never met any of them before.

Tim whispered to me after we had walked in the door, "The secret to dancing for guys is to pretend you really enjoy it." I nodded.

We took turns. Tim did his striptease first, with a dance song blaring on the stereo. He looked like a regular college student, in flannel shirt and khakis. He stripped these off to reveal boxer briefs, then peeled off the boxer briefs until he was wearing only a skimpy blue G-string. He lowered the G-string enough to reveal his pubic hair, then did a final bump and grind as the song ended.

"Your turn, partner!" he yelled to me and then turned to one of the men who was seated on a large sectional sofa. "Mind if I sit on your lap?" The man smiled as Tim straddled his knee.

I did my dance, pleased at the cheers I got when I took off my pants and again when I pulled off my boxers to reveal my red G-string. Wanting to be creative, instead of showing my bush, I turned around and flashed my ass. I got some scattered applause.

When I finished I looked to see what Tim wanted to do next. I hoped he would take the first step and get completely naked.

Instead, Tim was still sitting on one of the men on the couch, but he had at least five different guys feeling his body. Tim just closed his eyes and lay back as the partygoers massaged his chest and legs.

I realized that there was a whole group of men on the sofa staring at Tim, but sitting too far away to reach him. I walked over and planted myself on top of two of them. They took my cue and began to run their hands along my muscles, one guy even discreetly kneading my ass.

I looked over at Tim. One of the guys had a $10 bill out and was sliding it down Tim's chest. He pushed it past Tim's stomach and then down into his G-string. My eyes widened as he reached down into the well-filled pouch and fondled Tim's cock. Tim only moaned with pleasure. Within seconds two more hands were inside his underwear, feeling him up. Tim responded by pulling his G-string to his knees, freeing his hard, circumcised cock. It looked to be a hefty six or seven inches.

Suddenly, I felt a hand gripping my already-hard member. Then another and another found their way into my G-string, which was soon being pulled off my legs and unceremoniously thrown onto the floor.

Completely bare-assed now, I looked over to see Tim watching me. He smiled to show his approval of my compromising situation as a hand wrapped around his cock. Although heavy, hairy men typically are not my type, watching the horny daddies pet and stroke my friend was indescribably erotic.

After a few moments Tim stood up. Still naked, he walked over to me, his stiff dick swinging in front of him, and took my hand, pulling me off the couch and onto my feet.

"Well, that's our show," he said. There was a chorus of disappointment. "At least, that was the first half of our show. We can stay and do a second act if you want."

I stared at Tim dumbly. *Second act? What was he talk-ing about?*

"What do you guys do for an encore?" asked the guy who was throwing the party.

"For an extra 100 bucks my partner and I will do anything to each other you'd care to see." As if to prove his point, he put his arm around my waist and pulled me close to him.

As a few of the men pooled their money, he whispered in my ear, "So, are you up for it?"

I whispered back. "I didn't know you were into this."

"Dude," he said, "you can't tell me you haven't felt some-thing between us these past few weeks."

"I have," I said. "I didn't realize you felt it too."

He pulled me closer, embracing me. "Of course I did," he said. "I was just afraid to say anything. Now is our chance to relieve some of that tension." He grabbed my cock and began stroking it.

One of the guys handed Tim a wad of money and then pointed to me.

"You," he said, "I want to see you suck his cock."

Tim sat down on the couch, and I obligingly put my head between his legs. I started to lick his dick head.

"Deep-throat him!" one of the men shouted out. I did my best to get Tim's member into my mouth. Tim moaned as my head moved up and down between his legs.

"Rim him!" one guy yelled.

"Yeah," yelled another, "suck that asshole!"

Tim raised his butt to meet my lips, and I cautiously applied my tongue to his warm hole. To my surprise, it tasted almost sweet. His ass lips contracted involuntarily at the unfa-miliar sensation of my tongue, but as I worked him over, he began to relax. He gasped in surprise when I shoved my tongue deep into his hole, then groaned with pleasure as I fucked him with my tongue.

I glanced around to see that almost all of the partygoers had their penises out and were stroking themselves as they watched Tim and I going at it.

"Put your dick in his ass!" someone yelled.

A few more voices then chimed in, chanting, "Butt-fuck! Butt-fuck!"

Tim pulled my face toward his until we were eye to eye and my cock was just inches from his saliva-drenched anus.

He whispered in my ear, "I've never done this before."

"Is this how you want your first time to be?" I whispered back.

"Hell, yeah!" He winked at me.

I gently worked the head of my dick into his hole. He was tight, so it was with extreme care that I eased my shaft up his ass, inch by inch. Carefully, I pushed myself in to the hilt. One of the masturbating men lost control and shot his load all over my side. It dripped down onto Tim, who smiled and winked at the man.

"Are you taking it in all right?" I said to Tim.

He nodded and said. "Let's give 'em the show they deserve."

I started fucking Tim, slowly at first and then faster and faster, until I was slamming my balls against his ass. The expression on his face registered the pleasure he was feeling, and he never quit saying "Yeah" over and over.

I knew I couldn't take much more of this. After a few minutes I grunted and pulled my dick out. I grabbed my cock head, and the moment I touched it, I began spurting strands of thick white come onto Tim. There was a smattering of applause. Then Tim slid me down onto my back in one fluid motion.

"Turnabout is fair play," he said as he spread my legs wide and began sucking my cock while the partygoers looked on. After a minute or two, he moved down to lick my balls before pushing my legs up and leaning in to eat my ass, working his tongue into my hot hole. Another of the men ejaculated, this time onto Tim's back. I was amazed at how pleasurable getting rimmed is.

"Fuck him!" someone shouted. As Tim positioned his dick at my ass, I looked around at our audience. What a thrill, I realized, to have my body worshiped by this many men at one time.

After a brief bit of resistance, Tim's dick slid easily up my butt. He leaned in to kiss me, then started slamming his cock into me the way I had just done to him.

I allowed myself to enjoy the sensation. Our audience, realizing the show would soon be over, started pumping their cocks furiously, and Tim and I were soon awash in torrents of joy juice as each man shot his wad onto us.

I was impressed by Tim's staying power; he continued to fuck me like a rabbit for some time. *Will he come inside me?* I wondered. Finally, with a groan, Tim pulled his cock out and took it in his hand.

His semen hit me in the face at a surprising velocity, and we both grinned. Tim's come dripped onto my lips, and I licked it off, enjoying the flavor of my friend.

We embraced, naked, as the last of the onlookers deposited his sperm onto us.

The host of the party let us use his shower to wash all of the goo off us. (As a show of thanks, I let him grope my cock one last time before Tim and I went into the bathroom together.) I jumped into the shower first, letting the steaming water run down my body.

Tim poked his head into the shower.

"Buddy," he said, "that was the best fuck of my life." I pulled him by his penis into the shower.

"I wish all of my workdays ended like this," I said. "Do you think we'll ever get an assignment like this again?"

Tim, who had started soaping up my balls, leaned in to kiss me. "Someday, maybe."

He kissed me again. "I can promise you one thing," he said. "We're going to be spending a lot of time practicing our act."

f f f

Traveling Tailor

BY

SEAN WOLFE

"Goddamn it!" Adam slammed his fist down on his desk and kicked the heavy wooden leg. Of all the times for shitty luck to show its face.

He hadn't split the seam in his pants since he was a fat, awkward kid. It had been a common occurrence back then, and the other kids had been merciless in their teasing. To this day he could remember running home crying and slamming the door behind himself to shut out their laughter.

But that was 20 years ago, and now as he was approaching 30, things had all turned around. Later this afternoon, Adam Gomez was going to pitch the ad campaign that everyone knew would make him the youngest partner in Dallas's largest advertising agency—not to mention the only Latino partner. Smith, Davidson, and Young would soon become Smith, Davidson, Young, and Gomez.

This meeting was the last step before making it official.

This afternoon's presentation would surely clench the Bruce Callahan account that had eluded the agency for more than 10 years, and it was just two hours away. Adam was dressed in his finest suit—then, as he sat down at his desk just a few moments ago, he'd heard the undeniable rip of his inseam. When he moved his leg to look down in disgust at the tear, he saw that it spread even farther, stretching from mid thigh to just below his knee.

He cursed himself for all the hours he'd spent at the gym over the last three or four years. No longer the fat kid in town, Adam was now just over six feet of solid and lean but bulging muscle—muscle that had ripped his pants leg. He'd grown into a striking young man. His black hair, deep-brown eyes, smooth copper skin, and bright white smile were complemented by the strong jawline and cheekbones that had gradually appeared as he lost weight. Add that to his charm, talent, and strong ambition, and there was absolutely nothing working against him anymore—except for the goddamn tear in his pants.

"Karen," he shouted into his intercom to his secretary, "I need you in here now."

"I'm sorry, Mr. Gomez," came a tiny, scared voice. "Karen isn't here right now. She took some papers across the street for Mr. Davidson."

Adam switched the intercom button off and swore under his breath. Davidson had his own secretary, so why the hell was he always pulling Karen away to run his errands? Sweat began to bead his brow as he fumed.

It was then that he remembered the tailor shop that occupied the small space on the first floor of his office building, right before the elevators. He'd passed it every day for years, smiling politely at the elderly woman who was always busy behind the counter. Traveling Tailor, the shop was called, because it catered to downtown offices and sent tailors out on emergency "wardrobe malfunction" calls.

He rummaged through his desk drawer for the building directory and frantically flipped through the pages until he spotted the simple black-and-white ad. He dialed the number quickly, then took a deep breath in order to compose himself before speaking.

"Traveling Tailor," came a sweet elderly woman's voice over the line. It was thick with an accent Adam struggled to place. Russian maybe. Or German. He wasn't sure.

"Hi. This is Adam Gomez, with Smith, Davidson, & Young. We're in your same building up on the 58th floor."

"Yes, Mr. Gomez. How can I help you?"

"Well, I have somewhat of an emergency," Adam stammered. "Actually it's a really big emergency. I just ripped my pants, and I have a very important meeting in a couple of hours. I really need your help."

"Yes, sir. I am in the middle of another emergency right now. Ms. Cartwright on the 32nd floor has pulled her hem." Adam thought he heard a tone of sarcasm in her voice.

"But this is really important," he said, biting his bottom lip. "My meeting is in an hour," he lied and sat forward in his chair.

"Ms. Cartwright's meeting is in 20 minutes."

Adam swatted at the air around the phone and gave the old woman the middle finger.

"But I'm almost finished here. I can maybe come up there in about half an hour."

"That would be fine," Adam said between clenched teeth. He knew this was his only chance at fixing the huge rip in his pants. "Thank you."

"My pleasure, sir," the old woman said. "I'll be up as soon as I can."

Adam hung up the phone and counted to 10. It wouldn't do any good to brood or get angry. He had to keep his cool. He had to be ready for the most important pitch of his career.

Adam picked up the only file on the desk in front of him. While scanning the file's contents, he continued practicing the right combination of inflection and gestures that would close the biggest account in his company's history. The Callahan account was worth more than $60 million, and Adam wanted to be sure that his presentation would be perfect.

He was shocked when Karen buzzed him only 15 minutes later.

"Adam, Mr. Callahan is on line 2 for you. And the traveling tailor is here for you," she said with a puzzled tone.

"Great!" Adam said as he picked up the cordless phone and hit the button for line 2. "Send her in."

"Bruce, how are you?" he asked as the door to his office opened, and he stood up to walk around to the front of his desk.

A young blond boy of about 19 walked in carrying a small case and closed the door behind him. He was wearing a letter jacket from Texas A&M and looked like he must play for one of the school's athletic teams. His hair was slightly ruffled, and his cheeks had a blush to them that hinted of robust young sexuality.

Adam leaned against the front of his desk and spread his legs so that the young man could see the huge tear. The boy knelt down in front of Adam and pulled on the torn pants leg to see what he had to work with.

"I spoke with a woman," Adam whispered as he covered the mouthpiece of the phone. Bruce Callahan was in the middle of a long exhortation regarding the upcoming meeting.

"Yeah," the boy replied quietly, "Gramma said it was an emergency, so she sent me up. Don't worry, I know what I'm doing."

Adam nodded and went back to his conversation.

"I know, Bruce, but don't worry about a thing. I'm all set here," he said and looked down at the kid again.

The boy's face was inches from his crotch, and Adam felt his cock stir inside his pants as the kid's hot breath hit his bare leg through the ripped seam. The tailor's hands brushed his thigh a couple of times, and Adam panicked as he noticed the long line of his hardening cock spread across the front of his slacks. *Damn, I should've worn briefs instead of boxers today,* he thought.

"Yes, we're fully expecting they will be upset," Adam spoke into the receiver.

The blond kid reached inside the gaping hole in the leg of Adam's pants and caressed Adam's smooth, muscular thigh.

Was that an intentional squeeze? Adam blushed as his cock started to throb. The kid looked up and smiled, and his bright blue eyes sparkled as he licked his lips.

Adam swallowed hard and tried to keep his calm. "You know how much we appreciate this, Bruce," he stuttered out as the kid's hands found their way to his belt and began to unbuckle it. "Don't worry about a thing."

The front of Adam's pants unbuttoned quickly, and Adam felt the young tailor press his face against the bulging crotch as his arms wrapped around Adam's legs. Precome was already leaking out of the head of his cock when the blond boy slid the waist of the pants down Adam's long legs.

"Me too." Adam breathed heavily and closed his eyes. The college student had reached inside Adam's boxers and pulled out his throbbing uncut cock.

"Bruce, I've got to run," Adam said quickly. The boy wrapped his fist around Adam's long, fat pole and slowly slid the foreskin back and forth along the length. "Something unexpected has just come up. I'll call you back."

Adam reached around to hang up the phone just as the hot, wet mouth covered his cock head. The kid's tongue tickled his knob for a moment, then he sucked greedily on the thick shaft.

"Shit, kid. That feels good."

The tailor swallowed half of Adam's dick and looked up and winked. Adam slid his long cock all the way inside the boy's throat a couple of times.

"You're good," Adam said as he pulled completely out of the young man's hot mouth.

"Thanks," the college student–tailor said and stood up to face Adam. "I'm Rick," he said and leaned in to kiss Adam on the lips.

"Adam," Adam stammered out between deep kisses. He tasted himself on Rick's tongue.

"So, Adam," Rick said as he pulled away and began to undress himself, "I hear you have somewhat of an emergency."

"Um...yeah..." Adam replied absently, dumbfounded as the kid boldly stripped right there in his office.

"Well, now so do I," Rick said as he dropped his jacket and pulled off his T-shirt, revealing his well-muscled chest and hard, flat stomach.

"Really? And what exactly is your emergency?"

"This," Rick replied breathlessly as he unbuttoned his jeans and quickly pushed them to his ankles. He wore no underwear, and his hard cock sprung up, pointing directly at Adam. The trail of blond hair that started at Rick's navel and spread down into his pubic bush took Adam's breath away.

"That does look like it needs some immediate attention," Adam said, breathing heavily as he stroked his cock.

"It most certainly does," Rick replied, stroking himself as well. "If we're gonna get these slacks of yours fixed before your meeting, you'd better stop talking and start fucking me."

"Well, let's get to it," Adam growled, loosening his tie and pulling off his shirt, then sliding his boxers down and kicking them off.

Rick turned his back to Adam and leaned forward. His ass was extremely well-muscled and had a light coating of baby-fine blond hair. Adam squeezed the cheeks in both hands, then pressed his cock against the crack between them.

"That's it, Adam," Rick moaned, spreading his cheeks wider. "Fuck me."

Normally Adam would start by licking the ass he was about to fuck, getting it relaxed and wet, but Rick was obviously in no mood for foreplay. That suited Adam just fine, since he was pressed for time anyway. Retrieving a condom and some lube from his briefcase, he pulled on the rubber and juiced up his cock and then Rick's hungry ass. He spread some lube around the tiny puckered hole and moaned loudly as he rubbed his giant cock up and down the length of Rick's ass crack.

Rick reached behind him with one hand and moved Adam's throbbing dick right to his twitching hole. Then he took a deep breath and slowly slid backward onto the fat cock, until it was buried deep inside him.

"Damn, you're huge," he whispered, short of breath.

"You asked for it," Adam grunted and began sliding in and out of one of the hottest, tightest asses he'd fucked in years.

Rick's ass muscles squeezed the big dick, and Adam felt his foreskin moving across his long, thick shaft inside the rubber as he fucked the kid. He reached around and pinched Rick's nipples and ran his hand along the college kid's washboard stomach. They found a rhythm very quickly and fucked as if they'd been partners for years.

Adam could usually go for quite a while, but he knew it was going to be different with Rick. The kid was damn talented, working and squeezing Adam's hot cock with his muscles as Adam's dick burrowed deep into his ass.

When Rick reached down and stroked his own cock, his ass tightened even more strongly around Adam's fiery cock, and Adam felt the come churn in his balls as it prepared to shoot out his shaft.

"Fuck, Adam, I'm gonna shoot," Rick almost yelled. Before he even finished the sentence, Adam saw the kid's load spewing across the floor. Several jets flew out, and with each one the ass muscles enveloping Adam's cock grew tighter and hotter.

"Me too." Adam breathed deep and pumped faster and deeper.

Rick pulled himself off Adam's cock and fell to the floor, facing the huge brown dick as Adam ripped off the rubber. He closed his eyes just as the first shot squirted out and kept his head tilted back as Adam's load sprayed across his face, landing on his forehead and his cheeks.

"Man, you have a great cock," Rick said, leaning backward and resting on his hands.

"And you have a great ass."

Just then the intercom buzzed, and Karen's voice broke through.

"Adam, there's a Mrs. Schneider on line 1 for you. Something about a traveling tailor?"

"Tell her I'll be just one minute, please."

"Yes, sir."

Rick was already getting up and starting to dress.

Adam picked his pants up from the floor and handed them to the tailor. He would definitely have to give this kid a big tip, he noted to himself as he stood naked in the middle of the office, glistening with sweat, trying to catch his breath.

"I'll have these fixed for you in no time," Rick said. He kissed Adam on the lips and pushed him down into the big leather chair. "Gramma's on line 1," he smiled. "She doesn't like to be kept waiting."

"This is Adam Gomez," Adam said calmly into the phone as his heavy uncut dick lay limp between his legs. "Yes, he's here. He's getting me all fixed up right now."

Dangerous Liaisons

ƒ ƒ ƒ

†††

Family Affair

BY

BOB VICKERY

Nick rides up front with Maria in her beat-up '74 Buick convertible. Maria is driving like a lunatic, weaving in and out of the traffic. I'm wedged in the backseat with all the beach gear tumbling over me. The radio is turned on full blast, set to an oldies station belting out a Beach Boys tune. "I wish they all could be California girls," Nick sings along. He buries his face into Maria's neck and makes loud farting noises. Maria screams with laughter, and it's only by the grace of God that she avoids plowing us all into the highway's concrete median.

"Jesus Christ!" I cry out in terror.

Nick and Maria crack up—Nick wheezing, Maria's shoulders shaking spasmodically. "What the hell is wrong with you guys!" I shout. "You been sniffing airplane glue?"

"No," Nick says. "Drano." Maria breaks up again, laughing until she starts hiccuping.

"You two are fucking crazy," I say, shouting over the wind and the radio. "You're going to kill us all."

Nick turns his head and looks at me, grinning. "Lighten up, Robbie," he says. "We're supposed to be having a good time." I glare at him. He turns back to Maria. "I didn't know your little brother was such a tight-ass," he laughs.

"Oh, Robbie's OK," she says. She glances back at me in the rearview mirror and widens her eyes in comic exaggeration. I turn my head away sulkily and stare over on my left toward the ocean, which stretches out as flat and shiny as a metal plate.

We ride together for a few minutes in silence, then Nick reaches over and turns down the radio. He turns his head toward me. "So, Robbie," he says affably. "I hear you're gay."

"Jesus, Maria!" I exclaim.

Maria isn't laughing now. At least she has the decency to look embarrassed. "I didn't think you'd mind me telling him, Robbie," she says. But her guilty tone makes it clear she knew damn well I'd mind. She shoots a poisonous look at Nick. "You've got a big mouth," she hisses.

"He's not the only one," I say.

Nick's eyes shift back and forth between Maria and me. "Oops," he says. He laughs, unfazed. "It's no big deal. I'm cool. It's not like I'm a born-again Christian or anything." He looks at me. "So, are you just coming out or what?"

"I don't want to talk about it," I say frostily. Maria flashes me an apologetic glance in the mirror, but I just glower back at her. We ride the rest of the distance to the beach in silence.

It's still early. The sun has just started climbing high, and there's only a scattering of cars in the dirt parking lot. We start the trek to the beach—Nick and Maria leading the way, me lagging behind with the cooler. Nick leans over and says something to Maria, and she laughs again, her previous embarrassment all forgotten now, which makes my mood all the more pissy. At the top of the dunes the two of them wait for me to catch up. The sea stretches out before us, sparkling in the bright sun, the waves hissing as they break upon the sandy beach. "Bitchin'!" Nick says. He reaches over and squeezes the back of my neck. "You having a good time, Robbie?" he asks, smiling.

Though I hardly know the guy, I know that this is as close to an apology as I'll ever get. A breeze whips over the dunes, smelling of the sea; the sun beams down benevolently, and I see nothing but good humor in Nick's wide blue eyes. In spite of myself I smile.

"Attaboy," Nick laughs. "I knew you had it in you!" He lets go, and we start climbing down the dunes to find a stretch of beach isolated from everyone else.

After we've laid out the blanket, Maria and Nick start taking off their clothes. I hurriedly pull my bathing suit out of my knapsack. "I'm going to change behind the dune," I say.

Nick has one leg raised, about to pull off a sneaker. "I'll go with you," he says abruptly.

I have mixed feelings about this but don't know how I can dissuade him. We circle the nearest dune, leaving Maria behind on the broad expanse of beach. Nick peels off his shirt, and I can't help noticing the sleek leanness of his torso, the blond dusting of hair across his chest. My throat tightens, and I turn my attention to my fingers fumbling with the buttons of my jeans. Nick kicks off his shoes and shucks his shorts and Calvins. The honey-brown of his skin ends abruptly at his tan line, and his hips are pale-cream. Nick turns his back to me and stretches lazily like a jungle cat, arms bent. His ass is smooth and milky, downed with a light fuzz that gleams gold in the sun's rays. Nick turns around and smiles at me. His dick, half hard, sways heavily against his thighs.

I turn away and quickly pull my jeans off. When I look back at Nick, he's still standing there naked, only this time his dick is jutting out fully hard, twitching slightly in the light breeze. He sees my surprise and shrugs helplessly. "Sorry," he grins, his eyes wide and guileless. "Open air always makes me hard."

"This isn't a nude beach," I say, trying to sound casual. "You have to wear a suit."

"In a minute," Nick says. "I like feeling the breeze on my skin." His smile turns sly, and his eyes lose some of their innocence. He wraps his hand around his dick and strokes it slowly. "You like it, Robbie?" he asks. "Maria calls it my 'love club.'"

"What the hell are you trying to prove?" I ask.

Nick affects surprise. "I'm not trying to prove anything," he says, his tone all injured innocence. "I'm just making conversation." I quickly pull on my suit and walk back to the blanket. Nick joins us a couple of minutes later.

Nick and Maria race out into the waves. She pushes him into the path of a crashing breaker, laughing as he comes up sputtering. They horseplay in the surf for a while and then swim out to deeper water. Eventually, they're just specks in the shiny gun-metal blue. I close my eyes and feel the sun beat down on me. Rivulets of sweat begin to trickle down my torso.

Suddenly, I'm in shade. I open my eyes and see Nick standing over me, the sun behind him so that I can't make out his features—just an outline of broad shoulders tapering down. He shakes his head and water spills down on me. "Hey!" I protest.

He sits down beside me on the blanket. "The water feels great," he says. "You should go out in it."

"In a little while," I say. "Where's Maria?"

Nick gestures vaguely. "Out there somewhere. She didn't want to come in yet." He stretches out next to me, propped up on his elbows. "So why are you so upset about me knowing you're gay? You think I'll disapprove or something?"

"Jeez, what's with you! Will you just drop the subject?"

"I've gotten it on with guys," Nick goes on, as if he hadn't heard me. "It's no big deal." He grins. "You want to hear about the last time I did?"

"No," I lie.

"It was in Hawaii. Oahu, to be exact." Nick turns on his side and faces me, his head on his hand. "I was there on spring break last year. I started hanging out with this dude I'd met in a Waikiki bar, a surfer named Joe." He laughs. "Surfer Joe, just like in the song. Ah, sweet Jesus, was he ever beautiful! Part Polynesian, part Japanese, part German. Smooth brown skin; tight, ripped body; and these fuckin' dark, soulful eyes." He smiles. "Like yours, Robbie. Like Maria's too, for that matter," he adds, as if it's an afterthought.

"Anyway, I had a rented car, and we took a drive to the North Shore. Somehow we wound up lost on this little piss-ass road—nothing but sugarcane fields on both sides. It'd been raining, but the sun was just breaking out, and all of a sudden, wham! This huge Technicolor rainbow comes blazing out right in front of us." Nick sits up, getting excited. "It was fuckin' awesome! The motherfucker just arced overhead like some kind of neon bridge and ended not far off in this little grassy patch beyond the cane. Well, Joe leaps out of the car—I tell you, he was one crazy bastard—and he races across the field toward the rainbow, and because I couldn't think of anything better to do, I do the same."

Nick's eyes are wide, and he's talking faster now. "Joe makes it to where the rainbow hits the ground, he pulls off his board shorts, and he just stands there naked, his arms stretched out, the colors pouring down on him. Blue! Green! Red! Orange! I strip off my shorts too and jump right in."

Nick laughs, but his eyes drill into me. "It was the strangest damn sensation—standing in that rainbow, my skin tingling like a low-voltage current was passing through me." He blinks. "Joe wrestles me to the ground, one thing leads to another, and we wind up fucking right there with all the colors washing over us—me plowing Joe's ass, Joe's head red, his chest orange, his belly yellow, his legs green and blue. When I finally came, I pulled out of Joe's ass, raining my jizz down on him, the drops like colored jewels." Nick gazes down at me, his eyes laughing. "Like I said, fucking awesome!"

"You are so full of shit," I say.

Nick adopts an expression of deep hurt. "It's true. I swear it."

"Fuck you. You can't stand in a rainbow, for chrissake. It's against the laws of optics."

"'The laws of optics,'" Nick snorts. "What are you, an optician?"

"You mean a physicist. An optician prescribes glasses. Jesus, you're an ignorant fuck."

But Nick refuses to be insulted. He laughs and picks up my tube of sunblock. "Here," he says, "let me oil you up again. You've sweated off your first layer." Nick smears the goop on my chest and starts stroking my torso. His hand wanders down my belly and lies there motionless. I can feel the heat of his hand sink into my skin. The tips of his fingers slide under the elastic band of my suit. He looks at me, eyebrows raised. When I don't say anything, Nick slips his hand under my suit and wraps it around my dick. "Do the same to me," he urges.

"Maria..." I say.

Nick scans the ocean. "She's way out there," he says. "She can't see anything." His hand, still greased with sunblock, starts sliding up and down my dick. I close my eyes. "Come on," he whispers. "Do it to me too. Please."

My hand seems to have a mind of its own. It slides inside Nick's suit and wraps around his fat, hard dick. His love club. "Yeah, Robbie, that's good," Nick sighs. "Now stroke it."

We beat each other off as the sun blasts down on us, the ocean shimmering off in the distance like a desert mirage. After a few moments we pull our suits down to our knees. Nick smears his hand with a fresh batch of lotion and then slides it down my dick. I groan. "Yeah, baby," he laughs. "You like that, don't you?" I groan again louder, arching my back as the orgasm sweeps over me. Nick takes my dick in his mouth and swallows my load as I pump it down his throat. Even after I'm done he keeps sucking on my dick, rolling his tongue around it, playing with my balls. He replaces my hand with his and with a few quick strokes brings himself to climax, shuddering as his load splatters against his chest and belly.

Maria staggers out of the surf a few minutes later and races to the blanket, squealing from the heat of the sand on her soles. Nick and I are chastely reading our summer novels under the umbrella. She flings herself down on the blanket, grabs a towel, and vigorously rubs her hair. "You guys enjoying yourselves?" she asks.

"Yeah, sure," Nick says, his mouth curling up into an easy grin. "Except your degenerate little brother can't keep his hands off me." He winks. Maria laughs, but she shoots me a worried look, checking to see if I'm offended. I shrug and smile back. I feel like shit.

♩♩♩

Nick stops by my place a week later. It's the first time I've seen him since the beach. "Is Maria here?" he asks. "I swung by her apartment, but she wasn't home." He's dressed in a tank top and cutoffs, and he carries a summer glow with him that makes him shine like a small sun.

"No," I say, my heart beating furiously. "I haven't seen her all day."

Nick peers over my shoulder. "You alone?"

"Yeah," I say. My mouth has suddenly gone desert-dry. Nick regards me calmly, waiting. "You want to come in for a while?" I finally ask.

Nick smiles and gives a slight shrug. "Why not?"

As soon as I close the door behind us he's on me, pushing me against the wall, his hard dick dry-humping me through the denim of his shorts, his mouth pressed against mine. After the initial shock passes I kiss him back, thrusting my tongue deep into his mouth. Nick's hands are all over me, pulling at my shirt, undoing the buttons, tugging down my zipper. He slides his hands under my jeans and cups my ass, pulling my crotch against his.

I push him away, gasping. "This isn't going to happen," I say.

Nick looks at me with bright eyes, his face flushed, his expression half annoyed, half amused. "Now, Robbie," he says, smiling his old smile. "You're not going to be a cock tease, are you?"

I zip my pants up again and rebutton my shirt. I feel the anger rising up in me. "You're such an asshole," I say. I push past him and walk into the living room.

Nick remains in the hallway. I sit on the couch, glaring at him. He slowly walks into the room until he's standing in front of me. He looks out the window and then back at me again. "Why am I an asshole?" he asks. "Because I think you're fuckin' beautiful?"

"You may not give a shit," I say, "but Maria's crazy about you."

Nick sits down beside me on the couch. "Ah," he says quietly. A silence hangs between us for a couple of beats. "What if I told you I'm just as crazy about Maria?" he finally asks.

"You sure have a funny way of showing it."

Nick leans back against the arm of the couch and regards me with his steady blue gaze. He gives a low laugh. " 'Now, next on *Jerry Springer!*' " he says. " 'My sister's boyfriend is putting the moves on me!' " I look at him hostilely, not saying anything. He returns my stare calmly. "You know," he says, "lately every time I fuck your sister I think of you. It's getting to be a real problem."

"Will you knock it off!"

Nick acts like he hasn't heard me. "It's no reflection on Maria, believe me. She's a knockout. Great personality, beautiful..." He leaves the sentence hanging in the air, lost in thought. His eyes suddenly focus on me. "But there are things I want that she just can't give me."

I wait a while before I finally respond. "What things?" I ask sullenly.

Nick's smile is uncharacteristically wistful. "You, Robbie. That's 'what things.' " I don't say anything. Nick lays his hand on my knee. "It's fuckin' amazing how much you look like Maria sometimes. The same dark eyes, the same mouth, the same way you tilt your head. It's like the excitement of meeting Maria all over again." He leans forward, his eyes bright. "Only...you have a man's body, Robby. That's what Maria can't give me." His hand slides up my thigh. "She can't give me a man's muscles, a man's way of walking and talking." His hand slides up and squeezes my crotch. "A man's dick. I swear to God, if I had the two of you in bed together, I wouldn't ask for another thing for the rest of my motherfuckin' life!" He looks at me and laughs. "You should see your face now, Robbie. You look like you just sucked a lemon."

I feel my throat tightening. "You're fucking crazy if you think that's ever going to happen."

"Maybe I am crazy," Nick sighs. His eyes dart up to mine. "But I'm not stupid." His fingers begin rubbing the crotch of my jeans, lazily sliding back and forth. He grins slyly. "If I can't have you and Maria together, I'll settle for you both one at a time." He leans his face close to mine, his hand squeezing my dick. "Come on, Robbie, don't tell me I don't turn you on. Not after our little session on the beach."

I don't say anything. Nick's other hand begins lightly stroking my chest, fumbling with the buttons of my shirt.

"You want monogamy, Robbie?" he croons softly. "I promise I'll stay true to you and Maria. I'll never look at another family."

"Everything's a joke with you," I say. But I feel my dick twitch as his hand slides under my shirt and squeezes my left nipple.

"No, Robbie," Nick says softly. "Not everything." He cups his hand around the back of my neck and pulls me toward him. I resist but not enough to break his grip, and we kiss, Nick's tongue pushing apart my lips and thrusting deep inside my mouth. He reaches down and squeezes my dick again. "Hard as the proverbial rock!" he laughs.

"Just shut up," I say. We kiss again, and this time I let Nick unbutton my shirt. His hands slide over my bare chest, tugging at the muscles in my torso. He unbuckles my belt and pulls my zipper down. His hand slides under my briefs and wraps around my dick.

"We're going to do it nice and slow this time," Nick says. He tugs my jeans down, and I lift my hips to help him. It doesn't take long before Nick has pulled off all my clothes. He sits back, his eyes slowly sliding down my body. "So beautiful..." he murmurs. He stands up and shucks off his shirt and shorts, kicking them away. He falls on top of me, his mouth burrowing against my neck, his body stretched out fully against mine.

I kiss him again, gently this time, our mouths barely touching. His lips work their way over my face, pressing lightly against my nose, my eyes. His tongue probes into my ear, and his breath sounds like the sea in a conch shell. I feel his lips move across my skin, down my torso. He gently bites each nipple, swirling his tongue around them, sucking on them. I can see only the top of his head, the shock of blond hair, and I reach down and entwine my fingers in it, twisting his head from side to side. Nick sits up, his legs straddling my hips, his thick cock pointing up toward the ceiling. He wraps his hand around both our dicks and squeezes them together tightly. "Feel that, Robbie," he says. "Dick flesh against dick flesh." He begins stroking them, sliding his hand up and down the twin shafts: his, pink and fat; mine, dark and veined. Some precome leaks from his dick, and Nick slicks our dicks up with it. I breathe deeply, and Nick grins.

Nick bends down and tongues my belly button, his hands sliding under my ass. He lifts my hips up and takes my cock in his mouth, sliding his lips down my shaft until his nose is pressed against my pubes. He sits motionless like that—my dick fully down his throat, his tongue working against the shaft. Slowly, inch by inch, his lips slide back up to my cock head. He wraps his hand around my dick and strokes it as he raises his head and his eyes meet mine, laughing. "You like that, Robbie?" he asks. "Does that feel good?"

"Turn around," I say urgently. "Fuck my face while you do that to me."

I don't have to tell Nick twice. He pivots his body around, and his dick thrusts above my face: red, thick, the cock head pushing out of the foreskin and leaking precome. His balls hang low and heavy above my mouth, furred with light-blond hairs. I raise my head and bathe them with my tongue and then suck them into my mouth. I roll my tongue around the meaty pouch. "Ah, yeah," Nick groans. I slide my tongue up the shaft of his dick. Nick shifts his position and plunges his dick deep down my throat. He starts pumping his hips, sliding his dick in and out of my mouth as he continues sucking me off. I feel his torso squirm against mine, skin against skin, the warmth of his flesh pouring into my body. Nick takes my dick out of his mouth, and I feel his tongue slide over my balls and burrow into the warmth beneath them. He pulls apart my ass cheeks, and soon I feel his mouth on my asshole, his tongue lapping against the puckered flesh.

"Damn!" I groan.

Nick alternately licks and blows against my asshole. I arch my back and push up with my hips, giving him greater access. No one has ever done this to me before, and it's fucking driving me wild. Nick comes up for air, and soon I feel his finger pushing against my asshole and then entering me, knuckle by knuckle. I groan again, louder. Nick looks at me over his shoulder as he finger-fucks me into a slow-building frenzy. "Yeah, Robbie," he croons. "Just lie there and let me play you. Let's see what songs I can make you sing." He adds another finger inside me and pushes up in a corkscrew twist. I cry out, and Nick laughs.

He climbs off me and reaches for his shorts. "OK, Robbie," he says. "Enough with the fuckin' foreplay. Let's get this show on the road." He pulls a condom packet and a small tube of lube out of the back pocket and tosses the shorts back onto the floor.

I feel a twinge of irritation. "You had this all planned out, didn't you?"

Nick straddles my torso again, his stiff cock jutting out inches from my face. I trace one blue vein snaking up the shaft. "Let's just say I was open to the possibility," he grins. He unrolls the condom down his prick, his blue eyes never leaving mine. He smears his hand with lube, reaches back, and liberally greases up my asshole. Nick hooks his arms under my knees and hoists my legs up and around his torso. His gaze still boring into me, he slowly impales me.

I push my head back against the cushion, eyes closed. Nick leans forward, fully in. "You OK, baby?" he asks. His eyes are wide and solicitous.

I open my eyes and nod. Slowly, almost imperceptibly, Nick begins pumping his hips, grinding his pelvis against mine. He deepens his thrusts, speeding up the tempo. I reach up and twist his nipples, and Nick grins widely. A wolfish gleam lights up his eyes. He pulls his hips back until his cock head is just barely in my asshole, then plunges back in. "Fuckin' A," I groan.

"Fuckin' A is right," Nick laughs. He props himself up with his arms and fucks me good and hard—his balls slapping heavily against me with each thrust, his eyes staring into mine, his hot breath against my face. I cup my hand around the back of his neck and pull his face down to mine, frenching him hard as he pounds my ass. Nick leaves his dick fully up there, grinding his hips against mine in a slow circle before returning to the old in-and-out. He wraps a hand around my stiff dick and starts beating me off, timing his strokes with each thrust of his hips.

We settle into our rhythm: Nick slamming my ass, his hand sliding up and down my dick as I thrust up to meet him stroke for stroke. There's nothing playful or cocky about Nick now: His breath comes out in ragged gasps through his open mouth, sweat trickles down his face, and his eyes burn with the hard, bright light of a man working up to shoot a serious load.

I wrap my arms tight around his body and push up, squeezing my asshole tight around his dick at the same time. I look up at Nick's face and laugh; it's the first time I've ever seen him startled.

"Jesus," he gasps. "Did you learn that in college?"

I don't say anything—I just repeat the motion, squeezing my ass muscles hard as I push up to meet his thrust. Nick's body spasms as he moans strongly. "You ought to talk to Maria," he pants. "She could learn some things from you." The third time I do this pushes Nick over the edge, making him groan loudly and his body tremble violently. He plants his mouth on mine, kissing me hard as he squirts his load into the condom, up my ass. I wrap my arms around him in a bear hug, and we thrash around on the couch, finally spilling onto the carpet below—me on top, Nick sprawled with his arms wide out.

After a while he opens his eyes. "Sit on me," he says. "And shoot your load on my face."

I straddle him, dropping my balls into Nick's open mouth. He sucks on them noisily, slurping audibly as I beat off. Nick reaches up and squeezes my nipple, and that's all it takes for me. I give a deep groan, arching my back as my load splatters in thick drops onto Nick's face, creaming his nose and cheeks, dripping into his open mouth. "Yeah," Nick says, "that's right, baby." When the last spasm passes through me I bend down and lick Nick's face clean.

I roll over and lie next to Nick on the thick carpet. He slides his arm under me and pulls me to him. I burrow against his body and close my eyes, feeling his chest rise and fall against the side of my head. Without meaning to, I drift off into sleep.

When I wake up, the clock on the mantle says it's almost 1 in the morning. Nick is gone, but he's covered me with a quilt from my bed. I'm too sleepy to get up, so I just drift back into sleep again.

$$f \; f \; f$$

Nick, Maria, and I are all sitting on Maria's couch watching *Night of the Living Dead* on her TV. Maria sits between us, nestling against Nick. We're at the scene where the little girl has turned into a ghoul and is nibbling on her mother's arm like it was a hoagie sandwich. "Gross!" Maria says.

Nick grins. "You're so damn judgmental, Maria," he says. "I don't put you down when you eat those Spam-and-mayonnaise sandwiches of yours."

Maria laughs and burrows deeper against Nick. As we continue watching the movie I feel Nick's fingers playing with my hair, and I brush them away with a brusque jerk that I make sure Maria doesn't notice. After a while, though, he's doing it again. When I don't do anything this time, Nick entwines his fingers in my hair and tugs gently. From where she's sitting, Maria can't see any of this. The ghouls are surrounding the farmhouse now, closing in on the victims inside. Eventually, I lean back and sink into the feel of Nick's fingers in my hair.

f f f

Money

BY

DALE CHASE

"It's not about money," Johnny says. But, of course, it is. How could it not be? We both know we're driving into a pricey neighborhood that is well beyond our means.

Johnny had met Cyril at a party, during which Cyril invited Johnny to a small gathering at his home. "Intimate," Cyril said. "Bring a friend if you like."

"I just want to see his place," Johnny says as we turn onto Mulholland.

"Yeah, right," I reply.

"I mean it."

I don't press. Johnny is my best friend, a cute little number who wants to find a daddy to take care of him.

"What's he look like?" I ask.

"Cyril? Tall, slim, elegant, English-looking. You know, like old movies. Silver hair."

I know what happened at that first party because I know Johnny. I wasn't there, but I can easily imagine the scene: Johnny trolling not for action but for promise. If Cyril is attractive, so much the better for all concerned. But Johnny will never convince me it's about anything but security. "Money buys freedom," he has said more times than I have fingers and toes to count.

I go along now out of curiosity. And because I'm on the lookout too—not for a daddy, just for some good sex. I have no illusions about permanence; it's not on my agenda, which tends to give me the upper hand in a way. We're both eager in our respective quests. But Johnny has a sad air of quiet desperation.

Cyril's house is a hilltop aerie with an incredible view. The spread is all chrome and glass: sleek, like the young men lolling around the pool. I recall Cyril's calling the gathering intimate. Obviously, he didn't mean we'd have his undivided attention; there's quite a crowd both inside and out.

It's a late-October night; the air is hot and dry from the Santa Ana breeze that has been blowing all day. Guys glide through the pool or lounge at its edge. Most are naked. Cyril is clad in a white Speedo to highlight his deep tan and holds court near the shallow end. He immediately sweeps Johnny into his arms, and they exchange little whispers.

When the two of them end their clutch, Johnny introduces me. Cyril takes my hand in his and squeezes as he offers a welcome. "It's so hot. Why don't you get out of those clothes and make yourself comfortable?" he suggests. He keeps his eyes on me as he says this, and I see what Johnny means. The man is not merely attractive but exudes sensuality on a grand scale. His profligate gaze promises much more than money.

Johnny and I undress in a spare bedroom littered with clothes. A basket of swimsuits sits nearby, but we choose to remain naked. We stand side by side before a mirrored wall, making sure we look our best. "Isn't he something?" Johnny says as he runs his fingers through his thick blond hair.

"He certainly is," I reply flatly.

Since the party was in full swing when we arrived, there's already plenty of action in progress. One couple fucks on the steps of the pool, another on a mat near the deep end. Some lounge and watch the show, lazily stroking their own dicks or those of others. A couple of blow jobs are also in progress. From the corner of my eye I catch a glimpse of a fellow getting his ass eaten out. Apart from the usual distractions of an orgy, the event is a delicious parade of bodies. As Johnny and I enter the scene we enjoy the appreciative gazes that follow our movement. Johnny heads toward Cyril. After I get a drink at the bar, I turn toward my audience to display my rising cock.

Seconds later a gorgeous little thing sidles up next to me, gets a drink, and lets his bare ass brush my cock. He wiggles back into me and asks, "How do you know Cyril?"

"I don't," I reply. "My friend does."

"So you're on your own."

"Totally."

"Why don't we find ourselves a quiet corner?" he suggests.

I follow him to a patch of lawn off to one side of the house. He stretches out, then rolls onto his side. He pulls one leg over the other to showcase his firm little ass.

I lie down behind him, slide my dick up against his cheeks, and begin to hump him gently. He murmurs his approval and hands me a condom. This makes me laugh. He is stark naked but still well-provisioned. I roll the rubber over my prick, lube myself with spit, and ease into him. We lie on the lawn fucking while others splash in the pool.

Soon he begins to ride my dick, pushing back into me as he strokes himself. This does me in. I start to come, pumping juice into him. He lets go as well. We jerk and fuck, and when we're done we discover another naked guy has been watching us. I roll over on my back, pull off the rubber, and look up at him. His dick is big and hard.

"Nice show," he says.

My partner scrambles to his knees and sucks the guy's cock into his mouth. I head back to the bar for another drink.

At the pool I don't see Johnny or Cyril. I assume they've sought some privacy for themselves. Shyness strikes me as an amusing thing to want in the middle of an orgy. But maybe the host likes to watch but not to be watched. I take my drink to the pool and slide into the shallow end, where I lounge on the steps and get pleasantly drunk.

After a while a furry guy swims over to me, smiles, looks down at my dick, sucks in a breath, and submerges himself. I enjoy a brief underwater blow job. The bear surfaces and gasps for air. He has me hard again.

"Why don't you get out of the water?" he suggests.

"Not just yet," I reply, whereupon he swims away.

I see Johnny emerge from the house without Cyril. A hot number quickly moves in and Johnny, much to my surprise, doesn't resist. They move to a poolside mat and start to kiss and to play with each other. I wonder whether Cyril is watching.

Curious, I go into the house. I have to pee anyway, and once I'm done I explore a little. I find the library and begin to scan the bookshelves when I hear Cyril's voice.

"Are you a reader?" he asks.

"Not really," I reply. "More of a movie buff." I turn to find him naked. I'm impressed. His cock is big, uncut, and on the rise. He moves in.

"Bret, wasn't it?"

I nod.

"I have some wonderful volumes of pornography I'd like to show you," he tells me as he reaches past me to finger the books. "Videos as well." He slides a hand down onto my ass, runs a finger into my crack, finds my hole, and prods. "Of course, the real thing is so much better, don't you think?"

I spread my legs as I tell him yes, and he eases a finger into me. He begins to work it a bit. "Why don't I show you my bedroom?" he says.

I begin to ride his palm. I haven't had anything up there in a while, and his attention feels damn good. I follow him down the hall to a spacious bedroom with a huge bed. The painting over the bed catches my eye: a jumble of lines that seem to converge into an orgy scene the longer I study the image. Much is left to the imagination but further concentration banishes my doubts.

"Isn't it wonderful?" Cyril asks as he gets behind me and pushes his stiff dick between my legs. "The painter is an absolute genius. A few brushstrokes and suddenly everyone's fucking."

I close my thighs around his dick, and he begins to thrust gently. His cock head is wet. His hands move from my hips to my prick, and he begins to play with me, pulling at me and squeezing my balls. As he nuzzles my neck, he whispers, "I want you to fuck me."

I reach down to explore his cock, and he says, "Johnny's told you about me, hasn't he?"

"Yes," I reply.

"Well, Johnny doesn't quite know everything. Sometimes..." he stops and pulls me around to face him. "Sometimes I just need a good fucking. From the moment I saw your magnificent cock, I wanted it in me."

I slide my hands onto his ass and squeeze his cheeks, then run a finger into his crack. He murmurs his approval and squirms in eagerness. When I prod his pucker, he bears down and I push in.

"Oh, yes," he says, "all the way." He thrusts his ass back until my finger is buried in his ass. "Wonderful," he moans, "but let's do the real thing. Get your cock up there."

He pulls away and climbs onto the bed. He pulls at his dick while he rolls onto his side to present me with his eager ass. I can't believe this is Johnny's potential daddy. I pull a condom from the bedside bowl, grease myself with one of the assorted lubes, move behind him, and guide my prick into his ass. He groans and rides my dick as if he were doing the fucking—and not me. I establish a steady rhythm and reach around for his prick. It's dripping wet. Just as I take hold, I hear Johnny's voice behind me. "Lookin' good," he says.

I don't turn. I keep fucking Cyril, and I feel Johnny climb onto the bed behind me. "Want some company?" he asks.

"How about it, Cyril?" I ask as I tug at his dick and keep pumping his ass. "Johnny wants you."

Cyril's delight is irrepressible. "Darling boy," he gushes as we disengage. "By all means."

Cyril quickly dons a rubber and makes a production of lubing Johnny's ass. I lean back on my haunches and watch Cyril psyche himself into a sexual frenzy. He maneuvers Johnny into position. He rests Johnny's head facedown on a pillow with his legs tucked under him and his ass high. Then Cyril plunges in, letting out a long, gratified moan, but doesn't start to fuck. "Now, Bret..." he says.

Though he's buried in Johnny's ass he still manages to lean forward and to part his cheeks. "Fuck me," he says, flexing his muscle. I glance at the winking hole and get behind him again. I've never done this before; I've never been party to an honest-to-God fuck chain. As I push into Cyril I get an incredible rush.

Cyril lets out a cry and continues to vocalize loudly. I can't say I blame him. Fucking and being fucked—he's got the best of both worlds. He has embarked on quite a trip.

When I begin to thrust, he quickly matches my pace. Soon we establish a perfect rhythm. It's not long before the three of us are completely wet and slippery; runny lube dribbles from assholes and covers our balls. My familiar fuck-slap finds an echo, and I have to remark, "Listen to that: the sweetest sound there is."

Cyril goes silent, and for a while there is only fucking. "Hey, Johnny," I finally say, making him laugh. "I'm fucking Cyril's ass. How do you like it?"

"Dick city, man," Johnny chortles. "Go for it."

Cyril loves the banter and starts to come. "Fuck me, Bret," he cries. "Come inside me now!"

I pick up the pace and feel my own spunk rise. "I'm gonna fill your ass," I growl at him. He repeats the line to Johnny as he unloads.

He slams into Johnny and I continue to pound him relentlessly. I dig my fingers into his hips as I ride out an incredible climax. Cyril lets out a howl as I spend my load. I fill his ass with the power of my orgasm as his own energy roars into Johnny.

We keep at it for some time, reluctant to break our fuck chain until the last drop of jizz works its way out of us. Even then, the three of us cling together. Cyril's arms encircle Johnny, and mine encircle Cyril. "That was so good," Johnny finally manages to whimper.

"Hear, hear," Cyril says between gasps.

I pull out of Cyril, who pulls out of Johnny. We discard our condoms. The three of us lie side by side with Cyril in the middle.

When Cyril begins to snore, Johnny and I leave him there to go to the kitchen for water. As I drain half a bottle, it occurs to me that our three-way may not have been as spontaneous as it appeared. I consider saying something to Johnny, then decide against it. If the price of his entrance into Cyril's life is bringing along a partner, so be it. I had a good time and, after all, it's not about the money.

f f f

Red-Hot Valentine

BY

DALE CHASE

I'm not partial to redheads. Generally, they seem too all-American, too wholesome, and that's not what I'm after. So it surprises me when I notice this guy. I try to remind myself that I don't like his type—but I find I no longer feel that way.

His hair is a riot of red curls, but it works—it has a certain likable chaos. I wonder if maybe he plans it, if he stands in front of a mirror and gels it into place, then messes it up, doing an eggbeater thing with his fingers. I can see him at it. Naked, of course.

I've never had a redhead. Too pale, too pink, too Midwestern. But he's gorgeous, irresistible. He's with a date and so am I; it's Valentine's Day. Maybe that's why I'm so drawn to his fiery countenance, his redness. Come to think of it, he does look kind of like Cupid all grown up. I know I'd have no objection to him shooting me with his arrow. We're both having

218

dinner, and he's at the next table, facing me and looking over his date's shoulder—as am I. We're both carrying on conversations with our dates, and I wonder if his dick is getting hard. Mine sure is.

He's dressed casually in a white shirt and slacks. His date is bleached blond, dark at the roots—and elsewhere, I suppose. This encourages me, since I'm brown-haired with brown eyes. I think of the contrast as I eat my dinner, my olive skin against his pink.

I become animated with Rick, my date, because I want to show myself off to the redhead. I make Rick laugh. I look into his eyes—we're headed for bed after dinner—lean forward and tell him what I'm going to do to him, then let my gaze move past, carry the energy one table down. And then the redhead's date gets up and goes to the john, and I'm left with a clear view. I notice there's a little blue logo on his shirt, and I want to read it. The shirt fits him rather well, and I can see well-defined pecs under the fabric. Every time Rick looks down at his meal, I glance past him; one time the redhead, with great care so I'll take note, slides his hand across the table, off the edge, and down to his crotch. I look at it, then back up to his face, pass a few seconds of up-and-down gawking, then go back to Rick, who's saying, "Hey, you listening?"

"Sure," I lie, but I still don't pay attention because the redhead gets up just as his date returns. He doesn't look at me; he just heads for the john, and I interrupt Rick. "Gotta pee," I say, hoping he won't notice the bulge in my pants.

The redhead is at a urinal when I go in. I glance at his dick, which is long, pink. I head for a stall, and when the restroom is empty he joins me. I'm stroking my cock when he opens the door. He's left his fly open; his dick is on the rise. He takes hold, brings it to mine, and rubs the heads together. We play a bit, and precome is soon liberally smeared. Then his hand slips onto my cock, and my hand slips onto his cock, and we pull at one another while I gaze into eyes that are a vibrant blue. He's not freckled like most redheads, and I wonder if he's been kept indoors, cultivated into this magnificent specimen, grown up now, turned out into the world, fresh and eager. Cupid at 23.

It registers in the back of my mind that we're on the clock, but I know I'll think of some excuse if Rick gets pissed, because I need time with this guy. I stop stroking him and get his shorts down, get a look at his red pubes. I chuckle because they seem almost absurd, yet I kneel, get my nose into them and breathe in his scent. I lick the long pink cock, working my way to the tip, then slide it into my mouth. I look up as I begin to suck and see a grin on the redhead's face, beautiful white teeth, pink tongue skating across his lower lip.

He's a mouthful. I take all I can, but he's an absolute pole. I get a hand into his silky bush, pet him as I feed on his cock. Behind us, others come and go, toilets flush, water runs. A guy enters the next stall and takes a shit as I suck cock. Surely he sees four legs in our stall, two on knees. He spends a long time in his stall, and I wonder if he's imagining us in our stall—what we're doing, if he'd like a go. Will he wait till we emerge, meanwhile playing his own mind games? Maybe return to his table primed for fucking?

The redhead grabs the sides of my head and holds me still while he begins to thrust. I cradle him with my tongue, and soon we've got a good mouth-fuck going while I work my meat, thinking about getting into him, getting on him, riding the shit out of his sweet ass while he spews come all over the floor. Then he pulls out, waving his wet dick at me, and he starts rubbing it against my cheeks and my forehead, poking the head at my eyes. He's getting really worked up, and I know what he needs, but he seems to want to draw things out, torture himself a bit. He starts slapping his cock against me, hips working as if he's fucking rather than flailing. He's breathing hard, and I wonder if this is a regular thing for him, holding back when most of us would take that hot poker and put it where it needs to go.

Suddenly, he grips my shoulders, pulling me up, apparently having gotten to where he needs to be. I stand up, and he rasps, "Fuck me," and hands me a condom. I drop my pants, suit up, and lube myself with spit; only when I'm ready does he turn and spread his cheeks. And there it is, the pinkest pucker I've ever seen, a rosy little hole that's winking at me, begging. I push in a finger, then two, and he lets out a soft groan, and the guy in the next stall does too. I almost laugh, but I give the redhead a good little reaming while my dick drools in wait. And then I withdraw, get into position, and his eager ass wiggles in anticipation. I watch the dance for a second, then shove in, everything at once, maximum dick. He lets out a grunt, then a series of loud exhales as I start to fuck him.

His ass is hot, and I think about that as I ride him, that redness of his, like he's fiery inside. Maybe that's what the red hair means. He squeezes his muscle as I go in, clamping on to me, and it sends a wave up my dick and back into my ass, which fires me all the more. I start to pound him as a result, fleshy slaps echoing through the room, and I don't care who hears us. I'm totally gone, and the guy in the next stall must be too, because I hear the unmistakable sound of stroking dick, not to mention little groans of ecstasy that are beyond the expected sounds from a man in his position. And then he lets go, and I almost laugh, hearing his noisy climax while my own has yet to arrive. Then he's quiet, listening, I suppose, or mopping up before rejoining the family. I can just hear his companion asking, "What took you so long, dear?"

I hear his zipper, the toilet flushes, and he exits. There's the sound of him washing hands, then the swing of the outer door. I want to say something about it to the redhead but don't. Ours is to be a pure relationship: cock and ass. He's got his hands on the tile, his big cock unattended, and I like that. It's all about my dick plowing his ass. I start slamming into him, and I keep on reaming him until the ache starts in my balls, my spine. Everything in me tenses, drawing up, every ounce of energy centered in my crotch, and I can't help but utter a raspy "Oh, shit!" as I come. A monumental pulsing begins, and I unleash long streams of jism. It takes what seems like minutes to unload, and afterward my cock is still viable, as if this particular ass can take me above and beyond my limits. I'm gasping for breath, sweat is running down my face and my back, and I'm so blissed out that I'm almost delirious.

The redhead pulls away, turns, rolls the rubber off my cock and discards it, then strokes my meat, cupping my balls. "Turn around," he whispers. He takes another condom from his pocket and pulls it onto his rigid prick. "My turn," he says when he's ready.

We change places, and my hands are suddenly on the tile. I think of Rick as the redhead's cock head finds my hole. I see him fidgeting at the table, meal gone, and I hope to hell he doesn't get impatient enough to come looking for me. But then I've got a dick going up my chute, and I don't care about anything or anyone except getting fucked, that singular pleasure of a cock going up my rectum. And the redhead has a memorable one, far longer than Rick's, and as it pushes deep into my bowels, I grind back onto it to let him know I want it up there all the way, that I can take the longest of hoses.

And then he's doing it, fucking me full-out, making me wince as he blazes new territory. My dick is hard again, and I get a hand on it because he's pounding me so hard the juice is stirring.

His stroke is incredibly long. He uses every inch of that salami, pulling nearly out, then ramming back in, so it's kind of a slow-motion fuck, which is almost funny because up front I'm jerking frantically as a climax teases. I want so badly to come while he's doing me—there is nothing better than coming with a dick up your ass—and then, as if nature has answered my call, I start squirting juice, powerful shots of cream splattering the tile. The redhead offers a low chuckle as he watches, and then he sucks in a long breath and holds it, and I know he's coming.

When he exhales, it's in breathy grunts in time to his squirts. Again our fuck-slap echoes through the room.

I've still got a hand on my dick, even though I'm empty. I hold on as he unloads inside me, pumping steadily in his ultra-long strokes. He keeps on even when his breathing has returned to normal, slowing gradually. When he finally pulls out, I turn and watch him strip away the rubber. His prong is flushed red, come smeared over the head. I reach down, run a finger through it, play around the slippery crown, hating the fact that there are people waiting for us. I think about what his date is in for, feel a jealous pang, and it drives me back down to my knees. I get my face back into those wild red pubes, lick his spent prick, then go under to his balls where I suck one, then the other. I start thinking maybe he's done, but when I get a finger around back into his hole and start to prod, his prong comes alive. He starts riding my hand, and I add a second finger, reaming him while up front I'm slurping nuts and jerking dick. He starts moaning, and I'm pumping like crazy, then he lets out an "Oh, shit!" and cream oozes from his cock. His ass muscle clamps on to my fingers, and he works me as I work him, squeezing out the last of it. But, of course, that's not the last of it, at least not for me. When I stand up, he goes down, sucks my prick into his mouth, and we're off again, him doing to me what I did to him, fingers up my ass and me going at it back and front. I have a vague recollection of being on the clock, but a moment later I'm coming again, and time seems to stand still. As I empty, I find myself wishing again this didn't have to end.

The redhead finally stands, gives me a smile, and pulls up his shorts, and I do the same. I think about asking for his number but don't. Something tells me it wouldn't fly. He leaves the stall first, washes his hands, and exits. I stand there still reeling, wishing I didn't have to come down. After a few deep breaths, my thoughts are focused ahead. I exit the stall, wash up, and rejoin Rick.

"Where were you?" he asks.

"Sorry. I ran into someone from work. Couldn't get unstuck. You know how it is."

"Let's go."

My dinner is cold. The redhead is eating ice cream and talking to his date, more into it than before. When we stand, I steal a glance, as does he. *I'd do you again in a minute,* his face says. My dick twitches. I'd do him right there on the table in front of his date and Rick and the whole damned restaurant. The moment is exhilarating yet painful. Rick takes my arm and we leave. He's all over me in the car because he's ready for some major fucking, and I'll certainly oblige because it is Valentine's Day, after all, and I like Rick. I honestly do. But he's not what the redhead was. As I drive, I think about those red pubes, and later, as I pump my cock into Rick, I picture pristine pink instead of tawny gold, and I think about that long ropy dick that is probably at that very moment up a willing ass, doing Cupid proud.

f f f

Tuesdays, We Read Baudelaire

BY

BY R.J. MARCH

Mr. Gerard said he was going to Paris. Luke and I nodded. "Paris is cool," Luke said. How he'd know, I had no idea. Maybe he'd seen something on MTV about it.

I was wishing I had worn some other kind of underwear because I knew Luke was going to tell me to take off my jeans any minute now. The briefs I was wearing belonged to my brother—too big and not at all sexy except to me. I watched Luke playing with the buttons of his jeans. I could see the outline of his dick under the denim, the way it moved slyly down his thigh. Luke had a big one. Mr. Gerard pretended not to notice, but I knew he could see it, liked seeing it. He sat on his chair with a cup of tea balanced on his knee. He was tall and thin, wearing wire-rimmed glasses. His hair was combed back with some gel. There was a volume of Baudelaire on the table beside him. That's what he called it—it wasn't a book; it was a "volume."

Luke and I were drinking beers. Luke said, "Could I have another?" "Me too," I chimed in. I'd finished mine a while ago but didn't want to ask for more. Luke was good at asking for more. That's what I liked about him.

"Of course," Mr. Gerard said, and he started to get up, but I said I'd get them. I liked walking through his house. The hallway leading to the kitchen was lined with pictures of men. The walls were painted a mossy green, and the trim was red. The colors always made me imagine being inside a Christmas gift box.

The kitchen's ceiling was higher than the hall's, and there was a hanging fixture that looked like a streetlight. It had a soft shine, though, and everything looked neat and clean, the way it always looked. There was a box of cookies on the counter that wasn't opened, so I didn't take one, but I did look into a cupboard to see what was there. There wasn't anything but food. I don't know what I expected to find.

I got the beers and went back to where we were sitting. Mr. Gerard called it the sitting room. It was a living room and his bedroom all together, though. The bed was against the wall and piled with pillows, looking like a couch, kind of, and he had a couple of chairs that were huge and comfortable, roomy enough for Luke and me together, and a big table covered with things, mainly books and magazines. In this room the walls were red and the trim was green, and it wasn't like being in a box at all. It was more like some foreign country, what with the hanging silk-covered lamps, the odd drawings of chairs that hung on one wall, and a big gold-framed mirror. Luke liked standing in front of the mirror when he undressed. He was working out and was in love with his body, which seemed to change every day. I liked the mirror because it was like seeing a big picture of all of us together.

Luke and I worked together at Good Buys. He worked in the electronics department, and I worked mostly as a cashier. We had graduated from school together but didn't really know each other until we started working together; then it was like, "Hey, I know you," and we started hanging out together. He took me up to the top of the hill that overlooked Reading and pointed out where he lived now. He shared an apartment near the outlets with Kenny Farrell, who was turning out, Luke said, to be a real asshole. I didn't know it at the time, but the hill was real cruisy, and I noticed all the guys pulling up to us and sitting in their cars doing nothing, waiting for something to happen. Some of them waved at Luke. (One of them, it turned out, was Mr. Gerard. I didn't know it until later, though.) I didn't say anything because I still hadn't put two and two together, so Luke said, "Guys come up here to get their rocks off." He looked at me, and I could make out his face in the darkness but not what he was driving at. It must have shown on my face, though, the blankness, the "duh," because he laughed and said, "With other guys. In their cars or in the woods there, or you go home with them."

I said, "Oh," and he laughed again, harder this time, and I laughed too because I felt stupid, and he put his hand on my leg. It stayed there, and I got a boner. I was glad he started it because I never, ever would have, even though I liked him so much that I dreamed about him and pretended he was in bed with me at night, one of his hands on my hard-on, the other farther down between my legs, fingering my butt. I would stare at him from across the sales floor when I could, and he'd catch me and make a stupid face or a jack-off hand sign, like "I'm so fucking bored," and I'd nod, loving him.

He leaned over me that night and started licking my face like a dog. I wasn't expecting that, but it wasn't so bad, and when he started on my neck, it made me crazy with wanting him, and I put my arms around him, getting my hands into the back of his jeans, finding him without underwear. I pulled him onto me, but his legs were stuck between the seat and the steering wheel. His ass cheeks felt smooth, like river rocks. I squeezed them hard. "Take it easy, he-man," he said, undoing the buttons of his jeans. His fanny felt cold in my hands, and I rubbed his cheeks to warm them. My fingers touched into the rough of his crack—he was hot there and a little sweaty. The smell of his butt was going to stay on my fingers for hours that night since I refused to wash it off, sniffing them through the night and making myself come— two, three times.

What he did to me that night was rub his big cock against my stomach. He lifted my shirt and played with my nipples and pushed his groin against my gut and humped me that way. His balls rubbed against the waistband of my jeans, and I wanted to take them down, my jeans, to get my dick out too, but Luke held my hands up over my head, his elbows dug into my armpits. I squirmed under him, seeing the bars of headlights cutting through the night air all around us, Luke's hot breath falling down on me in blasts, some stupid song I hated on the radio. I pushed up with my crotch, my dick harder than steel, right up against his fanny. I'd never fucked anyone before, but I was sure that was what I wanted to do. He kept gut-fucking me, though, holding my hands and licking the insides of my arms, making these little noises that really turned me on, little grunts or something that made me think he was really getting into what he was doing. And then he said, "OK," and lifted himself, and I felt the spray of his come hit my face and the front of my shirt. He sat up, right on my crotch, and moved his butt around. Everyone could see him and knew what he was doing, even if they couldn't see me. He touched my nipples, just put his thumbs over them, finding them right away through my semen-spotted T-shirt, and I sauced in my jeans.

$$f\ f\ f$$

It was only a week or so later when he came up to me in the break room, touching the back of my neck even though there was a camera in the room up in the corner by the ceiling. (I think Good Buys even had cameras in the toilets.) He said we were going to visit a friend of his and that he brought a joint for the ride.

"Where does this guy live?" I asked.

"Just in Flying Hills, man," Luke said. He sat at the table with me and got one of his shoes off and put his foot up in my crotch, and I got a hard-on that lasted all fucking day.

He tried to explain it to me in the car on the way to Mr. Gerard's, but the dope made me stupid and lame, and I just wanted to put my hands in his jeans and touch his cock. "He likes watching," Luke said, unbuttoning his jeans to let me into the warm confines of his underpants. "You sit and have tea with him, and he reads a couple of poems, and then we fuck around."

"Does he fuck around too?" I asked.

Luke shook his head. It was dark now, and his cock glowed green under the dashboard. I had it in my mouth and was sucking on it, lapping up the sweet seepage that leaked out. "Shit," he said. "That feels awesome, Billy." He put a hand on the top of my head, forcing my mouth down into his pubes, and I swallowed him. I did some serious head bobbing, riding his veiny shaft and leaving a pool of my spit in the hairy hollow where his belly and dick met. He slipped his hand inside my shirt and fingered one of my nipples and made me feel wild, unable to get enough of him into my mouth. I wanted to eat him up. I growled and moaned, and he pinched my tit hard, and I had to stop because I was close enough to make a mess of myself, humping the seat piggishly.

"You're a fucking animal, man," Luke said, pulling off to the side of the road. "We're here." He got out of the car, putting

away his wet, sticky boner, and got himself ready to introduce
me to his friend Mr. Gerard.

f f f

I had expected someone older, I think, someone less
attractive. Mr. Gerard—I never learned his first name—looked
to me like someone who was really hot trying to look like a total
dweeb, like Clark Kent or something. He shook my hand, with
this prissy smile on his face, and led us into the sitting room,
asking Luke how he'd been, going on about how long it had
been since he'd seen him even though Luke told me they'd gotten together the previous week. There was a tray on an ottoman
set up for tea: the pot on top of some little burner, three cups
all ready for us. The room flickered with candles.

Mr. Gerard didn't talk; he chatted. Every third word out of
his mouth was "delightful," every fourth "fascinating," as he sat
cross-legged in a chair going on and on about this and that, his
eyes flicking between Luke and me.

And then he said, getting up, "I need to make a phone call.
Would you excuse me?"

When he left the room, Luke nudged me. He unzipped his
jeans, and his prong poked out from his shorts. "C'mon," he
said, "get undressed."

"What for?" I asked.

"It's time to frolic," Luke said, looking at me with a little
smile. "He'll be back to watch."

I stood up and took my pants down. Luke told me to leave
my socks on. "Next time you have to wear tighty-whiteys like
me." Luke left his briefs on, his dick sticking out through the
pee hole. He looked very sexy to me, and I lunged at him, but
he dodged me. I fell across the pillow-covered daybed, my rear
end swatted. He fell on top of me, his cock going hotly between
my butt cheeks. We hadn't fucked yet, but I was hoping we
would sometime and liked letting him know I thought the idea

was pretty awesome. He burrowed his dog into the channel of my crack, licking my back. I rolled over, flipping us so that I was on top, his cock still trapped between my cheeks. I wriggled my fanny, feeling the sudden ooze of slickness that had leaked out of his fat-tipped bone. He put his hands on my hips and slid me up and down against his shaft. He covered my belly, putting a finger into my belly button, rubbing me there, and then his hands moved up the ribbed cage of my middle to the chocolate kisses of my nipples. I had my eyes closed, my head tilted back. I could smell his hair, I could feel his lips against the back of my neck, and I heard him say, "Pretend you don't see him," and I looked up, and there was Mr. Gerard across the room with a gigantic hard-on sticking out of his pants. He was rubbing the end of it, peering at us like a museum exhibit. Candlelight reflected off the lenses of his glasses. "Suck my cock, man," Luke prompted, and I slowly got off him, feeling the loss of his burning prick against my rear. I turned so that my butt was pointing at Mr. Gerard, and I made my little hole wink and purse, but Luke moved me with a finger, allowing a clear view of his dick sliding into my mouth. I sensed movement in Mr. Gerard's corner and glanced over to see him edging closer, getting himself behind one of his enormous chairs, hiding his fat pecker and the jacking he was doing. I was thinking it would have been more fun if he joined in. From the corner of my eye, he looked awesome, his black hair like one of those British movie stars who play pirates and Shakespeare, long and wavy like that.

Luke spread his legs, and I played with the taut cotton that covered his balls, giving them a good squeeze. I petted his thighs, which were all feathery with hair and hard with muscle from playing soccer or whatever sport he'd played when he was in school. I chugged down on his boner, feeling my throat constrict around the head, feeling him throb alongside my tonsils, and he put his hands on my head and did some pretty impressive moaning, saying my name, rolling his head from side to side like I was taking him to the edge of ecstasy or something. I lifted my head to look him in the eye, a drippy string of drool and precome connecting us.

"Bring it here," he said.

Up until now Luke hadn't really gone near my cock. He might have licked it once or twice while we were locked in a sixty-nine and his prick was rooting around in my esophagus, but I couldn't have said he ever really sucked it. It didn't make much difference to me up until then, but the thought of it happening made my dick ache with wanting to feel his lips around it. I crawled up the bed on my knees, sinking into the pillows, bringing him my cock. When I got it close enough for him to kiss the end, he looked up at me and said, "Take it easy." He took hold of my prick like it was a finger sandwich and stuck out his tongue at it. I steadied myself with one hand on the wall behind Luke's head. Mr. Gerard had moved again, getting a better view. I could see his great penis, pale and huge, with its rolling skin and bright red head. He held it with both hands and still couldn't cover all of its shaft. He pulled on his trouser snake, pinching out a flood of leakage, baring and covering the bulbous head. But I forgot about Mr. Gerard when I felt the first heat of Luke's mouth and the slide of my dick head over his flattened tongue.

I did my best to keep still, but I couldn't help myself and had to fuck that soft wetness. It was better than anything I'd ever felt, better than the cool and slippery slide of the percale pillowcase I'd been fucking ever since I could remember, better than the space between Eric Moser's hairless thighs, better even than the spitty cup of my hand. I loved the friction of his chin on my balls and the terror of his slight underbite when his bottom teeth caught on the sensitive underside of my cock head. Together the sensations combined and doubled, tripled; I was practically shaking but banging into his mouth with a vengeance. I started breathing hard, and Luke was tapping my thighs, then hitting my stomach, choking on me. I pulled out,

out of control, and creamed across his face, practically bawling, and I felt the warm squirt of jizz on the backs of my thighs as Luke unloaded.

"That wasn't so bad," Luke said later in the car. "Was it?"

I shrugged. Actually it was the single most awesome experience of my life. I'd just had an orgasm that was like an explosion, and it was witnessed by a man wanking on a monster dick, watching me like I was on television. "Not bad," I agreed.

$$fff$$

I was surprised one day when I saw Mr. Gerard in the CD department of Good Buys. "I'm looking for a Puccini disc," he said when I came up to him. He looked different to me this day—his hair wasn't so gelled, his clothes not all black and woolly. He looked very much like a normal guy. "Luke is busy tonight, but I was wondering if you'd care to drop by."

I told him I didn't drive.

"I'd be happy to pick you up. Shall I? After work?"

I waited outside the store for half an hour and was just about ready to give up when he pulled up in a little black Jag. He apologized for being late. "I was at the gym," he said, and I noticed under his jacket that he wasn't wearing a shirt and tie but a stringy tank top. There was a dark brush of hair between his pecs, straight and shining. He had on a pair of sweats, old gray ones with a rip in one knee. He looked more normal than ever. I sank into the leather seat with a sort of awe. He hadn't shaved, and he was wearing, I thought, contacts. It was like being with another person altogether.

He kept quiet. Apparently he liked the song on the radio. He hummed bits and pieces of it, his eyes intent on the road.

Mr. Gerard excused himself to go to the bathroom once we arrived, and he took a really long time. I sat and leafed through some boring magazines. *Where's the porn?* I wondered and figured he was taking a bath or something. He came out the same way he went in, though, and sat down beside me on the bed made up as a couch.

"Take off your clothes for me," he said casually, as though he'd just asked me to get him a glass of water. I stood up, feeling a little shy, and moved away from him so he'd have a good view. I started stripping.

"Take your time," he said, leaning back on some pillows. The bulge in the crotch of his sweats was prominent, a mountain of a molehill. I unbuttoned my shirt slowly, getting down to my T-shirt. I still had shoes and socks and jeans and briefs to go, figuring it would be a long show, not really thinking about how fast clothes come off. I went for the shoes next, untying them, bent over, feeling the blood rush to my face. I saw his hand run over the lump in his sweats.

The shoes came off quicker than I'd expected. I straightened up and wondered what to take off next—shirt, socks, or pants. I did some mental head scratching and decided the socks would go next, but I was going to need some help. I stepped close to Mr. Gerard and put my foot on the cushion between his legs. He caught on quickly and didn't seem put off by the idea. He grasped my foot and gently peeled the sock off, rubbing the sole with his thumb, his other hand on my ankle and creeping higher. When I gave him the other foot to unsock, he pulled me onto him.

"You're better at this than you let on," he said, his mouth close to my ear. His hands went all over my backside, and it was becoming apparent that my cherry little behind wasn't meant for Luke after all. He ran his thumb along the seam of the ass of my jeans, applying pressure at my hole and again where my balls were flattened between my legs. His mouth worked all over mine, his tongue darting and stabbing, flat and slobbering, then hard and pointed, and he stuck it into my mouth so that it nearly went to the back of my throat, taking my breath away.

He let me up for air once, rolling us around so that he was on top, and then his sweats were gone, and he was humping me with that humongous tool of his. His legs were covered with fine black hairs. I could put my hands on the backs of his thighs and cup his ass cheeks, which were smooth and firm with muscle. He sighed when I put my fingers into his crack, and he pawed at my briefs, rolling them off my hips and pushing them down my thighs, and they turned into tight ropes around my knees. His cock rolled over mine, dwarfing it, leaking a sticky goo that made it slick between us. His balls dangled down in the V of my legs, banging against my little chestnuts, slapping against my pinched-up little hole.

He got up and stood over me. "Get on your hands and knees," he said quietly. He had his great prong in his hand, palming it, getting his juices flowing. I looked at the gigantic head and wondered how on earth he was going to get it into me without splitting me wide open. "Don't worry," he added. "I wouldn't dream of hurting you."

He got behind me and started eating out my butt. I could feel the ring of my anus flutter under the stroke of his tongue. He licked up and down my ditch, wild hairs springing up all over the place. He bit my ass cheeks and chinned my balls. He handled my prick gently, tugging on the end of it, his fingers smearing in the grease. I heard him say, "Ready?" and I thought, *I'll never be ready for that thing.*

He didn't fuck me, though—not with his cock, anyway. He fingered me with his left hand and jacked off with his right, and he told me to turn over. I think he was afraid I'd jizz up his bedspread; I'd already gotten plenty of dick drool on it. On my back I lifted my legs and put my feet on his chest. His finger poked at that spot I'd recently found on my own, and it was driving me crazy. Mr. Gerard looked down at me with this glazed look on his face, his eyes slitted. He licked his beautiful lips, working another finger in. He tapped my thigh with the heavy head of his dick, leaving wet marks.

"Jerk yourself off," he said, because I wasn't touching myself—I didn't need to, really. I was sure he was going to make me come, working his fingertips over that hardening ball up my ass. "I want to see you come," he said, and I said, "OK," and it just happened. I started squirting all over myself, clotty streams of white flying all over the place, landing on my face and in my hair and on the pillows behind me, which might have pissed him off if he hadn't been so horny.

Mr. Gerard bent over and started lapping up my come like a cat over spilled milk. I could feel his fisted cock between my legs, then the hot spray of jizz as his prick spit out all over my cock and bush and balls.

He fell back on the bed with a huge sigh, his stiffer looking like a candle dripping wax. I wanted to lick it off. He looked at me with sleepy eyes. I was fascinated by his cock, the enormity of it, the way it started falling, a tree in slow motion, big and white, across his thigh, slime still coming out of the fat head.

"You want to do it again, don't you?" he said to me. I nodded.

"Dinner first," he said. "We'll go to Joe's. And when we come back you can fuck my brains out. How does that sound?"

I shrugged. "OK, I guess," I said, though inside I was starting to boil. My dick was still hard, and I imagined what it would be like to be up inside that muscular ass and very nearly had a little accident.

Mr. Gerard got up and took my hand, pulling me up and leading me to the bathroom. He turned on the water and started filling the tub, pouring in this and that, turning the water a pretty green that smelled like limes and oranges and roses all together. He touched the pointed prong that wouldn't go away.

"Insistent," he said thoughtfully.

We got into the hot water, and he pulled me to him, getting me between his legs as though we were tobogganing, and he put his lips against my head.

"Have you read any Cavafy?" he asked me, and I carefully shook my head no.

"Oh, you must," he said. "You must."

It Could Happen

ƒ ƒ ƒ

f f f

All Big 'n' Shit

BY

R.J. MARCH

I wanted to fuck his brains out, I wanted to fuck him blind, but I was worried about the Canadians. I am always worrying about the Canadians. Who doesn't around here? This is fucking Buffalo, dude.

I gave Jeff a lift because he said he'd be late if I didn't, and I didn't want him to be late for his first day on the job. He'd just gotten hooked up at Shoes R Us. I've had a job for a while at U R Cool. We sold T-shirts with Farrah Fawcett pictures on them and Skechers and Fubu jeans. It was a good place to work because you got a 40% discount and there wasn't anything to do but fold the Farrah Fawcett T-shirts and ask people if they wanted to buy "some socks to go with that outfit" or a "really cool hemp necklace."

Jeff looked like the guy in Third Eye Blind. I think it's that guy, the one that sings. Or maybe it's the Better Than Ezra guy. I can't remember. I only know that I saw Jeff in his boxers once and sprouted myself some mighty wood and had to cover it with my dad's golf-club towel, which seemed kind of appropriate at the time.

So I like guys, but I don't like to talk about it, you know? I don't go around saying I'm gay or anything, because I'm really not too sure about that right now anyway, and my mom thinks I should make sure before I march in any gay pride parade. I think she's offering some good advice, but there's something about Jeff that would make me march down the middle of my hometown in my mom's bra and panties if I knew I was marching toward Jeff with his Abercrombie boxers around his ankles, ass flying high like any proud rainbow fucking flag, ready for some major plowing.

I've got a fattie, a cock like a third fucking arm, which would make a great name for a band, I'm thinking. Once me and this guy, Bryan—said he was the district manager of one of our biggest competitors—We Be Phat, we were fucking around in the store after hours. He'd been on my shit all day, telling me he was going to get me my own store and shit, and he liked the way my hair looked because I had the tips bleached, and wanting to know how much I benched—like 210 at the time, by the way, and practically 250 now. He hung out after 9 because he said he wanted to compare our closing procedures to the ones at his stores, and I was like, whatever, you know? The lights went out and he had me back in the office, his hands all over me. "You look so tense," he said, massaging my pecs, dropping down to my crotch, where I'd sprung a leak, if you know what I mean, and I'm saying, "Tense? You don't know tense." And he starts undoing my jeans and digging around in my boxers, getting my man in two hands and bringing it out into the open.

"At last" was all he said.

Jeff played with the radio and then he played with the end of his shirt. He had to wear this completely gay shirt that said Yo! Shoes R Us! which I thought was totally offensive, but there's marketing for you, and I was thinking of majoring in that next semester at Buff. U., and then I could get a job—uh, nowhere, you know what I mean? He looked better in a wife beater, because then you could see his Superman tat and the hand-sampled heart he'd drawn himself in sixth grade, long before I'd ever met him. He dug at himself, getting a good handful of his crotch and squeezing it hard, grinding the heel of his hand into himself, making even me wince and thinking he might have had crabs or something—scabies—whatever. I watched the road because my car wasn't exactly insured, but whatever he was doing or trying to kill down there got my attention. I got a bone myself that stuck up against the steering wheel and made my driving skills strictly retarded. *Shouldn't have worn the warm-ups without some protection*—that's what I was thinking, looking forward to the next turn I was going to make, my dick head wedged nicely.

Jeff said, "Dude, I am so not into this. Wouldn't it be cool if you could just keep on going? Why don't we drive to California—I hear everyone is cooler out there."

"Who told you that?" I asked.

"Some dude from L.A."

That district manager was from California. I liked thinking about him. I hadn't done anything since him and was feeling kind of backed up, which is why I nearly got off on the steering wheel, seeing Jeff scratch himself. I liked thinking about Bryan and Jeff together, what they might do. I liked thinking about Jeff bending himself over for this guy who wasn't much older than us and letting him fuck him. I was thinking that Jeff could, like, lean over a chair or something and completely open his ass for this guy, who was hot, really, a fucking sketchy hottie, all tall and black-haired like some *Vogue Homme*—French for *hottie*—model, his hair always getting into his eyes and his buzzed little goatee itching all the time, making him look thoughtful yet completely fuckable, which he was.

When he opened my jeans and pulled out my pole, he looked a little pale, a little beyond happy. He held me with both hands and said, staring at my cock's single eye, "At last." Considering the dime-size opening of my piss slot, I was about to consider this guy a bit gone. I never knew anyone to praise the beast so highly. It was a daunting piece—so said my history professor—a dick to fear, according to some of the other guys. It was an ass-stretcher, a mouth-wrecker. I'd come to think of hand jobs as the only way I would ever get off, hadn't met a girl or guy willing to actually insert it. I've heard it all when it comes to my dick, but never "At last."

The next thing he said was "We need some lube," his voice strangled. He flicked my dick head with his finger and I nearly came—lube? I was finally going to get some. I watched him undress, undoing his Gucci belt for him, unknotting his Hermes tie. He was too cool for this shithole store, but that didn't make much difference to me. He let his pants drop, and I eyeballed his hairy thighs and wanted to feel them against mine, and I stepped toward him.

Jeff said, "I need some Gatorade—I think I'm dehydrated." I stopped at 7-Eleven and stared at his ass as he walked into the store. That was one thing I hadn't ever seen, his bare butt, but it was something I was very interested in, like it was a hobby, something of a pursuit. In jeans it was a sweet bubble. Naked—who knew? Smooth cheeks? Fuzz-covered? It was a crapshoot, this second-guessing, but crap I wouldn't mind shooting, if you know what I mean.

"Get me something not—you know," I yelled out through the window.

"Canadian?" he called back.

Exactly, I thought.

The DM didn't really have hair that got into his eyes or a little goatee, and he'd never have made the pages of any fashion mag. He was actually kind of balding and a little on the fat side. And his clothes were all from, like, the Polo outlet. It didn't matter to me, though, because he was married and had two kids and used to play football in college. All of that was like some sort of aphrodisiac for me. I was the one that pawed him from the start, letting him know from minute one that he could do whatever he wanted to me, that I was his for the taking. He was crazy about my cock, though, cock-crazy like you wouldn't believe, throwing himself on it, first his mouth and then his ass. He was fired up and wanted to be tore up—wasn't like the old lady was going to notice or anything, he said to me. He took off his tasseled Cole Haans. "Do me a favor," he said, holding out a shoe for me. "Smell this and tell me what you think."

I took the shoe and took a big whiff. My cock dripped like a honeycomb. "I think you fucking stink," I said, and he said "Damn straight," smiling hard and punching my arm.

He started sucking my knob. It's a big old red thing, like a tomato hanging from a fucking thick-ass vine. He made some gurgling noises, some choking noises, some more gurgling noises. I saw him whip his own out: a nice-looking piece of meat, very pink, very straight, very long, rising up out of a thick patch of reddish hair. He swung it around like a bullwhip, and it sprayed out a golden thread of leakage that marked up his Ralph Lauren chinos. He got his mouth close to my halfway mark, a bulge in a vein that pretty much marked the 4.5 inches of dick, with that much to go to get to the base. He handled my 'nads hard, like a man, and I stayed quiet, enjoying the soft slip of his tongue, the firm grip of his lips. He tugged on my prick for a while, banging his nose into my bush, his fingers moving up toward my butt hole.

The one time I saw Jeff in his boxers, in his room at his parents' house before he got kicked out for selling acid to his cousins, I was drawn to the swinging bob of his cock as he walked across the room, fresh from a shower and in pursuit of something to put on, probably to cover that swinging bob, that juicy hang. He had a nice body, his stomach all boxed up with muscle, his tits not big like mine, but there, enough to want to put your mouth on them. He wasn't into bulk, wasn't bulky himself, no interest in fat hard tits or big wagging quads, but boasting some sweet ass cheeks and knuckle-biting thighs—sweet things, those thighs, fucking sweet.

We were listening to Ben Folds, getting ready to go see *Armageddon*. I had a secret bone for Ben Affleck because I figured he had a secret bone for Matt Damon, but I forgot about it, seeing Jeff in his shorts. He put his hands inside them as if I wasn't there. "Dude," he said, running his hands through his perfect fucking hair, "What am I going to wear?"

He came back to the car with a bottle of water for me and a can of Canada Dry—his idea of a joke. "Don't even," I said, not letting him into the car with the ginger ale. "Just get it the fuck out of here." He took it to a garbage can, holding it like a grenade or a turd.

"Dude," he said. "You are totally fixated on this Canadian thing. What is up with that?" He looked at me like I was fucking Winona Ryder, and I felt like a complete asshole, but what was I going to say? How could I explain myself?

"Fuck, man," I said, putting my face in my hands, feeling like Johnny Depp for a minute. "I don't even fucking know," which was about as close to the truth as I cared to go.

He had such sweet-colored hair, kind of blond, kind of not. Like how I wanted my own hair to look but couldn't, not really, anyway. I wanted to touch his hair, to put my nose into it, to smell him and lick his scalp and his neck and all the rest of him. All the fucking rest of him. He was narrow but thick, a guy with meat on his bones. He knew that Post Office was a game his parents used to play, an excuse to make out. He said to me once, "Dude, you ever hear of Post Office?" I shook my head, and he said, "It's like this excuse to make out. You go to the post office to get your letter, and the post office is like someone's bedroom, and the letter is SWAK'd, man. 'Sealed with a kiss.' You never heard of that?"

"Never ever," I said, but I would have like to have. I would have liked to play Post Office with Jeff.

ALL BIG 'N' SHIT

One of the things about Jeff that bothered me was that he had no idea about my cock, none that I knew of anyway. Like I said, not everyone said "At last" like my dick was a fire hydrant in the middle of a desert.

But all Jeff could say about it at this point was "What about it?" because he hadn't seen it. Now, Bryan, he's still talking about it, catching me online, calling me up every once in a while for some pretty hot phone. I can still see his squirming, hairy ass, blond fuzzy cheeks, grinding and chewing, eating up my fat cock slowly, taking the whole thing slowly the way a boa swallows up an armadillo. I was thinking then that he was going to take all of me into him that way. I leaned back in the chair I was sitting on, this dilapidated office chair from like the 40s or something, and watched his ass drop lower and lower, and more of me disappeared, ready to be sucked up into his ass like some sort of reverse baby. He had his shirt off by then, and I was playing with the hairs on his back, which I always thought would gross me out but found a little more than kind of sexy, like I was thinking, *This is a guy, man, a fucking guy.*

"I feel like I'm trying to fit someone's knee up my ass," he said over his shoulder, and I saw beads of sweat on his forehead and across his scalp, clinging to the sparse little hairs there like dew. "You are fucking big, babe," he said, and later, when I was fucking him, the two of us standing and him holding on to a wall because I was whaling on his ass, he kept calling me Big Man, Big Man, like, "Come on, Big Man, fuck my ass, yeah, fuck it, Big Man."

"Tell me about your wife," I said, my voice all hoarse and shit, and he started telling me about her tits and how often he fucked her and how she gave the best head, and I started getting dizzy and my cock felt dizzy too, and I grabbed his titties, these huge fucking red nips—fucking *cherries*, dude—and I started slamming him, and he said, "Give it to me, Big Man, give it to me." And I did.

He let me squirt off into him, his big shoulders heaving under me, and when I was done, shaking like a weasel, lying all sweaty across his big back, he shook me off and uncorked himself—the noise we made was fucking gross, I'll tell you— and told me to get down on my knees. I opened my mouth, ready for him, and he blasted my face. It wasn't excessive, though—just enough to get me off again, hosing his ankles with a meager yet admirable amount of what I call the reserves.

We were outside of the mall, and Jeff's shift started in like 20 minutes. He said to me, turning in his seat, bringing one leg up and putting his chin on his knee, "This is so fucking stupid."

I asked what, and he said, "Everything, man, everything."

I was wondering if he was scared, because he sounded kind of scared. He looked out at the parking lot. Security drove by, making me feel safe. It was some fucked-up-looking dude who looked like he was looking for his Siamese twin, and I started thinking about winter, because what the fuck did this guy do in the snow without his Siamese twin? Jeff leaned back in his seat, throwing his head back. He made a groan.

"What's up?" I said, because he was scaring me and I didn't feel safe anymore.

"I can't say," he said, looking at me with these eyes that, like, ripped my heart out, they looked so sad and wet. I wanted to reach out and grab him and hold him and I wanted to tongue-kiss him until we both died, and the dichotomy was so strong that I just sat there like a fucking mushroom.

"Who killed Kenny this time?" I asked.

"Not funny," he answered.

I decided to be bold for a change. I put my hand on the back of the seat in the general vicinity of his shoulder, close enough to be *around* him, and I asked him, all sincere and shit, "Dude, are you all right?"

He played with the scuffed hem of his stovepipes and whispered something I couldn't hear.

"What was that?" I asked.

"Never mind," he said quietly again, but this time I heard him. He licked the knee of his pants. I felt my thighs through my warm-ups, loving the feel of the nylon, thinking about running into the sporting goods store for another pair, these pants were so sexy. My dick rested against my belly, hot and fucking engorged, which was a pretty decent description as far as I was concerned.

"Will you pick me up after work?" he asked me, and I said, "Sure, no problem." And he got out of my car, not really closing the door. He looked like a kid going to the principal's office. He disappeared behind a Jeep Wagoneer and was gone.

I'll tell you about this Canadian thing. When I was a kid I had this dream that the U.S. was going to be invaded by Canada, and it was so fucking real that I woke up screaming. And every winter afterward, when the lake froze up, I'd think about that dream and how easy it would be for them to just walk across the ice and take over the whole fucking country, all these Canucks telling us what to do and making us pay more for cigarettes, changing the way we talked and shit. It's stupid, but it stayed with me. And then one day my dad had this job selling fruit juices and he crossed the border and I never saw him again, and now he's like some Canadian or something. It's like they grabbed him and washed his brain so that he forgot about us, me and my mom. Once I was drinking a beer and found out it was a Labatt's and I spit it out—that's how much I hate the Canadians.

Stupid, huh?

I waited for him at 9:30. He came out the doors with all the other mall workers, looking fried. "I ate dinner at Chik-fil-A," he said, an explanation.

I headed for home, and we almost got there, but he stopped me. "I've got to piss," he said.

"We're almost there," I told him, looking at him, wondering if he really wanted me to stop.

"Dude," he said. "Don't make me wet myself."

I pulled over—what else could I do?—and he stepped off to the side of the road and started pissing. I found a song we liked on the radio and turned it up, mostly to drown out the sound of him pissing, which had given me another bone, making me feel simple and a little like Pavlov's dog, something I learned about my one semester at Buff. U. He turned around when he was finished and put himself away, and I saw everything— his fucking cock, a drip of pee, his darker-than-his-head pubes, the slow zip of his stoves, and a trail of sparks from his fly.

When he got back into the car he moved in close to me, closer than he needed to, and I was wondering what was up with that when he told me he had to talk.

"Go ahead, dude," I said, fingering the keys in the ignition, not intending to go anywhere until he said so.

"Maybe we could go to your place," he said, because he was living at home again and felt kind of wussed-out as a result.

"Sure," I said. "Whatever."

At my place he flopped down on the couch, and I ran around throwing shit here and there, trying to look like half the pig I really was. Like, anything that was food and moldy went right in the trash, and the dirty clothes went into the coat closet, and the porn magazines—not many!—were all bundled up like old newspapers and thrown behind the bedroom door. I put on Rufus Wainwright on the CD player, followed by the new Luscious Jackson, and tried to chill but couldn't. Jeff was looking at the toes of his Skechers and making me nervous, looking all Party-of-Fived out.

"What's up," I said, wanting to put my arm around him again, as if I'd actually done it before. "Do you want to lie down?"

"What?" he said, looking at me as though I'd asked to eat his liver. And he was lying down already.

"I don't know," I said. I didn't. It was Jeff, here in my living room, in some kind of emotional turmoil. I fed on it and turned it into my own. Jeff with the perfect hair, the cute body, the best ass.

"This music," he said, making a face.

"You don't like it?"

"I want to die," he said.

"I can change it," I said back. "But I don't have any Foreigner, dude."

"This guy is totally Canadian, you know."

I went pale, feeling it. I could have fainted.

"No way," I said. "Don't fuck with me."

"I swear to God," Jeff said. "I have a friend at Discs 4 U. He fucking told me."

"Not true, not true."

"And one of the girls in Hole."

"Shut up," I said. "I can't hear you anymore." I put my hands over my ears.

He wiggled his fingers, some dumb kind of sign language I didn't get, and he said something I didn't hear, so I said, "What?" And he said, "I said I fucking love you."

"Shut the fuck up," I said.

"Whatever," he said, getting up.

"Where are you going?" I asked.

"Home, dude, I'm walking home."

"Why?"

He turned around. "I guess because you haven't asked me to stay."

It was weird because it was Jeff, but he let me undress him, and I got a hard-on that, like, oozed my pants. He didn't want any lights on, but I got him to let me at least light a candle I had from the Bath and Body Works, a gift from an ex-girlfriend. His skin was beautiful, his shoulders so pretty. I kissed them feeling kind of stupid but what the fuck, and I saw myself as a total Chester, all close and touchy, gross, the kind of friend you don't want to find yourself alone with.

"We could take a bath," Jeff said.

"Yeah," I said. "Sure."

He still had his boxers on, but I could see he had a boner

too. He walked to the bathroom, and I followed him, flicking on the switch. "No lights," he said, so I ran back for the candle that smelled like my fucking grandmother and reminded me of a girl I never wanted to see again.

I just want to jump ahead here because what I liked best about the whole thing—even though he, like, completely changed his mind the next day—was the way, when it was over and we were dripping onto sheets that smelled a little too much of me, if you know what I mean, the best fucking thing was the way that Jeff put his arms around me, holding my head to his chest, where I listened to the bass beat of his heart, the fill and empty of his lungs, and the little squeaks and gurgles your stomach makes after you eat something at Chik-fil-A.

I filled the bath, squirting in some shampoo for bubbles, and Jeff got himself out of his boxers, and I saw his hard-on for the first time. It was white and beautiful, banana-curved, a righteous sword. His balls dangled low, dark-skinned, almost red in the light of the candle. He stepped into the sudsy water and laughed. "It's fucking hot, dude," he said. "You trying to cook us?"

I still had my clothes on, all of them, although I was desperate to be naked. He squatted slowly in the foam until he could tolerate the heat. I just stood there watching him. He was like something out of a fucking movie, naked like that and beautiful the way he was always beautiful, and I felt like such a fag and I didn't even care, first of all because he said "I love you" first.

I took off my shirt, Jeff staring at me. I felt like a stripper but completely self-conscious. I ran my hand over my pecs because I couldn't help it, wanting to feel how full they felt and to touch my nipples, which always gave me a little rush anyway. "You're big and shit," Jeff said, and I said, "Yeah."

"It's cool, though," he said, playing with the candle. I played with the waistband of my warm-ups—that's all there was left. Jeff was completely engrossed with trying to burn himself and dripping hot wax into the water. I reached into my pants and tugged my woody, letting him know that I was totally hung and wicked-hard, but he was too busy making the bath bubbles disappear.

"Dude," I said, turning sideways casually, wanting him to get the full effect before I set the beast free, changing things forever between us. "Are you into this or what?" I guess I sounded kind of annoyed, because he dropped the candle into the bath. "Shit!" he said. "Fucking clocked my nuts, man."

I played with the cords that tightened my pants, thinking this was fucked-up, feeling as though my dick was going to burn through the nylon that covered it. I saw him glance at it, once, twice, the third time he started staring and his mouth went open, but he didn't say anything. It was time—I had his attention. I took off my pants, turning away from him, showing my bare ass first, giving him back. When I turned around again, the breath left him. "Dude," he said airlessly. I stepped toward him, the big stick wagging him. I knelt on the tub's edge, the heavy, sappy head dipping at his face. He looked around it at me. "Fucking amazing," he said.

"I guess," I said, shrugging. I'd seen bigger, actually, and more than once—once, up on Skyline Drive, this guy jacking off in his car, fucking whacking his dick against the steering wheel and making the horn blow, and then Donny Hays, this Indian kid I worked with at U R Cool before he got caught blowing a security guard in the public toilets.

What I had going for me was thickness and a huge fucking knob. I gripped the base and swung the hose around a little until I started pulling on my pubes, which kind of hurt. His mouth was close, and it was open, but he wasn't doing anything with it. He played with himself underwater. "Awesome dick, man," he said, sounding all sincere.

"You want me to come in?" I asked. I bobbed myself in front of him, feeling buzzed and juicy, ready for anything.

Jeff shrugged his shoulders.

"What do you feel like doing?" I said, and he shrugged again, staring at my prick.

"Lick it," I told him, dropping my voice, making it sound— I hoped—sexy. "Lick my dick, dude," I said.

I was shocked when I saw his tongue, more shocked when I felt it. It was hot like a flame, swirling into the fat piss slit, then dragging around the head. He turned his head and had my balls in his mouth and sucked them hard, making me feel queasy and real turned-on. He took his wet hands out the tub and grabbed my hips, holding them hard, and he got the head of me into his mouth, tongue dancing wild.

What the fuck! I was thinking. *What the fucking fuck!* Everything was normal one minute—as normal as things get with me—and then this shit happens. It was too much like a dream, too unreal, too good to be true. I started thinking about all those times I was laid up with an aching boner because he let his pants drop low on his ass, or reached up under his shirt to play with the feathery hairs there, or grabbed my tit and pinched the hell out of it just for the hell of it, or pissed right next to me like I wasn't there at all. And here he was now, struggling with my swollen knob, two-fisting it, giving me the chills and sweats all at once.

He rose up out of the tub all shiny and wet, suds dripping off him the way I wanted to, and he let my dick swing from his mouth. "Ever get fucked?" he wanted to know.

"Only once," I said, a painful confession and a lie too. I'd gotten rammed a few times, up on Skyline on those afternoons I had off, guys with pickups and dirty fingernails and little bent dicks wanting to pop my cherry—as if.

"Let me see it," he said, and I turned around and bent over for him. I put my hands on my cheeks and spread them for him, giving him an excellent view of my pink hole, knowing this because of the breeze he blew over it.

He licked me there—now that was a first, for real—and wiggled his tongue into the wrinkled opening, which he replaced with his finger. He grabbed my balls through my legs and started sucking on them at the same time, and I was ready to die because what else was there, man, what else?

When he slapped his own pointy pecker head against my pucker, I opened up big-time, leaning back against him and trying to get him inside me fast. I wanted all of him in me, as much as I could get, and he put his hands on my shoulders and slid in slow until I could feel his hips against my ass and his dick end somewhere in my guts. "How is it?" I wanted to know.

"You tell me," he said.

"Excellent?"

"Fucking right," he said, shoving in, his body taking over mine like I never imagined. His hands went all over my chest, squeezing my tits until they hurt and fucking me harder all the while. He roamed over my abs until he got hold of my big cock, taking it with both hands again and pulling on it, thumbing the sticky head, causing some serious leakage.

"You leak as much as I come," he said, laughing, and I banged my ass against him.

"Easy," he whispered. "Easy easy easy." But I didn't want it easy. I fucked myself on his bone, grooving on the fiery slide it made up into my asshole, digging his wild balls bucking against my own wet skin bag sticking between my legs. I reached behind me and took one of his pale nips into an easy pinch, tugging on it and making him moan. "Oh, fuck," he said, warning me, and I steadied myself, ready for whatever he was about to give up.

"Dude," he said. "I'm going to—"

"Whatever, man, whatever."

"It's cool?" he asked, missing a beat, and I helped him pick it up, sliding my butt down his shiny pole. "Fuck," he breathed, and started ripping me apart, shredding my ass with power thrusts, gripping my dick like it was what kept him alive, and I felt myself jell, ass cheeks puffing, cock cream flying out of his fists.

Like I said, he held me later on in my bed, doing it all over again—this time by hand, which was cool too—and I had my head against his chest and it was like fucking beautiful, just fucking beautiful.

And like I said, he changed his fucking mind the next day, waking up straight again and totally not into guys. We stayed friends for a while, but it was fucking strange, you know, having had his dick up my ass. It was kind of hard looking at him and not dropping a wasted load into my shorts.

I went to the lake one day and looked across it. You couldn't see Canada, and that kind of made me feel better. I knew I was going to find someone I liked as much as Jeff, it was just going to take some time. Meanwhile, the new guy at U R Cool was giving me some dirty vibes and staring at my crotch, like, every time we closed, so who knows.

ƒ ƒ ƒ

A Business Trip

BY

CHASE PETERS

I sit at a hotel bar at the end of a long, tiring day. I am in a strange city where I know no one. I have never been here before, and with luck I will never be here again. I am bored. It's dinnertime, but I'm not hungry. I sip on a scotch on the rocks, thinking about being bored. I don't want to do anything—don't want to see a movie or read a book or eat or listen to music. Sex might be nice, but I prefer my boredom to anything else. I am beginning to enjoy it; I am feeling sorry for myself. I deserve my pity; I have earned it.

I know there should be more in my life than this vast ennui, but at the moment I don't want it, whatever it might be.

The bar is fairly crowded, but I am quite alone. No matter where I might be, I remain alone. I am the quintessential introvert. I am not good at conversation, and I am especially inept at small talk with strangers. I do not relate well to people—only to numbers. I am an accountant.

I finish my drink and signal the young bartender for another as I put a $10 bill on the bar. The bartender is not particularly attractive, but he is energetic and smiling, extroverted. I think I might enjoy sucking his cock, but I don't know how to approach him, how to get around the societal taboos. One does not say "May I suck your cock?" to a stranger.

Two middle-aged men on my left are arguing about the bond market. I conclude that they know very little about it but say nothing to them. They leave.

A woman sits next to me; she has long black hair and long black lashes, which I assume she bought at Kmart. She has heavy makeup on her face, but the lines show through anyway.

"Would you like to buy me a drink?" she asks.

"No," I respond.

"Please?" she persists.

"I would rather be alone than with you," I reply. I am not tactful either.

"Asshole!" she retorts as she leaves.

I redirect my attention to my drink, but the exchange has made me aware of the word asshole. I think about the young bartender's asshole; then I think about my own.

I know I have a very attractive ass. I have seen it many times in my three-panel mirror at home, and it seems to appeal to many people of both sexes. I frequently see them staring at it, admiration in their eyes. It occurs to me that within a week my ass will be 23 years old. Few asses have a CPA ticket at 23.

An elderly gentleman sits on one of the barstools vacated by the men involved in the bond discussion. The one next to me remains vacant.

It occurs to me that if my ass is 23 years old, my cock has to be the same age.

I think about my cock. I have a nice cock, I think, of more than adequate dimension, and it's quite serviceable.

I think about my last orgasm. It was yesterday morning in the shower. I remember my semen running down the tile wall.

It was in this hotel, 36 hours ago. It felt good, though it was not a particularly remarkable orgasm. One seldom has truly memorable orgasms alone.

My thoughts return to my loneliness, the absence of any normal social relationships in my life. I am the only child of deceased parents, victims of an auto crash over two years ago. Since then I have been quite unfettered by other people. I finished college quite young—20—but the few friends I have from there and high school are widely scattered and have grown largely out of touch. As an introvert I find it difficult to form new alliances of any importance with people of either sex.

I remember selling the house, most of its contents, and one of the cars and collecting a number of substantial life insurance checks. I owe a debt of gratitude to the guy who invented double indemnity. I took a job half a continent away and began my solitary existence.

I put away the memories of my brief history and allow my boredom to return. I sip my scotch, paying little attention to the other patrons.

A man sits next to me on my left. I can see him in the mirror ahead of me over the back bar; he is slightly older than I am—upper 20s, I guess. He is a good-looking chap in a blue plaid shirt and a black jacket. He orders a bourbon and Coke—not the hallmark of a sophisticate.

He sees, in the reflection, that I have been inspecting him. He turns to me and smiles. I am forced to reciprocate; to do otherwise would be rude.

"Hi," he says. "I'm Brad." He extends his hand.

I wonder how big Brad's cock is, but I don't ask.

"Hello, Michael here," I answer and return my attention to my drink, as though dismissing him.

"Do you come here often?" he asks.

"No. Never. I'm staying here for a few days." I wonder when he last had an orgasm and how he came to have it—whether he'd been alone or with someone.

"Oh? Where are you from?"

"Southern New York state," I reply, trying to reveal as little as possible, for no reason except my instinctive reticence.

About then I feel his knee brush against mine. I believe it is not an accident. He moves his knee off; I do not. I position my leg slightly closer to him.

"How long are you going to be in town?" he asks.

"Leaving tomorrow afternoon."

The knee returns for a slightly longer visit. I do not retreat. If he is making an approach, I elect to hold his interest till I decide whether I am interested in a liaison.

I turn to look directly at him; he looks right into my eyes. Now I have no doubt what he intends.

"You come here regularly, I assume?" I ask, a bit more stiffly than I intended to.

"Two, three nights a week," he replies.

"Then you can tell me where the men's room is."

"Sure. C'mon, I'll show you."

I follow him out of the barroom across the hall to the men's lounge. I stand at a urinal, unzip, and pull out my cock, which is flaccid but slightly expanded. He stands next to me and looks from my eyes to my cock and back to my eyes as he unbuckles his belt, opens his pants, and pulls down the elastic top of his briefs. He exposes his cock: fully erect, slightly over seven inches, I guess. It's well-proportioned, cut, and crowned with a thick black bush.

The sight of it is exhilarating; my own is up to full size in a few seconds. I am about a half-inch larger, but in every other way we are fairly well-matched. My hair is light blond and my bush more curly but equally thick.

He is about to make a comment when someone else comes into the room. We lean forward so that the sides of the urinals shield us from the view of the new arrival. We tuck away, wash our hands perfunctorily, and go back to the bar.

When we are seated again, the knee quickly returns, with

significantly more vigor than before.

I face ahead, looking at my drink.

"What are you thinking?" he asks.

"Actually, I was wondering what you are thinking," I respond.

"I was thinking that I want to suck your cock," he says softly, matter-of-factly.

I pause, not sure what to say. "I...I, ah, I'm not really much of a conversationalist. I'm not very good at this."

"You mean you haven't ever done this before?"

"No. I don't mean that. I've done it a few times before. I just feel a bit awkward with total strangers."

"You'll feel better when we get a little better acquainted."

"Maybe. Shall we have another drink?"

"Why don't we just go to your room?"

"I suppose we could do that. I'm in room 1726. I'd rather we didn't leave together, though, if you don't mind. I'll go up. Give me about five minutes' lead time, OK?"

"You're going to disappear on me, aren't you?" he asks.

"No, of course not. If I didn't want to, I'd tell you flat out. I'm not a cockteaser."

"OK, five minutes," he says, smiling.

"I'll be waiting."

"You can use the time to get naked."

"Yes, I suppose I could."

Times like this always make me uncomfortable. I never know what to say. I have been with my firm for almost two years, and I travel on business once or twice a month. Something like this happens about a third of the time. I remember that it doesn't take long for conversation to become unnecessary.

I ride the elevator to the 17th floor. I go to my room, hang up my suit jacket, remove my tie and shirt, and throw them into my open suitcase. My T-shirt follows quickly.

I sit on the edge of a chair to take off my wing tips and dark-blue socks. I am anticipating getting my cock sucked. I remove my pants and put them on a hanger. I am anticipating taking Brad's cock into my mouth.

I am standing at the closet door in my Calvin Kleins when the knock on the door come softly. I slip off my briefs before I open the door. My cock is very hard. I open, and Brad comes in quickly and closes the door behind him.

"Oh! Wow! You're a hunk, Michael!" He puts his arms around me and kisses me hard on the mouth. Before the kiss ends his right hand is holding my cock, stroking it slowly but firmly.

"Let me take your coat," I say when he lets go of me. I hang up his jacket as he unbuttons his shirt. He throws the rest of his clothes on the floor as he hurries to strip them off.

He pulls off his briefs to free his magnificent, rock-hard cock. It snaps up against his flat, hairless belly and stands at an approximate 2 o'clock position. I am trying to think of something nice to say about his cock, but before I can say a word he kisses me again, his tongue probing into my mouth like a starving snake.

We break apart and, hand in hand, go farther into the room near the king-size bed. Brad turns me around in a circle, looking me over, his eyes eager, full of lust, passion.

"God, Michael, you're a gorgeous son of a bitch! You've got a beautiful ass and a cock to write home about."

"You're very good-looking too, Brad. Almost overwhelmingly so."

I urge him onto the bed and lie next to him, facing him. We hold each other and kiss again. I let my hand play with his cock, stroking its length gently, and fondle his balls, already tightening up in his scrotum.

His hand is on my chest, playing with my nipples; it goes to my cock and balls and over my hip to my ass. We push our throbbing cocks against each other and kiss again, hands on each other's firm ass.

"I'm going for your cock now," I say.

"Yeah, go for it, and let me at yours."

"Please don't come in my mouth," I tell him. "I won't come in yours either."

"Oh, do it," he says. "I want your jizz."

"That's not a good idea, Brad. I'm negative, but you never know."

"Oral is very low-risk, Michael. Practically none. Please. I want to taste it."

"It's your decision, but don't shoot in mine, OK?"

"Sure."

I assume a sixty-nine position and put my hand on his cock to draw it to my mouth. I lick its tip around the flange and flick my tongue in the groove on its underside. Then I take it fully down my throat with all the suction I can muster. I look at his balls as I suck. It is a truly delightful experience; my mind is full of a strange mixture of admiration and adoration of the incredible appendage in my mouth. I allow my hand to play gently with his balls, fingers very lightly touching on the side where they meet his thigh. I can't resist putting my tongue on them, and I try to take them into my mouth. I can manage only one at a time, not because of their size but because they are clinging so tenaciously to the base of his fabulous, towering cock.

As I revel in the joy of his indescribably beautiful cock and balls, he is doing many of the same things to me. The touch of his hot, wet mouth on my cock is sensational, sending endless thrills and tingles through my body from my groin to my spinning brain and back again. The wondrous experience is in sharp contrast to the gray ennui that enveloped me as I sat at the bar less than an hour earlier.

I take my mouth off Brad's bone to watch him as he sucks my cock, taking tight, firm strokes up and down my shaft. He stops and buries his nose and mouth in my curly blond bush. He runs his tongue up the delta of fine hair on my belly and explores my navel, as though seeking nourishment. He returns

IT COULD HAPPEN

to my thick bush and raises his head, stretching a mouthful of curls to their full length, then allowing them to snap back, wet with his saliva. He returns to my cock, vacuuming slowly with as much suction as he can manage. He is obviously enjoying his task. The intense sensations return to my bone as his tongue flutters, like a hummingbird's wings, across the groove on the underside of my cock head.

I return to his plum-like dick head and take a few rapid strokes before slowing into a smooth, steady rhythm, hoping that I am pleasing him as much as he is pleasing me.

In a few minutes I release him again and bury my nose in his magnificent, thick black bush. I marvel at its uniform width all across his groin, from thigh to thigh, climbing up about three inches beyond the base of his shaft, where it abruptly stops. Above that line his body is hairless: He has no trail up his flat belly; the area up to and beyond his navel is as smooth as an infant's. I wonder if he has shaved it and run my fingers slowly and carefully over his belly up to the navel but find no trace of bristle. He is naturally smooth—rare and, to me, very beautiful.

The tingles in my cock are very intense now, and I know I will come soon. I am about to tell him, but I feel his cock grow slightly in my grip and harden even more, which seemed impossible. "I'm gonna shoot, Michael!" he exclaims. I take my mouth off his cock in time to watch a white ribbon of his juice fly skyward. It soars over four feet in the air, hovers for a tiny fraction of a second, and falls to become a wide white line on his chest and belly. Another white streak follows, nearly as high; a third, with slightly less force; a fourth, a foot or so; a fifth, a few inches; and a sixth oozes down the side of his shaft. The whole display lasts only a few seconds, but it is a beautiful, thrilling sight.

He is moaning softly, his head resting on my thigh again, savoring the erotic thrill of his release. I am filled with wonder at the magnificence of it.

262

He rests only briefly and applies his mouth to my cock again, sucking hard and furiously up and down my bursting shaft. I am overwhelmed by an electric charge that soars through me, from my aching balls and my cock through my whole body to my brain, and I feel the surge of thick semen shoot through my shaft into his eager mouth. Again and again I send the viscous seed into his mouth, the thrill nearly unbearable. I cry out in unintelligible sounds of passion as my orgasm possesses my being.

As I begin to recover my senses, I look up at Brad. He is still swallowing my ejaculate, a globule of white on the corner of his mouth, a thin trail of my fluid running down his chin. I collapse and lie flat, breathing deeply, consumed by the joy of it, feeling completely content, peaceful.

In a moment I rise and swing around so that we are lying face-to-face again. We kiss deeply; his tongue invades my mouth; I taste my own discharge. Brad's semen is squished between our chests and bellies. It is still warm. We fondle each other's cock and balls. Our cocks are softened but still quite large. Our balls have loosened, hanging lower.

We smile at each other, knowing we have shared our bodies, that we have given each other the ultimate pleasure. We kiss again, gently, tenderly but firmly, then again with more vigor.

Brad runs his hand over my chest and belly. I am wet with his discharge, as is he. His hand is quickly coated with the ooze, and he strokes my cock with it, giving me shivers of delight. I have to laugh.

He stops stroking for a moment.

"You like that?" he asks, grinning.

"Yes, I like that."

I run my hand in a circle around his chest and belly until it is slippery too, and I stroke his cock in return.

"Ooh!" he moans.

Our cocks begin to harden again in response to the stimuli.

"I think we'd better get up and take a shower," I suggest.

"You don't want to do it again?" He asks, wistfully.

"Oh, yes!" I answer without hesitation, "But not quite yet."

"OK," he responds, a note of disappointment in his voice.

We get up and go to the bath; I am still fascinated by his body—its strength, its sensuality, its beauty.

I turn on the water. We wait for the temperature to adjust. We kiss while we wait, and his hand goes for my cock again, then my balls.

I unwrap a small bar of soap, and we step into the warm stream. When we are both wet, I soap his body, starting with his pubic hair to get some lather, and wash his cock and balls, his smooth belly and chest, and his underarms, where I find abundant, thick black hair. I turn him slightly and wash the crack of his ass and let my fingers pass over his asshole.

I give the soap to Brad, and he washes me in much the same way. He lathers my pubic hair and massages the lather on my cock and balls, then works his way up the trail of light-blond fuzz to my navel. He runs handfuls of lather over the hair in my armpits and down my back into the crack of my ass. He probes for my asshole but does not penetrate. He returns to my cock and gives it full, long, even strokes up and down its length while using his other hand to play with my balls.

I am fully hard when he is finished, and we allow the water to rinse the soap from our impatient bodies. He too is completely erect, his cock standing tall, an inch or two off his belly.

We step out of the tub and begin to dry each other with thick towels. He dries my upper body first, front and back, then sits on the edge of the tub to dry my cock, balls, ass, and legs. He drops the towel and returns to my cock and takes it deep into his mouth, strokes it, quickly runs his tongue around the flange of its head, and flicks his tongue on the groove again and directly over the opening at its very tip. I am reluctant to stop him, but I do and urge him to his feet so I can dry him. I finish quickly, and we race to the disheveled bed.

Standing next to it, we kiss and kiss again. Then we lie down, assuming a sixty-nine position, and engulf each other's sweetly scented cock, the soapy aroma adding a new delight to our coupling.

This time we are more patient, relishing the luxurious titillation of cock in mouth and mouth on cock. The feast will not end so quickly this time. I stroke his shaft with my tongue for a time, then allow myself to lick its head, all around it and down the underside to his shrinking nuts, which I lick all over. I lift them gently to get my tongue on their back side, loving the feel of them on my tongue. I take one of them into my mouth and let my tongue snake its way around it, first clockwise, then counterclockwise. I repeat the process with the other one. I stop and release them, staring in awe at them and at the grandeur of his towering ivory cock.

Suddenly, it is gone! He has pulled it out of my grasp. I look up in shock. Brad is kneeling between my legs, sucking my cock with passion. He releases it and comes up to give me a hot, clinging kiss. He kisses his way down my body, stopping first at my left nipple. He takes it into his mouth, bites it gently, then swishes his tongue around it. He moves to the right one and does the same. He kisses his way down my chest to my navel, puts his mouth over it, and sucks, as though to draw it into his mouth. He puts his tongue inside it and probes. He kisses my belly, flattening the fine little hairs with his saliva. He stops at my bush and bites at the hair, then licks eagerly all around the base of my cock. He attacks my balls with his tongue and licks his way down below them, pushing his tongue into my ass crack, then back up to inhale my entire cock. I am amazed—mystified—that he can take nearly eight inches of thick flesh into his throat without choking. He is in a frenzy! He is utterly consumed with a need to absorb my cock.

He stops, looks at my face, and speaks in a hoarse whisper.

"Michael, I can't tell you how very beautiful you are. Your cock is a sculpted work of art!"

"Thank you, Brad. Now come kiss me, then give your cock back to me. I want it back in my mouth."

He obeys. I take his shaft and rest my head on his thigh as I suck on it unhurriedly, taking the tip and half its length. He has regained control of himself and sucks my cock in short, tight, gentle strokes, seeking only to deliver pleasure.

I pull my cock away from him and position myself to kiss him hard. I suck on his nipples and bite them gently. I invade his navel with my tongue and lave his hairless belly en route to the thick black fur above his cock. I circle his cock as he watches me. I ingest his balls and eat them one at a time, then both together. I work my way back up his cock and twirl my tongue around the flange.

Brad is moaning softly.

"Michael?"

"Hmm?" I say, not stopping.

"Come up here and fuck my face."

"I want to watch you come first."

"No. Come up here and fuck my mouth until you shoot your cream down my throat."

"Give me a couple of minutes to get you off."

"Do it quick."

I go for his cock with a mission. I suck hard and fast on the upper half of his raging hard-on, and in a minute he is making high keening sounds. The sounds grow louder, and I increase my efforts.

"Mmm! Ah, ah, a-a-ah! I'm gonna blow, Michael."

I can feel the expansion in the bottom tube in his cock and the inevitable hardening for the powerful squirts of seed. I put a generous deposit of saliva on his sword and stroke it firmly with my hand.

After two or three strokes, he erupts like a volcano. A rope of thick white jizz shoots from his throbbing tip, high into the air, and falls back on his chest and belly. I collect some of his slippery juice in my hand and massage his cock. He screams at the unbearable pleasure.

"Argh! Stop! Michael, stop! Ooh! Argh! Stop!"

I do not stop. I continue to rub his sperm into his cock until he rolls over, taking it out of reach.

"You bastard!" he laughs. "God, that was un-fuckin'-real." He is panting for breath, grinning broadly. He recovers, smiling. "Now it's your turn. Come up here and fuck my mouth until you squirt it way into my belly."

He slides himself up the bed and props his head on the pillows. I move up and straddle his chest, offering him my hard bone. I know I will not last long.

He opens wide, and I stick my cock inside. He clamps on to it, pressing it between his tongue and the roof of his mouth. I slide farther in and pull back. Soon I know I am at the point of no return.

"Here it comes!" I almost shout. "I'm going off! Ahnnghng! O-o-oh! Mmm!"

I allow my cock to empty into his mouth. He puts his arms around my ass, holding me tightly. He begins furiously sucking my blasting cock. His mouth is filled with my come, but he doesn't stop to swallow it; he keeps up the tight, fast sucking until I am begging him to stop. I try to pull my cock free, but he is holding me tightly. I cannot get away. He is getting even with me for torturing his cock after he came. I hold his head against the pillow and manage to free my cock. I collapse and let my body slide back so I can lie on top of him, my chest pressing against his chest. We kiss, and I taste my semen again.

My chest is covered with his seed once more, and I have it on my ass and balls from when I sat on him to fuck his face. I don't care. The sheets will be wet with it, and I will happily sleep in it. "That was some of the best sex I ever had," he murmurs and kisses me again.

"I don't have to qualify it. That was the best sex I've ever had, beyond a doubt," I reply. "It was incredible, so beautiful."

It Could Happen

"Do you think you could make it one more time?" he asks. "I don't know," I answer. "I haven't had dinner yet. Let's clean off and get some food. We can see what happens then."

We shower together again but don't fool around. We dress and go downstairs. The main dining room is closed, but the coffee shop is open. We have steaks with salad, French fries, and coffee.

Our conversation is easier now, more relaxed, and I am still intoxicated by the memory of the fabulous sex. I tell him what I do for a living. He tells me he's a nurse. We exchange full names, addresses, and phone numbers. I agree to call him if I get near here again. He says he has a week of vacation he must take before the end of the year. He agrees to come to New York over Thanksgiving, only three weeks away.

I have a plane ticket for tomorrow afternoon, but tomorrow is Friday. It's a full-fare ticket; I can change it to Sunday without charge. We agree to call the airline when we go back upstairs. We have already agreed we will go back upstairs.

I order a chocolate eclair for dessert. It is about as thick as his cock, though shorter, and it doesn't taste as good. I tell him that, and he laughs. I smile at his laugh.

We leave the coffee shop. Brad waits for me near the elevators while I go to the front desk to extend my stay to Sunday.

I meet him at the elevator. We enter the car. I press the button for 17. The door closes, and we kiss, groping each other's rising cock as the car ascends. We agree that he will meet me in the bar tomorrow afternoon and that he will stop to pick up some rubbers and K-Y.

We have one more tryst that night and are both sucked totally dry. It is late when Brad leaves. I am not bored. There is no oppressive ennui. I go to sleep thinking that tomorrow I will fuck his beautiful ass, and my ass will lose its virginity to his magnificent cock.

I have a friend.

f f f

The Opportunist

BY

DEREK ADAMS

She was the first thing I saw when I entered the café. No, make that the first thing I *heard*. She was in a booth across from the jukebox, waving her arms, her voice shrill. I couldn't hear her exact words, but I could tell from the tone of them that she was ripping some poor bastard a new asshole. Once I got about even with the table I glanced over and, sure enough, there was a guy with a totally hangdog look on his face, shoulders drawn up, eyes cast down, peeling the label off a bottle of Bud.

I stuck a quarter in the jukebox, picked out a couple of tunes I hoped would be loud enough to drown out the ranting blond, then took a seat at the counter and ordered me an ice-cold beer.

"Here you go, handsome."

"Thanks, Reba." Reba and I had been in high school together and had always been good pals. We had us a little thing going a few years back, but decided that we made better friends than lovers. Reba assured me that there was absolutely nothing wrong with my performance in the sack—it was just that she knew my heart wasn't really in it. That had led to one of them all-night confessionals with me spilling my guts to Reba. Turned out she'd known all along. And here I'd thought I was being so clever about slipping away to the city on the weekends so I could enjoy a little man-to-man action.

"Things ain't sounding any too good over there, are they?" I hazarded.

"Maybe not," Reba allowed, "but they're not looking so bad, are they, Clay?" I shrugged my shoulders noncommittally. She rested her elbows on the counter and lowered her voice. "I've seen more than my share of men, but rarely have I seen one engineered quite so well from the ground up. God must've been in a fine mood the day that boy was born. Oh, yes."

I had to agree with Reba—there was no faulting the broad shoulders, the biceps straining against the sleeves of his shirt or the full curve of his denim-encased thighs. The fellow also had a nice profile—jutting chin, prominent nose, and smallish pink ears that I wouldn't have minded nibbling on for a starter course.

"Well, you can just shove it up your ass sideways, Lenny!" The blond gal jumped up from the booth, sending Lenny's beer flying. She spun on her heel and stalked toward the front door. "What the hell are you two looking at?" she snarled as she stormed past me and Reba.

"Y'all come on back now," Reba crooned. "And kiss my butt," she added under her breath. She grabbed a towel and went over to mop up the mess the blond had left behind. I slipped behind the counter and pulled a beer out of the cooler—one of the ones Reba kept tucked back by the refrigeration coils just for me. I practiced a smile in the mirror above the cash register, then made a beeline for Lenny.

"Here you go, buddy," I said, setting the beer down in front of him.

"Huh?" He looked up at me, obviously still dazed.

"I'd like to buy you a beer. Mind if I sit down?" I eased into the booth without waiting for his reply.

"Got no moss growing on your back, Clay Phillips," Reba muttered. "Not by a long shot." I flashed her a big grin and she shook her head. Before she walked off, she mouthed something at me and flicked her eyes toward Lenny.

Opportunist. That's what the word had been. Reba had first pulled it on me the other day. She'd been reading a magazine article and told me it fitted me to a tee. What it meant, near as I could figure, was a guy who recognized a situation and took advantage of it. Now, I don't know about you, but I don't think there's anything wrong with that. I mean, it's not like I was going around holding a gun to anybody's head or anything like that. I just recognized in Lenny a guy who was in need of some comfort. I thought of about 13 different kinds of comfort I could offer, and a cold beer was as good a place to start as any.

"Thanks for the beer, mister," Lenny said, eyeing me woefully.

"Clay," I replied, introducing myself. "Clay Phillips."

"Hey, Clay." Lenny shook my hand. He had a nice grip. "I'm afraid I ain't going to be much company. Me and my gal just broke up."

"Don't need to talk to be company, Lenny," I assured him. "I know what you're going through, buddy." I heard a muffled snort from Reba, but I didn't look over at her.

"I don't know what it is, but that Sue Ann..." Lenny was off and running. All I needed to do was supply a sympathetic ear and keep the beer flowing. About an hour into it, I signaled Reba and ordered us a couple of steaks. I sure didn't want Lenny to pass out on me. By the time we got to the end of Lenny's relationship, we had finished the steaks and pretty much put an end to Reba's supply of ice-cold beer.

"Why don't you come back to my place?" I asked while we were paying the bill. He had confided that he was going to be spending the night in the cab of his truck. I hated to think of a big strong guy like Lenny folded up in the cab of a truck like a pretzel. It just didn't seem right somehow.

"You sure it ain't a bother, Clay?"

"Hell, no," I assured him, clapping a hand on his shoulder. The man was a rock—a warm, flexible rock.

"You're a pal, Clay," he said, his fingers closing around my upper arm like a vise. I flexed and he gripped harder. I took that as a good sign.

When we got to my place, I left Clay in the living room while I made a trip to the can. Before returning, I detoured through my bedroom and stripped down to my boxers. What the hell—it was hot and I was hoping for it to get a lot hotter before the night was over.

"Just make yourself comfortable, Lenny," I suggested when I sauntered through the living room on my way to the kitchen. "I don't stand on no ceremony around here. Want a beer?"

"Sure, Clay." I popped the tops of a couple of longnecks and returned in time to watch Lenny peel his shirt off one of the prettiest torsos it had been my pleasure to see in many a day. Long, dark hairs feathered up over his collarbone and swirled around his fat brown nipples. A narrow trail of the same silk trickled down the middle of his flat belly.

"You mind if I take off my jeans?"

"Suit yourself, Lenny," I replied nonchalantly, watching as buttons slowly popped, revealing a crotch bulge upholstered in scarlet.

"Sue Ann got me these," Lenny announced, eyeing his shorts uncertainly. "Ain't much to 'em." He wriggled out of his jeans, pushing them down over his thighs, then his calves. When he bent down to take off his boots, I got me a dynamite view of the twin mounds of pale flesh that had been left high and dry by the tiny triangle of fabric that made up the back of his briefs.

When he stood up again, I saw that the designers hadn't wasted a lot of material up front either.

"Hey, man, on you they look good." I handed Lenny his beer. He took it, then his eyes zeroed in on my chest.

"Whoa, Clay! That is wild, man!" I'd had my left nipple pierced on one of my recent trips to the city. "Does it hurt?"

"Hell, Lenny, it was like paving a four-lane highway from my tit to my crotch."

"Can I...can I touch it?" This was almost too good to be true. I nodded, watching his fingers as he slowly reached out to me. When he touched the thick steel ring, every muscle in my body flexed. He slipped his forefinger through the hoop, rubbing his nail against the rubbery point of my tit. He tugged gently and my pec twitched. "I've got no feeling in my tits," he remarked, twisting the hoop from side to side.

"I don't believe that," I countered, wondering whether he'd give me a chance to prove my point. "You know how good it feels when you play with your nuts?" His eyes got wide and he blushed scarlet. "Well, your tits feel every bit as good." He shook his head stubbornly. "I can prove it to you."

He didn't speak, so I took the initiative. I reached up and grazed the thick points of his nipples with my callused thumbs. From the way he jumped, you'd have thought somebody'd crammed a cattle prod up his ass. I half expected him to put the couch between us, but he didn't. Once he'd stopped weaving around, he was right back where he'd started. I touched him again, only this time I pinched his thick tits and held on so I wouldn't lose him.

Lenny's eyelids drooped, and he let out a low moan when I began gently tugging on the sensitive tabs of flesh. I kept waiting for him to grip my wrists and pull my hands away, but he didn't. All he did was lean forward slightly when I tugged, then rock back when I pushed him away from me.

After a couple of minutes of this, Lenny grunted and I felt something hot and wet pressed against my belly, right above the waistband of my boxers. I looked down. Lenny's cock had escaped from his skimpy shorts and was now spanning the distance from his body to mine. It was a nice cock, thick and stubby, jutting out of a bush of gleaming brown curls.

"Uh...sorry," he stammered, grinning at me goofily. If he was embarrassed, it wasn't slowing him down any. "I...uh...I must be a little drunk."

"Yeah, Lenny," I replied. "Me too." Just so I wouldn't look like a piker, I reached into my shorts and fished my cock out through the fly. It was growing but hadn't quite risen to attention.

"Oh." Lenny was looking down. "Yours is bigger than mine."

"Not so much," I replied modestly. "Yours is prettier."

"Huh?"

"What I mean is, it's more in proportion. I think it's a real nice dick."

"I...uh...I like yours, too." Lenny all of a sudden got this real serious look on his face. "I...uh...I don't think I should be doing this, Clay."

"You ain't doing anything, Lenny," I countered, more or less truthfully. "You're horny, right?" He nodded. "This feels good, right?" I twisted his nipples. He nodded again. "I just want you to feel better, man. You've had a hell of a day." He blinked his big brown eyes at me. "Tell you what, you give me about 10 minutes of your time, and we'll see whether or not I can put a big old smile on that mug of yours. OK?"

Lenny nodded one last, fateful time, and I sank to my knees, stripping his red shorts off in one smooth move. I gripped him firmly by the waist, letting my fingers curl against his delectable, rock-hard buns. I took a deep breath, bobbed forward, and started working on the fat purple knob that capped his spike. When I made contact, he sucked air so hard it damn near made my hair stand on end, but he made no effort to extract himself from my hot mouth. I tightened my lips around the rim of the crown and began to poke at his piss hole with the tip of my tongue.

One pretty consistent thing about straight guys—they don't get much first-rate head. That, once you get 'em in the right setting, makes 'em easy pickings for a dude who knows how to suck cock. Well, the setting was right, and Lenny's hot little rod had come to the attention of a real pro. I lunged forward and butted his belly with my forehead. He grunted, and his balls clipped my chin.

While I was doing my best to suck Lenny's brains out through his dick, I was also letting my fingers take a walk over the silky terrain of his backside. I had no doubt that the flawless globes of flesh were uncharted territory. As my wandering digits got closer and closer to his crack, the atmosphere got warmer and more humid. When I touched the tightly puckered ring of muscle that kept him from taking on water when he sat in the tub, his dick damn near poked a hole in the roof of my mouth. He wiggled around a little but made no effort to stop me.

Encouraged, I sucked his bone a few minutes longer, then left it standing tall while I burrowed between his furry thighs. I polished his knotted balls for a bit, then pushed along the swollen ridge that ran back to ground zero. I coaxed his feet apart and wriggled my way between his legs, spreading them like a wishbone. When I flipped myself around and looked up, there it was, all tight and pink, encircled by a mossy ring of brown fuzz, throbbing with his pulse. Paradise dead ahead!

I tore into his ass like a pig rooting for truffles. Poor bastard didn't have a clue what was happening till I had my tongued jammed in deep. Just to make sure I didn't lose him, I reached between his legs and grabbed his cock, pulling it down and back. He leaned forward and braced his hands on the coffee table, head down, eyes closed, mouth gaping. I punched my tongue up his chute, then took a long slow lick down the length of his cock. It flexed and drooled a big glob of thick, clear lube. I lapped it up and licked my way back up to his twitching asshole.

After several similar round-trips, Lenny's hole was loose enough for me to slip a finger into him beside my plunging tongue. I glanced at his upside-down face. The fucker was in total bliss, shaking his head from side to side, moaning incoherently. I blew a little air up him and sneaked in a second digit, then a third. I twisted the plug of fingers deep and wiggled them. I made contact with his prostate and he quivered.

"Lenny," I cooed, still pumping my hand in and out of his ass. His eyes fluttered open. "Reach in that box on the table and grab me one of those packets." He fumbled for the box, pulled out a foil-wrapped rubber, and eyed it dubiously. "Wanna open it for me?" He gripped a corner of the packet between his teeth and ripped it open, cupping the glistening rubber in his palm. "Wanna put it on me?"

"Huh?"

"You know how to put a rubber on, don't you?" Another nod. "Just like doing one on yourself, only you grab my dick." He hesitated briefly, but once he touched me his grip was firm. He plopped the lubed circle on the tip of my prick and rolled it till he ran out of rubber.

"Looks like a big old sausage, man," he said, chuckling softly. "What you gonna...aahhh!" I cut off his question when I jammed my fingers in him up to the webbing. I finger-fucked him briefly, then stopped moving. Lenny's hips took over, and he continued to bounce up and down on my hand.

I don't think he could've sworn to the exact moment I substituted cock for fingers. I simply switched tools and slid up into his hungry hole, pushing ahead slow and easy. He was hot and tight inside, his ass ring gripping me firmly so I wouldn't accidentally slide out. Lenny continued to wiggle, and I started wiggling myself, watching my latex-sheathed prick disappear between those milky globes of flesh.

Lenny started tipping forward, and I grabbed him by the hips. He put his hands on top of mine and took a quick inventory. "What...?" he muttered.

"Just massaging that old hot spot, buddy." I crammed my knob hard against his prostate, and the muscles in his back danced. He looked back at me uncertainly. I pumped him again.

"Oh, man." His head drooped, and his subsequent conversation was confined to a series of increasingly noisy groans as I kept on savaging his lush ass.

I stopped one pump shy of shooting, focusing on the tickle in my gut that mounted in intensity till it became unbearable. I pulled out slow, felt the pressure build, then shoved it back in up to the hilt as I started to spew. I reached under Lenny, grabbed his stiffer in both hands, and pumped him off, savoring the sensations as his whole body quivered and convulsed. I stayed behind him, smearing jism over his belly till he spasmed and spit my cock out of his hole.

The following Saturday I was sitting at the counter talking to Reba when Lenny and Sue Ann moseyed in and slid into the booth across from the jukebox. Lenny waved at me and smiled. Sue Ann glanced my way but did neither.

"Looks like those two are speaking again," Reba observed, propping her elbows on the counter. Sue Ann's voice rose in volume. "For now." Reba pulled her order pad out of her apron. "Better go over there and take their order while I've got the opportunity."

"Good idea," I agreed. "It's very important not to let opportunity pass you by. Never can tell when you'll get another chance."

"Maybe not, Clay," Reba replied, "but I'm sure you'll be ready and waiting." She shook her head, grabbed a coffeepot and set sail across the café. While I sat there listening to Sue Ann's voice rise and watching Lenny's shoulders droop, a big old shit-eating grin struggled to take over the bottom half of my face.

fff

Plaza del Sol

BY

SEAN WOLFE

I had been in Guadalajara, Mexico, for nine months. I had a good job teaching English at a private school. Made lots of money, had lots of friends, got lots of sun. Being 25 years old and having blond hair and blue eyes made me more than a little popular with the cute Mexican boys and, to my horror, even the girls. I did my best to put the girls off as much as possible—and to get it on with as many of the cute boys as possible. It wasn't hard. I never dated a student of mine, but once I was no longer their teacher, it was open territory and there was never a shortage of volunteers. The clubs were always packed with lines way out the doors, and I never went home alone unless I wanted to.

Not that it was all about sex. I did make a lot of really good friends—coworkers, straight and gay friends from the theater and dance groups I often went to see perform, friends from the clubs.

But after nine months I began to become a little bored. That, and I was a little homesick. I worked 10 hours a day during the week and five on Saturdays. Though I loved my job, I was getting a little burned-out and started thinking about returning to the States.

We had two-hour lunch breaks at the school. There were a number of fast-food restaurants right around the school that I visited every once in a while. But I usually went to a little family-owned restaurant located in Plaza del Sol, a shopping mall three blocks from the school. Every day they had three homemade meals you could choose from as entrées. They were all cheap, delicious, and served with fresh tortillas and endless glasses of *agua fresca,* a delicious drink made with water and fresh fruit. After eating lunch I would take a book and sit in the open courtyard and read for an hour or so until it was time to return to the school.

I was always so engrossed in my books that I never realized the intense cruising that went on in that open-air mall. On this sweltering day in July, however, I finished my book very early after lunch and contented myself with watching the action and scenery around me. Sitting on one of the park benches that surrounded a fountain at the main crossroad in the mall, I was given a fantastic view of the goings-on around me: mall employees rushing back to work or, like me, taking a leisurely break; high school kids and working moms getting in some shopping; little old ladies sipping lemonade.

And then there were "the boys." It amazed me how many young men, anywhere from 15 or so to about 30, roamed aimlessly up and down the sidewalk, staring each other down. There was nothing subtle about their movements. They nodded at one another, raised their eyebrows, licked their lips, and groped their crotches. Several of them cruised me very openly, some of them even daring to sit at one of the benches next to mine and flirt with me there. I was amused but had no place to take them, since I lived quite a ways from the mall, so I pretty much ignored most of them. I watched with fascination, as they performed their mating rituals in front of me, and thought about returning to San Francisco.

Then Javier sat down right next to me. I'd seen him a couple of times before eating lunch at the same little restaurant. He was always wearing a name tag that tattled he was a sales clerk at Suburbia, the Mexican equivalent of Target. He was tall and very solidly built, with straight black hair and hazel eyes accented by long curly eyelashes. Twin dimples pierced each cheek that was braced by a strong jawline and a cleft chin. He was young, probably about 19 or 20, and adorable. I'd stared shamelessly at him when I saw him, trying to get his attention, but whenever I looked at him he was either not looking at me or he'd look away suddenly. I never pursued it more than that.

But now here he was, sitting right next to me. He was reading a book and finishing his lemonade. I nodded at him as he sat down, and he nodded back before he began reading— no smile, no licking of the lips or groping of the groin. So I went back to my people-watching, trying hard not to think about Javier.

I wasn't very successful. I kept sneaking a peek at him through the corners of my eyes. I could smell his sweet cologne, and after a while I swear I could distinguish his body heat from the 98-degree humid heat of Mexican summer. I'd sat there for about 15 minutes when I suddenly felt his knee brush mine. The first time, it was just a quick brush, and he pretended to reposition his feet. The next time, he let it rest there for a few minutes before moving it. The third time, it rested against mine for a moment, and then he began applying pressure against my leg.

I looked over at him. He continued reading his book as his leg pushed harder against mine. I looked away quickly and kind of gave my head a quick little shake. I looked back at Javier, and this time he looked me right in the eyes and smiled. His beautiful pink lips parted to reveal perfect pearl-white teeth and those drop-dead gorgeous dimples. My heart did a triple beat, and I quickly looked away. With just the batting of his eyelashes and the dimple display, he was causing my dick to stir in my jeans.

When I looked back at him, he marked his place in the book he was reading and closed it as he got up to leave. I panicked. My heart dropped to my stomach, I stopped breathing, and I felt my face flush hotly. Where was he going? Why didn't I talk to him when I had the chance? Why couldn't I live much closer?

He brushed my leg again as he deliberately walked in front of me rather than going around his side of the bench. I watched him leave, and saw that after a few steps he turned back around to look at me. He smiled that lethal smile again and nodded for me to follow him.

I couldn't breathe. This was one of the most gorgeous men I'd seen while in Mexico. He seemed shy and sweet and sexy and mysterious, all at once. And now he was motioning for me to follow him. I turned to see which direction he was heading. He stopped right outside a door marking the men's room, made sure I saw where he'd gone, and then disappeared into the door.

I stood up slowly and took a couple of deep breaths before forcing my feet to move, one foot in front of the other. When I reached the restroom door, I saw it was a stairway that went up a narrow hallway, winding around one corner before opening up into the rest room. I took the steps two at a time and walked into the rest room before I could chicken out. Once inside, I had to stop and catch my breath. It was a fairly large bathroom: eight urinals on either side of the room at the far end, with six stalls between the door and the beginning of the urinal section on one side. Across from the stalls was a bank of sinks and paper towel dispensers .

The doors to each of the stalls were locked, and I could hear slurping noises coming from behind them. Javier stood alone at the wall of urinals on one side, and two young guys stood next to each other on the other side. They'd moved their hands back to their own tools when I walked in, but it took them only a few seconds to size me up and move back to jerking each other off in their urinals.

Javier smiled when he saw me walk in and then moved the shy smile down to his cock. He was standing a few inches from the urinal, showing me his cock. It was still soft but already long and thick, with a soft sheath of foreskin covering its head. He watched it himself as he shook it a couple of times and then looked up at me, still smiling, as he began moving his foreskin slowly back and forth over the shaft.

He nodded at me to take the urinal next to him. I gulped deeply as I noticed his cock hardening in front of my eyes, then walked dazedly to the pisser next to him. I pulled out my half-hard dick and pointed it into the urinal, looking straight ahead and pretending to pee.

Javier gave a quiet "psst," and when I looked up he winked at me, his eyebrows motioning toward his cock. I ventured a look down there, and my knees almost buckled beneath me. His cock was fully hard now, and a drop of precome hung loosely at the head. It was long, maybe nine inches or so, and very thick. When he pulled the foreskin back, I saw a long throbbing vein run the length of the top of his dick. My mouth was dry as cotton, and I forced my eyes back to the wall in front of me.

I heard some of the stall doors open, and their occupants began to meander out one by one. I was getting nervous and started to put my cock back into my jeans when I heard Javier cough conspicuously. I looked over at him, and he shook his head no and nodded toward my dick. Another man, about 40, came into the rest room and took the last urinal on our side of the room. He peed quietly as I leaned as far as I could into the urinal so he couldn't see my shriveling dick. Javier didn't seem to care one way or the other and remained where he was. The older man finished relieving himself and left the rest room along with the last of the stall occupants.

The two boys behind us were still there. The shorter of the two was on his knees sucking his friend, who was leaning against the stall next to him. The sucker kept darting his eyes toward the door, watching out for anyone coming in. They apparently did not think of Javier or myself as a threat.

Javier turned away from me and, with his dick still hard and sticking out of his jeans, walked to the restroom door. He pulled a piece of paper from his back pocket and used a piece of gum from his mouth to stick it to the door. Then he shut the door and stuck the chair which was occupied by a lavatory attendant except during lunch under the handle.

I watched this with stunned silence and listened to my heart pounding in my chest as Javier walked smoothly back toward me, his huge, uncut dick leading the way. When he reached me, he put his hands on either of my shoulders and slowly pushed me back until I was leaning against the wall.

My cock was fully hard now and throbbing uncontrollably in front of me. Javier looked me directly in the eyes, smiled, and leaned forward to kiss me. His lips were soft and warm. I parted my lips slowly as he licked them and slid his tongue into my mouth. The room grew very hot, and I felt a little dizzy as he kissed me passionately. I don't usually precome, but I felt a drop slithering out of my cock head. I was afraid I'd come just from Javier's kiss, but he broke it before I did.

The two kids behind us were moaning and groaning, and Javier and I looked over at them. The kid on his knees was shooting his load onto the floor as he continued to suck his friend furiously. The taller guy let out a loud grunt and pulled his dick out of the shorter guy's mouth. He yanked on it twice, and we saw him shoot a huge load onto his friend's face. Spurt after spurt of thick white come covered the kid's face. He turned his face away after three or four sprays, and the jism shot past his ear and onto the floor.

IT COULD HAPPEN

Watching this turned Javier on more than I could ever have imagined, and before I knew what was happening, Javier pushed my shoulders down, forcing me to the floor. Before I could stand back up or figure out what was going on, I felt a shot of hot sticky come land between my nose and my mouth. I looked up at Javier's dick. He wasn't even touching it at all, yet it was shooting a load almost equal to that of the tall guy across from us, all onto my face. He moaned loudly and just let it shoot onto me without touching his dick. I didn't turn my head away; I loved the feel of the hot wet come as it hit my face.

Javier hooked his hands under my arms and pulled me up to my feet again. He kissed me on the lips, licking his own come from my face and sliding his tongue covered with his cooling jizz back into my mouth. I sucked on his tongue hungrily, swallowing his come and making my own cock throb spastically.

The two guys who'd shot their loads just a minute earlier walked over to us and began undressing us both. I looked around nervously, and the younger and shorter of the two boys took my chin in his hand and kissed me strongly, letting me know we were safe and wouldn't be bothered. When we were completely naked, our two new friends dropped to their knees and began sucking us at the same time.

I can't vouch for the kid sucking on Javier's huge dick, but the one with his lips wrapped around mine must have had a Ph.D. in cock sucking. He swallowed my thick cock in one move and somehow had eight or 10 tongues licking the head, the shaft, the balls, all while he moved his mouth up and down the length of it.

Javier leaned over and kissed me while we fucked the boys' mouths in front of us. It didn't take long before I felt the come boiling in my balls. I moaned softly and sucked harder on Javier's tongue as the kid on his knees in front of me sucked and swallowed my dick like it had never been sucked before.

Javier sensed that I was close and broke our kiss as he pulled the young guy off my dick and onto his feet.

He turned me around so that my back was to him and pushed me gently up against the wall. He told our friends to do the same, and they did as they were told; the older and taller boy against the wall as the younger guy moved behind him. He and Javier bent down and played follow-the-leader.

Javier began kissing behind my right knee, nibbling and licking his way up the back of my legs until he got to my ass. He kissed and licked my ass cheeks one by one, then gently spread them apart. I was so hot by then, I could barely breathe. I wanted him to fuck me so badly, but when I pushed my ass closer to his face, he just licked it again and blew a cool breath on the exposed hole.

I looked over and saw the short kid was playing the same cat-and-mouse game with his partner, who was as delirious as I was. His eyes were closed, and he was moaning loudly as he pushed his tight, smooth ass closer to his partner's teasing mouth.

Javier reached between my legs and pulled gently on my hard cock as his fingers spread my ass cheeks and teased my hole. I grunted my delight, and he finally decided to reward me with what I wanted. I felt his nose press against the small of my back and a second later felt his hot tongue tickling the outside ring of my sphincter. I almost shot my load right then, but tensed up my body and counted to 10 to avoid it. Javier moved his left hand from my cock so he could use both hands to keep my cheeks spread open. He slowly worked his tongue around the outside of my ass for a couple of minutes, and then slid it very slowly inside, snaking it in, then out, then back in a little deeper each time. I was going nuts and noticed the guy next to me was too.

The younger of our new friends was really getting into licking his friend's ass. I looked down and saw his cock was rock-hard and dancing wildly between his legs. He had a nice cock, about the size of mine but uncut. Huge amounts of pre-come dripped from the head of his dick, enough to make me wonder if he'd come again.

Javier and his counterpart stood up simultaneously. They must have had some secret code, because they moved together as one from the moment Javier turned me around. The younger kid turned his partner around just as Javier did the same to me and directed me and my counterpart to kiss. We did, very deeply and passionately, as Javier and our other friend dug through their jeans pockets for condoms. As we kissed, the guy in front of me reached for my hand and placed it on his cock. It was huge, almost as large as Javier's. I wrapped my hand around his dick and began sliding his foreskin up and down his thick pole.

He moaned and gyrated his hips, grinding his cock into and out of my fist. His dick was hot and throbbing strongly. My mouth watered with desire. I wanted to suck him so badly, I could almost taste him in my mouth, even as my hand pumped him gently closer to orgasm.

Javier leaned forward across my back and kissed my ear.

"¿Qué quieres, papi?" he whispered huskily in my ear. He had his nerve—asking me what I wanted as he gently pressed his huge dick against my ass.

I shuddered in response and pressed my ass harder against his hot cock. He gave me a tiny laugh and bit my ear softly to let me know he'd gotten the message. Then he moved his head back down to my ass and licked the hole some more, lubing it up to take his mammoth dick. As he stood up again and positioned the huge head of his cock against my twitching hole, he bent me over, indicating he wanted me to suck the guy next to me.

Never one to argue with authority, I leaned over and licked the head of the cock of the guy next to me. It was covered with precome as well, salty and sweet at the same time, and slick as silk. I'd never been with anyone in the States who dripped much precome, but at that very moment I decided I was quite fond of the sweet, sticky stuff. I licked the guy's head until it was clean from stickiness, then took a deep breath as I swallowed his cock all the way to his balls.

On my second time swallowing the giant cock I felt Javier shove the head of his big dick just inside my ass. I tensed up and knew the boys in front of me were doing exactly the same thing, judging by the deep animal groan escaping from the throat of the guy I was sucking off. It took me a moment to relax with Javier's throbbing pole up my ass, but I finally did and resumed the task of sucking my new friend dry.

I think it may have been a little awkward for the kid fucking the guy next to me, since my guy had to stand up straight so I could suck and swallow his dick. The kid fucking him kept pulling out of his ass and trying to find better positions to fuck him in. He must have signaled Javier, because after only a couple of minutes Javier pulled me into a standing position. He had absolutely no problem whatsoever staying inside me. My ass wrapped itself around his long, thick pole and sucked it further inside. He slid into me in long, slow strides, as the shorter guy to my side smiled gratefully and bent his friend down toward my cock.

I closed my eyes as I felt Javier's cock slide into my hungry ass and a hot, wet mouth envelop my dick. I'd never been fucked and sucked at the same time, but it took no time whatsoever to realize it was my new favorite position. The kid getting fucked while sucking me was every bit the expert cocksucker his friend was. He and Javier found their rhythm with me almost instantly. Javier's thick cock sliding into my ass just as the guy sucking me slid off my cock.

I looked over at the guy with his dick inside my cocksucker's ass. He was pumping wildly, sweat dripping from his brow. He closed his eyes and moaned loudly, just as Javier was doing. I could tell they were both close. I was too—and trying desperately to hold back my orgasm.

It Could Happen

I was up to about eight in my silent counting game when the guy fucking my cocksucker pulled out suddenly. He ripped the condom from his cock and pointed it at his friend's back. The first shot rushed past his friend's head and landed on Javier's chest. Javier grunted loudly, and I felt his cock grow unbelievably thicker inside my ass. It started contracting wildly inside me, and I knew that he was shooting a huge load into my ass as the kid across from me shot his hot load all over his friend's back and ass.

Javier kept his cock inside my ass as he came. That, and seeing the other kid shoot, was all it took for me. I pulled my cock from the other guy's reluctant mouth, shooting my own load in every direction. Some of it landed on the guy's face, some on the floor, some in the air, and some even on the kid fucking my cocksucker. I'd never shot such a large, wild load, and I laughed a little as it just kept pouring out of my dick. When I laughed, my ass muscles squeezed Javier's cock and sent shocks of pleasant pain up my ass and back.

The guy who had been sucking my dick suddenly stood up and tensed his entire body. He cried out loudly as wave after wave of thick white come shot out of his dick and splattered against the wall in front of him. We all just watched in amazement as it kept coming and coming. It seemed there was enough to fill a glass.

I started laughing first, which caused me so much pain, I had to pull Javier's cock out of my ass. Unbelievably, he was still hard. Then the others started laughing as well. We all leaned against a wall or sink and caught a few breaths. There was come everywhere; on the wall, the floor, a sink, all of us. The air smelled strongly of it. Pity the next people who came in here to actually use the rest room!

Javier removed his condom carefully and laid it on the sink next to the paper towel holder. It was almost completely filled with his load, and as he laid it on the sink, a good amount spilled out onto the counter. All four of us looked at it and began to giggle again as we got dressed.

We all kissed one another and walked out the door together. As I passed through the door, I pulled off the note Javier had placed there earlier. I wanted a memento of the best fuck of my life. I stuck it in my pocket and watched as Javier ran back to his work and the other two friends departed in separate directions. I started walking back to school and pulled the paper out to read it on my way: TEMPORARILY OUT OF SERVICE.

I smiled to myself, doubting the rest room had seen that much service in quite a while.

$f\,f\,f$

Str8 Guyz

BY

DOMINIC SANTI

I was starting to wonder if I'd been watching too many pornies. Sure, my JO sessions were great. Seeing all those naked dicks really turned me on. I was getting worried, though. At 22, I still hadn't figured things out. I mean, I liked having sex with girls. But I shot buckets watching guys get fucked. I imagined it was me—a buff, blond, and maybe a little bi-curious football player—throwing my legs in the air and getting my ass plowed. Since I'd never been with another guy, I didn't know if I really wanted what I thought I wanted. But I loved jerking off while watching guys have sex. I'd rented every pornie the local video store carried.

"You realize these are, um, all different?" the slender red-headed clerk had asked politely the first time he scanned a mixed basket of het, gay, bi, and "all-anal orgies" for me.

"I'm versatile," I mumbled, blushing as I grabbed my bag and hurried out the door. After a few weeks, though, Stan and

I got to know each other pretty well. He was gay, and he got off on recommending all the hottest new vids to me. I kind of practiced cruising with him, making eye contact, trying to scope out his crotch without looking away or blushing too much despite how cute he was.

Stan was the one who'd put the flier for the local gay chat line in my bag, along with a couple of het vids and the new all-male flick *Silver Foxes*. I was trying to hide the boner I'd gotten from looking at the cover. Hunky older guys turned me on something fierce.

"One of my online buddies worked on this video, dude. He's the film editor for Studline Video—a real daddy type in his 40s." Stan stared pointedly at my crotch as he handed me my change. "I told him I knew somebody who was going to love *Silver Foxes*—a straight boy who rented every kind of smut video and had a real thing for older guys. That's you, Michael, my friend."

"Oh, man," I blushed, moving my hard-on even closer to the counter. "Why did you tell him that?" I wanted to grab my stuff and run, but I needed to wait until my dick settled down so that I wouldn't embarrass myself going past the old ladies perusing the G-rated section.

"Studclippr thought it was way kinky, dude. He said he'd like to meet you." Stan smiled innocently as he passed me my vids. "We'll be online around 11 tonight. Address is with your receipt—if you're not, um, too busy with these."

My face flaming, I clutched the bag in front of my crotch and rushed out the door. To make a long story short, the videos got me so turned on that I went to the chat room. Stan made the introductions. Studclippr and I really hit it off online and also later when I called him on the phone. I came twice before I finally blurted that I wanted him to really fag me out.

Studclippr laughed until he almost choked. He promised to turn me into "a perfect little pussy boy." Since I was so nervous about actually doing it, though, we agreed to wait until Saturday night to get together so that his boyfriend would be out with some buddies and we'd be alone.

Studclippr—Don, actually—lived a couple of towns over. When I got to his house I was surprised that he looked just the way he'd described himself in his profile: a trim, muscular 6 foot 4 with quiet hazel eyes and thick black hair streaked with silver—on his head and peeking out of the front of his half-open cotton shirt. I'd thought everybody lied in their profiles. I mean, there's no way my cock is 10 inches! But Don was a real hunk. My dick started twitching the minute I saw him.

Even his house reflected his style. It was relaxed and comfortable, with bookcases lining the walls and a large overstuffed leather couch facing a huge oak entertainment center. The electronic equipment filling the shelves was awesome. It had all the latest bells and whistles. LEDs blinked everywhere, and a killer sound system was playing cool techno tunes, just like in the sound tracks to my favorite pornies. The whole room reminded me of a kick-ass movie set.

I was getting really nervous, though. My hand shook a little as I took the bourbon Don offered me. I sipped slowly, trying to calm my jitters, concentrating on the familiar, reassuring burn in my throat. We sat together on the couch, me perched stiffly on the edge of the cushion. Don casually rested his arm on the couch's back while I fidgeted next to him.

Finally, he set his drink on the coffee table and said, "Do you want to talk for a while first?"

"Um, about what?" I asked, rubbing a sweaty hand on my jeans.

"Never mind," he laughed softly. He lifted the glass from my fingers and put it down next to his. Then he leaned over, took my chin in his hand, and lowered his face to mine. And he kissed me.

Oh, wow! I hadn't thought about kissing—I mean, with a guy. People don't kiss much in the pornies; they go straight to the fucking. But Don pulled down on my lower jaw, poked his tongue between my lips, and my gut flip-flopped all the way down to my dick. Man, did he know how to kiss! It wasn't like anything I'd ever done with a chick. Don's mouth was strong and greedy, like he was hungry to taste me. And his tongue was so hot! I felt like I was melting against him. Without thinking, I kissed him back, exploring the inside of his mouth. I jumped when he started sucking on my tongue. The rhythmic tugs vibrated all the way down to my nads.

"Wow, dude," I whispered, suddenly wondering if his mouth would feel that hot on my cock.

"It's OK to hug me, Michael," he said. Surprised that he called me by my name, I just realized he'd wrapped his long arms loosely around me while we'd been kissing. I fumbled against him, pressing my hands to the smooth, firm flesh of his back. His kisses were driving me nuts. My dick was stretching out into my jeans, bending almost painfully. Finally, I had to resituate myself.

Don grabbed my hand and shook his head. "Let me."

I closed my eyes as he carefully manipulated the thick denim, straightening my dick out so it could stretch up along my belly. I'd never had another man touch me like that. Don's fingers moved so easily, like he really knew how to handle a cock. And it was going to make me shoot.

"Oh, shit!" I gasped, my whole body stiffening. Don's hand immediately fell away. I panted against him, holding him tight as I climbed back from the edge.

"Take it easy, sport," he laughed. "We've got plenty of time. I'm certain that handsome 10-incher of yours will shoot more than once tonight."

I tried to unobtrusively hide my face in his shoulder. "Um, it's not really 10 inches. I, uh, embellished a bit for my profile."

"Really?" he laughed. "I never would have guessed."

My face blushed hot against him as I inhaled the rich, warm man-sweat scent of his shirt. "I figured nobody would be interested if I said I'm only six inches."

"Anything more than a mouthful is a waste," he said. This time he rubbed my thigh as his lips descended on mine. It was a long time before I could think clearly again. God, I could get addicted to kissing like that. The next thing I knew, his tongue was trailing down my neck, swirling over my Adam's apple, gliding over my chest. I hadn't even felt him unbuttoning my shirt before it was already off and he was licking my bare skin. I jumped when he swiped his tongue over my nipples.

"Wow, dude," I moaned, pulling his head closer. "That feels good."

"You'll be sore tomorrow," he laughed, his breath cool on my damp skin, "but it will still feel good. Think of me when your shirt moves against your skin."

Before I could answer, Don pushed me down on the couch and started really chewing my tits. I winced and squirmed as he teethed, my cock twitching at every sharp nip. Pretty soon, my whole chest tingled, and I was so tender and turned on that I could hardly stand it. I pushed him away and yanked his shirt open, flattening my hands against the furry, muscular wall of his chest.

Don's nipples stood out like stiff pink buttons. He sighed contentedly as I pinched one firm point and gently twisted it.

"They sure are sensitive," I whispered.

Don's laughter rumbled under my fingers. "Yours will get that way too—with practice." He leaned over and started tonguing the bulge in my crotch, and I almost stopped breathing. His breath was hot and wet, even through the heavy denim. I was still panting when he sat back, tugged my jeans open, and slowly pulled them down. My cock popped up immediately, waving wildly in the air, the head completely bared as Don worked my shoes and socks and pants off.

"Very pretty," he said, smiling as he stood and stripped. "I like uncut dicks."

I was too busy staring at him to answer. Don's tool wasn't monster-size, not by porno standards, but it had to be at least eight inches—dark red, thick, and heavily veined. I swallowed hard, suddenly uncertain about where I wanted that sword of flesh to go.

"Um, you're really big," I said nervously.

Don threw back his head and laughed. "Don't worry, sport. When the time comes, everything will fit where it's supposed to." He knelt on the floor next to the couch and slid his long, strong fingers purposefully up my thighs, massaging deep into my tense muscles. As I relaxed, he carefully lifted my scrotum into his hand and rubbed my balls between his fingers.

"Very nice," he said, his firm pink tongue swirling slowly over my nuts. The hair on my ball sac was wet with his spit as he sucked first one, then the other sensitive orb into his mouth and washed them with his tongue. "These feel primed to shoot."

I moaned as he probed the base of my shaft and slowly licked up. Don looked like he was eating an ice cream cone, tasting me, peppering me with soft little kisses. I shook when he delicately probed the tender slit in the head of my cock. I was so hard I thought my dick was going to break. With no warning, Don opened his soft, warm lips and slid them all the way down my shaft, sucking me over the heat of his tongue and into his hot, tight, wet throat.

I yelled as I exploded. Don pulled off just in time, my come spraying his face as I bucked and spurted beneath him. *Fuck! Oh, fuck! That felt good!*

Don rubbed his cock against my thigh as he wiped the creamy white ropes into his hand and lifted his spermy fingers to my open lips.

"Lick," he ordered.

Still panting like a fiend, I sucked his dripping fingers clean with the fervor of the possessed. My come was sweet and slippery, and I loved the way it slid down my throat.

"You have a very talented tongue, Michael. Your mouth is going to make my dick very happy."

I groaned, my face heating with embarrassment and over-powering lust as Don rose up over me, gliding over my still-twitching meat. He carefully straddled my chest, his huge cock now resting lightly against my cheek.

"Get acquainted. Take your time. I'm not going to move. Just watch your teeth. If you do something I don't like, I'll tell you."

I felt shy. I felt kind of embarrassed. And I wanted to touch that big red cock and those low-hanging furry balls more than anything I'd ever wanted in my life. I ran my hands over him, exploring, moving his velvety soft dick skin over the pulsating flesh beneath. I tugged softly on his wrinkled sac, rubbing his heavy balls between my fingers.

"Feels nice, Michael," Don moaned. "Taste them if you want to."

Blushing, I slid down and opened my mouth. I licked the crinkly hair into whorls, inhaling his thick, musky all-male scent. Don's balls were too big to fit in my mouth, so I grabbed his hips and bathed his sac until his breathing got faster and he was wiggling above me. Then I slowly worked my way up, tasting the slightly salty skin of his rock-hard shaft, tracing the path of the full blue veins that traversed his heated red flesh. I'd wanted to suck a man's dick for so very, very long. Don jumped when I tickled my tongue into the V of his glans.

"Keep going," he panted. "Kiss it. Let it know you want to be friends." He shivered as I wrapped my hand around his shaft and slid the skin back and forth. "Fuck, yeah," he moaned.

I wanted to be good friends with Don's cock. I opened my mouth wide and sucked the velvety soft head in, slowly and tenderly, just the way he'd pulled me into his hot, wet mouth.

Don's whole body tensed.

"Stop!" he gasped, grabbing my head. "And stop sucking!"

I froze, holding myself perfectly still as he pulled him-self free.

"Damn, boy," he panted. "I can't remember the last time one dick kiss brought me that close to coming."

"Thanks," I blushed, inordinately pleased with myself and my newfound cocksucking skills. I liked what I was doing. I loved the feel of his heavy cock on my tongue and the masculine taste and smell of his skin. When he told me it was OK, I cupped his ass and pulled him back into my mouth, letting the saliva run down my chin as I slurped and sucked and played to my heart's content with his wonderful human man toy. Even making myself gag felt good in a weird sort of way. I kept teasing the back of my throat with his dick—a little bit, then more and more—seeing how much I could take, relishing the way Don groaned and his cock got even stiffer each time I gagged and my throat clenched around him.

I whimpered in frustration when he pulled back. His chest heaved as he moved down between my legs.

"You learn quick," he laughed shakily. He pulled my legs up, grabbing the pillow out from under my head and stuffing it under my butt. Then he reached under the table and pulled out a huge bottle of lube and a pile of rubbers. "Now it's my turn to play. You comfortable?"

"Yeah," I said nervously.

Don's eyes twinkled as he winked at me. "I'm going to stretch your hole open now." He shook his head as I shivered at his words. "Don't worry. It's not going to hurt. In fact, it's going to feel really good. When you want more, just grab your legs and pull them back toward your shoulders so you can open your ass up better for me."

I nodded, skeptically certain that I wouldn't be doing that. I jumped as the lube squirted into his hand, jerked again as his cool, slicked fingers brushed into my crack. In spite of myself, I moaned, instinctively pushing my ass toward him as he started massaging my asshole.

Don's fingers played my ass like a musical instrument, rubbing and stretching, loosening my sphincter until it fluttered against his fingertips. He looked me right in the eye, his grinning face framed by my upthrust cock and tight balls, and slid one finger slowly into my hole. I cried out, lifting my hips toward him, greedy for his touch, as he teased in and out, gradually pressing deeper a second, then a third finger. When his other hand joined in a lone digit pulling me firmly open in the other direction, I closed my eyes, grabbed my legs up tight to my shoulders, and spread my ass as wide as I could.

Don finger fucked me senseless, stretching me loose and open for his cock. I wallowed in the sensations flooding my asshole, writhing and panting as my dick oozed each time he massaged my prostate. I didn't open my eyes until his hands left me.

Don was sliding a rubber over his huge, hard, deep-red pole, slathering the latex with lube. He looked me straight in the eye as he squirted out another handful and pressed it up into my butt. I clamped down hard against his fingers.

Don shook his head at me. "Don't tighten, Michael. That will only make it hurt, and I'm going to fuck you now."

I nodded sheepishly. I wanted it. My asshole twitched with craving for him, but I was still embarrassingly afraid. Fortunately, Don seemed to pick up on that.

"Don't worry," he smiled. "I'll go slowly. There's no rush. Relax and let your body adjust to the feel of a good fuck. It's going to stretch, it's going to burn, and if you tighten up, it's going to hurt like hell." I shuddered as the head of his dick pressed against my asshole. "But no matter what, then it's going to feel great."

I gasped as Don's dick started in and my hole reluctantly stretched to accommodate him. His face was a tight grimace as one strong arm braced over me and the other directed his cock into my suddenly clenched sphincter.

"Damn, you're tight. Pull your legs back farther and don't fight me, boy! Your ass lips are kissing my dick—they want to be fucked. Listen to them!"

I tried, concentrating on the feelings in my asshole, gasping at the stretch and the burn as Don slid in a tiny bit more. He wasn't pressing fast, but he wasn't backing off either. I lifted my head high and saw just the tip of Don's dick poking inside the ring of my hole. My guts clenched at the sight. Fuck, that looked hot! It was my favorite penetration scene, the one I so rarely saw in the pornies—when the top first slid in and the bottom gasped and opened for him. My asshole spasmed, reaching out. In that second, the head of Don's dick popped all the way in.

And the pain hit. I yelled, my eyes watering as my sphincter tightened around him like a rubber band and squeezed.

"Easy." Don's voice was soft and soothing as he leaned over and kissed me. He backed out slowly. Just as fast, he was right back in. It hurt. But not as much. My asshole couldn't clench quite as hard around him. He stroked in and out again and again. It took me a minute to realize he was going deeper each time.

The pain was more like a low burn now, stretching me open to take the iron hard shaft impaling me. Suddenly, my ass lips gave way, like they'd finally decided to quit fighting me. I watched in wonder as my stretching, burning asshole quivered one last time, and Don's glistening red shaft slid all the way into my ass.

It was the hottest fuck shot I'd ever seen in my life. Even better, it was my butt hole being stretched full with a warm, living dick. I groaned as Don started fucking me—I mean, really deep-fucking me. My eyes fed each sensitized stroke and my asshole's hungry grasping kisses to my brain and cock until I felt like I had to pee and my piss slit oozed man juice each time Don's shaft slid in deep. I jerked my precome-slicked foreskin over the head of my dick, the added sensation echoing down to my ass lips and back up again as I twitched in ecstasy.

"That's it, boy," Don gasped as he ground into me. "Beat off while I fuck you. It'll be a helluva come." He laughed as I wrapped my hand around my dick and pulled up hard, my fluttering asshole sucking him in deep. "Damn, you have a sweet pussy. You've opened up right nice for an uptight little straight boy."

I didn't care what I was. I wanted to be fucked, hard and long and rough. And Don was moving too slowly.

"Faster," I gasped. "Please." I groaned out loud as Don rabbit-punched into me a half-dozen times. My hand flew over my dick. I arched my ass up to him, opening myself as wide as I could. "Fuck me," I panted, loving the way the words rolled over my tongue, pleading for what my hungry asshole needed. "Fuck me! Fuck me! Fuck me! Fuck me! Please!"

Don's laughter filled my ears as my body drew in on itself. The climax was starting deep in my guts, where his strong, thick cock was pounding the orgasm out of my joy spot. My balls crawled up my throbbing dick as Don's steel-hard shaft slid over my hypersensitive sphincter. My ass lips kissed him uncontrollably, begging for his touch.

Don shouted and ground into me, the fuck sensation surging through my prostate as I passed the point of no return and my ass clamped down tightly around him. I yelled as my dick spurted into my furiously pumping hands, and my whole body convulsed, my hot juice splatting onto my chest and into my open mouth and next to my ear. I thought I'd died and gone to heaven.

I could only watch, gasping like a landed fish, as Don pulled out, threw off the rubber, and shot his wad onto my belly. His grunts of satisfaction echoed in my ears as his dick emptied itself in thick pools of white cream covering my body. Don leaned over and rubbed his body over mine, my over-sensitized dick jerking as he smeared our joined jizz together between us and collapsed on top of me.

He didn't move for a long time. I had no complaints. Don was taking most of his weight on his arms, and I was totally blissed out, my suddenly very tender—but very happy—little boy pussy winking and purring beneath me. I laughed as I realized I was no longer "bi-curious." I wanted to get fucked again—soon!

"What's so funny?" Don smiled, raising up over me and planting a kiss on my lips.

"Me," I grinned, hugging him to me hard. "Thanks for making my first time great."

"My pleasure," he said.

"I had a mighty fine time myself." I moaned, totally satisfied, as he sat up and our sticky cocks pulled apart.

While I was getting dressed, Don walked over to the entertainment center and rummaged around with the electronics. When I looked up again, he tossed a videotape into my hands.

"Only copy in the world, pal: *Straight Boy Vid Kid Loses His Virginity to the Studline Editor.* But if you ever want to check out the business, bring your demo here back to me, and I'll arrange some introductions. You're a natural."

I was too stunned to know what to say. Don gave me a quick hug on my way out the door. I hugged him back ferociously, wincing as my shirt moved over my sore and super-tender nipples. Then I was laughing again.

I laughed all the way home. I couldn't wait to watch the video. I knew it would always be the hottest thing I'd ever see. Maybe I'd break down and show it to Stan. Shoot, maybe I'd even show it to some of Stan's buddies. And maybe, just maybe, I'd take it back to Don and let him show it to *his* friends.

About the Authors

f f f

DEREK ADAMS is the author of a popular series of erotic novels featuring intrepid detective Miles Diamond. He has also penned over 100 short stories, which he insists are ongoing chapters in his autobiography. Adams lives near Seattle and keeps in shape by working out whenever he can find a man willing to do a few push-ups with him.

DALE CHASE has been writing gay fiction for seven years and has had more than 100 short stories appear in various magazines and anthologies, including the *Harrington Gay Men's Fiction Quarterly.* Chase's novel *The Great Man* is due out this year, as is *The Company He Keeps,* a collection of Victorian erotica.

T. HITMAN has written features for several national magazines and newspapers as well as short fiction, several novels and nonfiction books, and a few television episodes, of which he hopes to do more. In his spare time, he freely admits to watching professional sports such as baseball, hockey, and football—and extreme sports in the way that most men watch porn.

KEVIN JOHNSON is 29 years old and moved to the States from the United Kingdom four years ago with his boyfriend of 10 years. He is now a professional porn reviewer for *HX* magazine in New York City, where thousands of men hang on his every word to know what to jerk off to. Johnson's boyfriend works for an airline, which allows them to fly around the world together and seduce as many boys as possible.

ABOUT THE AUTHORS

PIERCE LLOYD lives in Southern California, where he has too little time and too much fun. He began writing erotica in college because it beat studying for tests.

R.J. MARCH wrote his first erotic story in the sixth grade. Since then, he has won wide acclaim as one of the most talented and prolific writers of gay erotic fiction. His erotica collection *Looking for Trouble* was a national best-seller, and his work appears regularly in magazines such as *Men, Freshmen,* and *Unzipped.*

NICK MONTGOMERY is a playwright and novelist who lives in New Jersey. "Spice Up Your Life" is his first piece of erotic fiction.

CHASE PETERS is a retired lawyer who lives in Milwaukee. From 1971 to 1974 he worked on Selective Service induction-prevention cases and at obtaining honorable discharges for servicemen by habeas corpus. His erotic fiction work has appeared in *Inches, Mandate, First Hand,* and *Freshmen.*

DOMINIC SANTI is a former technical editor turned rogue whose latest erotic work is the German-language collection *Kerle im Lustrausch (Guys in Lust Frenzy),* published by Bruno Gmünder in August 2004. Santi's fiction is available in English in several volumes of the Friction series as well as in *Best Gay Erotica, Best American Erotica 2004, Bi-Guys, Best Bisexual Erotica, Tough Guys, His Underwear,* on www.nightcharm.com, and in dozens of other smutty anthologies, magazines, and Web sites. Read more about his work at www.nicksantistories.com.

BOB VICKERY has five short-story collections, including *Play Buddies* and his audio book, *Manjack,* both from Quarter Moon Press. Vickery is a regular contributor to *Freshmen* and

Men magazines, and his stories have appeared over the years in numerous anthologies, magazines, and Web zines. To read more about his work, visit his personal Web site at www.bobvickery.com.

SEAN WOLFE has been writing gay erotica for a decade and has published more than 50 short stories in just about every gay magazine on the market. His stories have appeared in most of the Friction series anthologies as well as in *Twink*, *Three the Hard Way*, and *My First Time*, Volume 3. He has also penned the monthly video review Rushes for *Torso* magazine. Wolfe has three novellas published by Kensington Publications and his work has been included in the Lambda Literary Award–nominated anthologies *Masters of Midnight*, *Man of My Dreams*, and *Midnight Thirsts*. He has a single-author collection of his erotic stories, *Close Contact*, and he is now working on three gay novels.

SUBSCRIBE to
freshmen
and get this FULL-LENGTH DVD FREE!

☐ **YES! Here's my $29.99 payment. Start my subscription and send my FREE DVD immediately!**

SELECT YOUR SAVINGS:
☐ **2 years (24 issues) - you pay $45** **BEST DEAL!**
☐ 1 year (12 issues) - $29.99

☐ Amount enclosed $_____

CHECK ONE: ☐ Check enclosed   ☐ Bill me later
Charge my: ☐ Visa ☐ MasterCard ☐ AmEx

Card # _____

Exp. date _____

NAME_____

ADDRESS_____

CITY/STATE/ZIP_____

E-MAIL_____

Send to: **freshmen** P.O. Box 511, Newburgh, NY 12551
Or call 1-800-757-7069

For orders outside the U.S. please add $15 per year, payable in U.S. funds only. Magazines are mailed in an opaque wrapper for your privacy. This subscription offer is *not available* to persons under the age of eighteen (18).By ordering a subscription, you are representing that you are 18 years of age or older. The annual newstand price is $95.88.

*Offer expires 6/1/06

DVD not available outside of the U.S. or in the states of AL, MS, NC, TN, UT, and zip codes 32001-32699, 45201-45299, 73345-75200, 75300, 75400-76100, 76200-77000, 77100-77200, 77300-78400, 78481-78700, 78800-79900, 80000-88509

P45ALY